PORTALS
OF TOMORROW

The Best Tales of Science Fiction and Other Fantasy

PORTALS
OF TOMORROW

The Best Tales of Science Fiction and Other Fantasy

edited by

August Derleth

Rinehart *and Company, Inc.* New York Toronto

The Hypnoglyph, by John Anthony. Copyright 1953, by Fantasy House, Inc., for *The Magazine of Fantasy and Science Fiction*, July 1953.

Testament of Andros, by James Blish. Copyright 1952, by Columbia Publications, Inc., for *Future Science Fiction*, January 1953.

The Playground, by Ray Bradbury. Copyright 1953, by Esquire, Inc., for *Esquire*, October 1953. Copyright by Ray Bradbury, for FAHRENHEIT 451. Reprinted by permission of the Harold Matson Agency.

Gratitude Guaranteed, by R. Bretnor & Kris Neville. Copyright 1953, by Fantasy House, Inc., for *The Magazine of Fantasy and Science Fiction*, August 1953.

Rustle of Wings, by Fredric Brown. Copyright 1953, by Fantasy House, Inc.; reprinted by permission of the author and *The Magazine of Fantasy and Science Fiction*, August 1953.

The Other Tiger, by Arthur C. Clarke. Copyright 1953, by King-Size Publications, Inc., for *Fantastic Universe*, June–July 1953.

Civilized, by Mark Clifton and Alex Apostolides. Copyright 1953, by Galaxy Publishing Corporation, for *Galaxy Science Fiction*, August 1953.

Stickeney and the Critic, by Mildred Clingerman. Copyright 1953, by Fantasy House, Inc., for *The Magazine of Fantasy and Science Fiction*, February 1953.

The Word, by Mildred Clingerman. Copyright 1953, by Fantasy House, Inc., for *The Magazine of Fantasy and Science Fiction*, November 1953.

Hermit on Bikini, by John Langdon. Copyright 1953, by McCall Corporation, for *Bluebook*, March 1953.

Jezebel, by Murray Leinster. Copyright 1953, by Better Publications, Inc., for *Startling Stories*, October 1953.

D. P. from Tomorrow, by Mack Reynolds. Copyright 1953, by Hanro Corporation, for *Orbit*, Fall 1953.

The Altruists, by Idris Seabright. Copyright 1953, by Fantasy House, Inc., for *The Magazine of Fantasy and Science Fiction*, November 1953.

Potential, by Robert Sheckley. Copyright 1953, by Street and Smith Publications, Inc., for *Astounding Science Fiction*, November 1953.

Eye for Iniquity, by T. L. Sherred. Copyright 1953, by Galaxy Publishing Corporation, for *Beyond*, July 1953.

Kindergarten, by Clifford Simak. Copyright 1953, by Galaxy Publishing Corporation, for *Galaxy Science Fiction*, July 1953.

Acknowledgments to Forrest J. Ackerman
and Anthony Boucher, whose assistance in
this project was unstinted.

CONTENTS

INTRODUCTION

In view of the rapid growth in popularity of fantasy in general and science fiction (which is a form of fantasy) in particular in the last two decades, it is fitting that an annual assessment of this form of writing be made. Hence *Portals of Tomorrow*—which comes into a populous field as an anthology covering the entire genre of the fantastic: not only supernatural and science-fiction tales, but also every kind of whimsy and imaginative concept of life in the future or on other planets.

There are now no less than thirty-five magazines devoted wholly to the publication of fantasy, beginning with *Weird Tales*, established in 1923 (thus the oldest in point of time) and ending with *Spaceway*, the most recent addition to the group. Moreover, an increasing number of magazines in the general field now publish occasional stories which fall within the definition of fantasy. Of those magazines devoted solely to fantasy in the calendar year of 1953, the highest literary average was maintained by *The Magazine of Fantasy and Science Fiction*, closely pressed by *Galaxy Science Fiction, Beyond, Fantastic,* and *Astounding Science Fiction.*

The emergence of science fiction continued to attract attention during the year, so much so that, apart from the customary pages given to the subject of space travel and moon bases in the picture magazines and *Collier's,* special articles treating of various aspects of the subject appeared in magazines as varied as *The Atlantic Monthly, The Commonweal, The American Mercury,* and *The Catholic World,* though some of these were singularly inept. Perhaps the most informative articles available were "The Philosophy of Science Fiction" and "The Plot-Forms of Science Fiction," both by James E. Gunn, published in *Dynamic Science Fiction.*

If there was one marked development in the stories which fall into the classification of "fantastic" published during the calendar year of 1953, it was that the much-vaunted line between science-fiction fantasy and nonscience-fiction fantasy is becoming more tenuous than ever; indeed, there was a steadily increasing blend of science fiction with more orthodox fantasy even in magazines which purport to contain stories purely of science fiction or of the supernatural.

The development toward more orthodox fantasy in what is called science fiction only demonstrates what every intelligent reader, whose awareness goes beyond the limited field of fantasy, has always known: that science fiction is only another form of fantasy, and not a genre in its own right. Graham Hough, reviewing a collection by Ray Bradbury, in the London *Listener,* might be speaking of many authors in the genre when he says that the writer "takes the stuff of modern folk-lore—interplanetary travel, time machines and all that—and makes a variety of small objects of it—strange, beautiful, witty or critical. Some stories are of magic, some are not supernatural, some of the stories are sociological parables . . . but their morals are always on the side of life and humanity."

It is also possible to say that the general literacy level of the fantastic story has risen from the woeful depths that were its milieu for so many decades, and at the same time to point out that the average fantastic story is still far from the plane of the average non-fantastic story published in the United States.

The stories in this collection are representative of the best in the genre of fantasy. Thirteen of them classify as science fiction, and only three as fantasy of other kinds; and the science fiction falls into several sub-classifications as well.

These stories are manifestly not all the best published during the calendar year of 1953, but I am inclined to think they are a majority of them. The overwhelming bulk of fiction in the form being published today, even though it is more literate than it was two decades ago, still fails to measure up to the criteria by which I have been guided—literary merit, originality of story and/or treatment, freshness of theme, above all, a good story well told.

Here then is the first collection in a series in which we shall hope to do for the fantastic story what has been done so admirably by Martha Foley and her predecessor, the late Edward J. O'Brien, for the short story in general.

—August Derleth

1 December, 1953
Sauk City, Wisconsin

THE HYPNOGLYPH

by John Anthony

John Anthony is the pen name of a distinguished American poet, the author of several collections of verse, and, at present, an editor of Twayne Publishers. "The Hypnoglyph" is one of his earliest ventures into the field of the fantastic.

Jaris held the object cupped in his hand while his thumb stroked the small hollow in its polished side. "It's really the prize of my collection," he said, "but there isn't any real name for it. I call it the hypnoglyph."

"Hypnoglyph?" Maddick said, putting down a superbly rick-racked Venusian opal the size of a goose egg.

Jaris smiled at the younger man. "Hypnoglyph," he said. "Here, take a look at it."

Maddick held it in his palm stroking it softly, letting his thumb run gently over the little hollow. "This, the prize of your collection?" he said. "Why, it's nothing but a chunk of wood."

"A man," Jaris said, "may be described as not much more than a chunk of meat, but he has some unusual properties."

Maddick, his thumb still stroking the little hollow, swept his eye over the treasure room. "I'll say he has. I've never in my life seen more property in one room."

Jaris' voice gently brushed aside the edge of greed in the younger man's voice. "It has not been the longest life to date. Perhaps it even has something left to learn."

Maddick flushed a moment, then pursed his lips almost imperceptibly and shrugged. "Well, what's it for?" he said. He held the thing in front of him and watched his fingers stroke it.

Jaris chuckled again. "It's for exactly what you're doing. The thing is irresistible. Once you've picked it up, your thumb just automatically strokes that little hollow, and it just automatically hates to stop stroking."

Maddick's voice took on the tone that the very young reserve for humoring the very old. "It's a pleasant gadget," he said. "But why the rather pretentious name?"

"Pretentious?" Jaris said. "I had simply thought of it as descriptive. The thing actually is hypnotic." He smiled watching Maddick's fingers still playing with the thing. "You may recall a sculptor named Gainsdale who fooled with such things toward the end of the Twentieth Century. He founded a school of sculpture called Tropism."

Maddick shrugged, still absorbed in the object. "Everyone and his brother started a school of something back there; I guess I missed that one."

"It was an interesting theory," Jaris said, picking up an Arcturian space-crystal and watching the play of light rays from it. "He argued—soundly enough as I see it—that the surface of every organism has certain innate tactile responses. A cat innately likes to be stroked in certain ways. A heliotrope innately moves to face the light."

"And the leg," Maddick quipped, "innately likes to be pulled. So far we've covered some basic facts about tropism with a small *t*. What of it?"

"It isn't the facts so much as the application that's interesting," Jaris said, ignoring the younger man's rudeness. "Gainsdale simply carried his awareness of tropism farther than anyone had before. Anyone on earth at least. He argued that every surface of the body innately responds to certain shapes and textures and he set out to carve objects that—as he put it—made the bodily surfaces innately happy. He made objects for rubbing up and down the neck, objects for rubbing across the forehead. He even claimed he could cure headaches that way."

"That's nothing but old Chinese medicine," Maddick said. "I bought an Eighth Century talisman for rubbing out rheumatism just last week. Curio stuff."

"Gainsdale must certainly have known the Oriental glyptics," Jaris agreed, "but he was trying to systematize the idea behind them into a series of principles. He took a fling at reviving the Japanese netsuke, those polished hand-pieces the old Samurais dangled from their belts. But Gainsdale wanted to carve for the whole body. He tried psychic jewelry at one point and designed bracelets that innately pleased the arm. For a while he got to designing chairs that were irresistible to the buttocks."

"Quite an art," Maddick said, turning the object in his hand, working the little hollow around and around in his fist and then bringing it back to where his thumb could stroke along the tiny hollow. "You might say he got right down to fundaments." He smiled at Jaris as if looking for acknowledgment of his wit, but found no response there.

"He was, in fact, quite a man," Jaris said seriously. "Maybe the chairs and buttocks gave him the idea but after that he got to experimenting with gimmicks that would preserve sexual potency. The League of Something or Other made him stop that, but it is worth noting that his last child was born when he was eighty-four."

Maddick leered. "At last—a practical application!"

Jaris looked down at Maddick's hand still stroking the hypnoglyph, the fingers moving as if they had entered a life of their own. "After that," he said, ignoring Maddick's still lingering leer, "he got to designing sleeping blocks—wooden pillows something like the Japanese porcelain block, but molded to give the head pleasure. He claimed it produced good dreams. But most of all he sculptured for the hand, just as the Japanese carvers of talismans finally settled on the netsuke for their definitive work. After all, the hand is not only the natural tactile organ in one sense; it also has the kind of mobility that can respond to texture and mass most pleasurably."

Jaris put down the space-crystal and stood watching Maddick's hand. "Just as you're doing," he said. "Gainsdale was after the object the human hand could not resist."

Maddick looked down at the thing in his hand, the fingers working over it as if they were alone with it somewhere apart from the arm and mind they grew from. "I must say it is pleasant," he said. "But isn't all this just a bit far-fetched? You'd hardly argue that pleasure is absolutely irresistible. If we have no control over our lust for pleasure why aren't we strangling one another for the pleasure of stroking this thing?"

"Maybe," Jaris said gently, "because I want less than you do."

Maddick let his eyes sweep the treasure room. "Maybe you can damn well afford to," he said, and for a moment there was no suavity in his voice. He seemed to be aware of the gaff himself, for he changed the subject immediately. "But I thought you collected nothing but extraterrestrial stuff. How come this?"

"That," said Jaris, "is the curious coincidence. Or one of the curious coincidences. The one you're holding *is* extraterrestrial."

"And the other curious coincidences?" Maddick said.

Jaris lit one of his poisonous cheroots. "I might as well begin at the beginning," he said through the smoke.

"Something told me there was a story coming," Maddick said. "You collectors are all alike. I've never known one that wasn't a yarn spinner. I think it's the real reason for the collection."

Jaris smiled. "A professional disease. Do we collect so we can tell yarns, or tell yarns so we can collect? Maybe if I tell the yarn well enough I'll collect you. Well, sit down and I'll do my best: a new audience, a new opportunity."

He waved Maddick into an elaborately carved bone chair, placed the humidor, the drug sachets, and a decanter of Danubian brandy within easy reach of him, and sat down behind the desk with a wave of the hand that told Maddick to help himself.

"I suppose," he said after that pause-before-the-yarn that no story teller can omit, "I suppose one of the reasons I prize the thing is because I got it on my last blast into deep space. As you see," he added, waving his hand about him lightly, "I made the mistake of coming back rich, and it killed the wanderlust. Now I'm earthbound by my own avidity."

Maddick sat stroking the smooth little hollow with his thumb. "Being filthy rich is hardly the worst fate imaginable, I should think."

But Jaris' mind was on his story. "I'd been prospecting for space-crystals out toward Deneb Kaitos," he continued, "and I'd really struck bonanza, an asteroid belt just popping with the luscious things. We had the ship bulging with enough of them to buy Terra twice over, and we were starting back when we found that Deneb Kaitos had a planetary system. There had been several expeditions out that way before with no mention of the system and we had been so busy hauling in space-crystals that we hadn't been doing much looking. But I realized then that what I had thought was just an asteroid belt was really a broken-up planet orbiting around its sun. With the fragments running about eight per cent pure diamond, it was no wonder we'd hit the mother lode of them all.

"We ran a quick survey on the system and decided to put into DK-8 for the specimen run-over and life-forms data. DK-6 gave some indications of life-forms but hardly enough to be worth the extra stop. DK-8, on the other hand, ran high. So high it looked like a good chance for Federation Prize Money. With a ship load of space-crystals, even a million Units seemed small change, but it would be a kick to turn up a new Intelligence Group. The Columbus complex, you know.

"At any rate we put into DK-8, and that's where I got that thing you're holding. On DK-8 it's a hunting implement."

Maddick looked puzzled. "Hunting," he said. "You mean the way David got Goliath? Zingo?"

"No," Jaris said. "It's not a missile. It's a snare. The natives set them out and trap animals with them."

Still stroking it, Maddick looked at the gadget. "Oh come now," he said. "You mean they just set them out, wait for termites to invade, and then eat the termites? That kind of snare?"

Jaris' voice stiffened for an instant. "There are queerer things than that in space." Then his voice softened. "You're young yet," he said. "You have time enough. That gadget, for instance: you wouldn't believe a culture was founded on it. You're not ready to believe."

Maddick's smile said: "Well, after all you can't expect me to swallow this stuff, can you?" Aloud he said, "A yarn's a yarn. Let's have it."

"Yes," Jaris said, "I suppose it is incredible. In a way, that's what space is: the constant recurrence of the incredible. After a while you forget what a norm is. Then you're a space hand." He looked off a moment across the shining collection around him. "DK-8, for example. Once the indicator told us to expect intelligence, it was no surprise to come on side-humans. By that time it had been universally established that you can expect intelligence only in primate and quasi-primate forms. Unless you've got the prehensile hand and the supraorbital arch there's just no way for intelligence to get started. A monkey develops a hook for swinging through the trees and an eye for measuring distances between leaps and he's fitted for his environment. But it just happens that the hand is good for picking things up and the eye is good for looking at them closely, and pretty soon the monkey is picking things up and examining them and beginning to get ideas. And pretty soon he's beginning to use tools. An ungulate couldn't use a tool in a billion years; he has nothing to hold it with. There's no reason why there mightn't be some sort of lizard intelligence I suppose, except that it just doesn't seem to happen. Probably too low-grade a nervous system."

Jaris suddenly caught himself, realizing that his voice had been running away with the enthusiasm of his argument. "I really haven't been back very long," he said with a smile. "That's the sort of argument that gets hot in space." His voice softened again. "I was saying we weren't much surprised to come on side-humans once we'd got an intelligence indication. . . ."

"Odd that I've never heard of it," Maddick said. "I keep pretty well posted on that sort of thing. And surely a really close siding——"

"The fact is," Jaris said, interrupting in his turn, "we didn't make a report."

Maddick's voice sharpened with surprise. "Good heavens, man, and you're telling me? What on earth's to keep me from turning you over to Federation Space Base and getting your mind picked for it?" Once again his eyes swept the treasure room as if running an inventory and his lips pursed shrewdly for an instant. Then his voice loosened. "If I believed you, that is."

Jaris leaned back in his chair as if buried in thought and for a moment his voice seemed to be coming up from a cave shaft. "It doesn't really matter," he said. "And besides," he added with a smile, his voice growing near again, "you don't, as you say, believe me."

Maddick looked down at his hand still stroking the polished sides of the gadget. The thumb snaked out over the little polished dimple. In, up and back, in, up and back. Without raising his head, he raised his eyes to meet Jaris'. "Should I?" he said. Once more his eyes flicked over the treasure room, resting longest on the cabinet of space-crystals.

Jaris noted his look and smiled. "I've often thought myself what a lovely target I'd make for a blackmailer."

Maddick looked away quickly. "If the blackmailer could believe you."

Jaris smiled. "Always that doubt," he said. "What would you say if I told you the siding was so close that Terrans can mate with DKs?"

Maddick paused a long minute before answering, his eyes fixed on the thing in his hand, watching his fingers curl about and stroke it. He shook his head as if putting something out of his mind. "I seem to be beyond surprise at this point. Strangely, I believe you. And strangely, I know I should be arguing that it's impossible."

Suddenly his voice flared up. "Look here," he said, "what is all this rigmarole?" Again his voice calmed abruptly. "All right. Yes, sure. I believe you. I'm crazy, God knows, but I believe you."

"Enough to turn me in?"

Maddick flushed without answering.

"I'm afraid they'd only tell you it's impossible," Jaris said. "Pity too," he added wearily. "As I was saying I'd be such lush pickings for a blackmailer." He paused a moment, then added gently, "Don't worry about it, son."

Maddick's voice did not rise to anger. He looked down at his hand still stroking the thing. "Is that a threat?" he said indifferently.

Jaris shook his head. "A regret," he said. He blew out a cloud of smoke and spoke again more brightly. "Besides, all the arguments against its being possible are too sound. Life-forms can mate across some of the branches of divergent evolution if the species are related by some reasonably proximate common ancestor. The lion and the tiger, for instance, or the horse and the jackass. But it doesn't work for convergent evolution. You can evolve a species somewhere in space that resembles man, and with space enough and time enough you can evolve a lot of them, but the chemistry and physiology of egg and sperm are too tricky to come close enough without a common ancestor. Nevertheless, Terrans can mate with DK women, and have mated with them. That may sound incredible, said in this room, but after a while you find nothing is incredible in deep space."

"Deep space," Maddick said softly. His voice sounded as if it were stroking the words with the same sensuous pleasure his fingers found in stroking the polished thing in his hand.

Jaris caught the movement of his voice and nodded. "You've time yet. You'll get there. But to get back to DK-8. The only real difference between DKs and humans is the hair and the skin structure. DK-8 has a dense and tropical atmosphere. It's rather high in CO_2 and perpetually misty. The sun's rays have a hard time getting through the atmosphere. Also, the planet is all-tropical. Consequently, the animal life from which the DKs evolved never had to develop a fur covering. Hair is unknown on the planet. Instead, the DK life-forms developed a skin structure extremely sensitive to whatever diffused sun rays they can get. The skin is soft and pallid as a slug's. If a DK were exposed to the direct rays of Sol for a few minutes, he'd die of sunburn."

Jaris held up the cheroot before him and blew a puff of smoke over its lit end. "Nature," he said, "always has a trick of trying to deal two cards at once. The prehensile hand developed for one reason and became useful for something else. Just so, the DK's tremendously sensitive skin developed originally to absorb the most possible sun, but became in time the basis for a tremendously developed tactile sense."

"That goes for the lower animals too. Their tropisms are fantastically dominant over their other responses. Once an animal starts stroking one of those gadgets as you're doing, it simply cannot stop."

Maddick smiled and looked at his hand without answering. The polished sides of the thing gleamed dully, and his thumb ran down into and over the little hollow. Down into and over. Down into and over.

"You might almost say," Jaris continued, "that the DKs have developed a tactile science to a degree unknown to us. The energy we have put into a tool culture, they have put into a tactile culture. It isn't a highly developed society in our terms: a rigid tribal matriarchy with a few basic tools that only the women are permitted to operate, and at that only a special clan of the women. The other women lounge about on delicately arranged hill terraces and just lie motionless soaking up sun energy or working up a little voodoo mostly based on hypnotism and tactile gratification."

His voice grew softer and slightly distant. "As you might expect, they grow incredibly obese. At first it seemed repulsive to see them lying so. But on DK-8, obesity is really a survival characteristic. It makes for more surface to absorb sun energy. And the women have such perfect control of their skin surfaces that their bodies remain strangely well-proportioned."

He leaned back and almost closed his eyes. "Amazing control," he half whispered. Then suddenly he chuckled. "But you're probably wondering how they work such hard wood so perfectly with practically no tools. If you look closely you'll find that what you're holding is really grainless. Actually it isn't wood at all, but a kind of huge seed, something like an avocado nut. As you know, you can carve a fresh avocado nut almost as easily as you mold clay, but when you let it dry, it becomes extremely hard. Extremely hard."

"Extremely hard," Maddick agreed distantly.

"The women of the proper clan work these things, and the men set them out in the forests. As you might suppose, the men are a rather scrawny lot, and would starve soon enough if they had to depend on their own muscular prowess as hunters. These gadgets take care of all that, however. The animals, with their extremely high tactile suggestibility, come through the forest and find one of these things in their way. They begin to stroke it and feel it, and they just can't stop. The men don't even kill them; all slaughtering is handled by the ruling clan of women. The men simply wait till the animal has worked itself into the right state, and then lead it back to the slaughtering compound—still under hypnosis of course."

"Of course," Maddick agreed, his fingers working softly and rhythmically.

Jaris leaned back. His politeness was unfaltering, but now there was a touch of triumph in his voice. "There's really only one other thing you need to know. The men used to have unmanageable spells. As a result, it has become traditional to hypnotize them practically at birth. The practice is untold centuries old.

"Unfortunately, however, nature still deals a tricky hand. Keep the species in abeyance long enough and it stops thrusting toward its own development. The generations of hypnosis have had the effect of breeding the life-wish out of the males. It's as if the genes and the sperm were just slowly quitting. When we landed on DK-8 there were hardly enough men left to work the traps."

He leaned forward, smiling. "You can imagine what a treasure our crew must have seemed to the tribal leaders, once it was discovered that we could interbreed: new vigorous males, a new start, fresh blood for the life stream."

He paused and his tone became steady and dry. "I think perhaps you will understand now why I came back alone. The only male ever to leave DK-8. Although," he added, "in one sense I've never really left it."

". . .never. . .really. . .left. . .it. . ." Maddick said.

Jaris nodded and came around the desk. Leaning over Maddick, he blew a puff of smoke directly into his open eyes. Maddick did not stir. His eyes remained fixed straight ahead and he remained fixed motionless in the chair. Only the fingers of his right hand continued to move, curling about the polished thing, while his thumb flicked out and over the little hollow.

Jaris straightened, still smiling sadly, picked up a curiously wrought little bell from the desk and tinkled it once.

Across the room, a door swung open on a darkened alcove in which something huge and pale showed dimly.

"He is ready, darling," Jaris said.

TESTAMENT OF ANDROS

by James Blish

JAMES BLISH one of the most prolific writers in the so-called pulp-fiction field. He has written sports stories, whodunits, Western tales, and he is one of the most original writers in fantasy and allied fiction. He has been widely anthologized in such collections as *Shadow of Tomorrow, Beyond Human Ken,* and others.

My name is Theodor Andresson. I will write my story if you wish. I was at one time resident in astrophysics at Krajputnii, which I may safely describe as the greatest center of learning in the Middle East, perhaps of the entire Eastern Hemisphere. Later—until the chain of incidents which brought me to this *Zucht-Haus*—I was professor-emeritus in radio-astronomy at Calimyrna University, where I did the work leading to the discovery of the solar pulsation cycle.

I am sure that this work is not credited to me; that is of no importance. I would like it clearly understood that I am not making this record for your benefit, but for mine. Your request means nothing to me, and your pretense of interest in what I may write cannot deceive me. My erstwhile colleagues in the so-called sciences were masters of this kind of pretense; but they, too, were unable to prevent me from penetrating the masquerade at the end. How then does a simple doctor hope to succeed where the finest charlatanry has failed?

And what is allocation of credit—of what importance is priority of discovery before the inexorability of the pulsation cycle? It will work to its new conclusion without regard for your beliefs, my colleagues', or mine. Neither the pretended solicitude nor the real metal bars with which you have surrounded me will matter after that.

I proceed, therefore, to the matter at hand. My position at Calimyrna in that remote time before the cycle was discovered, befit my age (eighty-four years) and the reputation I had achieved in my specialty. I was in excellent health, though subject occasionally to depressions of spirit, readily ascribable to my being in a still-strange land and to those scars inflicted upon me in earlier times.

Despite these fits of moodiness, I had every reason to be happy. My eminence in my field afforded me the utmost satisfaction; despite poverty and persecution in youth, I had won to security. I had married Marguerita L——, in her youth and mine the toast of twelve continents, not only for her beauty but for her voice. I can still hear now the sound of her singing as I heard it for the first time—singing, on the stage of La Scala in Moscow, the rapturous quartet from the second act of Wagner's *Tristan et Messalina.*

It is quite true—I admit it immediately and calmly—that there were certain flaws in my world, even at Calimyrna. I do not mean the distractions which in old age replace, in the ordinary man, the furies of youth, but rather certain faults and fissures which I found in the world outside myself.

Even a man of my attainments expects at some time to grow old, and to find that process changing the way in which he looks at the world around him. There comes a time, however, when even the most rational of men must notice when these changes exceed the bounds of reason— when they begin to become extraordinary, even sinister. Shall I be specific? Consider, then—quite calmly—the fact that Marguerita did not herself grow old.

I passed into my eighth decade without taking more than perfunctory notice. I was deeply involved in the solar work we were then carrying on at Calimyrna. I had with me a young graduate student, a brilliant fellow of about thirty, who assisted me and who made certain original contributions of his own to the study. His name, and you will recognize it, was Mario di Ferruci. Calimyrna had completed its thousand-inch radio-telescope, the largest such antenna anywhere in the world—except for the 250-foot Manchester instrument. This was at once put to work in the search for so-called radio stars—those invisible bodies, many of them doubtless nearer to Earth than the nearest visible star, which can be detected only by their emission in the radio spectrum.

Completion of the thousand-inch freed the 600-inch paraboloid antenna for my use in solar work. The smaller instrument had insufficient beam-width between half-power points for the critical stellar studies, but it was more suitable for my purpose.

I had in mind at that time a study of the disturbed sun. Hagen of the Naval Research Laboratory had already done the definite study on the sun in its quiet state. I found myself more drawn to what goes on in the inferno of the sunspots—in the enormous, puzzling catastrophes of the solar flares—the ejection of immense radioactive clouds from the sun's interior high into its atmosphere.

It had already become clear that the radio-frequency emission from the disturbed sun was not, and could not be, thermal in origin, as in the RF emission of the quiet sun. The equivalent temperature of the disturbed sun in selected regions at times rises to billions of degrees, rendering the whole concept of thermal equivalency meaningless.

That the problem was not merely academic impressed me from the first. I have, if you will allow me the term, always had a sense of destiny, of *Schicksal,* an almost Spenglerian awareness of the pressure of fate against the retaining walls of human survival. It is not unique in me; I lay it to my Teutonic ancestry. And when I first encountered the problem of the disturbed sun, something within me felt that I had found destiny itself.

For here, just *here* was the problem in which destiny was interested, in which some fateful answer awaited the asking of the omnipotent question. I felt this from the moment when I had first opened Hagen's famous paper—NRL Report 3504—and the more deeply I became interested in the sun as an RF radiator, the more the sensation grew.

Yet how to describe it? I was eighty-four, and this was early in 1956; in all those preceding years I had not known that the mortal frame could sustain such an emotion. Shall I call it a sensation of enormous unresolvable dread? But I felt at the same time an ecstasy beyond joy, beyond love, beyond belief; and these transports of rapture and terror did not alternate as do the moods of an insane man, but occurred simultaneously—they were one and the same emotion.

Nor did the solar flares prove themselves unworthy of such deep responses. Flares have been observed in many stars. Some of them have been major outbursts, as indeed they would have to be to be visible to us at all. That such a flare could never occur on our own sun, furthermore, could not be said with certainty, for flares are local phenomena —they expend their energy only on one side of a star, not in all directions like a nova—and we had already seen the great detonation of July 29, 1948, on our own sun, which reached an energy level one hundred times the output of the quiet sun, which showed that we did not dare to set limits to what our own sun might yet do.

It was here, however, that I ran into trouble with young di Ferruci. He persistently and stubbornly refused to accept the analogy.

"It's penny-dreadful," he would say, as he had said dozens of times before. "You remind me of Dr. Richardson's stories—you know, the ones he writes for those magazines, about the sun going nova and all that. Whenever it's cloudy at Palomar he dreams up a new catastrophe."

"Richardson is no fool," I would point out. "Other suns have exploded. If he wants to postulate that it could happen to ours, he has every right to do so."

"Sure, Dr. Andresson, in a story," di Ferruci would object. "But as a serious proposition it doesn't hold water. Our sun just isn't the spectral type that goes nova; it hasn't ever even approached the critical instability percentage. It can't even produce a good flare of the Beta Centauri type."

"I don't expect it to go nova. But it's quite capable of producing a major flare, in my opinion. I expect to prove it."

Di Ferruci would shrug, as he always did. "I wouldn't ride any money on you, Dr. Andresson. But I'll be more than interested in what the telescope shows—let's see what we have here right now. The thermocouple's been calibrated; shall I cut in the hot load?"

At this point—I am now reporting a particular incident, although it, too, was frequently typical of these conversations—I became aware that Marguerita was in the observatory. I swung sharply around, considerably annoyed. My wife is innocent of astronomical knowledge, and her usually ill-timed obtrusions upon our routine—although I suppose they were of the desire to "take an interest" in her husband's profession—were distracting.

Today, however, I was not only annoyed, but stunned. How had I failed to notice this before—I, who pride myself on the acuity of my observation? What stood before me was a young woman!

How shall I say how young? These things are relative. We had married when she was thirty-six and I was forty-four; a difference of eight years is virtually no difference during the middle decades, though it is enormous when both parties are young. Marguerita had been in no sense a child at the time of our marriage.

Yet now, as I was finding, a spread as small as eight years can again become enormous when the dividing-line of old age insensibly approaches. And the difference was even greater than this—for now Marguerita, as she stood looking down at our day's three-dimensional graph of solar activity, seemed no older to me than the day on which I had first met her: a woman, tall, graceful, lithe, platinum-haired, and with the somber, smoldering, unreadable face of Eve—and yet, compared to me now, a child in truth.

"Good morning, Mrs. Andresson," di Ferruci said, smiling.

She looked up and smiled back. "Good afternoon," she said. "I see you're about to take another series of readings. Don't let me interrupt you."

"That's quite all right; thus far it's routine," di Ferruci said. I glanced sidewise at him and then back to my wife. "We'd just begun to take readings to break up the monotony of the old argument."

"That's true," I said. "But it would be just as well if you didn't drop in on us unexpectedly, Marguerita. If this had been a critical stage——"

"I'm sorry," she said contritely. "I should have phoned, but I'm always afraid that the telephone will interrupt you, too. When I'm here I can hope to see whether or not you're busy—and you can see who's calling. The telephone has no eyes."

She touched the graph, delicately. This graph, I should explain, is made of fourteen curves cut out in cardboard, and assembled so that one set of seven curved pieces is at right angles to the other set. It expresses the variation in intensity of RF emanation across the surface of the sun at the ten-centimeter wave length, where our readings commonly are taken; we make a new such model each day. It shows at a glance, by valley or peak, any deviation from the sun's normal output, thus helping us greatly in interpreting our results.

"How strange it looks today," she said. "It's always in motion, like a comber racing toward the shore. I keep expecting it to begin to break at the top."

Di Ferruci stopped tinkering with the drive clock and sat down before the control desk, his blue-black helmet of hair—only a little peppered by his memories of the Inchon landing—swivelling sharply toward her. I could not see his face. "What an eerie notion," he said. "Mrs. Andresson, you and the doctor'll have me sharing your presentiments of doom any minute now."

"It isn't a question of presentiments," I said sharply. "You should be aware by now, Mario, that in the RF range the sun is a variable star. Does that mean nothing to you? Let me ask you another question: How do you explain Eta Carina?"

"What's Eta Carina?" Marguerita said.

I did not know quite how to begin answering her, but di Ferruci, who lacked my intimate knowledge of her limitations, had no such qualms.

"It's a freak—one of the worst freaks of the past ten years," he said eagerly. "It's a star that's gone nova three times. The last time was in 1952, about a hundred years after the previous explosion. Before that it had an outburst in the 1600's, and it may have blown up about 142 A. D., too. Each time it gains in brightness nearly one hundred thousand times—as violent a stellar catastrophe as you can find anywhere in the records." He offered the data to her like a bouquet, and before I could begin to take offense, swung back upon me again. "Surely, Doc, you don't maintain that Eta Carina is a flare star?"

"All stars are flare stars," I said, looking steadily at him. His eyes were in shadow. "More than that: all stars are novas, in the long run. Young stars like our sun are variable only in the radio spectrum, but gradually they become more and more unstable, and begin to produce small flares. Then come the big flares, like Beta Centauri outburst; then they go nova; and then the cycle begins again."

"Evidence?"

"Everywhere. The process goes on in little in the short-term variables, the Cepheids. Eta Carina shows how it works in a smaller, non-cluster star. The other novas we've observed simply have longer periods—they haven't had time to go nova again within record history. *But they will.*"

"Well," di Ferruci said, "if that's so, Richardson's visions of our sun exploding seems almost pleasant. You see us being roasted gradually instead, in a series of hotter and hotter flares. When does the first one hit us, by your figures?"

Mario was watching me steadily. Perhaps I looked strange, for I was once again in the grip of that anomalous emotion, so impossible to describe, in which terror and ecstasy blended and fused into some whole beyond any possibility of communication. As I had stated for the first time what I saw, and saw so clearly, was ahead for us all, this deep radical emotion began to shake me as if I had stepped all unawares from the comfortable island of relative, weighable facts into some blastingly cold ocean of Absolute Truth.

"I don't know," I said. "It needs checking. But I give us six months."

Marguerita's and di Ferruci's eyes met. Then he said, "Let's check it, then. We should be able to find the instability threshold for each stage, from RR Lyrae stars right through classical Cepheids, long-periods, and irregulars to radio-variables. We already know the figure for novas. Let's dot the i's and cross the t's—and then find out where our sun stands."

"Theodor," Marguerita said, "what—what will happen if you're right?"

"Then the next flare will be immensely greater than the 1948 one. The Earth will survive it; life on Earth probably will not—certainly not human life."

Marguerita remained standing beside the model a moment longer, nursing the hand which had been touching it. Then she looked at me out of eyes too young for me to read, and left the observatory.

With a hasty word to di Ferruci, I followed her, berating myself as I went. Suspecting as I did the shortness of the span left to us, I had not planned to utter a word about what was to be in store for us in her presence; that had been one of the reasons why I had objected to her visits to the observatory. There had simply been no reason to cloud our last months together with the shadow of a fate she could not understand.

But when I reached the top of the granite steps leading down to the road, she was gone—nor could I see either her figure or any sign of a car on the road which led down the mountain. She had vanished as completely as if she had never existed.

Needless to say, I was disturbed. There are cabins in the woods, only a short distance away from the observatory proper, which are used by staff members as temporary residences; we had never made use of them —radio-astronomy being an art which can be carried on by day better than by night—but, nevertheless, I checked them systematically. It was inconceivable to me that she could be in the main observatory, but I searched that too, as well as the solar tower and the Schmidt shed.

She was nowhere. By the time I had finished searching, it was sunset and there was no longer any use in my returning to my own instrument. I could only conclude that I had miscalculated the time lag between her exit and my pursuit, and that I would find her at home.

Yet, somehow I did not go home. All during my search of the grounds another thought had been in my head! What if I was wrong? Suppose that there was no solar pulsation cycle? Suppose that my figures were meaningless? If this seems to you to be a strange thing for a man to be thinking, while searching for an inexplicably vanished wife, I can only say that the two subjects seemed to me to be somehow not unconnected.

And as it turned out, I was right. I have said that I have a sense of fate.

In the end, I went back to the observatory, now dark and, I supposed, deserted. But there was a light glowing softly inside: the evenly lit surface of the transparency viewer. Bent over it, his features floating eerily in nothingness, was Mario di Ferruci.

I groped for the switch, found it, and the fluorescents flashed on overhead. Mario straightened, blinking.

"Mario, what are you doing here? I thought you had left before sundown."

"I meant to," di Ferruci said slowly. "But I couldn't stop thinking about your theory. It isn't every day that one hears the end of the world announced by a man of your eminence. I decided I just had to run my own check, or else go nuts wondering."

"Why couldn't you have waited for me?" I said. "We could have done the work together much quicker and more easily."

"That's true," he said slowly. "But, Dr. Andresson, I'm just a graduate student, and you're a famous man; young as you are. I'm a little afraid of being overwhelmed—of missing an error because you've checked it already, or failing to check some point at all—that kind of thing. After all, we're all going to die if you're right, and that's hardly a minor matter;

so I thought I'd try paddling my own canoe. Maybe I'll find the world just as far up the creek as you do. But I had to try."

It took me a while to digest this, distracted as I already was. After a while I said, as calmly as I could: "And what have you found?"

"Dr. Andresson—*you're wrong.*"

For an instant I could not see. All the red raw exploding universe of unstable stars went wheeling through my old head like maddened atoms. But I am a scientist; I conquered it.

"Wherein am I wrong?"

Di Ferruci took a deep breath. His face was white and set under the fluorescents. "Dr. Andresson, forgive me; this is a hard thing for me to say. But the error in your calcs is way the hell back in the beginning, in your thermodynamic assumptions. It lies in the step between the Chapman-Cowling expression, and your derivation for the co-efficient of mutual diffusion. Your derivation is perfectly sound in classical thermodynamics, but that isn't what we have to deal with here; we're dealing instead with a completely ionized binary gas, where your quantity D_{12} becomes nothing more than a first approximation."

"I never called it anything else."

"Maybe not," di Ferruci said doggedly. "But your math handles it as an absolute. By the time your expanded equation fifty-eight is reached, you've lost a complete set of subscripts and your expressions for the electron of charge wind up all as odd powers! I'm not impugning your logic —it's fantastically brilliant—but insofar as it derives from the bracketed expression D_{12} it doesn't represent a real situation."

He stared at me, half-defiantly, half in a kind of anxiety the source of which I could not fathom. It had been many years since I had been young; now I was gravid with death—his, mine, yours, Marguerita's, everyone's. I said only: "Let's check it again."

But we never had the chance; at that moment the door opened soundlessly, and Marguerita came back.

"Theodor, Mario!" she said breathlessly. "Are you trying to work yourselves to death? Let's all live to our appointed times, whenever they come! Theodor, I was so frightened when you didn't come home—why didn't you call——"

"I'm not sure anyone would have answered," I said grimly. "Or if someone had, I would have suspected her of being an impostor—or a teleport."

She turned her strange look upon me. "I—don't understand you."

"I hope you don't, Marguerita. We'll take that matter up in private. Right now we're making a check. Dr. di Ferruci was about to knock the solar pulsation theory to flinders when you entered."

"Doc!" di Ferruci protested. "That wasn't the point at all. I just wanted to find——"

"Don't call me 'Doc'!"

"Very well," di Ferruci said. His face became whiter still. "But I insist on finishing my sentence. I'm not out to kick apart your theory; I think it's a brilliant theory and that it may still very well be right. There are holes in your math, that's all. They're big holes and they need filling; maybe, between us, we could fill them. But if you don't care enough to want to do the job, why should I?"

"Why, indeed?"

He stared at me with fury for a moment. Then he put his hand distractedly to his forehead, stood up slowly, and began to pace. "Look, Doc—Dr. Andresson. Believe me, I'm not hostile to the idea. It scares me, but that's only because I'm human. There's still a good chance that it's basically sound. If we could go to work on it now, really intensively, we might be able to have it in shape for the triple-A-S meeting in Chicago two months from now. It'd set every physicist, every astronomer, every scientist of any stripe by the ears!"

And there was the clue for which, all unconsciously, I had been waiting. "Indeed it would," I said. "And for four months, old Dr. Andresson and young Dr. di Ferruci would be famous—as perhaps no scientists had ever been famous before. Old Dr. Andresson has had his measure of fame and has lost his faith in it—but for young Dr. di Ferruci, even four months would be a deep draught. For that he is willing to impugn his senior's work, to force endless conferences, to call everything into question—all to get his own name added to the credits on the final paper."

"Theodor," Marguerita said. "Theodor, this isn't like you. If——"

"And there is even a touch of humor in this little playlet," I said. "The old man would have credited young Dr. di Ferruci in the final paper in any case. The whole maneuver was for nothing."

"There was no maneuver," di Ferruci ground out, his fists clenched. His nervous movements of his hand across his forehead had turned his blue-black hair into a mare's nest. "I'm not an idiot. I know that if you're right, the whole world will be in ashes before the year is out—including any research papers which might carry my name, and any human eyes which might see them.

"What I want to do is to pin down this concept to the point where it's unassailable. The world will demand nothing less of it than that. *Then* it can be presented to the AAAS—and the world will have four months during which the best scientific brains on Earth can look for an out, a way to save at least a part of the race, even if only two people. What's fame to me, or anyone else, if this theory is right? Gas, just gas.

But if we can make the world believe it, utterly and completely, then the world will find a loophole. Nothing less than the combined brains of the whole of science could do the job—and we won't get those brains to work unless we convince them!"

"Nonsense," I said calmly. "There is no 'out', as you put it. But I'll agree that I looked deeper into you than I needed for a motive. Do you think that I have overlooked all these odd coincidences? Here is my wife, and here are you, both at improbable hours, neither of you expecting me; here is young Dr. di Ferruci interrupted at his task of stealing something more than just my work; here is Marguerita Andresson, emerged from wherever she has been hiding all evening, unable to believe that Earth's last picture is all but painted, but ready to help a young man with blue-black hair to steal the pretty notion and capitalize on it."

There was a faint sound from Marguerita. I did not look at her.

After a long while, di Ferruci said: "You are a great astronomer, Dr. Andresson. I owe you twenty years of inspiration from a distance, and five years of the finest training a master ever gave a tyro.

"You are also foul-minded, cruel-tongued, and very much mistaken. I resign from this University as of now; my obligation to you is wiped out by what you saw fit to say of me." He searched for his jacket, failed to find it, and gave up at once in trembling fury. "Goodbye, Mrs. Andresson, with my deepest sympathy. And Doc, goodbye—and God have mercy on you."

"Wait," I said. I moved then, after what seemed a century of standing frozen. The young man stopped, his hand halfway to the doorknob, and his back to me. Watching him, I found my way to a chart-viewer, and picked up the six-inch pair of dividers he had been using to check my charts.

"Well," he said.

"It's not so easy as that, Mario. You don't walk out of a house with the stolen goods under your arm when the owner is present. A strong man armed keepeth his house. You may not leave; you may not take my hard-won theory to another university; you may not leave Hamelin with pipes in your hand. You may not carry both my heart and my brains out of this observatory as easily as you would carry a sack of potatoes. In short—*you may not leave!*"

. I threw the points of the dividers high and launched myself soul and body at that hunched, broad back. Marguerita's sudden scream rang deafeningly as a siren in the observatory dome.

The rest you know.

I have been honest with you. Tell me: where have you hidden her now?

I, Andrew, a servant of the Sun, who also am your brother, he who was called and was sanctified, say unto you, blessed be he that readeth, and keepeth the word; for behold, the time is at hand; be thou content.

2. For behold, it was given to me, in the City of Angels, upon a high hill, to look upon His face; whereupon I fell down and wept;

3. And He said, I am the Be-All and End-All; I am the Being and the Becoming; except that they be pure, none shall look on Me else they die, for the time is at hand. And when He had spoken thus, I was sore afraid.

4. And He said, Rise up, and go forth unto the peoples, and say thou, Unless thou repent, I will come to thee quickly, and shine My countenance upon thee. I shall loosen the seals, and sound the trumpets, and open the vials, and the deaths which shall come upon thee will be numbered as seven times seven.

5. The Sun shall become black as sackcloth of hair, and the moon become as blood; and the stars of heaven shall fall onto the earth, and the heaven depart as a scroll when it is rolled together, and every mountain and island be moved out of their places. And all men shall hide themselves, and say to the mountains and rocks, Fall on us, and hide us from the face of Him that sitteth on the throne.

6. There will be hail and fire mingled with blood, and these cast upon the earth; a great mountain burning with fire shall be cast into the sea; and there will fall a great star from heaven, burning as it were a lamp, upon the fountains of waters; and the third part of the Sun shall be smitten, and the third part of the moon; and there shall arise a smoke out of the pit, so that the air and the day be darkened.

7. And if there be any who worship not Me, and who heed not, I say unto you all, woe, woe, for ye shall all die; ye shall feast without sacraments, ye shall batten upon each other; ye shall be clouds without water, driven by dry winds; ye shall be dry sterile trees, twice dead, and withered; wandering stars, to whom is given the dark of the emptiness of eternity; verily, I say unto you;

8. Ye shall be tormented with fire and brimstone, the third part of trees shall be burnt up, and all green grass be burnt up, and the third part of creatures which were in the sea, and had life, shall die; and the waters shall become blood, and many men die of the waters, because they be bitter; and the smoke of your torment shall ascend up for ever and ever, and thou shalt have no rest, neither day nor night; for the hour of judgment is come.

9. And saying thus, He that spake to me departed, and His dread spirit, and I went down among the people, and spoke, and bade men beware; and none heeded.

10. Neither those who worshipped the stars, and consulted, one

among the others; nor those who worshipped man and his image; nor those who made prayers to the invisible spirits of the air; nor those who worshipped any other thing; and the spirit of Him who had spoken was heavy upon me, so that I went unto my chambers and lay me down in a swound.

11. And the angel of the Sun spoke to me as I lay, and spake with a voice like trombones, and said, Behold, all men are evil, but thou shalt redeem them, albeit thou remain a pure child of the Sun, and thou alone. Thou shalt have power; a two-edged sword shall go out of thy mouth, and thou shalt hold seven times seven stars in thy palm, and be puissant; this I shall give thee as thine own, if only thou remainest, and thou alone. And I said: Lord, I am Thine; do with me as Thou wilt.

12. And I went forth again, and spoke, and the nations of men harkened, and the kings of the world bent the knee, and the princes of the world brought tribute, seven times seven; and those who worshipped the stars, and the spirits of the air, and all other things, bowed down before Him; and it was well with them.

13. Now at this time there appeared a great wonder in heaven: a star clothed in a glory of hair, like a woman; and the people gathered and murmured of wonder, saying, Beware, for there is a god in the sky, clothed in hair like a woman, and with streaming of robes and bright garments; and behold, it draws near in the night, and fears not the Sun; the hem of this robe gathers about us.

14. And there arose a woman of the world, and came forward, preaching the gospel of the wild star, saying: Our god the Sun is a false god; his mate is this great star; they will devour us. There is no god but man.

15. And this woman, which was called Margo, summoned the people and made laughter with them, and derision, and scorned the Sun, and gave herself to the priests of the voices in the air, and to those who worshipped numbers, and to the kings and princes of the world; and there was whirling of tambourines in the high towers of the Sun.

16. And the angel of the Sun spoke to me with the sound of trombones, saying, Go with thy power which has been given to thee, and crush this woman else thou shalt be given to the wild star, and to the flames of the wild star's hair, and with thee the world; I command thee, slay this woman, for thou hast been given the power, nor shall it be given thee again; I have spoken.

17. And I went, and the woman called Margo spoke unto me saying: Thou art fair, and hath power. Give me of thy power, and I will give you of mine. Neither the wild star nor the Sun shall have such power as we have.

18. And I looked upon her, and she was fair, beyond all the daughters

of the earth; and when she spoke, her voice was as the sounding of bells; and there was a spirit in her greater than the souls of men; and a star, clothed in a glory of hair, with streaming of robes and bright garments; and I kissed the hem of her robe.

19. And the voice of the angel of the Sun was heard like a sounding of trombones, saying, Thou hast yielded thy power to an harlot, and given the earth to the fire; thy power is riven from thee, and all shall die;

20. So be it.

My name is George Anders. I have no hope that anyone will read this record, which will probably be destroyed with me—I have no safer place to put it than on my person—but I write it anyhow, if only to show that man was a talkative animal to his last gasp. If the day of glory which has been foretold comes about, there may well be a new and better world which will cherish what I put down here—but I am desperately afraid that the terrible here-and-now is the day the voices promised, and that there will be nothing else forever and ever.

This is not to say that the voices lied. But since that first night when they spoke to me, I have come to know that they speak for forces of tremendous power, forces to which human life is as nothing. A day of glory we have already had, truly—but such a day as no man could long for.

It was on the morning of March 18, 1956, that that day dawned, with a sun so huge as to dominate the entire eastern sky—a flaring monster which made the memory of our accustomed sun seem like a match-flame. All the previous night had been as hot as high summer, although not four days before we had a blizzard. Now, with the rising of this colossal globe, we learned the real meaning of heat.

A day of glory, of glory incredible—and deadly. The heat grew and grew. By a little after noon the temperature in the shade was more than one hundred fifty degrees, and in the open—it is impossible to describe what an inferno it was under the direct rays of that sun. A bucket of water thrown into the street from a window boiled in mid-air before it could strike the pavement.

In some parts of the city, where there were wooden buildings and asphalt or tarred-black streets, everything was burning. In the country, the radio said, it was worse; forests were ablaze, grasslands, wheatfields, everything. Curiously, it was this that saved many of us, for before the afternoon could reach its full fury the sky was gray with smoke, cutting off a least a little of the rays of that solar horror. Flakes of ash fell everywhere.

Millions died that day. Only a few in refrigerated rooms—meat-coolers, cold-storage warehouses, the blast-tunnels of frozen-food firms, underground fur-storage vaults—survived, where the refrigation apparatus itself survived. By a little after midnight, the outside temperature had dropped to only slightly above one hundred degrees, and the trembling and half-mad wraiths who still lived emerged to look silently at the ruined world.

I was one of these; I had planned that I would be. Months before, I had known that this day of doom was to come upon us, for the voices had said so. I can still remember—for as long as I live I will remember, whether it be a day or forty years—the onset of that strange feeling, that withdrawal from the world around me, as if everything familiar had suddenly become as unreal as a stage-setting. What had seemed commonplace became strange, sinister: What was that man doing with the bottles which contained the white fluid? Why was the uniform he wore also white? Why not blood in the bottles? And the man with the huge assemblage of paper; why was he watching it so intently as he sat in the subway? Did he expect it to make some sudden move if he looked away? Were the black marks with which the paper was covered the footprints of some miniscule horde?

And as the world underwent its slow transformation, the voices came. I cannot write here what they said, because paper would not bear such words. But the meaning was clear. The destruction of the world was at hand. And beyond it——

Beyond it, the day of glory. A turn toward something new, something before which all men's previous knowledge of grandeur would pale; a new Apocalypse and Resurrection? So it seemed, then. But the voices spoke in symbol and parable, and perhaps the rising of the hellish sun was the only "day of glory" we would ever see.

And so I hid in my shelter, and survived that first day. When I first emerged into the boiling, choking midnight smoke I could see no one else, but after a while something white came out of the darkness toward me. It was a young girl, in what I took to be a nightgown—the lightest garment, at any event, which she could have worn in this intolerable heat.

"What will happen to us?" she said, as soon as she saw me. "What will happen to us? Will it be the same tomorrow?"

"I don't know," I said. "What's your name?"

"Margaret." She coughed. "This must be the end of the world. If the sun is like this tomorrow——"

"It *is* the end of the world," I said. "But maybe it's the beginning of another. You and I will live to see it."

"How do you know?"

"By your name. The voices call you the mother of the new gods. Have you heard the voices?"

She moved away from me a little bit. There was a sudden, furious gust of wind, and a long line of sparks flew through the lurid sky overhead. "The voices?" she said.

"Yes. The voices of the powers which have done all this. They have promised to save us, you and I. Together we can recreate——"

Suddenly, she was running. She vanished almost instantly into darkness and the smoke. I ran after her, calling, but it was hopeless; besides, my throat was already raw, and in the heat and the aftermath of the day I had no strength. I went back to my crypt. Tomorrow would tell the tale.

Sleep was impossible. I waited for dawn, and watched for it through my periscope, from the buried vault of the bank where, a day before, I had been a kind of teller. This had been no ordinary bank, and I had never taken or issued any money; but otherwise the terms are just. Perhaps you have already guessed, for no ordinary vault is equipped with periscope to watch the surrounding countryside. This was Fort Knox, a bed of gold to be seeded with promise of the Age of Gold under this golden fire.

And, at last, the sun came up. It was immense. But I waited a while, and watched the image of it which was cast from the periscope eyepiece onto the opposite wall of the vault. It was not as big as it had been yesterday. And where yesterday the direct rays from the periscope had instantly charred a thousand-dollar bill, today they made only a slowly-growing brown spot which never found its kindling-point.

The lesson was plain. Today most of what remained of mankind would be slain. But there would be survivors.

Then I slept.

I awoke toward the end of the day and set about the quest which I knew I must make. I took nothing with me but water, which I knew I could not expect to find. Then I left the vault forever.

The world which greeted me as I came to the surface was a world transformed: blasted. Nearly everything had been levelled, and the rest lay in jumbled, smoking ruins. The sky was completely black. Near the Western horizon, the swollen sun sank, still monstrous, but now no hotter than the normal sun at the height of a tropic day. The great explosion, whatever it had been, was nearly over.

And now I had to find Margaret, and fulfill the millennium which the voices had promised. The tree of man had been blasted, but still it bore one flower. It was my great destiny to bring that flower to fruit.

Thus I bring this record to a close. I leave it here in the vault; then I shall go forth into the desert of the world. If any find it, remember: I am your father and the father of your race. If not, you will all be smoke.

Now I go. My knife is in my hand.

My name is Andy Virchow, but probably you know me better as Admiral Universe. Nowhere in the pages of galactic history has there ever been a greater champion of justice. Who do you know that doesn't know Universe, ruler of the spaceways, hero of science, bringer of law and order in the age of the conquest of space? Not a planetary soul, that's who.

Of course not everybody knows that Andy Virchow is Admiral Universe. Sometimes I have to go in disguise and fool criminals. Then I am Andy Virchow, and they think I am only eight years old, until I have them where I want them and I whip out my Cosmic Smoke Gun and reveal my identification.

Sometimes I don't say who I am but just clean the crooks up and ride off in my rocket, the *Margy II*. Then afterwards the people I have saved say, "He didn't even stay to be thanked. I wonder who he was?" and somebody else says, "There's only one man on the frontiers of space like him. That's Admiral Universe."

My rocket is called the *Margy II* partly because my secret interstellar base is on Mars and the Mars people we call Martians call themselves Margies and I like to think of myself as a Margy *too,* because the people of Earth don't understand me and I do good for them because I am champion of justice, not because I like them. Then they're sorry, but it's too late. Me and the Margies understand each other. They ask me for advice before they do anything important, and I tell them what to do. Earth people are always trying to tell other people what to do; the Margies aren't like that, they ask what to do instead of always giving orders.

Also Admiral Universe calls his rocket *Margy II,* because my patron saint is St. Margaret who gets me out of trouble if I do anything wrong. Admiral Universe never does anything wrong because St. Margaret is on his side all the time. St. Margaret is the patron saint of clocks and is called the Mother of Galaxies, because she was a mother—not like my mother, who is always shouting and sending me to bed too early— and mothers have milk and *galaxy* is Greek for milk. If you didn't know I was Admiral Universe you'd ask how I know what's Greek for anything, but Admiral Universe is a great scientist and knows everything. Besides, my father was a teacher of Greek before he died and he was Admiral Universe's first teacher.

In all the other worlds in the universe everything is pretty perfect except for a few crooks that have to be shot. It's not like Earth at all. The planets are different from each other, but they are all happy and have lots of science and the people are kind and never raise their hands to each other to send each other to bed without their supper.

Sometimes there are terrible accidents in the spacelanes and Admiral Universe arrives on the scene in the knick of time and saves everybody, and all the men shake his hand and all the girls kiss him and say mushy things to him, but he refuses their thanks in a polite way and disappears into the trackless wastes of outer space because he carries a medal of St. Margaret's in his pocket over his heart. She is his only girl, but she can't ever be anybody's girl because she is a saint, and this is Admiral Universe's great tragedy which he never tells anybody because it's his private business that he has to suffer all by himself, and besides if anybody else knew it they would think he was mushy too and wouldn't be so afraid of him, like crooks I mean.

Admiral Universe is always being called from all over outer space to help people and sometimes he can't be one place because he has to be in some other place. Then he has to set his jaw and do the best he can and be tough about the people he can't help because he is helping somebody else. First he asks St. Margaret what he should do and she tells him. Then he goes and does it, and he is very sorry for the people who got left out, but he knows that he did what was right.

This is why I wasn't there when the sun blew up, because I was helping people somewhere else at the time. I didn't even know it was the sun, because I was so far away that it was just another star, and I didn't see it blow up, because stars blow up all the time and if you're Admiral Universe you get used to it and hardly notice. Margaret might have told me, but she's a saint, and doesn't care.

If I'd of been there I would have helped. I would have saved my friends, and all the great scientists, and the girls who might be somebody's mothers some day, and everybody that was anybody except Dr. Ferguson, I would have left him behind to show him how wrong he was about me.

But I wasn't there at the time, and besides Admiral Universe never did like the Earth much. Nobody will really miss it.

My name is T. V. Andros. My father was an Athenian immigrant and a drunkard. After he came here he worked in the mines, but not very often because he was mostly soused.

Sometimes he beat my mother. She had TB but she took good care of us until I was eight; early that year, my father got killed in a brawl in a bar, and the doctor—his name I forget—sent her back to the little town in Pennsylvania where she was born. She died that March.

After that I worked in the mines. The law says a kid can't work in the mines but in company towns the law don't mean much. I got the cough too but the other miners took care of me and I grew up tough and could handle myself all right. When I was fourteen, I killed a man with a pick-handle, one blow. I don't remember what we were fighting about.

Mostly I kept out of fights, though. I had a crazy idea I wanted to educate myself and I read a lot—all kinds of things. For a while I read those magazines that tell about going to other planets and stuff like that. I didn't learn anything, except that to learn good you need a teacher, and the last one of those had been run out by the company cops. They said he was a Red.

It was tough in the mines. It's dark down there and hot, and you can't breathe sometimes for the dust. And you can't never wash the dirt off, it gets right down into your skin and makes you feel black even at noon on Sundays when you've scrubbed till your skin's raw.

I had a sixteen-year-old girl but I was too dirty for her. I tried to go to the priest about it but he wasn't looking for nothing but sin, and kept asking me had I done anything wrong with the girl. When I said I hadn't he wasn't interested no more. I hadn't, either, but he made me so mad he made me wish I had. After that I sort of drifted away from going to church because I couldn't stand his face. Maybe that was bad but it had its good side, too; I missed it and I took to cracking the *Bible* now and then. I never got much of the *Bible* when I was going to church.

After a while I took to drinking something now and then. It wasn't right for a kid but I wasn't a kid no more, I was eighteen and besides in the company towns there ain't nothing else to do. It helped some but not enough. All the guys in the bar ever talk about are wages and women. You got to drink yourself blind and stupid to keep from hearing them, otherwise you go nuts. After a while I was blind and stupid a lot of the time and didn't no longer know what I did or didn't.

Once when I was drunk I mauled a girl younger than I was; I don't know why I did it. She was just the age I had been when my mother left me to go home and die. Then it was all up with me at the mines. I didn't mean her any harm but the judge gave me the works. Two years.

I got clean for once in my life while I was in the jug and I did some more reading but it just mixed me up more. Two years is a long time. When I got out I felt funny in my head. I couldn't stop thinking about the girl who thought I was too dirty for her. I was at the age when I needed girls.

But I wasn't going to mess with girls my age who could see the prison whiteness on the outside and all that ground-in coal dust underneath it. I couldn't forget Maggy, the girl that got me into the jam. That had been a hot night in summer, with a moon as big as the sun, as red as blood. I hadn't meant her any harm. She reminded me of myself when my mother had gone away.

I found another Maggy and when the cops caught me they worked me over. I can't hear in one ear now and my nose is skewed funny on my face. I had it coming because I hurt the girl. When they let me out again I got a job as a super, but there was another girl in the apartment above, and I went to fix a pipe there while her mother was away. It was a hot day with a big sun and no air moving, just like the day my mother left. I didn't really know nothing had happened until I saw that one of my hands was dark red. Then I tried to get her to talk to me but she wouldn't move. After a while I felt some woman's hands beating at my neck. She said, "Stop, you!"

This time they took me to a hospital and a Dr. Ferdinand talked to me. Write it all down, he said. It may help you. So I wrote it all down, like you see it here. Then they put me in a cell and said I would have to stay for a while. I don't talk to them much any more.

It is a real hot day. Outside the cell the sun is bigger. I don't breathe good any more but there's something wrong with the air. I pulled my mattress to pieces but I didn't find nothing. Maybe something is going to happen. Something is going to happen.

My name is Man. I will write my story if you wish.
I was. . . .
Here the ashes blow away. The voices die.

THE PLAYGROUND

by Ray Bradbury

RAY BRADBURY (1920–   ) was born in the Middle West, but has spent most of his life in California. Since his early emergence in *Weird Tales,* he has taken his place among the best contemporary writers of the short story in English. He has contributed to magazines ranging from *The Reporter* and *The New Yorker* to *Mademoiselle* and *Collier's* from *Harper's* to *Esquire,* from *The Saturday Evening Post* to *Charm.* He has been widely anthologized and is the author of several books—*Dark Carnival, The Martian Chronicles, The Illustrated Man, The Golden Apples of the Sun, Fahrenheit 451*—and will have a new version of his first book in 1954. At this writing, he and his wife and daughters are in Ireland where he is writing script for John Huston's *Moby Dick.*

A thousand times before and after his wife's death, Mr. Charles Underhill ignored the Playground on his way to and from his commuter's limited train. He neither liked nor disliked the Playground; he hardly knew it existed.

But only this morning his sister Carol, who had occupied the empty space across the breakfast table from him each day for six months, quietly broached the subject.

"Jim's almost three years old now," she said. "So tomorrow I'm going to start him at the Playground."

"Playground?" said Mr. Underhill.

At his office, he underlined a memorandum with black ink: *Look at Playground.*

That afternoon, the thunder of the train subsiding in his body, Underhill struck up through town on his usual path home, newspaper tucked crisply under his arm to prevent reading himself past the park. So it was, at five-ten in the late day, that he came to the cool iron fence and the open gate of the Playground, and stood for a long, long time, frozen there, gazing in at it all. . . .

At first there seemed absolutely nothing whatever to see. And then as he adjusted his attention outward from his usual interior monologue, the scene before him, a grey, blurred television image, came to a slow focus.

Primarily, he was aware of dim voices, faint underwater cries emerging from a series of vague streaks and zigzag lines and shadows. Then, as if someone had kicked the machine, screams jumped at him in full throat, visions leaped clear. Now he saw the children! They were dashing across the Playground meadow, fighting, pummeling, scratching, falling, every wound bleeding or about to bleed or freshly caked over. A dozen cats thrown among sleeping dogs could not have shrieked as loud! With incredible clarity, Mr. Underhill saw the tiniest cuts and scabs on knees and faces.

He weathered the first blast of sound, blinking. His nostrils took over when his eyes and ears retired in panic.

He sniffed the cutting odors of salve, raw adhesive, camphor, and pink mercurochrome, so strong it lay bitter on his tongue. An iodine wind blew through the steel fence wires which glinted dully in the grey light of the overcast day. The rushing children were hell cut loose in a vast pinball table, a colliding, and banging, and totaling of hits and misses, thrusts and plungings to a grand and as yet unforeseen total of brutalities.

And was he mistaken or was the light within the Playground of a peculiar intensity? Every child seemed to possess four shadows: one dark, and three faint penumbras which made it strategically impossible to tell which way their swift bodies were racing until they bashed their targets. Yes, the oblique, pressing light made the Playground seem deep, far away, and remote from his touching. Or perhaps it was the hard steel wire fence, not unlike those barriers in zoos, beyond which *anything* might happen.

A pen of misery, thought Underhill. Why do children insist on making life horrible for each other? Oh, the continual torture. He heard himself sigh with immense relief. Thank God, childhood was over and done for him. No more pinchings, bruisings, senseless passions and shattered dreams.

A gust of wind tore the paper from his hand. He ran after it down the Playground steps. Clutching the paper, he retreated hastily. For in that one brief instant, stranded in the Playground's atmosphere, he had felt his hat grow too large, his coat too cumbersome, his belt too loose, his shoes too big; he had felt like a small boy playing businessman in his father's clothes; the gate behind him had loomed impossibly tall, while the sky pressed a huge weight of greyness at his eyes, and the scent of iodine, like a tiger's breath exhaled upon him, blew his hair. He tripped and almost fell, running back.

He stood outside the Playground, like someone who has just emerged, in shock, from a terrible cold sea.

"Hello, Charlie!"

He heard the voice and turned to see who had called him. There on top a metal slide, a boy of some nine years was waving. "Hello, Charlie . . . !"

Mr. Charles Underhill raised a hand. But I don't *know* that boy, he thought. And why should he call me by my first name?

The boy was smiling high in the misty air, and now, jostled by other yelling children, rushed shrieking down the slide.

Underhill stood bemused by what he saw. Now the Playground was an immense iron industry whose sole product was pain, sadism and sorrow. If you watched half an hour there wasn't a face in the entire enclosure that didn't wince, cry, redden with anger, pale with fear, one moment or another. Really! Who said childhood was the best time of life? When in reality it was the most terrible, the most merciless era, the barbaric time when there were no police to protect you, only parents preoccupied with themselves and their taller world. No, if he had his way, he touched the cold fence with one hand, they'd nail a new sign here: TORQUEMADA'S GREEN.

And as for that boy, the one who had called out to him, who was he? There was something familiar there, perhaps in the hidden bones, an echo of some old friend; probably the son of a successfully ulcered father.

So this is the playground where my son will play, thought Mr. Underhill. So this is it.

Hanging his hat in the hall, checking his lean image in the watery mirror, Underhill felt wintry and tired. When his sister appeared, and his son came tapping on mouse-feet, he greeted them with something less than full attention. The boy clambered thinly over him, playing KING OF THE HILL. And the father, fixing his gaze to the end of the cigar he was slowly lighting, finally cleared his throat and said, "I've been thinking about that playground, Carol."

"I'm taking Jim over tomorrow."

"Not really? *That* playground?"

His mind rebelled. The smell and look of the place were still vivid. That writhing world with its atmosphere of cuts and beaten noses, the air as full of pain as a dentist's office, and those horrid tic-tac-toes and frightening hopscotches under his feet as he picked up his newspaper, horrid and frightening for no reason he could see.

"What's wrong with *that* playground?" asked Carol.

"Have you seen it?" He paused in confusion. "Damn it, I mean, the children there. It's a Black Hole."

"All the children are from well-to-do families."

"Well, they shove and push like little Gestapos," said Underhill. "It'd be like sending a boy to a flour-mill to be crushed into meal by a couple of two-ton grinders! Every time I think of Jim playing in that barbaric pit, I freeze."

"You know very well it's the only convenient park for miles around."

"I don't care about that. All I care is I saw a dozen kinds of bats and clubs and air guns. By the end of the first day, Jim would be in splinters. They'd have him barbecued, with an orange in his mouth."

She was beginning to laugh. "How you exaggerate."

"I'm serious!"

"You can't live Jim's life for him. He has to learn the hard way. He's got to take a little beating and beat others up; boys are like that."

"I don't *like* boys like that."

"It's the happiest time of life."

"Nonsense. I used to look back on childhood with great nostalgia. But now I realize I was a sentimental fool. It was nothing but screaming and running in a nightmare and coming home drenched with terror, from head to foot. If I could possibly save Jim from that, I would."

"That's impractical and, thank God, impossible."

"I won't have him near that place, I tell you. I'll have him grow up a neurotic recluse first."

"Charlie!"

"I will! Those little beasts, you should've seen them. Jim's my son, he is; he's not yours, remember." He felt the boy's thin legs about his shoulders, the boy's delicate fingers rumpling his hair. "I won't have him butchered."

"He'll get it in school. Better to let him take a little shoving about now, when he's three, so he's prepared for it."

"I've thought of that, too." Mr. Underhill held fiercely to his son's ankles which dangled like warm, thin sausages on either lapel. "I might even get a private tutor for him."

"Oh, Charles!"

They did not speak during dinner.

After dinner, he took Jim for a brief walk while his sister was washing the dishes. They strolled past the Playground under the dim street lamps. It was a cooling September night, with the first dry spice of autumn in it. Next week, and the children would be raked in off the fields like so many leaves and set to burning in the schools, using their fire and energy for more constructive purposes. But they would be here after school, ramming about, making projectiles of themselves, crashing and exploding, leaving wakes of misery behind every miniature war.

"Want to go in," said Jim, leaning against the high wire fence, watching the late-playing children beat each other and run.

"No, Jim, you don't want that."

"Play," said Jim, his eyes shining with fascination, as he saw a large boy kick a small boy and the small boy kick a smaller boy to even things up.

"Play, daddy."

"Come along, Jim, you'll never get in that mess if *I* can help it." Underhill tugged the small arm firmly.

"I want to play." Jim was beginning to blubber now. His eyes were melting out of his face and his face was becoming a wrinkled orange of color.

Some of the children heard the crying and glanced over. Underhill had the terrible sense of watching a den of foxes suddenly startled and looking up from the white, hairy ruin of a dead rabbit. The mean yellow-glass eyes, the conical chins, the sharp white teeth, the dreadful wiry hair, the brambly sweaters, the iron-colored hands covered with a day's battle-stains. Their breath moved out to him, dark licorice and mint and juicy-fruit so sickeningly sweet, so combined as to twist his stomach. And over this the hot mustard smell of someone tolerating an early chest cold; the greasy stink of flesh smeared with hot camphorous salves cooking under a flannel sheath. All these cloying, and somehow depressing, odors of pencils, chalk, grass and slateboard erasers, real or imagined, summoned old memory in an instant. Popcorn mortared their teeth, and green jelly showed in their sucking, blowing nostrils. God! God!

They saw Jim, and he was new to them. They said not a word, but as Jim cried louder and Underhill, by main force, dragged him like a cement bag along the walk, the children followed with their glowing eyes. Underhill felt like pushing his fist at them and crying, "You little beasts, you won't get *my* son!"

And then, with beautiful irrelevance, the boy at the top of the blue-metal slide, so high he seemed almost in a mist, far away, the boy with the somehow familiar face, called out to him, waving and waving.

"Hello, Charlie . . . !"

Underhill paused and Jim stopped crying.

"See you later, Charlie . . . !"

And the face of the boy way up there on that high and very lonely slide was suddenly like the face of Thomas Marshall, an old business friend who lived just around the block, but whom he hadn't seen in years.

"See you later, Charlie."

Later, later? What did the fool boy mean?

"I know *you*, Charlie!" called the boy. "Hi!"

"What?" gasped Underhill.

"Tomorrow night, Charlie, hey!" And the boy fell off the slide and lay choking for breath, face like a white cheese from the fall, while children jumped him and tumbled over.

Underhill stood undecided for five seconds or more, until Jim thought to cry again and then, with the golden fox eyes upon them, in the first chill of autumn, he dragged Jim all the way home.

The next afternoon Mr. Underhill finished at the office early and took the three o'clock train, arriving out in Green Town at three-twenty-five, in plenty of time to drink in the brisk rays of the autumnal sun. Strange how one day it is suddenly autumn, he thought. One day it is summer and the next, how could you measure or tell it? Something about the temperature or the smell? Or the sediment of age knocked loose from your bones during the night and circulating in your blood and heart, giving you a slight tremble and a chill? A year older, a year dying, was *that* it?

He walked up toward the Playground, planning the future. It seemed you did more planning in autumn than any other season. This had to do with dying, perhaps. You thought of death and you automatically planned. Well, then, there was to be a tutor for Jim, *that* was positive; none of those horrible schools for him. It would pinch the bank account a bit, but Jim would at least grow up a happy boy. They would pick and choose his friends. Any slambang bullies would be thrown out as soon as they so much as touched Jim. And as for this Playground? Completely out of the question!

"Oh hello, Charles."

He looked up suddenly. Before him, at the entrance to the wire enclosure, stood his sister. He noted instantly that she called him Charles, instead of Charlie. Last night's unpleasantness had not quite evaporated. "Carol, what're you doing *here*?"

She flushed guiltily and glanced in through the fence.

"You didn't," he said.

His eyes sought among the scrabbling, running, screaming children. "Do you mean to say . . . ?"

His sister nodded, half amused. "I thought I'd bring him early——"

"Before I got home, so I wouldn't know, is *that* it?"

"That was it."

"Good God, Carol, where *is* he?"

"I just came to see."

"You mean you left him there all afternoon?"

"Just for five minutes while I shopped."

"And you *left* him. Good God!" Underhill seized her wrist. "Well, come on, find him, get him out of there!"

They peered in together past the wire to where a dozen boys charged about, girls slapped each other, and a squabbling heap of children took turns at getting off, making a quick run, and crashing one against another.

"That's where he is, I *know* it!" said Underhill.

Just then, across the field, sobbing and wailing, Jim ran, six boys after him. He fell, got up, ran, fell again, shrieking, and the boys behind shot beans through metal blowers.

"I'll stuff those blowers up their noses!" said Underhill. "Run, Jim! Run!"

Jim made it to the gate. Underhill caught him. It was like catching a rumpled, drenched wad of material. Jim's nose was bleeding, his pants were ripped, he was covered with grime.

"*There's* your playground," said Underhill, on his knees, staring up from his son, holding him, at his sister. "*There* are your sweet, happy innocents, your well-to-do, piddling Fascists. Let me catch this boy there again and there'll be hell to pay. Come on, Jim. All right, you little bastards, get back there!" he shouted.

"We didn't do nothing," said the children.

"What's the world coming to?" Mr. Underhill questioned the universe.

"Hi! Charlie!" said the strange boy, standing to one side. He waved casually and smiled.

"Who's that?" asked Carol.

"How in hell do *I* know?" said Underhill.

"Be seeing you, Charlie. So long," called the boy, fading off.

Mr. Underhill marched his sister and his son home.

"Take your hand off my elbow!" said Carol.

He was trembling; absolutely, continually trembling with rage when he got to bed. He had tried some coffee, but nothing stopped it. He wanted to beat their pulpy little brains out, those gross Cruickshank children; yes, that phrase fit them, those fox-fiend, melancholy Cruickshank children, with all the guile and poison and slyness in their cold faces. In the name of all that was decent, what manner of child was this new generation! A bunch of cutters and hangers and bangers, a drove of bleeding, moronic thumb-screwers, with the sewage of neglect running in their veins? He lay violently jerking his head from one side of his hot pillow to the other, and at last got up and lit a cigarette, but it wasn't enough. He and Carol had had a huge battle when they got home. He had yelled at her and she had yelled back, peacock and peahen shrieking in a wilderness where law and order were insanities laughed at and quite forgotten.

He was ashamed. You didn't fight violence with violence, not if you were a gentleman. You talked very calmly. But Carol didn't give you a chance, damn it! She wanted the boy put in a vise and squashed. She wanted him reamed and punctured and given the laying-on-of-hands. To be beaten from playground to kindergarten, to grammar school, to junior high, to high school. If he was lucky, in high school, the beatings and sadisms would refine themselves, the sea of blood and spittle would drain back down the shore of years and Jim would be left upon the edge of maturity, with God knows what outlook to the future, with a desire, perhaps, to be a wolf among wolves, a dog among dogs, a fiend among fiends. But there was enough of that in the world, already. The very thought of the next ten or fifteen years of torture was enough to make Mr. Underhill cringe; he felt his own flesh impaled with b-b shot, stung, burned, fisted, scrounged, twisted, violated, and bruised. He quivered, like a jelly-fish hurled violently into a concrete-mixer. Jim would never survive it. Jim was too delicate for this horror.

Underhill walked in the midnight rooms of his house thinking of all this, of himself, of the son, the Playground, the fear; there was no part of it he did not touch and turn over with his mind. How much, he asked himself, how much of this is being alone, how much due to Ann's dying, how much to my need, and how much is the reality of the Playground itself, and the children? How much rational and how much nonsense? He twitched the delicate weights upon the scale and watched the indicator glide and fix and glide again, back and forth, softly, between midnight and dawn, between black and white, between raw sanity and naked insanity. He should not hold so tight, he should let his hands drop away from the boy. And yet—there was no hour that looking into Jim's small face he did not see Ann there, in the eyes, in the mouth, in the turn of the nostrils, in the warm breathing, in the glow of blood moving just under the thin shell of flesh. I have a right, he thought, to be afraid. I have every right. When you have two precious bits of porcelain and one is broken and the other, the last one, remains, where can you find the time to be objective, to be immensely calm, to be anything else but concerned?

No, he thought, walking slowly, in the hall, there seems to be nothing I can do except go on being afraid and being afraid of being afraid.

"You needn't prowl the house all night," his sister called from her bed, as she heard him pass her open door. "You needn't be childish. I'm sorry if I seem dictatorial or cold. But you've got to make up your mind. Jim simply cannot have a private tutor. Ann would have wanted him to go to a regular school. And he's got to go back to that playground tomorrow and keep going back until he's learned to stand on his own two feet and until he's familiar to all the children; then they won't pick on him so much."

Underhill said nothing. He got dressed quietly, in the dark and, downstairs, opened the front door. It was about five minutes to midnight as he walked swiftly down the street in the shadows of the tall elms and oaks and maples, trying to outdistance his rage and outrage. He knew Carol was right, of course. This was the world, you lived in it, you accepted it. But that was the very trouble! He had been through the mill already, he knew what it was to be a boy among lions, his own childhood had come rushing back to him in the last few hours, a time of terror and violence, and now he could not bear to think of Jim's going through it all, those long years, especially if you were a delicate child, through no fault of your own, your bones thin, your face pale, what could you expect but to be harried and chased?

He stopped by the Playground, which was still lit by one great overhead lamp. The gate was locked for the night, but that one light remained on until twelve. He wanted to tear the contemptible place down, rip up the steel fences, obliterate the slides, and say to the children, "Go home! Play in your backyards!"

How ingenious, the cold, deep playground. You never knew where anyone lived. The boy who knocked your teeth out, who was *he?* Nobody knew. Where did he live? Nobody knew. How to find him? Nobody knew. Why, you could come here one day, beat the living tar out of some smaller child, and run on the next day to some *other* playground. They would never find you. From playground to playground, you could take your criminal tricks, with everyone forgetting you, since they never knew you. You could return to this playground a month later, and if the little child whose teeth you knocked out was there and recognized you, you could deny it. "No, I'm not the one. Must be some other kid. This is my first time here! No, not me!" And when his back is turned, knock him over. And run off down nameless streets, a nameless person.

What can I possibly do? thought Underhill. Carol's been more than generous with her time; she's been good for Jim, no doubt of it. A lot of the love she would have put into a marriage has gone to him this year.

I can't fight her forever on this, and I can't tell her to leave. Perhaps moving to the country might help. No, no, impossible; the money. But I can't leave Jim here, either.

"Hello, Charlie," said a quiet voice.

Underhill snapped about. Inside the Playground fence, seated in the dirt, making diagrams with one finger in the cool dust, was the solemn nine-year-old boy. He didn't glance up. He said "Hello, Charlie," just sitting there, easily, in that world beyond the hard steel fence.

Underhill said, "How do you know my name?"

"I know it." The boy crossed his legs, comfortably, smiling quietly. "You're having lots of trouble."

"How'd you get in there so late? Who are you?"

"My name's Marshall."

"Of course! Tom Marshall's son, Tommy! I *thought* you looked familiar."

"More familiar than you think." The boy laughed gently.

"How's your father, Tommy?"

"Have you seen him lately?" the boy asked.

"On the street, briefly, two months ago."

"How did he look?"

"What?"

"How did Mr. Marshall *look?*" asked the boy. It seemed strange he refused to say "my father."

"He looked all right. Why?"

"I guess he's happy," said the boy. Mr. Underhill saw the boy's arms and legs and they were covered with scabs and scratches.

"Aren't you going home, Tommy?"

"I sneaked out to see you. I just knew you'd come. You're afraid."

Mr. Underhill didn't know what to say.

"Those little monsters," he said at last.

"Maybe I can help you." The boy made a dust triangle.

It was ridiculous. "How?"

"You'd give anything, wouldn't you, if you could spare Jim all this? You'd trade places with him if you could?"

Mr. Underhill nodded, frozen.

"Well, you come down here tomorrow afternoon at four. Then I can help you."

"How do you mean, help?"

"I can't tell you outright," said the boy. "It has to do with the Playground. Any place where there's lots of evil, that makes power. You can feel it, can't you?"

A kind of warm wind stirred off the bare field under the one high light. Underhill shivered. Yes, even now, at midnight, the Playground seemed evil, for it was used for evil things. "Are all playgrounds like this?"

"Some. Maybe this is the only one like this. Maybe it's just how *you* look at it, Charlie. Things are what you *want* them to be. A lot of people think this is a *swell* playground. They're right, too. It's how you look at it, maybe. What I wanted to say, though, is that Tom Marshall was like you. He worried about Tommy Marshall and the Playground and the kids, too. He wanted to save Tommy the trouble and the hurt, also."

This business of talking about people as if they were remote, made Mr. Underhill uncomfortable.

"So we made a bargain," said the boy.

"Who with?"

"With the Playground, I guess, or whoever runs it."

"Who runs it?"

"I've never seen him. There's an office over there under the grand-stand. A light burns in it all night. It's a bright, blue light, kind of funny. There's a desk there with no papers in it and an empty chair. The sign says *Manager*, but nobody ever sees the man."

"He must be around."

"That's right," said the boy. "Or I wouldn't be where I am, and some-one else wouldn't be where they are."

"You certainly talk grownup."

The boy was pleased. "Do you want to know who I really am? I'm not Tommy Marshall at all. I'm Tom Marshall, the father." He sat there in the dust, not moving, late at night, under the high and faraway light, with the late wind blowing his shirt collar gently under his chin, blowing the cool dust. "I'm Tom Marshall, the father. I know it'll be hard for you to believe. But it *is* true. I was afraid for Tommy. I was the way you are now about Jim. So I made this deal with the Playground. Oh, there are others who did the same, here. If you look close, you'll see them among the other children, by the expression in their eyes."

Underhill blinked. "You'd better run home to bed."

"You want to believe me. You want it to be true. I saw your eyes just then! If you could trade places with Jim, you would. You'd like to save him all that torture, let him be in your place, grownup, the real work over and done."

"Any decent parent sympathizes with his children."

"You, more than most. You feel every bite and kick. Well, you come here tomorrow. You can make a deal, too."

"Trade places?" It was an incredible, an amusing, but an oddly satis-fying thought. "What would I have to do?"

"Just make up your mind."

Underhill tried to make his next question sound very casual, a joke, but his mind was in a rage again. "What would I pay?"

"Nothing. You'd just have to play in the Playground."

"All day?"

"And go to school, of course."

"And grow up again?"

"Yes, and grow up again. Be here at four tomorrow afternoon."

"I have to work in the city tomorrow."

"Tomorrow," said the boy.

"You'd better get home to bed, Tommy."

"My name is *Tom* Marshall." The boy sat there.

The Playground lights went out.

Mr. Underhill and his sister did not speak at breakfast. He usually phoned her at noon to chat about this or that, but he did not phone. But at one-thirty, after a bad lunch, he dialed the house number. When Carol answered he hung up. Five minutes later he phoned again.

"Charlie, was that you called five minutes ago?"

"Yes," he said.

"I thought I heard you breathing before you hung up. What'd you call about, dear?" She was being sensible again.

"Oh, just called."

"It's been a bad two days, hasn't it? You *do* see what I mean, don't you, Charlie? Jim *must* go to the Playground and get a few knocks."

"A few knocks, yes."

He saw the blood and the hungry foxes and the torn rabbits.

"And learn to give and take," she was saying, "and fight if he has to."

"Fight if he has to," he murmured.

"I knew you'd come around."

"Around," he said. "You're right. No way out. He must be sacrificed."

"Oh, Charlie, you *are* odd."

He cleared his throat. "Well, that's settled."

"Yes."

I wonder what it would be like, he thought.

"Everything else okay?" he asked the phone.

He thought of the diagrams in the dust, the boy seated there with the hidden bones in his face.

"Yes," she said.

"I've been thinking," he said.

"Speak up."

"I'll be home at three," he said, slowly, piecing out the words like a man hit in the stomach, gasping for breath. "We'll take a walk, you and Jim and I," he said, eyes shut.

"Wonderful!"

"To the Playground," he said and hung up.

It was really autumn now, the real chill, the real snap; overnight the trees burnt red and snapped free of their leaves, which spiraled about Mr. Underhill's face as he walked up the front steps, and there were Carol and Jim, bundled up against the sharp wind, waiting for him.

"Hello!" they cried to one another, with much embracing and kissing. "There's Jim down there!" "There's Daddy up there!" They laughed and he felt paralyzed and in terror of the late day. It was almost four. He looked at the leaden sky, which might pour down molten silver any moment, a sky of lava and soot and a wet wind blowing out of it. He held his sister's arm very tightly as they walked. "Aren't you friendly, though?" She smiled.

"It's ridiculous, of course," he said, thinking of something else.

"What?"

They were at the Playground gate.

"Hello, Charlie. Hi!" Far away, atop the monstrous slide stood the Marshall boy, waving, not smiling now.

"You wait here," said Mr. Underhill to his sister. "I'll be only a moment. I'll just take Jim in."

"All right."

He grasped the small boy's hand. "Here we go, Jim. Stick close to Daddy."

They stepped down the hard concrete steps and stood in the flat dust. Before them, in a magical sequence, stood the diagrams, the gigantic tic-tac-toes, the monstrous hop-scotches, the amazing numerals and triangles and oblongs the children had scrabbled in the incredible dust.

The sky blew a huge wind upon him and he was shivering. He grasped the little boy's hand still tighter and turned to his sister. "Goodbye," he said. For he was believing it. He was in the Playground and believing it, and it was for the best. Nothing too good for Jim. Nothing at all in this outrageous world! And now his sister was laughing back at him, "Charlie, you idiot!"

Then they were running, running across the dirt Playground floor, at the bottom of a stony sea that pressed and blew upon them. Now Jim was crying, "Daddy, Daddy!" and the children racing to meet them, the boy on the slide yelling, the tic-tac-toe and hop-scotches whirling, a sense of bodiless terror gripping him, but he knew what he must do and what must be done and what would happen. Far across the field footballs

sailed, baseballs whizzed, bats flew, fists flashed up, and the door of the
Manager's office stood open, the desk empty, the seat empty, a lone light
burning over it.

Underhill stumbled, shut his eyes and fell, crying out, his body
clenched by a hot pain, mouthing strange words, everything in turmoil.

"There you are, Jim," said a voice.

And he was climbing, climbing, eyes closed, climbing metal-ringing
ladder rungs, screaming, wailing, his throat raw.

Mr. Underhill opened his eyes.

He was on top of the slide. The gigantic, blue metal slide which
seemed ten thousand feet high. Children crushed at his back, children
beat him to go on, slide! slide!

And he looked, and there, going off across the field, was a man in a
black overcoat. And there, at the gate, was a woman waving and the man
standing there with the woman, both of them looking in at him, waving,
and their voices calling, "Have a good time! Have a good time, Jim!"

He screamed. He looked at his hands, in a panic of realization. The
small hands, the thin hands. He looked at the earth far below. He felt
his nose bleeding and there was the Marshall boy next to him. "Hi!"
cried the other, and bashed him in the mouth. "Only twelve years here!"
cried the other in the uproar.

Twelve years! thought Mr. Underhill, trapped. And time is different
to children. A year is like ten years. No, not twelve years of childhood
ahead of him, but a century, a century of *this.*

"Slide!"

Behind him the stink of Musterole, Vick's Vaporub, peanuts, chewed
hot tar, spearmint gum and blue fountain-pen ink, the smell of kite-twine
and glycerin soap, a pumpkin smell of Hallowe'en and a papier-mâché
fragrance of skull masks, and the smell of dry scabs, as he was pinched,
pummeled, shoved. Fists rose and fell, he saw the fox faces and beyond,
at the fence, the man and woman standing there, waving. He shrieked,
he covered his face, he felt himself pushed, bleeding, to the rim of nothingness. Headfirst, he careened down the slide, screeching, with ten
thousand monsters behind. One thought jumped through his mind a
moment before he hit bottom in a nauseous mound of claws.

This is hell, he thought, *this is hell!*

And no one in the hot, milling heap contradicted him.

GRATITUDE GUARANTEED

by R. Bretnor and Kris Neville

REGINALD BRETNOR is equally widely known for his stories with a light touch in *The Magazine of Fantasy and Science Fiction* as for his book *Modern Science Fiction: Its Meaning and Its Future*, published last year. Like many another writer in the genre, he lives on the West Coast.

KRIS NEVILLE is a Californian who has but recently entered the lists. His concern is chiefly for social and psychological evolution of mankind in the possible futures of science fiction. His stories have appeared in many of the magazines devoted to the genre, as well as in such anthologies as *The Best from Fantasy and Science Fiction, Beyond Human Ken*, etc.

On the morning of December fifth, Mr. E. Howard Harrison showed up at the processing labs of Cuddlypets Corporation promptly at eight-forty-five. He hung up his coat, scrubbed his hands, and put on his smock, mask, and gloves. Then, as he had every working day for seven long years, he joined the two other surgical technicians who made up his team.

As always, Mr. Olson was sitting on the operating table, singing Cuddlypets commercials in his concrete-mixer baritone:

> "Cudd-lee-pets, Cudd-lee-pets,
> Snuggle up to Cudd-lee-pets!
> They'll love Mom and Dad and you
> Like they're GUAR-AN-TEED to do!
>
> "Tweak their whiskers, pull their fur,
> Cuddlypets just grin and purr!
> Cuddlypets just purr and grin—
> Love and gra-ti-tude's BUILT-IN!"

As always, Mr. Kerfoid was standing across from him, beating time on a sterilizer with his forceps. When Mr. Harrison entered the room, Mr. Kerfoid glanced up, nodded, and winked like a vulture with sand in its eye. Mr. Olson just kept on singing:

> "Cuddlytiger's big and classy,
> Cuddlypanther's really snazzy,
> Cuddlyleopard, Cuddlylion—
> YOU can buy them all ON TIME!
>
> "Cudd-lee-pets, Cudd-lee-pets,
> Snuggle up to ——"

It had been Mr. Harrison's habit to ignore these renditions as politely as possible, keeping his long, tight rectangle of a face carefully averted, and busying himself with minor adjustments to the encephaloscreen, or the disposal unit, or to the little glass cabinet that held their day's supply of Schroeder Bypasses and Dappleby Blocks. On the morning of December fifth, however, he did nothing of the sort. Instead, he took three brisk paces to bring himself face to face with Mr. Olson, and snarled, "Shut up!"

Mr. Olson jerked his head back, emitted a hoarse "—Cudd-l——," gasped, and was silent. Mr. Kerfoid dropped his forceps, and said, "Now, now, Mr. Harrison," plaintively several times.

"You shut up too," growled Mr. Harrison, turning on him. "It's bad enough having to waste my time working on these goddam big cats, cats, cats—that's all we get nowadays, is cats—lions, tigers, panthers, jaguars, cougars, ocelots—what'll it be next, I want to know, sabre-tooths?" He confronted Mr. Olson again. "It's so bad I can smell 'em in my sleep."

"I—I don't see how you can," protested Mr. Olson nervously. "We've a swell Cuddlylion at home ourselves. Got him for the kid. He's clean and neat, just like it says in the com——. Anyhow, he doesn't smell even a little bit. Uses his little old lion-box every time." He looked toward his colleague for support. "Isn't that right, Mr. Kerfoid?"

"It certainly is," croaked Mr. Kerfoid. "Everybody knows that Cuddlypets are—well, as Dr. Schroeder puts it, they are 'personally dainty.' Besides they're all of them deodorized before shipment. It's the policy of the firm, and a very good policy too, I may say."

Mr. Olson sniffed. "And anyhow," he said, "it seems to me, Mr. Harrison, that even if you don't like my singing, you might at least have the courtesy not to be offensive about it. Maybe Mr. Kerfoid and I *don't* have our B. S.'s in Cyber-Surgery; maybe we aren't qualified to work on human beings like you say you are—but at least *we* don't let our conduct become *subprofessional.*"

As unobtrusively as possible, Mr. Harrison sneaked a glance at the big clock on the wall. Everything, so far, had gone just as he'd planned it, and Mr. Olson had been adequately provoked——

Very deliberately, he allowed an expression of uncertainty to come over his features. "Wh-what do you m-mean, subprofessional?" he stuttered.

Mr. Olson was encouraged. He rose threateningly. "You know damn' well what I mean, Mr. Harrison. If you don't watch yourself, I'll report you to the Association—and likely as not they'll have you degraded. See?"

And at that point, as Mr. Harrison had known it would, the red light above the encephaloscreen flashed on to warn them that their first patient would arrive in just thirty seconds.

Automatically, they slipped their masks up over their faces. Mr. Olson took up his position near the hindfoot and tail clamps. Mr. Kerfoid moved to the clamps at the frontfoot and head end. Mr. Harrison, grinning under the gauze, clicked the trephining saw and the encephaloscreen pickup into place.

Right on the dot, the overhead conveyor trap opened, and down came a fine young male lion, snoring away under profound anesthesia, and displaying a small tonsured area just over his forehead. Mr. Olson and Mr. Kerfoid snapped the clamps. Mr. Harrison pressed the button that lowered the foot of the table. Mr. Olson made his incisions, hinging back a few square inches of scalp. Mr. Kerfoid let the saw buzz for a moment, and lifted a section of skull with his forceps. Then Mr. Harrison adjusted the pickups until the encephaloscreen diagrammed the precise path for his instruments. He reached for the delicate electronic scalpel with which Stage One was performed, moved it along the division between the two lobes, noted its indicated position on the screen, and——

> "Ta-da-dum, ta-da-dum,
> Tada-tada-ta-da-dum——"

sang Mr. Olson cheerfully.

Mr. Harrison's hand stopped.

> "Ta-da-ta-da ta da dum
> Tum-tum-tum-tum-tum-tum-tum."

Mr. Harrison rested hand and scalpel on the lion's nose, frowned, and said, *"Please!"* with great self-restraint.

"Can't I even hum?" protested Mr. Olson. "I was just humming. I didn't even say the words."

Mr. Harrison went back to his labors. He completed Stage One and Stage Two, took the Schroeder Bypass which Mr. Kerfoid had broken out of its sterile plastic capsule, waited while its number was recorded together with his own and the lion's, and installed it. By the time Dr. Schroeder and Dr. Dappleby entered the room on their routine morning inspection, he had completed Stages Three, Four, and Five, and was ready to put in the Dappleby Block. Mr. Olson had hummed the Cuddlypets tune twice more, and had whistled it once.

As always, Dr. Schroeder and Dr. Dappleby walked round the table and stopped beside Mr. Harrison. Dr. Schroeder patted the lion's cheek with a long, hairy hand. "Soon," he chirped, "you will be a *good* little lion. Soon you will lie down with the lamb. It is the Schroeder Bypass that does all this, gentlemen—yes, indeed. It conditions the animal to feel permanent gratitude—*gratitude*, gentlemen. Ah, yes, and we mustn't forget the Dappleby Block, must we? It was so clever of Dr. Dappleby to invent it, so that our nice little friends can't get *too* grateful and hurt people."

Dr. Dappleby's ears turned red, and he mumbled that it really wasn't anything much. Mr. Kerfoid said loyally that it was too. Dr. Schroeder made his usual remark about the good work they were doing, and how it made him feel all warm inside and not at all sorry that he and Dr. Dappleby had abandoned the most lucrative veterinary practice west of the Mississippi to start the Cuddlypets Corporation.

"I know *just* how you feel, Dr. Schroeder," declared Mr. Olson sentimentally. "It's inspiring, that's what it is. Every time I see one of our TV shows, well, I'm grateful to you for the chance of working here." He glanced at Mr. Harrison. "And our commercials—say, they're really *sharp*. They really stay with you. Did you hear that swell one last night?"

Dr. Schroeder said that maybe he hadn't. Mr. Harrison tensed slightly. Mr. Olson threw back his head and sang:

> "Cuddlypets are clean and tidy,
> Cuddlypets don't need a didy.
> Junior's ooky? Junior's wet?
> Trade him for a CUDD-LEE-PET!

> "Cudd-lee-pets, Cudd-lee-pets,
> Snug——"

"SHUT *UP!*" Mr. Harrison bawled. He took two long steps toward Mr. Olson. Then, with a roar like an unprocessed Cuddlypet, he leaped for his throat. Together, they fell against the little glass cabinet, sending it crashing down, sending a shower of Schroeder Bypasses and Dappleby Blocks into the funnel-shaped sink at the bottom of which the jaws of the disposal unit whirred hungrily.

It took a minute or two to separate them, to restrain Mr. Harrison, and to restore some sort of equilibrium. Dr. Schroeder was the first to regain his poise. *"Well!"* he said. "You have attacked Mr. Olson. You have destroyed our valuable bypasses, our valuable blocks. You have spoiled our system of records completely! I'm really afraid that we can't keep you."

"Cow-mechanic!" spat Mr. Harrison.

Dr. Schroeder scarcely blinked at the insult. "The fact that you are qualified to operate on human beings," he explained, "cannot change my decision. Since the new psychiatric techniques made you unnecessary, you B. S.'s in Cyber-Surgery are a dime a dozen—a dime a dozen, Mr. Harrison. Besides, you are emotionally unstable, are you not? Maybe you need a Schroeder Bypass yourself. Now Dr. Dappleby will finish this lion, and then I will send another man to your place. Go away."

Mr. Harrison stamped to the door. He threw his mask down, and kicked it into a corner. "Nuts to you, monkey-plumber!" he shouted. "I *quit!*"

Fifteen minutes later, he left the Cuddlypets building by the front entrance, his last check in his wallet. His professional status was doomed; his career was ruined—but there was a new spring in his walk. What was that crack of the doctor's about needing a Schroeder Bypass himself? He chuckled. He felt in his pocket. There it was, safe in its small plastic capsule—*unrecorded*—just as he'd planned from the start.

> "Cudd-lee-pets, Cudd-lee-pets,
> Snuggle up to Cudd-lee-pets—"

sang Mr. Harrison happily as he went away.

Mr. Harrison disliked cats much more than he did singing commercials, and he disliked cats actually present more than cats at a distance. Now that professional pride was no longer involved, he scarcely objected when his wife watched her favorite Cuddlypets program each evening, and often he came in and watched it himself—at least until it reminded her of their problems, and of his own plans, about which she was doubtful.

It was just three weeks later, on the day after Christmas, that these plans finally came to fruition. The program ended, and Mr. Harrison switched off the set. Nodding critically, he remarked, "Well, I don't like cats—but that was pretty good. That was *rich*—the part where the door was going to open, and he didn't know who would come out."

"In the *story*," replied Mrs. Harrison, pursing her over-ripe lips, "it ended right there. You never did learn who it was, the lady *or* the tiger.

Of course, it's a very old old story, maybe pre-Twentieth Century, when the tigers were fierce and ate people up. So he *couldn't* have turned out to be just an old Cuddlytiger, not really, and *both* of them couldn't have come out. Anyway, I think it's better the way it was written. I think they ought to be left the way Nature made them, in the jungle and all—though at least you *were* a professional when you were doing the work, and I must say no one in *my* family has ever been *sub*professional before. That was why they all said I ought to have married Elmer Maginnis, because he was a real Ph.D."

Mr. Harrison sighed. "Look, Chickadee," he said patiently, "I've explained till I'm blue in the face. It's just for a while. The world owes me something—me, a Cyber-Surgery B. S., working seven years in a goddam cat factory, making 'em grateful!" He snorted. "Well, a Schroeder Bypass'll work just as well in an electronic brain as it will in a cat's. Those cheap poodle-fixers don't know it, but I do. That's why I'm working for Jonson, Williamson, Selznick, and Jones. One of these days, they'll send me on just the right job. Then we'll live off the fat of the land."

"Well, I suppose you know best," his wife said, "but I can't for the life of me see how a mechanical brain can be *grateful* even if you do something for it. And this morning I met that frowzy Eppinger woman —she tries to make out she's thirty-three, but she's forty at least—and she said, 'I hear your husband's a *mechanic* now, Mrs. Harrison, on mechanical brains? Now, isn't that *nice*.' And I said——"

Before she could finish, the phone rang in the hall; and Mr. Harrison, grumbling, pushed into his slippers and went off to answer it.

She heard him snap, "Hello, Harrison speaking." Then, after a moment, in a much sweeter voice: "We're *fine,* Mr. Selznick. A fine Christmas, too. Yes, *sir,* yes indeed. . . . *Who?* . . . Sure I know where they are! . . . Yes . . . Yes, sir, right away. . . . Thank *you,* Mr. Selznick. Goodbye."

He strode back. "Guess who that was!" he crowed. "It was Mr. Selznick, that's who it was. Babe, our troubles are over. This is *it.*"

"This is what?" Mrs. Harrison asked.

"The big chance. We won't have to wait. Say, isn't it lucky he called me instead of one of the others? I'll bet you can't guess where it is."

"Eberhard," Mrs. Harrison said, "stop beating around the bush and come to the point."

"Ha!" Mr. Harrison strutted. "Well, I'll tell you. It's Moss-Eagleberg, Chickadee. *Moss-Eagleberg,* the biggest store in the West. Forty-six floors. They sell tailor-made suits and new cars, turbocopters, crown jewels and ermines and things, the best Scotch you can get, Oriental rugs, real antiques, pheasants already cooked by French chefs, swimming pools, readymade barbecue pits—— They sell *everything*."

"Their prices are always too high," Mrs. Harrison said. "I like Monkey Ward's best."

"And they're *fully* automatic—order, accounting, and shipping departments all run by one brain. *One*—just like a lion or tiger or something. And now it's gone dead—and I'm the guy who's going to fix it." Mr. Harrison danced three steps of a jig. "Get it, honeybunch? After tomorrow, that great big Moss-Eagleberg brain will be grateful to *me*. We'll pick up the phone and order whatever we want—all for free."

"Well, you make it sound very nice, but I still don't see how a lot of condensers and things——"

"It's a cinch," Mr. Harrison said, reaching for his troubleshooter's kit and his hat. "I won't even have to put in a Dappleby Block."

Deep inside Moss-Eagleberg's broken-down brain, Mr. Harrison spent most of the night doing what Jonson, Williamson, Selznick, and Jones paid him to do. In the whole vast, silent warehouse, there was no one to bother him; and, as he worked, he made mental notes. *Order Record, Delivery Record, Charge Debit, Collection Routine*—all these could be by-passed just as if they'd been labelled *Aggression* (*against Human*), *Aggression* (*against Animal*), *Hunger* (*for Human*), *Hunger* (*for Animal except Syntho-horse*). That was simple. Of course, the *Semiannual Inventory* circuits would take a little finagling——

At six in the morning, Mr. Harrison climbed the ladder to the control room. He locked the door just to be on the safe side, plugged a mike and a typer in on the *Charge Accounts* bank, tapped out his name and address, gave himself a Triple-A credit rating, and activated the unit. He repeated name and address into the mike so that the brain could record his individual voice pattern for future identification over the phone. He went down the ladder again and traced out the new circuit. Then, expertly, he installed the Schroeder Bypass where it would do the most good, running fifty-six fine little tantalum wires to the grafting points on its gelatinous skin, and attaching all the appropriate shunts.

"Love and gra-ti-tude's BUILT-IN!" sang Mr. Harrison triumphantly as he went back to his work.

By eight o'clock, when the two subprofessionals who kept tab on the brain showed up, he had it all finished and was seated in the control room writing his bill.

They came in, a plump, pink little man and a long, lean, leathery one. "Hi," said the long one. "I'm Winkler, and this here's Swartz. You get everything fixed?"

Mr. Harrison looked up coldly. "I am *Mr.* Harrison," he informed them. "Repairs have been made, and I'll have the bill ready in a minute or two if I'm not interrupted."

"Sure, sure," Swartz said. He inspected the room, nodding and rubbing his hands. He patted the panels. He stroked the master switch gently. "Boy, oh boy. It sure will be good to have old Bessie perking again."

"Eleven hours at twelve dollars and twenty cents an hour," Mr. Harrison muttered, "makes one hundred thirty-four dollars and twenty cents."

"Worth every cent of it, too," Winkler asserted. "Mr. Harrison, you done wonders. I tell you, Swartz and me were real worried when we found out about it. We thought she was just dead and gone, like a person. We felt like we'd killed her."

Mr. Harrison tore off the original bill and two carbons. "That's all nonsense," he stated. "Giving this brain a name doesn't make it at all like a person. It's an electronic device, and it's very much simpler even than a Cud—— even than an animal's brain, let alone a human's."

"You don't know Bessie." Swartz shook his head. "She's got ten million units, and she thinks a thousand times faster than we do. She's a real personality, Bessie is."

Mr. Harrison reached for his wrenches and printed circuits and blob-like germanium transistors. He put his graphite pencils in the tray and his two pocket meters in their receptacles and snapped shut his kit. "You're wrong," he said flatly. "But I won't waste time arguing with you. Machines can't think. They don't live. They can't die. And that's final."

"I don't see how you can say that," Winkler protested. "Look here. When Swartz cut all the current off Bessie Christmas Eve, wasn't she exactly like a dead human, except for decaying, I mean? Just now it took you nearly twelve hours to bring her back to life, didn't it? Seems to me that was the same as artificial respiration, or heart massage maybe."

"It was just unit by unit shock. There's no connection."

"There!" Swartz exclaimed. "Didn't I tell you? It was *shock therapy.* Bessie does too think. I've worked with her from the start. *I* ought to know."

"Then you ought to know never to cut the current all the way off," Mr. Harrison snapped.

Winkler and Swartz looked at each other. "She needed the rest," Swartz explained patiently. "That new unit they put in to send individual Christmas cards to the customers worked her to death on top of the holiday rush and all. Besides, it was Christmas Eve."

"When you get through the day, set the dial on 'Stand-by'; *never* cut the current all the way off," Mr. Harrison said through his teeth.

"Since we carry cards for *every* occasion," observed Winkler, "she ought to be grateful we only make her send them out once a year. Don't you think so?"

Most of the circuits in Mr. Harrison's mind were busy with thoughts of the Shroeder Bypass, and the very extensive Moss-Eagleberg stock, and how to get home in a hurry. Now, however, he came up with a jerk.

"She—she ought to be *what?*"

"*Grateful,*" Winkler repeated obligingly. "She sometimes is. You can feel it."

"God damn it, machines *can't* be grateful!" shouted Mr. Harrison, waving his arms.

"Bessie can," Swartz told him. "She'll be grateful to you too, Mr. Harrison, for bringing her back from the dead like you did. She'll love you for that." He reached for the master switch; pulled it all the way down. "You just wait and see."

Conveyor belts came to life from one end of the giant warehouse to the other. Under Bessie's direction, mechanical arms sorted packages, loaded them on the right belts and unloaded them at their destinations. In the delivery and mailing room, address stencils dropped in flawless order from the rotating customer drums, and steel arms slammed the stencils against oncoming crates and cartons, and machine-guided brushes applied smears of stencil ink, and the moving belts carried the crates and cartons away to waiting driverless trucks.

At this evidence of Bessie's revivification, Winkler blew his nose sentimentally; Swartz dabbed at his eyes. Neither of them even noticed Mr. Harrison hurrying out.

Mr. Harrison drove through a red light and two stop signs before he completely convinced himself that neither Winkler nor Swartz suspected the presence of the Schroeder Bypass; that their talk about gratitude was purely coincidental. He remembered that subprofessionals were all stupid bastards, with compulsions to personalize their machines, to—he fished for the word—to *anthropomorphize* them. Yes, that was it. Stupid bastards. The very idea of a machine that was grateful, all by itself, was absurd. It was laughable.

Mr. Harrison was still chuckling when he reached his apartment. His wife had their breakfast unpackaged and ready; and, over their coffee, they thumbed eagerly through the latest edition of the four-inch-thick Moss-Eagleberg catalog. There were things for every conceivable purpose and purse, from every conceivable part of the world. There were even a few souvenir ashtrays and lampbases made out of pumice brought back at terrific expense from the Moon.

"Number 62-A-547-01," Mrs. Harrison read aloud. "Rope of pearls, triple strand, fine Oriental. N-ninety-nine thousand, five hundred. Now, that would be *nice*."

"Don't bother reading the price, ha-ha." Mr. Harrison laughed. "*We* can afford it."

"62-C-202-49, Ring, emerald, thirty-two carats." She held up her hand, crooked the ring finger, and sighed. "Well, I'll note them both down for later—when we've made sure, that is."

"Chickadee, we *are* sure."

"I'm not," Mrs. Harrison said. "So we'll just buy a few things at first, things we can pay for if something goes wrong and they send us a bill. Anyhow, it's near the end of the month, and we'll find out in four or five days."

A few minutes later, Mr. Harrison called up Moss-Eagleberg's charge department. He gave his name and address. Bessie checked against his recording; okayed it. The human operator said, "Your circuit is open now, sir. You can dial your order." And, very carefully, he dialed the catalog numbers: a big tri-di TV set, a Chinchilla trimmed hostess gown, a flacon of *En Chaleur No. 5*, a silver service for eight, a banquet for two with ortolans, truffles, and other strange goodies from the Rotisserie, a case of champagne, and a box of expensive cigars.

They didn't have to wait long. At eleven-fifteen, the delivery port in the hall buzzed its warning, and cartons and packages began to come out. As they appeared, Mr. Harrison opened each one and checked up on its contents. Every item was there. In fact, there were two tri-di sets.

"My finger must've slipped dialing that one," he remarked. "Well, no harm's done. Anyhow, it works just as I told you. I'll hang onto my job for awhile so nobody'll get any funny ideas, but from now on Moss-Eagleberg's going to support us in style. Let's celebrate!"

They celebrated right through the weekend, enjoying their champagne hangovers thoroughly, and spending almost as much time over the catalog as in watching their new tri-di sets. They celebrated all over again on New Year's Eve. Then, as the first days of January went by without any bill, Mrs. Harrison began to say less and less about what might happen if something went wrong, and to think more and more about a future of opulent ease provided by Bessie.

On January tenth, unable to wait any longer, she phoned Moss-Eagleberg, asked for a statement on her husband's account, and was informed that no purchases had been made. When he came home that evening, she had her new shopping list all made out.

"I want you to order all these things in the morning, Eberhard dear," she told him. "It's too soon after Christmas to buy jewelry and clothes; they'll be almost sold out. So this time I'll simply get things for the house: a grand piano, a Louis the something-or-other bedroom suite, and a dear little electronic organ, and new curtains all around, and a freezer, and a real antique spinning-wheel, and a marbletop dresser, and—oh, and all *sorts* of things."

"Better not go getting too much big stuff," Mr. Harrison warned, "at least not at one time. It won't come up through the port; the janitors'll have to bring it in the service elevator. We don't want them geting suspicious."

"Don't worry," Mrs. Harrison said. "I've thought of all that. We aren't going to order more than once in two weeks, even things like our meals. If the police found it out, goodness knows what they'd do! They'd probably use that psychiatric technique on you, the one that made Cyber-Surgery on people out of date. Then where would we be?"

Mr. Harrison laughed. "I'd be sort of a zombi. I'd be just like a Cuddly-pet only more so. But they'll never find out because Bessie won't tell them. She loves me too much, ha-ha-ha! It's BUILT-IN!"

Next day, just before noon, the delivery came through. As the smaller objects were being stacked up in the hall, the telephone rang; and Mr. Harrison, breaking off the catchy commercial he was humming, answered it.

"Hello? Mr. Harrison?" The building manager sounded a little upset. "We've got a raft of stuff for you down here, Mr. Harrison. You—you want to come down?"

"No, indeed, Mr. Quandt. Just send it up."

"*All* of it?"

"Of course, all of it!" Mr. Harrison snapped. "Why shouldn't you send all of it up?"

"Well, okay if you say so. If you can figure where to put *three* grand pianos in that apartment of yours, I guess it's your busi——"

"What's that? *How* many pianos?"

"Three, Mr. Harrison, like I said. The store must of made a mistake."

Mr. Harrison covered the mouthpiece. "They—they sent *three* grand pianos," he said to his wife.

"Well, we'll have to send two of them back."

"We—we *can't* send them back, Chickadee. There'd be too many questions. My God, we can't even sell them! We'll have to fit them in someplace, that's all. I—I must've dialed a three instead of a one when I ordered. That must've been it. Whew!" He turned back to the phone. "There's been no mistake, Mr. Quandt," he declared a little too loudly. "I checked with the wife. She—she likes music a lot."

The Harrisons put the three grand pianos in the living-room, where they took up eighty per cent of the space. They hoisted the tri-di TV's onto one of them, and the spinning-wheel onto another; and they squeezed the organ into the bedroom between the new bedroom set and the marbletop bureau. The next time Mr. Harrison ran into Mr. Quandt in the hall, he dropped a hint that his wife had these *moods* when she had to be humored; doctor's orders, he said. And he made up his mind to double-check every digit he dialed in the future.

As for Mrs. Harrison, she accepted the crowding philosophically. When she wasn't out window-shopping at Moss-Eagleberg's, she kept herself busy making out and revising her lists, running happliy through such compositions as *Pretty Redwing* and *The Golliwog's Cakewalk* on her pianos, and regretting that she couldn't tell that frumpy Eppinger woman about Bessie.

On January twenty-fourth, they ordered again, and again Mrs. Harrison put off getting her jewels and her wardrobe. "You order this time," she said. "All I want is one of those iridium-mink coats, and some silver things for my dresser, and a little more perfume, so it won't matter much if you do make another mistake. But when I get the really valuable things, I want to do it myself. Now that I think of it, you always do seem to get the wrong number when you phone."

When the order arrived, "There!" she cried out. "Didn't I tell you? I said *one* iridium-mink coat, and you went and got *four*."

"I'll be damned," Mr. Harrison said. "I could've sworn I dialed that right. If I didn't *know* that machines simply can't——" He shrugged. "Well, anyway, it's lucky they had four in stock."

Then, without protest, he called up Moss-Eagleberg and arranged to have Bessie record his wife's voice so that she could charge against his account—and he warned her not to order a thing for two weeks at least.

Mrs. Harrison assured him that she wouldn't, adding that he needn't worry about *her* dialing half-a-dozen when she meant only one; and she kept her promise for all of five days. On January twenty-ninth, though, she happened on an ad in the paper where it said that Moss-Eagleberg were having a sale on star sapphires, up to thirty per cent off the regular price. Even though she knew there wouldn't be any charge, somehow she couldn't resist it. Giving herself the excuse that she might as well charge the next order of food now as later, she picked out a medium-sized stone of about eighteen carats and circled its number. She dialed it last, very slowly and carefully.

When the delivery arrived, Mrs. Harrison hurriedly searched for the one little package. Not finding it, she controlled her impatience and began checking off all the boxes of food by their numbers. When she had moved every one of them into the kitchen, she found one package left. But it wasn't a small one. It was about four feet high, and exceedingly heavy. Her heart fluttering, she tore off the paper and exposed a big wooden box with ELL-AY ARTY-CRAFTS, INC. stencilled on the side. She obtained a screwdriver, and pried off the top, and exposed a combination sundial and birdbath in genuine simulated bronze, with fat cherubim peeping up over the edge, and North, South, East, and West marked with arrows, and a motto cut into the rim: *Honi Soit Qui Mal Y Pense.*

Mrs. Harrison sat down. She wept for two solid minutes. She tried to remember whether she could have made a mistake on the very first number of the sapphire. Then, straining mightily, she pushed the birdbath-cum-sundial into a closet and covered it up. When her husband came back from work, she said nothing about it.

Four days later, she made another try for the sapphire. This time, she received several pairs of long winter woolies, size fifty long stout. A little hysterically, she hid them back of the birdbath, and said not a word.

On February fifth, the telephone broke up her afternoon nap. When she answered it, a feminine voice sang loudly and clearly:

> "Happy birth-day, to you-u-u,
> Happy BIRTH-day to you-u-u,
> Happy BIRTH-DAY, dear Eber-hard,
> Happy birth-day to YOU-U-U!"

And, within half an hour, something arrived from Moss-Eagleberg—a huge, heart-shaped box of candied fruit with WON'T YOU BE MY VALENTINE? across the outside. As the day was neither Mr. Harrison's birthday nor St. Valentine's Day, she deduced that her husband was playing a joke, and she mentioned it to him on his return.

". . . and it seems to me," she concluded, "that you'd be *above* things like that, especially after lecturing *me* on not ordering so often. All that candied fruit—it'll take weeks to eat up!"

After the initial shock of the news, Mr. Harrison had decided, logically enough, that Winkler and Swartz were trying to prove to him that Bessie was grateful. This, however, was hardly a subject he wished to debate with his wife, so he simply assured her that he hadn't ordered a thing, that he was as puzzled as she was.

"Nonsense!" cried Mrs. Harrison shrilly, still unnerved by the birdbath and the long underwear. "I refuse to believe it. And you aren't being funny at all. I'm sure Elmer Maginnis wouldn't ever have stooped to being so—so *childish.* Don't you dare to do it again!"

When they retired that night, she was still very angry; and the events of the following day did nothing at all to mend matters. The telephone rang. The feminine voice sang its message. Presently, Moss-Eagleberg delivered a pair of large potted cacti.

Mr. Harrison's protestations went unheeded. His wife turned the Cuddlypets program up louder than ever before, and ignored him icily. He began to wonder whether he hadn't better do something about Winkler and Swartz.

Next morning, he stopped wondering. As it was Saturday, he answered the phone himself. He heard its gay greeting. An hour or so later, after reading the card enclosed with the package, he unwrapped one dozen athletic supporters. On the card was a drawing of a woman in uniform, and under the drawing were the words: *Lots of Love to my Aunt in the Service.*

Mr. Harrison decided that on Monday he would approach Winkler and Swartz and take drastic action.

Mrs. Harrison also reached a decision. With Eberhard making such a fool of himself, there was no point in *her* waiting for the good things of life. On Monday——

On Monday, just before lunch, Mrs. Harrison ordered a score of the most expensive items in the jewelry department. She also dialed a small but select wardrobe of the sort which might have been chosen by a particularly wealthy and generous maharajah's favorite wife. As she hung up, she told herself reassuringly that in no previous delivery had there been more than a single mistake, and that one mistake now wouldn't really make very much difference—though she did hope it wouldn't be on the rope of pearls, triple strand.

At about the same time, Mr. Harrison sneaked out of the office of Jonson, Williamson, Selznick, and Jones, and went to a pay phone. An angry gleam in his eye, the phrases with which to demolish Winkler and Swartz all set in his mind, he called up Moss-Eagleberg and asked for Bessie's control-room. As soon as it answered, he shouted, "Winkler? Winkler, you listen to me——"

"*Who* you want?" shouted the receiver back at him.

"I want *Winkler.*"

"Not here."

"Okay then—Swartz."

"*Who?*"

"*Swartz!*"

"*He ain't here neither!*"

"THEY GO OUT TO LUNCH?" Mr. Harrison bellowed. "WHEN YOU EX-PECTING THEM BACK?"

"THEY WON'T BE BACK!" bawled the receiver. "THEY BEEN TRANSFERRED. THEY'VE WENT OUT TO DALLAS! GODDAMMIT, STOP SHOUTING!"

Mr. Harrison stopped shouting. His stomach felt as though it had suddenly passed through a very cold wringer. He said, "H-how long ago?"

"Three weeks!" barked the phone.

Mr. Harrison groaned. He replaced the receiver, and staggered away from the booth. He found his way to a bar, and had two double bourbons. Then he went back to Jonson, Williamson, Selznick, and Jones, and pretended to work for the rest of the day. He thought of the Valentine present and the cacti and the athletic supporters. He wondered whether his wife might not have ordered them all for a gag, and decided against it. He remembered what Winkler and Swartz had said about Bessie, and cursed both of them for a pair of dumb bastards. Finally he recalled that sometimes a new Cuddlypet took awhile to adjust—that a couple of months might go by before the Schroeder Bypass stabilized properly. It was pretty rare, but it happened. Maybe——

By the time he got home, he had persuaded himself that something like this had happened to Bessie, that all he and his wife had to do was sit tight for another few weeks and it would all straighten out.

"Hello! Hello-oh!" he called as he opened the door. "Chickadee, I'm home."

He halted abruptly. The hall was full of crates, cartons, boxes, and bundles. Some had been opened, wholly or partially; others were intact. Some were small; some were big; several were simply enormous. And there were more of them showing in the visible part of the living-room.

"H-Honeybunch?" Mr. Harrison called in alarm. "Where *are* you? Hey, Chickadee!"

He was answered by a loud and very moist sob from the bedroom. There, stretched out on the Louis-the-something-or-other bed, he discovered his wife. Dashing in, he tripped over a tangle of paper and string on the floor, swore, sat down on the edge of the bed, put an arm round her. "Sweetheart!" he cried. "Mignonetta! What's happened? What's *wrong?*"

Mrs. Harrison quaked. She shook off his arm. She sat up, revealing a very red nose and some badly eroded makeup. "What's *h-happened?*" she wailed. "Wh-what's *wrong?* Just l-look what you *di-i-id!*"

She pointed, and a new freshet of tears came forth. Mr. Harrison, following her finger, beheld a dark cylindrical object partly concealed by the wrappings over which he had stumbled. He lifted it out. It was about two feet high, leathery, hollow, and more than ten inches across.

"I j-just dialed some jewels and a f-few things to wear—and *loo-o-k* what I got. Ei-*eighteen* of them!"

Mr. Harrison looked. He saw that, down at the bottom, the object splayed out very slightly into four recognizable toes. He lifted the tag.

On one side it said, CONGO NOVELTIES, *Original! Exclusive!*; on the other, HIPPOPOTAMUS FOOT UMBRELLA STAND, *Guaranteed Real.*

Mr. Harrison let it slide to the floor. He peered at his hands, found they were shaking, put them away in his pockets. "Hippo feet," he muttered aloud, "for umbrellas. Must be a mistake. That's what. Just a mistake."

Mrs. Harrison threw herself back on the pillow with a shrill cry of anguish.

"——ha-ha-ha! Machines make mistakes all the time. No harm done, ha-ha! Be all right. Yes, indeed. Don't you worry." He patted her clumsily. He went out. He attempted to take a brief inventory. Besides the eighteen hippopotamus feet, he found a bale of peat moss, a turret-top lathe, two lobster traps, a case of Adventist hymnbooks, five or six crates of lettuce, a hayrake, a portable duck blind with decoys, a small Japanese automobile, and a cage containing a family of Belgian hares.

At that point, definitely dazed, he gave up and went back to the bedroom. Mrs. Harrison was sitting up. She had dried her eyes, and looked combative.

"*S-something* went wrong," Mr. Harrison mumbled.

She did not reply.

"M-maybe I ought to have put in a Dappleby Block," he continued. "Chickadee, maybe that's what——"

"Don't you Chickadee me, you—you *beast!*" Mrs. Harrison leaped to her feet. "*I'll* tell you what's wrong! That mechanical brain or whatever it is—that thing you call Bessie. She *loves* you! She loves you—and she's jealous of *me!* That's what's wrong. When you ordered the piano, she sent you two extras. It was the same with the coats, because it was you. But whenever *I* ordered something, just look what I got—rabbits and birdbaths and hippopotamus feet!" She stamped on the floor. "Well, you just get all that junk out of my house, do you hear? Send it back to your Bessie. Oh, if you could've seen the look on that Mr. Quandt's face when they brought it all up! Like—like we'd *stolen* it! Oh! Oooh, Eberhard dear, what will we *do-o-o?*"

She collapsed on his chest. Again she burst into tears. They clung to each other. Presently, between sobs, "That awful m-machine," Mrs. Harrison moaned. "She l-loves you. And I l-love you too. The nerve of the thing, s-sending me all that old trash! And s-sending you p-p-presents like that! Well, you can just choose between us, that's all. If you want me to stay, you can just send every bit of it back!"

Mr. Harrison was trying desperately not to think of the expression on Mr. Quandt's face—and of his probable fate if the police got wind of his little affair with Bessie. However, he got a grip on himself. He pointed out that Bessie was just a machine. He explained that she didn't really *love* him, not even as much as a Cuddlypet would have. It was merely a matter of circuits, of condensers and things. He also explained that, much as he wanted to get rid of the stuff that was cluttering the place, it would be taking too big a risk. Of course, he could drop all that lettuce down the garbage disposer, and he guessed he could sneak out some night and let the rabbits loose in the park. But they'd just have to live with the rest of the stuff for a year or two, maybe selling it off or giving it away bit by bit. If they did that, and didn't let anyone in the apartment, and didn't have any friends in, maybe they'd be safe enough. Mr. Quandt couldn't have talked to the police; if he had, they would've been there by now. And tomorrow he himself would go down to Moss-Eagleberg's, and he'd take the Schroeder Bypass right out, and erase all the records, and they'd have no more trouble—because Bessie was just a machine after all.

While Mr. Harrison was explaining all this, he had to take time out fairly frequently to declare that he did *too* love his Chickadee; to protest that he'd done it for her, and *not* just because he didn't like cats; to point out that after all she *did* have four iridium-mink coats.

Finally, a relative calm was restored. They kissed and made up. Together, they spent several hours in pushing and hauling. They stuffed all the closets. The duck blind went under a piano with the rabbits. The small Japanese automobile was parked in the bathroom. When, exhausted, they crept into bed, a navigable channel had been dredged through the hall, and part of the living-room carpet was actually visible.

"Oh, I do hope things'll work out," Mrs. Harrison sighed, as she turned out the light. "I'm still sort of scared. I can't believe that your Bessie is just a mechanical brain. I—I think she's *alive*."

Mr. Harrison slept rather poorly. First he dreamed that he was working on Bessie, installing Schroeder Bypasses and Dappleby Blocks. The Dappleby Blocks kept blowing up like balloons and exploding, and every time one would blow up, Bessie would purr and purr, and he'd reach for a wire and find whiskers instead, or a handful of fur. And then Winkler and Swartz would come in, and they'd dance around him carrying umbrellas over their heads. And Mr. Olson was there, singing Cuddlypets commercials in his concrete-mixer voice. And finally the fur and the whiskers came up all around Mr. Harrison, like tall grass, and Mr. Quandt opened up a big door and out came these critters wearing athletic supporters. And Mr. Olson was one of them, somehow, and he was singing:

"Cudd-lee-pets, Cudd-lee-pets,
Snuggle up to Cudd-lee-pets!
Sweet as sugar, big as busses—
CUDDLYHIPPOPOTAMUSES!"

Mr. Harrison woke up, in an icy sweat. He took two sleeping tablets. Fifteen minutes later, he found himself in a police station, under a big, bright light which had something to do with the new psychiatric technique. Dr. Schroeder and Dr. Dappleby were dressed up as policemen, and they were holding him down while Mr. Olson read aloud from a list of the things Bessie had sent him, and every time he read one out Mr. Kerfoid erased a word from his B. S. diploma in Cyber-Surgery, until there weren't any left and the diploma was blank. Then a steam whistle went off in his head, and his mind went all whirly, and the next thing he knew he was out on the street, on all fours, and he felt *different* somehow. He looked around at himself and saw that he was covered with iridium-mink fur. There was a collar around his neck, and a leash, and Dr. Schroeder was leading him—hop, skip, jump, hop, skip, jump. And he felt so grateful to Dr. Schroeder for feeding him all that wonderful, juicy, raw Syntho-horse that he rubbed up against him and purred. And then it wasn't Dr. Schroeder any more, but a little Japanese auto pulling him into Bessie's control room, which was a mouth full of teeth, and behind every tooth was a policeman, and they were all purring, purring, purr——

Mr. Harrison was not in good shape when he rose. He gulped down his coffee, pretended to shave, and went off to Jonson, Williamson, Selznick, and Jones. He found Mr. Jonson, who looked at him queerly and made some remark about "godawful benders."

"Mr. Jonson," he asked, as casually as he could, "did you ever hear of Charge Reference records getting into the permanent memory bank of one of those big department store brains? I mean so there'd be no control over what the machine did?"

"That just couldn't happen," Mr. Jonson assured him. "It's impossible. Only living creatures can function that way."

Mr. Harrison sighed.

He forced himself to wait until noon. Then he hurried down to Moss-Eagleberg's. Sure enough, there was only one subprofessional on duty in the control room, a wide, red-faced, cheerful sort of a fellow.

"I'm from Jonson, Williamson, Selznick, and Jones," Mr. Harrison said. "Did a job on this brain a while back. How's she getting along?"

"Say, you must be Mr. Harrison!" The man grinned, got to his feet, held out his hand. "Filmore's the name. I heard all about you. Winkler told me all about how you brought Bessie back from the dead. Well, she's just fine—she's just *purring* along."

Mr. Harrison bit his lip. "That's good. But maybe I'd better give her a checkup anyhow. There'll be no extra charge. It's part of our regular service."

"That's mighty white of you, Mr. Harrison. Bessie'll appreciate that."

Mr. Harrison counted to ten. He managed a smile. "Oh, by the way," he said, opening his kit. "I seem to have forgotten my replacement transistors. They're in a box on the seat of my car. It's parked on the third-level lot. If I give you the key could you——?"

"Get 'em for you? Say, I'll be glad to, Mr. Harrison."

As soon as the man had departed, he closed the door, locked it, went down the stairs as fast as he could, and tore out the Schroeder Bypass and all its connections. Then he came up again, plugged in the mike, asked for the file on Mr. and Mrs. E. Howard Harrison. As soon as the numbers showed up on the typer, he flipped the switch from RECORD over to TOTAL ERASURE. The Machine clicked and whirred. A little red light blinked three times. All the Harrison data had been removed, deleted, expunged.

"Boy, *that* does it!" Mr. Harrison murmured in triumph. Joy and relief surged in his heart. He burst into song:

> "Pussycats are full of germs,
>   Dogs have nasty fleas and worms,
>   That's not what *I* want to get—
>   Mom, I want a CUDD-LEE-PET!"

And, on the final note, he unplugged the typer, flipped the switches back where they belonged, and pulled out the mike. When the sub-professional came back with the spare transistors, he was packing his kit.

Mr. Harrison went away whistling. He stopped at a phone on the way to the shop, and called up his wife, and told her that their troubles were over. All that afternoon, he worked like a beaver.

He came home at his regular time. He rang the bell. Nobody answered. He knocked. When he thought he heard someone stirring inside, he called, "Chickadee, are you home?" several times. Finally, he took out his key and tried to open the door. Something seemed to be blocking it, something too heavy to shove.

He frowned. He began to feel frightened. After hesitating a minute or two, he went downstairs to the apartment under his own, and persuaded the inquisitive elderly lady who lived there to let him through to the fire escape, promising to let her know *right away* if he found anything wrong.

Luckily, the kitchen window hadn't been latched. He crawled in. A glance was enough to inform him that something quite dreadful had happened. One end of the kitchen was filled with identical packages. They were stacked round the freezer, and they reached almost up to the ceiling. And that wasn't all. On the table, weighted down, was a note.

Slowly, with a horrible feeling of doom, Mr. Harrison read it.

> Dear Eberhard,
>
> I have been a good wife to you the best I know how even if you aren't a real professional any more like Elmer Maginnis. If it was another woman I could forgive you I guess—but this is *too much*. I have gone home to Mother. I have taken only what really is mine, like my mink coats. You won't be lonely, because your Bessie has *everything*. If you don't believe me, just look in the living-room.

> Your wife, Mignonetta (Chickadee)

Like an automaton, Mr. Harrison went into the hall. He found it filled with huge square objects, and he clambered up over them. At the living-room door he paused, struggling feebly against the compulsion to open it. He watched his hand reach for the knob, turn it, push the door ajar. He went in.

There they were, as he had known they would be when he walked through the Syntho-horse packages in the kitchen and over the king-sized cat-boxes in the hall. They were everywhere—on and under the pianos, on the chairs, on the mantelpiece. They were sitting there happily, small, medium, and large, striped and mottled and spotted.

The Cuddlypets saw Mr. Harrison. All together, they rose. They all started purring. They came padding toward him——

There was love in their eyes.

RUSTLE OF WINGS

by Fredric Brown

FREDRIC BROWN (1906–   ) was born in Cincinnati but now
lives in the Los Angeles area. He is more widely known in the field
of the whodunit for such books as *The Fabulous Clipjoint* (an
Edgar winner as the best mystery of 1947), *We All
Killed Grandma,* and half a dozen others, but he has also published
his science fiction in such collections as *What Mad Universe, Space
on My Hands,* and *The Lights in the Sky Are Stars.*

Poker wasn't exactly a religion with Gramp, but it was about the nearest
thing he had to a religion for the first fifty or so years of his life. That's
about how old he was when I went to live with him and Gram. That
was a long time ago, in a little Ohio town. I can date it pretty well,
because it was just after President McKinley was assassinated. I don't
mean there was any connection between McKinley's assassination and
my going to live with Gram and Gramp; it just happened about the
same time. I was about ten.

Gram was a good woman and a Methodist and never touched a card,
except occasionally to put away a deck that Gramp had left lying somewhere, and then she'd handle it gingerly, almost as though it might explode. But she'd given up, years before, trying to reform Gramp out of
his heathen ways; given up trying *seriously,* I mean. She hadn't given
up nagging him about it.

If she had, Gramp would have missed the nagging, I guess; he was
so used to it by then. I was too young, then, to realize what an odd
couple they made—the village atheist and the president of the Methodist
missionary society. To me, then, they were just Gramp and Gram, and
there wasn't anything strange about their loving and living together despite their differences.

Maybe it wasn't so strange after all. I mean, Gramp was a good man
underneath the crust of his cynicism. He was one of the kindest men I
ever knew, and one of the most generous. He got cantankerous only

when it came to superstition or religion—he refused ever to distinguish between the two—and when it came to playing poker with anyone, anywhere, any time.

He was a good player, too; he won a little more often than he lost. He used to figure that about a tenth of his income came from playing poker; the other nine-tenths came from the truck farm he ran, just at the edge of town. In a manner of speaking, though, you might say he came out even, because Gram insisted on tithing—giving one-tenth of their income to the Methodist church and missions.

Maybe that fact helped Gram's conscience in the matter of living with Gramp; anyway, I remember that she was always madder when he lost than when he won. How she got around his being an atheist I don't know. Probably she never really believed him, even at his most dogmatic negative.

I'd been with them about three years; I must have been about thirteen at the time of the big change. That was still a long time ago, but I'll never forget the night the change started, the night I heard the rustle of leathery wings in the dining-room. It was the night that the seed salesman ate with us, and later played poker with Gramp.

His name—I won't forget it—was Charley Bryce. He was a little man; I remember that he was just as tall as I was at the time, which wouldn't have been more than an inch or two over five feet. He wouldn't have weighed much over one hundred pounds and he had short-cropped black hair that started rather low on his forehead but tapered off to a bald spot the size of a silver dollar farther back. I remember the bald spot well; I stood back of him for a while during the poker and recall thinking what a perfect fit that spot would be for one of the silver dollars—cartwheels, they were called—before him on the table. I don't remember his face at all.

I don't recall the conversation during dinner. In all probability it was largely about seeds, because the salesman hadn't yet completed taking Gramp's order. He'd called late in the afternoon; Gramp had been in town at the broker's with a load of truck, but Gram had expected him back any minute and had told the salesman to wait. But by the time Gramp and the wagon came back it was so late that Gram had asked the salesman to stay and eat with us, and he had accepted.

Gramp and Charley Bryce still sat at the table, I recall, while I helped Gram clear off the dishes, and Bryce had the order blank before him, finishing writing up Gramp's order.

It was after I'd carried the last load and came back to take care of the napkins that poker was mentioned for the first time; I don't know which of the men mentioned it first. But Gramp was telling animatedly of a hand he'd held the last time he'd played, a few nights before. The stranger—possibly I forgot to say that Charley Bryce *was* a stranger; we'd never met him before and he must have been shifted to a different territory because we never saw him again—was listening with smiling interest. No, I don't remember his face at all, but I remember that he smiled a lot.

I picked up the napkins and rings so Gram could take up the tablecloth from under them. And while she was folding the cloth I put three napkins—hers and Gramp's and mine—back into our respective napkin rings and put the salesman's napkin with the laundry. Gram had that expression on her face again, the tight-lipped disapproving look she wore whenever cards were being played or discussed.

And then Gramp asked, "Where are the cards, Ma?"

Gram sniffed. "Wherever you put them, William," she told him. So Gramp got the cards from the drawer in the sideboard where they were always kept, and got a big handful of silver out of his pocket and he and the stranger, Charley Bryce, started to play two-handed stud poker across a corner of the big square dining-room table.

I was out in the kitchen then, for a while, helping Gram with the dishes, and when I came back most of the silver was in front of Bryce, and Gramp had gone into his wallet and there was a pile of dollar bills in front of him instead of the cartwheels. Dollar bills were big in those days, not the little skimpy ones we have now.

I stood there watching the game after I'd finished the dishes. I don't remember any of the hands they held; I remember that money seesawed back and forth, though, without anybody getting more than ten or twenty dollars ahead or behind. And I remember the stranger looking at the clock after a while and saying he wanted to catch the ten o'clock train and would it be all right to deal off at half-past nine, and Gramp saying sure.

So they did, and at nine-thirty it was Charley Bryce who was ahead. He counted off the money he himself had put into the game and there was a pile of silver cartwheels left, and he counted that, and I remember he grinned. He said, "Thirteen dollars exactly. Thirteen pieces of silver."

"The devil," said Gramp; it was one of his favorite expressions.

And Gram sniffed. "Speak of the devil," she said, "and you hear the rustle of his wings."

Charley Bryce laughed softly. He'd picked up the deck of cards again, and he riffled them softly, as softly as he had laughed, and asked, "Like this?"

That was when I started to get scared.

Gram just sniffed again, though. She said, "Yes, like that. And if you gentlemen will excuse me— And you, Johnny, you better not stay up much longer."

She went upstairs.

The salesman chuckled and riffled the cards again. Louder, this time. I don't know whether it was the rustling sound they made or the thirteen pieces of silver, exactly, or what, but I was scared. I wasn't standing behind the salesman any more; I'd walked around the table. He saw my face and grinned at me. He said, "Son, you look like you believe in the devil, and think I'm him. Do you?"

I said, "No, sir," but I must not have said it very convincingly. Gramp laughed out loud, and he wasn't a man that laughed out loud very often.

Gramp said, "I'm surprised at you, Johnny. Darned if you don't sound like you *do* believe it!" And he was off laughing again.

Charley Bryce looked at Gramp. There was a twinkle in his eye. He asked, "Don't you believe it?"

Gramp quit laughing. He said, "Cut it out, Charley. Giving the boy silly ideas." He looked around to be sure Gram had left. "I don't want him to grow up superstitious."

"Everybody's superstitious, more or less," Charley Bryce said.

Gramp shook his head. "Not me."

Bryce said, "You don't think you are, but if it came to a showdown, I'd bet you are."

Gramp frowned. "You'd bet what, and how?"

The salesman riffled the deck of cards once more and then put them down. He picked up the stack of cartwheels and counted them again. He said, "I'll bet thirteen dollars to your one dollar. Thirteen pieces of silver says you'd be afraid to prove you don't believe in the devil."

Gramp had put away his folding money but he took his wallet out again and took a dollar bill out of it. He put the bill on the table between them. He said, "Charley Bryce, you're covered."

Charley Bryce put the pile of silver dollars beside it, and took a fountain pen out of his pocket, the one Gramp had signed the seed order with. I remember the pen because it was one of the first fountain pens I'd ever seen and I'd been interested in it.

Charley Bryce handed Gramp the fountain pen and took a clean seed order blank out of his pocket and put it on the table in front of Gramp, the unprinted side up.

He said, "You write 'For thirteen dollars I sell my soul,' and then sign it."

Gramp laughed and picked up the fountain pen. He started to write, fast, and then his hand moved slower and slower and he stopped; I couldn't see how far he'd written.

He looked across the table at Charley Bryce. He said, "What if——?" Then he looked down at the paper a while more and then at the money in the middle of the table; the fourteen dollars, one paper and thirteen silver.

Then he grinned, but it was a kind of sick grin.

He said, "Take the bet, Charley. You win, I guess."

That was all there was to it. The salesman chuckled and picked up the money, and Gramp walked with him to the railroad station.

But Gramp wasn't ever exactly the same after that. Oh, he kept on playing poker; he never did change about that. Not even after he started going to church with Gram every Sunday regularly, and even after he finally let them make him a vestryman he kept on playing cards, and Gram kept on nagging him about it. He taught me how to play, too, in spite of Gram.

We never saw Charley Bryce again; he must have been transferred to a different route or changed jobs. And it wasn't until the day of Gramp's funeral in 1913 that I learned that Gram had heard the conversation and the bet that night; she'd been straightening things in the linen closet in the hall and hadn't gone upstairs yet. She told me on the way home from the funeral, ten years later.

I asked her, I remember, whether she would have come in and stopped Gramp if he'd been going to sign, and she smiled. She said, "He wouldn't have Johnny. And it wouldn't have mattered if he had. If there really is a devil, God wouldn't let him wander around tempting people like that, in disguise."

"Would you have signed, Gram?" I asked her.

"Thirteen dollars for writing something silly on a piece of paper, Johnny? Of course I would. Wouldn't you?"

I said, "I don't know." And it's been a long time since then, but I still don't.

THE OTHER TIGER

by *Arthur C. Clarke*

ARTHUR C. CLARKE is the President of the British Interplanetary Society. He writes widely under his highly respected name both fiction and nonfiction about scientific matters. His book, *The Exploration of Space,* was a best-seller and a book club choice. He has also written such science fiction as *Prelude to Space, Childhood's End, Sands of Mars, Against the Fall of Night,* and *Expedition to Earth.* He has been widely anthologized as one of the best among writers of fantastic tales.

"It's an interesting theory," said Arnold, "but I don't see how you can ever prove it." They had come to the steepest part of the hill and for a moment Webb was too breathless to reply.

"I'm not trying to," he said when he had gained his second wind. "I'm only exploring its consequences."

"Such as?"

"Well, let's be perfectly logical and see where it gets us. Our only assumption, remember, is that the universe is infinite."

"Right. Personally I don't see what else it *can* be."

"Very well. That means there must be an infinite number of stars and planets. Therefore, by the laws of chance, every possible event must occur not merely once but an infinite number of times. Correct?"

"I suppose so."

"Then there must be an infinite number of worlds *exactly like Earth,* each with an Arnold and Webb on it, walking up this hill just as we are doing now, saying these same words."

"That's pretty hard to swallow."

"I know it's a staggering thought—but so is infinity. The thing that interests me, though, is the idea of all those other Earths that aren't exactly the same as this one. The Earths where Hitler won the War and the Swastika flies over Buckingham Palace—the Earths where Columbus never discovered America—the Earths where the Roman Empire has lasted to this day. In fact the Earths where all the great *if's* of history had different answers."

"Going right back to the beginning, I suppose, to the one in which the ape-man who would have been the daddy of us all, broke his neck before he could have any children?"

"That's the idea. But let's stick to the worlds we know—the worlds containing *us* climbing this hill on this spring afternoon. Think of all our reflections on those millions of other planets. Some of them are exactly the same but every possible variation that doesn't violate the laws of logic must also exist.

"We could—we *must*—be wearing every conceivable sort of clothes—and no clothes at all. The Sun's shining here but on countless billions of those other Earths it's not. On many it's winter or summer here instead of spring. But let's consider more fundamental changes too.

"We intend to walk up this hill and down the other side. Yet think of all the things that might possibly happen to us in the next few minutes. However improbable they may be, as long as they are *possible*, then somewhere they've got to happen."

"I see," said Arnold slowly, absorbing the idea with obvious reluctance. An expression of mild discomfort crossed his features. "Then somewhere, I suppose, you will fall dead with heart failure when you've taken your next step."

"Not in *this* world." Webb laughed. "I've already refused it. Perhaps *you're* going to be the unlucky one."

"Or perhaps," said Arnold, "I'll get fed up with the whole conversation, pull out a gun and shoot you."

"Quite possibly," admitted Webb, "except that I'm pretty sure you, on this Earth, haven't got one. Don't forget, though, that in millions of those alternative worlds I'll beat you on the draw."

The path was now winding up a wooded slope, the trees thick on either side. The air was fresh and sweet. It was very quiet as though all Nature's energies were concentrated, with silent intentness, on rebuilding the world after the ruin of winter.

"I wonder," continued Webb, "how improbable a thing can get before it becomes impossible. We've mentioned some unlikely events but they're not completely fantastic. Here we are in an English country lane, walking along a path we know perfectly well.

"Yet in some universe those—what shall I call them?—*twins* of ours will walk around that corner and meet anything, absolutely anything that imagination can conceive. For as I said at the beginning, if the cosmos is infinite, then all possibilities must arise."

"So it's possible," said Arnold, with a laugh that was not quite as light as he had intended, "that we may walk into a tiger or something equally unpleasant."

"Of course," replied Webb cheerfully, warming to his subject. "If it's possible, then it's got to happen to someone, somewhere in the universe. So why not to us?"

Arnold gave a snort of disgust. "This is getting quite futile," he protested. "Let's talk about something sensible. If we don't meet a tiger round this corner I'll regard your theory as refuted and change the subject."

"Don't be silly," said Webb gleefully. "That won't refute anything. There's no way you can——"

They were the last words he ever spoke. On an infinite number of Earths an infinite number of Webbs and Arnolds met tigers friendly, hostile or indifferent. But this was not one of those Earths—it lay far closer to the point where improbability urged on the impossible.

Yet of course it was not totally inconceivable that during the night the rain-sodden hillside had caved inward to reveal an ominous cleft leading down into the subterranean world. As for *what* had laboriously climbed up that cleft, drawn toward the unknown light of day—well, it was really no more unlikely than the giant squid, the boa constrictor or the feral lizards of the Jurassic jungle. It had strained the laws of zoölogical probability but not to the breaking-point.

Webb had spoken the truth. In an infinite cosmos everything must happen somewhere—including their singularly bad luck. For *it* was hungry—very hungry—and a tiger or a man would have been a small yet acceptable morsel to any one of its half dozen gaping mouths.

CIVILIZED

by Mark Clifton and Alex Apostolides

MARK CLIFTON (1906–   ) is a comparative newcomer to science fiction. He has been a teacher, a personnel caseworker, and an industrial worker. He began writing but three years ago and has since completed his first novel. He has contributed to many magazines, including If: Worlds of Science Fiction, Astounding Science Fiction, and many others. His most recent anthology appearance was in The Best Science Fiction Stories: 1953.

ALEX APOSTOLIDES has appeared principally thus far as a collaborator with Mark Clifton. He lives and works on the West Coast.

The females and children worked among the lichen growth, picking off the fattest, ripest leaves for their food and moisture, completing their arc of the circle of symbiosis.

The males worked at the surface of the canals, or in open excavations. Their wide, mutated hands chipped into the rock-hard clay, opening a channel which was to be filled with sand and then sealed off with clay on all sides and surface. That water might seep through the sand without evaporation, without loss, from the poles to the equator of Mars—seep unimpeded, so that moisture might reach the lichen plants of everyone, so that none might thirst or hunger.

The seepage must flow. Not even buried in the dim racial memory had there ever been one who took more than his share, for this would be like the fingers of one hand stealing blood from the fingers of the other.

Among the Mars race there were many words for contentment, kinship of each to all. There were words to express the ecstasy of watching the eternal stars, by night and by day, through the thin blackish atmosphere. There were words to express the joy of opening slitted nostrils to breathe deeply in those protected places where the blowing sands did not swirl, of opening folds of rubbery skin to catch the weak rays of the distant Sun.

But there were no words for "mine" as separate from "yours." And there was no urge to cry out, "Why am I here? What is the purpose of it all?"

Each had his purpose, serene, unquestioning. Each repaired or extended the seepage canals so that others, unborn, might know the same joys and ecstasies as they. The work was in itself a part of the total joy, and they resisted it no more than healthy lungs resist clear, cool air.

So far back that even the concept of beginnings had been forgotten, the interwoven fabric of their symbiotic interdependence seeped through their lives as naturally as the precious water seeped through the canal sands. As far back as that, they had achieved civilization.

Their kind of civilization.

Captain Griswold maintained an impassive face. (Let that, too, be a part of the legend.) Without expression, he looked through the screen at the red land flashing below the ship. But unconsciously he squared his shoulders, breathed deeply, enjoying the virile pull of his uniform over his expanding chest. Resolutely he pushed aside the vision of countless generations of school children, yet to come, repeating the lesson dutifully to their teachers.

"Captain Thomas H. Griswold took possession of Mars, June 14, 2018."

No, he must not allow any mood of vanity to spoil his own memories of this moment. It was beside the point that his name would rank with the great names of all time. Still, the history of the moment could not be denied.

Lieutenant Atkinson's voice broke through his pre-occupation, and saved him the immodest thought of wondering if perhaps his cap visor might not be worn a little more rakishly to one side. He must father a custom, something distinctive of those who had been to Mars——

"Another canal, sir."

Below them, a straight line of gray-green stretched to the horizon, contrasting sharply with the red ferrous oxide of the landscape. An entire planet of ferrous oxide—iron—steel for the already starving technology of the Western Alliance. The Captain felt a momentary irritation that even this narrow swath displaced the precious iron ore.

Obviously these canals served no purpose. His ship had circled the planet at its equator, and again from pole to pole. Canals everywhere, but nothing else. Enough time and fuel had been wasted. They must land. Obviously there was no intelligent life. But the history of the moment must not be marred by any haste. There must be no question within the books yet to be written. There must be no accredited voice of criticism raised.

"My compliments to Mr. Berkeley," he said harshly to Lieutenant Atkinson, "and would he kindly step to the control room?" He paused and added dryly, "At his convenience."

Mister Berkeley, indeed. What was it they called the civilian—an ethnologist? A fellow who was supposed to be an authority on races, civilizations, mores and customs of groups. Well, the man was excess baggage. There would be no races to contact here. A good thing, too. These civilian experts with their theories—show them a tooth and they'll dream up a monster. Show them a fingernail paring and they'll deduce a civilization from it. Nonsense!

"You wanted to see me, Captain?" The voice was young, quiet, controlled.

Without haste, Captain Griswold turned and faced Berkeley. Not only a theorist, but a young theorist. These super-bright young men with their sharp blue eyes. A lot of learning and no knowledge. A lot of wisdom and no common sense. He carefully controlled his voice, concealing his lack of respect for the civilian.

"Well, Mr. Berkeley, we have quartered the globe. We have seen no evidence of civilization."

"You discount the canals, Captain?" Berkeley asked, as if more from curiosity than refutation.

"I must discount them," the Captain answered decisively. "Over all the planet we have seen no buildings, not even ruins, no evidence at all that intelligence exists here."

"I consider straight lines, running half the length of a world, to be evidence of something, sir." It was a flat statement, given without emphasis.

Arguments! Arguments! Little men who have to inflate themselves into a stature of importance—destroy the sacred history of the moment. But quietly now. There must be no memory of petty conflict.

"Where are their buildings, Mr. Berkeley?" he asked with patient tolerance. "Where are their factories? The smoke from their factories? The highways? The transportation facilities? Where are the airplanes? Even this thin air would support a fast jet. I do not require they have space-ships, Mr. Berkeley, to concede them intelligence. I do not require they be the equal of Man. I also have some scientific training. And my training tells me I cannot recognize the existence of something where there is no evidence at all."

"The canals," Berkeley answered. His voice also was controlled, for he, too, knew the history of this moment. But his concern was not for his own name in the history books. He knew only too well what its writers did to individuals for the sake of expediency. His concern was that this moment never be one of deep shame for Man. "Perhaps they have no buildings, no factory smoke, because they don't need them. Perhaps they don't have highways because they don't want to go anywhere. Perhaps their concept of living is completely unlike ours."

Griswold shrugged his shoulders. "We speak an entirely different language, Mr. Berkeley."

"I'm afraid you're right, Captain," Berkeley sighed. "And it might be a tragic thing that we do. Remember, European man spoke a different language from that of the American Indian, the Mayan, Polynesian, African, Indonesian——" He broke off as if the list were endless. "I ask only that we don't hasten into the same errors all over again."

"We can't hover here above the surface forever," Griswold said irritably. "We have quartered the globe. The other experts are anxious to land, so they can get to their work. We have made a search for your civilization and we have not found it."

"I withdraw all objections to landing, Captain. You are entirely correct. We must land."

The intercom on the wall squawked into life.

"Observation to Control. Observation to Control. Network of canals forming a junction ahead."

"Prepare for landing, Lieutenant Atkinson," Griswold commanded sharply. "At the junction." He turned and watched the screen. "There, Mr. Berkeley, dead ahead. A dozen—at least a dozen of your canals joining at one spot. Surely, if there were a civilization at all, you would find it at such a spot." Slowly and carefully, he constructed the pages of history. "I do not wish the implication ever to arise that this ship's commander, or any of its personnel, failed to coöperate in every way with the scientific authorities aboard."

"I know that, Captain," Berkeley answered. "And I agree. The junction, then."

The sigh of servo-mechanism, the flare of intolerably hot blue flame, and the ship stood motionless above the junction of canals. Ponderously, slowly, she settled; held aloft by the pillars of flame beneath her, directly above the junction, fusing the sand in the canals to glass, exploding their walls with steam. Within their warm and protected burrows beside the canals, slitted nostrils closed, iris of eyes contracted, fluted layers of skin opened and pulled tight, and opened again convulsively in the reflexes of death.

There was a slight jar only as the ship settled to the ground, bathed in the mushrooming flame.

"A good landing, Lieutenant," Captain Griswold complimented. "A good landing, indeed."

His head came up and he watched the screen to see the landscape reappear through the dust and steam.

"Prepare to disembark in approximately six hours, Lieutenant. The heat should have subsided sufficiently by then. The ship's officers, the civ—er—scientific party, a complement of men. I will lead the way. You, Lieutenant, will carry the flag and the necessary appurtenances to the ceremony. We will hold it without delay."

Berkeley was watching the screen also. He wondered what the effect of the landing heat would be on the canals. He wondered why it had been considered necessary to land squarely on the junction; why Man always, as if instinctively, does the most destructive thing he can.

He shrugged it away. Wherever they landed might have been the wrong place.

Farther along the canals, where the heat had not reached, the Mars race began to emerge from their protecting burrows. They had seen the meteor hurtling downward, and it was part of their conditioning to seek their burrows when any threatening phenomenon occurred.

Flaming meteors had fallen before, but never in the interlocked racial mind was there memory of one which had fallen directly on a canal junction. Within the fabric of their instinct, they sensed the fused sand, the broken clay walls, the water boiling through the broken walls, wasted. They sensed the waters on the other side of the barrier seeping onward, leaving sand unfilled. Within the nerves of their own bodies they felt the anticipated pangs of tendril roots searching down into the sand for water, and not finding it.

The urgency came upon them, all within the region, to remove this meteor; restore the canals as soon as the heat would permit. They began to gather, circling the meteor, circling the scorched ground around it. The urgency of getting at it before there was too much water lost drove them in upon the hot ground.

The unaccustomed heat held them back. They milled uncertainly, in increasing numbers, around the meteor.

Since Captain Griswold had not asked him to leave the control room during landing operations, Berkeley still stood and watched the screen. At the first appearance of the Mars race emerging from the soil, he exclaimed in great excitement:

"There they are! There they are, Captain!"

Griswold came over and stood beside him, watching the screen. His eyes widened.

"Horrible," he muttered in revulsion. The gorge arose in his throat and stopped his speech for a moment. But history took possession of him again. "I suppose we will get accustomed to their appearance in time," he conceded.

"They're the builders, Captain. Wonderful!" Berkeley exulted. "Those shovel-shaped forelimbs—they're the builders!"

"Perhaps," Griswold agreed. "But in the way a mole or gopher—still, if they were intelligent enough to be trained for mining operations—but then you certainly cannot call these things intelligent, Mr. Berkeley."

"How do we know, Captain?"

But the Captain was looking about vainly for buildings, for factory smoke, for highways.

"Lieutenant Atkinson!" he called.

"Yes, sir."

"Send an immediate order throughout the ship. The Mars things are not to be molested." He glanced at Berkeley as he gave the order, and then glanced away. "Double the complement of men on the landing party and see that they are fully armed." Then back to Berkeley, "A good leader guards against every contingency. But there will be no indiscriminate slaughter. You may be assured of that. I am as anxious as you that Man——"

"Thank you, Captain," Berkeley answered. "And the planting of the flag? The taking possession?"

"Well, now, Mr. Berkeley, what shall we do, now that we have seen some—things? Go away? Leave an entire planet of iron ore to be claimed later by the Eastern Alliance? The enemy is not far behind us in their technology, Mr. Berkeley."

He warmed to his theme, his head came up, his shoulders back.

"Suppose these things are intelligent. Suppose they do have feelings of one kind or another. What would happen to them if the Eastern Alliance laid claim to this planet? Under us, at least, they will have protection. We will set aside reservations where they may live in peace. Obviously they live in burrows in the ground; I see no buildings. Their total food supply must be these miserable plants. What a miserable existence they have now!

"We will change that. We will provide them with adequate food, the food to fill their empty stomachs—if they have stomachs. We will clothe their repulsive nakedness. If they have enough sense to learn, we will give them the pride of self-employment in our mines and factories. We would be less than human, Mr. Berkeley, if we did not acknowledge our duty."

The light of noble intention shone in his face. He was swept away with his own eloquence.

"If," he finished, "we take care of the duty, the destiny will take care of itself!"

That was very good. He hoped they would have the grace to quote him on that. It was a fine summing up of his entire character.

Berkeley smiled a rueful smile. There was no stopping it. It was not a matter of not planting the flag, not taking possession. The Captain was right. If not the Western Alliance, then certainly the Eastern Alliance. His quarrel was not with the Captain nor with the duty, but with the destiny. The issue was not to be decided now. It had already been decided—decided when the first ape-man had crept into the tree nest of another and stolen his mate.

Man takes. Whether it be by barbaric rapine, or reluctant acceptance of duty through carefully contrived diplomacy, Man takes.

Berkeley turned and made his way out of the control room.

Outside, the soil shifted in its contortions of cooling. The wind whispered dryly over the red landscape, sending up little swirls of dust, eternally shifting it from one place to another. The soil was less hot, and as it cooled, the Mars race pressed inward. Theirs was the urgency to get at this meteor as quickly as possible, remove it, start the water flowing once more.

"Observation reports ground cool enough for landing!" The magic words seemed to sing into the control cabin.

"Summon all landing party," Captain Griswold commanded immediately.

The signal bells rang throughout the ship. The bell in the supercargo cabin rang also. With the other scientists, Berkeley dressed in his protecting suit, fitted the clear glassite oxygen helmet over his head, fastened it. Together with the rest, he stood at the designated airlock to await the Captain's coming.

And the Captain did not keep them waiting. At precisely the right moment, with only a flicker of a side glance at the photographic equipment, the Captain strode ahead of his officers to the airlock. The sealing doors of the corridor behind them closed, shutting off the entire party, making the corridor itself into a great airlock.

There was a long sigh, and the great beams of the locks moved ponderously against their weight. There was the rush of air from the corridor as the heavier pressure rushed out through the opening locks, to equalize with the thin air of Mars. With the air rushed outward fungus spores, virus, microbes; most of them to perish under the alien conditions, but some to survive—and thrive.

The red light above the lock was blinking on-off-on-off. The officers, the scientists, the armed men, watched the light intently. It blinked off for the last time. The locks were open. The great ramp settled to the ground.

In ordered, military file, the Captain at their head, the landing party passed down the corridor, through the locks, out upon the ramp beneath the blueblack sky; and down to the red soil. Captain Griswold was the first man to set foot on Mars, June 14, 2018. The photographers were second.

Now the Mars race was moving closer to the ship, but the ground was still too hot for their unprotected feet. The pressing need for removing the meteor possessed them. The movement of the men disembarking from the ship was to them no more than another unintelligible aspect of this incredible meteor.

The sound of a bugle pierced the thin air, picked up by the loudspeaker from the ship, reverberating through their helmets. The landing party formed a semicircle at the foot of the ramp.

Captain Griswold, his face as rigidly set as the marble statuary of him to follow, reached out and took the flag from Lieutenant Atkinson. He planted it firmly, without false motion, in the framework one of the men had set upon the baked ground to receive it.

He pointed to the north, the south, the east, the west. He brought his hands together, palms downward, arms fully outstretched in front of him. He spread his arms wide open and down, then back together and up; completing a circle which encompassed all the planet. He held out his right hand and received the scroll from Lieutenant Atkinson.

With a decisive gesture, not quite theatrical, he unfurled the scroll. He read in a voice firm enough to impress all posterity:

"By virtue of authority vested in me from the Supreme Council of the Western Alliance, the only true representatives of Earth and Man, I take possession of all this planet in the name of our President, the Supreme Council, the Western Alliance, Earth, and in the name of God."

The ground was cool enough now that their feet might bear it. The pain was great, but it was lost in the greater pain of feeling the killing obstruction the great meteor had brought to their canals. The Mars race began to press inward, inexorably.

It was the anticlimactic moment, following the possession ceremony, when men milled around in uncertainty, that Lieutenant Atkinson saw the Mars race had come closer and was still moving.

"The monsters!" he exclaimed in horror. "They're attacking!"

Berkeley looked, and from the little gestures of movement out of his long training he deduced their true motive.

"Not against us!" he cried. "The ship."

Perhaps his words were more unfortunate than his silence might have been; for the ship was of greater concern to Captain Griswold than his own person.

"Halt!" Griswold shouted toward the approaching Mars race. "Halt or I'll fire!"

The Mars race paid no heed. Slowly they came forward, each step on the hot ground a torture, but a pain which could be borne. The greater torture, the one they could not bear, was the ache to press against this meteor, push it away, that they might dig the juncture clean again. As a man whose breath is stopped fights frantically for air, concerned with nothing else, so they felt the desperation of drying sands.

They came on.

"For the last time," Griswold shouted, "halt!" He made a motion with his hands, as if to push them back, as if to convey his meaning by signs. Involuntarily, then, his eyes sought those of Berkeley. A look of pleading, helplessness. Berkeley met the glance and read the anxiety there, the tragic unwillingness of the man to arouse posterity's rage or contempt.

It was a brief glance only from both men and it was over. Captain Griswold's head came up; his shoulders straightened in the face of the oncoming monsters. They were close now, and coming closer. As always, the experts were free with their advice when it was not needed. When the chips were down, they could do no more than smirk and shrug a helpless shoulder.

He gave the command, and now there was no uncertainty.

"Fire!"

The celebration was being held in the Great Stadium, the largest, most costly structure that Man had ever built. It was a fitting structure for the more important football games; and used on occasion, if they could be fitted in without upsetting the schedule, for State affairs. Now the stadium was filled to capacity, its floor churned by the careless feet of thousands upon thousands who had managed to obtain an entrance.

From the quarter-mile-high tiers of seats, from the floor of the stadium, the shouts welled up, washing over the platform at the north end.

"Griswold! Griswold!"

It was not yet time for history to assess the justice of the massacre.

The President raised his hand. The battery of video cameras picked up each move.

"Our hopes, our fears, our hearts, our prayers rode through every space-dark, star-flecked mile with these glorious pioneers." He turned then to the Captain. "For the people of Earth, *Admiral* Griswold, this medal. A new medal for a Guider of Destiny, Maker of Empire, Son of Man!"

The voice faltered, stopped.

The crowd on the floor of the stadium was pressing outward from the center, screaming in pain and terror. At the moment when the people should be quiet, rapt in reverence, they were emptying the floor of the stadium. But not willingly. They were being pressed back and out, as a great weight pushes its way through water. Those who could move outward no farther were crushed where they stood.

And then the ship appeared.

Hazy of outline, shimmering with impossible angles, seen by its glinting fire of light rather than by its solid form, as if its reality were in some other dimension and this only a projection, the ship appeared.

The President's hand reached out and gripped Griswold's shoulder as he leaned back and back, trying to determine its vast height. A silence then clutched the crowd—a terrified silence.

A full minute passed. Even on the platform, where all the pioneers of Mars were assembled with Earth's dignitaries, even there the people cowered back away from this unseeable, unknowable horror.

But one man leaned forward instead, frantically studying the shimmering outline of the ship. One man—Berkeley.

With the training of the ethnologist, a man who really can deduce an entire civilization from mystifying data, he recognized the tremendous import.

At the end of that minute, without warning, a group of figures hovered in the air near the floor of the stadium.

Quickly, Berkeley's eyes assessed their form, their color, the increasing solidity of the humanoids. There are some movements, some gestures, common to all things of intelligence—the pause, the resolution, the lift of pride.

"No!" he screamed and started forward. "Oh, no! We're civilized. We're intelligent!" He was pulled back, as in his terror he tried to leap from the platform to get at the humanoids.

Held there, unable to move, he read the meaning of the actions of the group hovering near the ship. One flashed a shining tentacle around, as if to point to the stadium, the pitifully small spaceship on display, the crowds of people.

The leader manifestly ignored him. He flowed forward a pace, his ovoid head held high in pride and arrogance. He pointed a tentacle toward the south end of the stadium, and a pillar of leaping flame arose; fed with no fuel, never to cease its fire, the symbol of possession.

He pointed his tentacles to the north, the south, the east, the west. He motioned with his tentacles, as if to encircle all of Earth.

He unfurled a scroll and began to read.

STICKENEY AND THE CRITIC

by Mildred Clingerman

MILDRED CLINGERMAN has appeared primarily in *The Magazine of Fantasy and Science Fiction* thus far, and in but one or two anthologies. She is first and foremost a wife and mother, but her stories indicate freshness and originality in a crowded field, and the aficionado looks forward to more of them. She lives in Tuscon, Arizona.

I wish I had thought to throw Stickeney a live chicken on Midsummer Eve. There's no sense in doing it now, but if I'm still alive next year, I'll be sure to remember. I've been tossing live chickens at Stickeney for over fifty years, once a year around Midsummer Eve, give or take a day. Stickeney is no stickler for the absolutely correct day. (Now is as good a time as any to tell you that I hate and despise puns, but I'm getting old, and as my joints stiffen I seem to grow lax in other ways.)

I've been sitting out on the east veranda, staring down the road that leads to town, smoking my pipe and waiting for the law to show up. I've been expecting the Town Marshal, but it could just as well be the F.B.I. because this affair has international complications. But the road is empty and dusk is drawing down, so here I am in the parlor writing out the whole thing while there's time. I wish I could believe the disappearance of the Englishman will go unnoted, but the truth is Mr. Cecil Cholmondeley was very well known in some circles. But I go on hoping, knowing full well "man lives in hope and dies in despair." This is a direct quotation from my father, who settled here in Oklahoma when it was Indian Territory; who, in fact, already had Mother staked out here on this very land while he lined up with the others in the Land Rush and pretended he wasn't one of those "Sooners" who had sneaked in before the signal. My mother had orders to shoot anybody who came nosing around and did shoot Father in the leg before she recognized him.

The reason Father wanted this land so much has a lot to do with Stickeney, though nobody knew about Stickeney at the time. Indians had camped on this land before the soldiers moved them out, but somebody had been here before—long before. Certainly it wasn't the Indians who had built the ancient stone barn or dug the huge stone-lined well. Father, in his forays into the forbidden territory, spotted the barn, the well, and the cleared acres and was determined he'd have the place come hell or the U.S. Army. He got it, with Mother's help, and, moreover, steered his brothers and their wives onto nearby homesteads so that I grew up surrounded by kinfolk, thinking I was cousin to every mortal soul on earth. After a while I even had Indian relatives as the Indians drifted back among us, and it was from one of these, a very wrinkled old squaw (relative by marriage) who named for us the thing in the well.

"Stickeney," she pointed at the well, backing away and twisting her face into horrible shapes. She chomped her toothless old gums together and repeated the word. "Stickeney . . . bad Stickeney."

Father found out soon enough that there was something strange about the well, stranger even than its size or its stonework or its location in what was supposed to be unsettled wilderness. At first he used the barn to stable the team, and the well for a watering trough for all the stock, since Mother refused to use the water from it, even for scrubbing. The well wasn't like any well she had ever seen, and she didn't like the look of the water. In the first place the water level came within inches of the ground surface and had an oily, black look. The stone coping around the well was just over a foot high, and you could see deep enough into the water to note the green-slimed stones that lined it. The whole thing had a diameter of fifteen feet, and when Father tried to sound it he had to give up. The well was as near bottomless as a hole could get in this world, he said. Before a week went by Father lost a mule to the well.

It happened just about twilight, as I've heard Father tell it. He heard this mule squealing and splashing and got there just in time to see the mule dragged under. *Dragged* under. The water in the well swirled for an hour before it finally quieted down. Father insisted the mule had fallen in and been dragged to the depths of the earth by a whirlpool. Just a plain, cussed whirlpool, he said, that happened to rise up in his well from subterranean rivers or something. That's what he told Mother. But that night he screamed in his sleep, and the next day he started fencing the well away from the barn. Eventually he tore the old barn down and our big house (this very one) has a foundation of its stones —stones with strange carvings. The well was fenced off in one corner of the acre used for the kitchen garden. My father's new barn was as far away from the old well as he could conveniently place it.

I am the fourth son of my father and was, I am told, a very ordinary Bottle baby. I forgot to tell you that my family name is Bottle. My full and real name is Abstain Bottle, because my mother had a fiendish sense of humor. I have been called Ab all my life, and I forgave Mother long ago. An ordinary Bottle baby walks at eight and one-half months, talks fluently and clearly at no later than ten months, and teaches himself to read before the age of four years. This last is accomplished by the reading aloud of Hawthorne's *Tanglewood Tales* by some adult, over and over until the child knows them by heart. Then comes the glad day when light is shed over the mystery of words, and the child comprehends instantly the relationship between letters and sounds, and is ever afterward capable of reading anything but modern criticism. (This method is no longer practised except by far-flung remnants of the Bottles, though I once divulged the entire procedure to the University of Oklahoma with no thanks received whatsoever.)

You have all heard of my cousin DeWitt Quintan Bottle.

That is, you have heard of him if you have heard of people like T. S. Eliot, E. E. Cummings, or of poetry or poets. Just let somebody mention poets, poetry, or even the words *avant garde* and eventually my cousin's name will bob up. I am not claiming he is worthy of mention with the poets I have named, but other people have certainly named him in exactly the same tone and the same breath. DeWitt Quintan Bottle, for all that, was not up to the standard for Bottle babies. In the first place, he didn't walk until he was thirteen months old, and even at eighteen months of age still talked baby talk and his grammar was atrocious. I happened to be around to hear the first poem he ever composed, which turned into a family joke so well remembered that it helped to drive DeWitt away from his family and country to settle in England and write poetry just for spite.

DeWitt used to visit at our house as a child, and it was the duty of all the children around the place to keep the chickens out of the kitchen garden, and particularly out of the enclosure that held the old well and Stickeney. Chickens were known to disappear with loud squawks if they hopped upon the old well curbing, and it was no good covering the well, because Father tried that. The boards just got smashed, somehow.

De Witt was terrified of Stickeney and loathed chasing chickens anyway. He was just eighteen months old, with long yellow curls, and his pants falling off when he stood in front of Mother defiantly refusing to help. He cried:

> "Poor little baby,
> Tan't walk hard'y
> *Won't* drive tzickies
> Out of Auntie's gardy."

There you are. DeWitt's first poem. He never lived it down. Bottles everywhere knew all about it and at family reunions and dinner parties and funerals it is still repeated with laughter. When he was fifteen DeWitt couldn't stand it any longer. He ran away. Quit farming for good. We were near enough the same age that DeWitt sneaked over to our house to tell me goodbye. Said I was his only friend in the family. All the other Bottles, he said, were down on him because he was backward. He'd show them, he said. All the other Bottle cousins thought he was a coward because he was scared to death of Stickeney. What he said was true enough. All the other Bottle kids would stand around the old well and chant until the water started swirling—gently at first, then faster and faster. When the water was really whirling good we'd toss in a live chicken. It was a favorite Sunday afternoon sport while the grown people napped in the parlor. But not DeWitt. We told him over and over that Stickeney liked us kids, and if he'd just throw in one chicken Stickeney would like him, too. But DeWitt went chasing off to England and became a poet.

That was nearly fifty years ago. DeWitt's dead now, and famous as all get out. And poor old Stickeney just gets one live chicken a year. The new crops of Bottle kids don't even know about him. I've sort of kept him quiet, a personal pet, you might say. I never married, and kinfolk don't visit the way they used to. As a matter of fact, I've only had one visitor in the last few weeks. Cecil Cholmondeley was the fellow's name. Fussy little man who wrote modern criticism. Wanted to do a book, he said, all about DeWitt's early influences. Wanted to drink in DeWitt's background, walk in DeWitt's footsteps, so to speak. I welcomed him. Told him to look around. Recited DeWitt's first poem. Warned him away from the old well. He wanted to know why. Told him DeWitt was always scared to death of it. Just that. We had an early dinner, and I was feeling sleepy, but Cecil wanted to stroll around the place.

"It's all so unspoiled," he said. "So primitive, really. One forgets that America is not all glitter and dazzle. I shall walk about, quoting Bottle's better bits and feel my way into the place. All right, sir?"

"Sure," I said. "Help yourself. Just stay away from the old well, though. It's not a healthy spot—too damp and weedy. Might be snakes."

That was the second time I warned Cecil away from the well. Just for the record. Cecil left with me a copy of a new magazine he'd brought along called *New Articulations,* open at a page which featured one of DeWitt's poems, and underneath it a critical review by Cecil himself. I read DeWitt's poem first, before I went on to read Cecil's review. I was astonished. Not at the poem. De Witt's poems are all much of a muchness to me, I confess. But Cecil's review . . . well, I wanted to tell him a thing or two when he came back. Here is the whole thing, poem and review, just so you'll know what I mean.

Early Departure

by DeWitt Quintan Bottle

In the well
 feathers?
Floating (oily)
 wretched
 The swirling swelling
 The voiceless YELLing
 All the down-yonder(ing)
 Infinitely pondering
 fear-blown the future
 wafts one away (clackety-trackety)
 Don't forget to tip the porter.

DeWitt Quintan Bottle in Perspective

A Review of Early Departure by Cecil Cholmondeley

The discovery of this Bottle poem, found in his papers after his death, should in the opinion of this reviewer, secure DeWitt Quintan Bottle's position as the most penetrating commentator on this age. Other poets have, it is true, commented (in a minor key) on the same theme—the inflated ground-swelling trauma of man face to face with himself—but none has shown so much stature, poise, and peculiar excellence of craftsmanship. The "well" symbol (obviously the Existentialist mirror image) combined with the shockingly distraught "feathers" impales with one word a vast social fallacy (men's flight-wish exposed for what it is). "Floating" and "oily" are magnificently playful examples of Bottle's expanding metaphor technique. The stark "wretched" uncoils like a naked snake to hiss at us before we invoke the sensuous beauty of "The swirling swelling"—alliteration being one of Bottle's most incremental effects, achieving great density in a many-doored room. "The voiceless YELLing" is a key passage. For sheer wantonness this is unsurpassed. There is good meat (and some lovely gristle) in the next two lines. Here we discover unity imposed upon experience, demonstrating a powerful sense of self-involvement. The last line is a poignant prayer. A great poet's last and most strenuous act towards self-discipline.

I read this review over once again and got so mad I couldn't wait for Cecil to come back, but started out looking for him. I wanted to tell him about Stickeney, and then chant at Stickeney until the water started whirling, and then ask smart-aleck Cecil if he hadn't read a whole hell of a lot into DeWitt's poem that DeWitt had no notion of. It was just a fancied-up poem about Stickeney, and about DeWitt's leaving home and riding a train for the first time.

I went stomping along until I heard Cecil declaiming DeWitt's last poem in the kitchen garden. In spite of all I told him, Cecil was out there beside the well. Dark was coming on and I tried to hurry, but my knees were stiff and I heard the splashing and YELLing before I could get there.

One thing I'd like to know is just what angered Stickeney. Was it De-Witt's poem, or the critic's English accent, or just that I'd forgotten to toss him a chicken for a long, long while? One thing I know, I'm not going to go ask Stickeney. Not while the water's whirling like that. He's just too doggone excited. That water's been whirling a full week. Ever since Cecil was taken, so sudden-like. And the old chant we used to chant at Stickeney keeps coming back to mind.

> "Fee, fie, foe, fum
> I smell the blood of an Englishman.
> Be he alive, or be he dead,
> I'll grind his bones to make my bread."

I'm downright ashamed of Stickeney. But it's my fault—I should have tossed him a chicken on Midsummer Eve. The thing is, now he's had a taste of English blood, I'm not sure he'll be content with chicken.

All the Bottles are of English descent.

I do hope, though, it's just a taste for modern criticism Stickeney has acquired. God knows, he's quite capable of swallowing it.

THE WORD

by Mildred Clingerman

MILDRED CLINGERMAN has appeared primarily in *The Magazine of Fantasy and Science Fiction* thus far, and in but one or two anthologies. She is first and foremost a wife and mother, but her stories indicate freshness and originality in a crowded field, and the aficionado looks forward to more of them. She lives in Tucson, Arizona.

I can tell you we were frightened when that woman opened the door. Goddess-tall, she was, like all those people. It is only when they are children their size does not frighten one . . . much. Even hunger, I think, could not have driven us forth from our hiding place to mingle with those giants in their crowded streets, but on that night Lodi had slipped back to report that the streets were thronged only with the little ones. We decided to chance it. Dorion would be yet three days repairing the ship, he said, and his fingers had slowed and grown clumsy because of his hunger.

Lodi blamed himself bitterly for the hunger that gnawed at the four of us. Lodi is a good leader, and I, for one, would follow him anywhere, but Mun and I sometimes have to sit on Lodi. Literally, I mean. For instance, while Dorion grumbled over his repairs and paid no attention at all to anything else, Mun and I had been forced to listen to Lodi explaining over and over just how it happened that he forgot to fill the emergency food bins. At last Mun nodded wearily at me. So Mun sat on Lodi's head and I sat on his feet and we took turns feeding back his own sad story, with variations.

"Old Yaud called you in to explain an entry in our ship's log. How could you explain it when you couldn't even read it?" said Mun.

"There we were," I took up the refrain, "just ready to take off from Big Ship with a million details to attend to, and you off in old Yaud's office buttering up the old idiot instead of checking the loading!"

But we couldn't keep Lodi down.

That's why I'd rather be on his observer ship than any of the twenty-three others attached to Big Ship. What if his crew is always being called to scuff the green carpet in the council chamber? With Lodi as our leader (and he tromping all over rules and regulations) we bring back the clearest, closest viewings of all. Tiu, who never leaves the Big Ship, but sits before the view screens day after day, blesses Lodi for his daring and pleads for us in the council chamber.

Now Lodi squirmed out from under us and got to his feet. "Shut up a minute," he said, and looked at Dorion who was driving himself at the repairs despite his slowing fingers. Then Lodi beckoned for Mun and me. We left the comparative safety of the ship and stumbled after him. I almost envied Dorion left groaning over his work. It was very dark outside the ship, but Lodi knew the way. Every night since the forced landing Lodi had sneaked into the nearby town with the small, portable view-taker he'd persuaded Dorion to make for him. Tiu, we knew, would be delighted with these views. While we walked we imagined among ourselves how his round belly would shake with his whoops of joy, and of how he would speak up in the council chamber, slowly and powerfully in our defense. It was comforting to remember Tiu at this moment. Because we were breaking the strictest rule of all. Lodi was ignoring it, and my empty belly and I saw no reason to remind him of the fact that crews are supposed under all circumstances to *stay inside the ship*.

It was a long walk. But at last Lodi halted us and made us lie down in some deep shadows while he crawled ahead to assess our position. Mun and I communicated our nervousness silently and lifted our heads to peer at the lights ahead. I remembered the giants who lived there, and I shuddered. I had never seen one any closer than ship's length away, staring goggle-eyed at us through the window of his aircraft.

Suddenly, I felt something rubbing against my hand. My heart almost stopped before I saw it was a small, mewing animal that meant no harm. I scratched its neck as I would have scratched the neck of a *pprrr* at home. I liked it.

Lodi sounded the clear-ahead whistle. Mun and I stood up and walked forward into the lights. I saw, from afar, Lodi standing calmly on a walk jostled by a crowd of children. All along the street the light standards showed dozens of strolling children, but none of the frightening big ones. Not one of the children paid much attention to Lodi, I saw, other than to point at him and stare a moment, smiling, before they moved on.

"It's all right, Cleel," Lodi reassured me, though he did not speak aloud. Lodi, too, was nervous. "They all have food. All of them. Smell it?" He waved his arm encompassingly. "Do you see they are all carrying sacks full of food? Watch them. They go up to a house, knock, say a certain word, and more food is put in their sacks. It's a curious procedure, and I am even now recording it with the view-taker." As he talked silently, coaxingly, we edged nearer to him. Lodi grabbed Mun impatiently and pulled him along by the hand. I was shaking with fright all the way to my toenails, but I plodded beside them.

"And are we, God forbid, to rob these children of their full sacks?" I have followed Lodi into many a trouble-making, council-shaking act, but I would not rob even a giant's child.

"No, no!" Lodi glared at me. "Have I yet led you into the unlawful?"

Mun and I clutched each other and snickered. Lodi dropped Mun's hand and stalked ahead. Another kind of animal, much larger than the mewing one (or we), came running up to Lodi, wagging its tail and licking Lodi on the chin. Lodi kept pushing it away and patting it timidly all at the same time. The animal then ran around and around Lodi keeping him prisoner and almost knocking him off his feet. Ahead of us a child turned and whistled. The animal went bounding away.

"Thank God," Lodi muttered. "I thought I had been chosen for Only-Love. Think how Dorion would have cursed if I'd been forced to return to the ship with that great beast. Now watch and extend your hearing." We all paused before a lighted house, and sheltered by the hedge, watched a group of children who waited before the open door. The light poured out on their upturned faces, and I gasped at the sight. One of the children bore the face of a man aged in wickedness. Another that of a polished skull. One child straddled a broom and wore a high, peaked hat and had the face of a toothless crone.

"Oh pity their parents!" I cried out. Lodi hushed me so that we might hear the secret word. A man giant came to the open door. The children all screeched together, so that it was difficult to sort out the syllables.

"How sad that they have the voices of children with such faces!"

Lodi shushed me again while we watched. The man put a piece of food into each sack. The children pushed and shoved each other in their eagerness. One child spilled all the contents of his sack and, wailing, stooped to retrieve them. And, oh then! His face fell off. I myself wailed at the horror of it. Lodi stuffed his hand against my mouth, and then I saw that underneath the face-that-fell dwelt another gentler face, like any child's.

"Did you hear the word?" Lodi hissed.

"No, did you?" Mun reached out and dragged Lodi into the shadow.

"Clang-heads!" Lodi whispered heatedly. "I will give you the word, but where oh where are *your* ears? Cleel must needs make the night ghastly with howling. Oh, yes, your lungs are ever-present, your mouth is ever-moving, your belly ever-calling, but who, *who* is it that does the head work, always and forever? *Who*, I say, makes it possible for you two honk-heads to stay in Observation? *Who?*"

"Tiu," I answered him. Lodi stopped raving and started giggling. We all sat down in the midst of the hedge and giggled. When we could stop, we got up and walked to the last house with a light. Lodi whispered the word to us, but we pushed him into the leading position, so that it was he who knocked on the door.

A light came on over our heads. The door opened. Goddess-tall was that woman standing in the doorway. Mun grabbed my hand, and my heart almost stopped again. But she was beautiful, that giant woman. She smiled down at us, and Lodi, who is susceptible to all the nuances of love, flapped his antennae in shy acknowledgment.

"Triggertree?" His thin, sweet voice gave him away. Lodi was in love again and, as usual, it was mutual. He lifted his eyes to the woman and she knelt before him. Just like that. That's Lodi for you. I poked Mun in the ribs. Mun started to giggle again.

"Oh, you darlings!" the woman's mind said. And I'd swear it was the same kind of thing she said aloud. She kept murmuring at us, and we caught the no-sack concept, and you should have seen Lodi pulling his face into a mournful no-sack-poor-little-thing to match her mind-talk. She loved it, that one. And Lodi wasn't half trying. Just then in the middle of all that exclamatory murmuring of hers I caught a concept that froze me to the marrow. Translated into words it was enough to set us all trembling again. Do you know what that woman's mind was saying to us, not above us, but right to us?

"Oh, the darling little men from Mars! See their cunning little costumes. . . . Your mother must have worked hours. . . . And did you come in a lit-tle space ship all that way just to say 'trick or treat' at my house? And did you think I wouldn't give you anything just because you forgot your sacks? Wait, just wait. I've got just the things little Martians like!"

She stood up suddenly. Mun and I fell back in fright. But she didn't seem to notice. She went darting deeper into the house, while we stood there frantically communicating, all mind-talking at once, with Lodi louder and stronger than Mun or I, trying to keep us from bolting and running like hell shipwards. We stayed, but you can't always trust Lodi's judgment when he's newly in love. He was stamping his foot and silently cursing us when the woman came back. She had three enormous sacks stuffed with food. We staggered as she placed them in our arms. I could smell the food, and some of my panic stilled. Food does that, you know.

"Now go home, darlings," the woman said in effect. "It's getting late, and your mothers will worry." I thought of Dorion sweating back in the ship with never a thought for us. But I was too scared to giggle. I ran with the heavy sack. Out on the street I stopped to look back. Mun was right behind me, but that Lodi! He had his arms around the woman's neck. She was kneeling before him and kissing him right between the antennae! I heard her call as he broke away from her at last. "Be sure to come back next year. Don't forget!"

And do you know, we may do that, if Tiu ever gets us out of disciplinary confinement. He's working at it. We had some of the food left when we got back to Big Ship. Tiu says any civilization that can cook like that can't be all bad . . . or mad. Lodi, who was too full of love to be afraid, kept his ears open, and he says the woman mind-named the things as she placed them in the sacks. Every day now while he plucks glucklings for Morden he names them over like a love song. "Popcorn, peanuts, apples, candy, doughnuts, cookies, cupcakes, *dandy!*" I don't know which was which. Neither does Lodi. But I'm going to remember that word Triggertree. Nobody has ever kissed me right between the antennae. Lodi says it's wonderful.

HERMIT ON BIKINI

by John Langdon

JOHN LANGDON's most recent work is a novel of suspense, *Vicious Circuit*, published last autumn. He writes a variety of fiction, and is not primarily a writer of fantasy, for all that his *Bluebook* story, reprinted here, has a timeliness and immediacy not often found in the genre.

From the files of the Disability and Vessel Personnel Division, U. S. Shipping Board, July 9, 1952. Statement of Captain Param F. Erickson, Master of the *M. V. Thalia*, appended to the ship's log of March 8, 1952.

When we first sighted the native craft and perceived through the glasses that the sole occupant appeared to be a white man, I gave orders to change course and stand by for a possible rescue. We were passing north of the Ratak chain of the Marshall Islands, almost within sight of the northernmost island of Bikini, uninhabited since the atomic-bomb tests of July, 1946. Any craft therefore in these waters would have been most unusual.

It was a calm day. We were able to approach close to the craft, which was oddly and crudely constructed. A light line was thrown across it and with this the occupant pulled himself to the side of the ship.

I had been observing him through the binoculars all this time, aware that his white hair and beard and the pallor of his skin, most unusual in anyone exposed for any length of time to this tropic sun, could be those of a rare albino native. But when he was alongside, holding on to the Jacob's-ladder that had been lowered, I saw that his eyes were a clear blue and not the eyes of an albino. He was extremely thin, almost a skeleton.

I called out to ask him if he was strong enough to climb the ladder or should I lower a lifeboat.

"I can manage the ladder, Captain."

His voice was surprisingly strong and resonant. And when he came up the ladder, kicking the craft away from the side of the ship, it was with a swiftness and a strength that did not go with his apparent age.

From the first his behavior was extremely odd. He did not at once come to the top of the ladder, but stopped mid-way and looked up at the men waiting to help him and asked in his ringing voice that no one please touch him or come any closer to him than ten or fifteen feet.

The men looked to me for instructions and I signaled them to stand back. Only then would he come on board, lifting himself lightly and easily over the gunwale as if his body had no weight, as if the mere pressure of his hands on the edge of the gunwale was enough to propel him up and over. He stood on the after-deck looking around uncertainly, but when a couple of men took a step toward him he sprang back with an amazing, effortless bound, and held up a hand.

"Don't!" he cried out. "For your own safety don't come any nearer!"

His actions were so strange that I left the bridge and came down to the after rail of the boat-deck. He turned to me.

"Captain, please order your men not to come any closer to me than they are now."

"Very well," I said. "But perhaps we had better go into my office and get this straightened out."

He shook his head. "I'm afraid to take the chance."

"Afraid to take the chance?"

"I have been living over there for six months."

"On Bikini?" I said.

"On Bikini, Captain. Bathing in its waters, eating what I found on its islands and the fish I caught in its lagoon."

I said I still did not understand.

"Captain, I'm afraid that I am radioactive. Highly—perhaps danger-ously—so. I am not sure, but I do not want to take a chance on anyone else becoming infected."

I told him I thought there was little danger of that. I had done some reading on the subject and as far as I knew, radioactivity could not be communicated by proximity or even by direct contact. This made no impression on him, however. He persisted in saying that he had probably absorbed more radioactive substances than any man on record and that no one could possibly tell, without scientific tests, just what effect this could have. In any case, he asked, why take a chance? Why not let him travel back to the United States in isolation or semi-isolation, at least? I could see no harm in agreeing to this.

He then identified himself as Matthew A. Hummel, formerly carpen-ter on the S. S. *Cambrian* which had capsized in a typhoon and gone down in these waters about six months ago. He was not sure of the date, but there had been no other survivors.

I remembered something about it in the way one will remember those mysteries of the sea where a few weak distress signals are received, then nothing more is heard of the ship.

Later, observing him at a somewhat closer range during the trip home, I was struck by the spring to his step, the way he moved and held himself, and by the firmness and resiliency of his muscles, and I could believe he was twenty-eight years old and not the sixty-some years I had first taken him to be. Also, there was a quality to his skin that I find hard to define— a translucence, a glistening or shimmering texture I have never before seen on any human being.

A small unused storeroom on the stern of the ship was cleared and cleaned up. He was provided with an army cot, bedding, eating utensils, towels and soap, a five-gallon bottle of drinking-water, and he was furnished a bucket with a line on it to haul up sea water for his washing. He was to take care of his own dishes, placing them on the edge of the hatch near the galley at mealtime and when food was put in them he would come and get it. He asked for pen and ink and a pad of writing paper. He said he had observations on his stay on Bikini that might be of interest to scientists and he wished to get them written down during the voyage home.

On the trip he kept to his room, writing, coming out only for his meals or to haul up a bucket of sea water. He might not have been on the ship at all except for the attitude of the crew who referred to him as "The Spook," and avoided the stern of the ship as much as possible. A few of them refused to go back there at all and there were, of course, the expected stories of strange ghostly lights to be seen in his room at night. One persistent story that had some minor basis in fact concerned a large luminous area far down in the water that seemed to be following in the wake of the ship. Undoubtedly over-active imagination plus the presence of a rather unusual amount of phosphorescence in the water accounted for this. And one of my mates reported solemnly that when he had glanced in the porthole of the storeroom while passing by one night he had actually seen the fellow writing by the glow that came from his body.

I had two conversations with him, seated several feet apart on the after hatch. In the first, appended to the log, I obtained essential information from him such as the name and address of his wife in Oregon and of his father and mother in Baltimore, Maryland, his place and date of birth, and so forth. He was well educated and had received a Bachelor of Arts degree from an Eastern university.

The second conversation occurred on the afternoon of March seventeenth. We were due to arrive in San Francisco shortly after six A.M. the following morning. On this occasion he placed a roll of papers, neatly tied, on the hatch between us and asked, should anything happen to him, to see it was delivered to the proper authorities.

I wondered why he thought anything might happen to him but he avoided a direct answer to my questions, repeating that this was merely a precaution and said something I did not understand about his work being finished.

"I have left in there a card with a complete set of my fingerprints on it in case it becomes necessary to establish my identity," he said. "There is also a small piece of metal, a scrap of iron I picked up off the deck. I have kept it about me constantly and it might prove my claim of being highly radioactive. So I would not handle it too much if I were you. Of course you have my permission to read what I have written, if you wish. But please see that those personal letters are delivered."

His manner struck me as strange, but there was no sign of derangement. In fact, he seemed quite calm, self-possessed and at peace with himself.

These are all the facts I can attest to. I have also been asked to state my impressions in view of his disappearance from the ship—which must have occurred in the early morning hours shortly before we reached the pilot station at San Francisco. He had stripped clean of everything the storeroom where he had been staying. The army cot and bedding, the utensils and towels, the waterbottle and even the bucket and the handline had been thrown overboard. There was no evidence that he had ever been on the ship—except, of course, for the unusually clean storeroom and the bundle of papers which he had turned over to me.

In stating my impressions I must say that as soon as I could, I read what he had written. It is obvious to me that he was insane. I am not versed in psychiatry, but the nature of his hallucination must have been such that he could appear to be rational.

I am familiar with the reports of the radiation research laboratories at Stanford and the University of California: that the scrap of iron he kept in his possession and even the steel bulkheads of the storeroom where he stayed did emit a peculiar type of high-intensity radiation that has so far defied identification, as did the card bearing his fingerprints, which proved to be those of a Matthew A. Hummel, born September 23, 1923, and the last registered on the articles of the S. S. *Cambrian* as its carpenter. I might also add that the roll of papers of the document he had given me remained in my desk drawer for several hours. In the same drawer I kept my Leica camera with a nearly-used roll of film. On finishing the roll I sent it to be developed but the entire roll was ruined by over-exposure.

Nevertheless, it is my firm conviction that Matthew A. Hummel was suffering from strong, obsessive hallucinations caused by the loneliness and deprivations of his stay on Bikini and possibly by his radioactive contamination. In my opinion the document is a hoax, though not a deliberate one. I do not doubt that he believed in it himself—so firmly, in fact, that he took his own life.

(Signed) *Param F. Erickson*
Master, *M. V. Thalia*
June 12, 1952

Document Attributed to Matthew A. Hummel

Near the end of last September our ship, the S. S. *Cambrian,* was running southeast from a typhoon, or rather, into the fringe of it, trying to circle it since the typhoon was moving in a general southwesterly direction. For two days the sky was overcast. We did not see the sun, and the sea boiled up around us in waves whose peaks easily reached as high as the boat-deck, nearly thirty feet above the waterline, and seemed to come at us from four different directions at once. Our instruments recorded short gusts of wind up to ninety-five and one hundred miles an hour.

During this time no work was done except that absolutely necessary for the running of the ship. It was impossible to keep anything on top of the galley ranges. The cooks had to move around with the aid of handlines we had strung, and we had no hot meals at all. Several lockers were ripped from their moorings by the force of the ship's roll whipping over and back and a few of the men who did not barricade themselves securely enough in their bunks were thrown out. We slept in quick snatches, awakening certain with each big roll that we were going on over this time. The limit-marker hand on the wheelhouse inclinometer had stopped at a fifty-five and one-half degree roll to the port side, far beyond our safety factor, and nothing but a high wave or several of them coming up under the port side at the peak of our roll at that moment, could have saved us from going on over and capsizing, since we were riding light and empty.

On the morning of the third day the winds began to slacken and by early evening it was fairly calm. Although the sky was still solidly overcast we resumed our normal cruising speed. Around eight o'clock that night the clouds were reported to be breaking up and at ten o'clock the bridge was able for the first time in nearly three days to fix our position. We were far south of our regular course.

It was near midnight when I was awakened by my roommate, the bosun, shaking me and saying, "Come on out, Chips! Come on out on deck!"

He left without giving any explanation. He had sounded so urgent that I dressed and followed.

Never will I forget the spectacle that struck my eyes when I stepped out on the fore-deck.

The ocean extending around the ship on all sides as far as I could see was one luminous, shimmering mass of green-white fire. The ship's lights, the running-lights, the circles of the portholes and the rectangles of open doorways all seemed pale and feeble by comparison. It was beautiful yet terrifying. I could feel my heart pounding. A chill that was not from actual cold swept over me.

This was not the usual phosphorescence of waves breaking on a beach and cresting the shoreline with frothing green-white luminescence. Nor was it like the patches I had seen at sea, running and spreading where the swells broke. Nothing I had ever seen remotely approached this. Not even standing one night on the deck of a ship fogbound a few miles offshore, listening to the bellowing of the ship's whistle and watching luminous blobs of light, literally thousands of them, float up and surround the ship like huge sightless eyes. This was utterly different. There were no swells; the sea was glassy; I could see the surface of the water and a short distance beneath it, and this glow neither brightened nor dimmed but spread its brilliant radiance evenly, making every detail of the *Cambrian* clearly visible.

Then I saw the low dark line of an island lying ahead off our starboard bow, and I joined a group of men standing at the rail.

"What island is that?" I asked.

Sykes, a seaman who had just been relieved at the wheel, said, "Bikini, I heard."

"Bikini!"

"Yeah. They're sure having one hell of a hassle up there."

"Who is?"

"All of 'em. The old man, the chief and the second mate, and the chief and the first engineer. The chief engineer swears he's got the engine wide open with all it'll take and the way it's turning over, he says we should be making fourteen and a half to fifteen knots. The second mate's ready to be tied. He claims we're not doing anywhere near that. Says he's got bearings on the island now and in an hour or two we'll know who's right."

"Who do you think is right?" someone asked.

"Now how in hell would I know?" Sykes said.

I asked Sykes if he had heard any explanation for this glow.

"All of 'em say they've never seen anything like it before," he said. "They don't know any more about it than we do."

Other groups were gathered on the fore-deck and up on the boat-deck. I could hear the murmur of hushed, excited voices. Ordinarily, after two days of constant buffeting by the typhoon, we would have wanted only to sleep. But now none of us thought of sleep. We were still out on deck as the luminosity began to fade slowly from the sky in the first faint dawn, then swiftly as the sky filled with light.

Shortly after dawn it was established by direct bearings on points of the island that our speed had dropped to something less than half. This, in spite of a full throttle and all nozzles open delivering a forward thrust of sixty-five hundred horsepower to the propeller.

Only strong headwinds or powerful tidal currents could have affected our speed that much. Even then, the current would have had to approach the proportions of a tidal-race or bore, and that was unheard of in open ocean or among these low Pacific atolls. Nor was there any wind except a slight off-shore breeze.

One seaman had the theory that we were in the grip of a powerful and until-now-unknown magnetic field. We laughed at this.

"Go ahead and laugh," he said. "But just the same, during my trick at the wheel the magnetic compass was acting up."

On modern ships the magnetic compass is infrequently referred to and so it was not strange he had been the only one to notice it. Nevertheless, we went up to the monkey-house on the flying bridge where the other binnacle was and the compass-card was pointed a quarter of a circle —ninety degrees—off our true heading.

The bosun was delegated to relay this information to the captain who verified it and said it was very strange but it explained nothing. There was no magnetic force on earth capable of slowing up a ship under full power, he said.

By noon, however, there could no longer be any doubt. We had stopped moving entirely. Whatever was holding us, magnetic force or not, we had come to a dead stop. The island, which should have been out of sight by now, was directly abeam of us. Nor was there any tide and only the faintest breeze. Boxes and bits of wood dropped over the side continued to float slowly forward past us and the magnetic compass-card had swung a full half-circle, directly opposite the direction of our heading.

It was then I began to feel fear, real fear, in myself and in the others.

No one spoke of it but we gathered together now in larger groups. Now and then one of the mates or an engineer muttered something reassuring, but their words sounded hollow. The three wipers refused to go below, saying they were not needed for the running of the ship and were going to stay topside until it was moving again. The rest of us did not work. We waited, feeling the throb of the engine as the propeller went on churning and churning. We stood at the rail and stared down at the clear blue-green water. Occasionally schools of small fish or the long dark shape of a larger one darted through the water. The bleached white bone of the island with the few splinters of coconut palms on it hung stationary off the starboard, shimmering in the hot sun. Now and then someone tossed a bit of wood or a cardboard carton over the side and we followed it with our eyes until it disappeared beyond the bow.

Then something happened which the four of us who saw it finally decided must have been a trick of the dazzling sunlight on the water. We were on the stern at the time, myself, the bosun and two sailors, when about a quarter of a mile off, a wave—one single wave in the midst of that calm expanse of sea—lifted itself. We all saw it at the same time. It rose to a height of six or eight feet in a long, thin, curved arm. Then the tip of it broke off and the next instant there was a bird, a large bird like a white albatross, flying low over the water.

For several seconds none of us could say anything. It had looked exactly as if the tip of the wave that had broken off had *become* the albatross. But that was impossible.

We finally figured out, as we watched the albatross circle the ship about a quarter of a mile away and disappear in the direction of the island, that it had been resting on the water all along and had chosen that moment to take off. The only trouble with that was that we had not seen one single bird or any living thing in the sky or water except the fish, since we had been here.

We decided not to say anything to the others about it.

At three o'clock that afternoon the oiler on watch in the engine-room came up to the messroom for coffee and announced that we might not have the main turbine working much longer. We were losing the vacuum on it. It had been dropping steadily since noon and had gone from twenty-eight inches of vacuum down to twenty-one.

"The sea water just won't cool," he said. "Yet it hasn't changed temperature since I came on watch. Not by one degree. I've been checking it every fifteen minutes since noon and it's always the same—eighty-two degrees. The chief and the first are going crazy down there."

"What'll happen if we lose vacuum?" someone asked.

The oiler stared at him.

"What'll happen?" he said. "We'll lose the plant, that's what'll happen —the turbines for the screw and the generators. You can't keep 'em turning without a vacuum."

No one asked any more questions. We avoided looking at each other. A couple of men got up quickly and went out. A little later in the eight-to-twelve watch-room I saw the ordinary seaman packing his belongings, folding his clothes and putting them away in a suitcase and a canvas duffel bag, oblivious, concerned only for his possessions. From behind the closed door of the steward's room I heard sounds of angry cursing. There were several voices. Some of the men were wearing their life-jackets.

On the fore-deck I stopped beside the bosun who said, "If only we were back in that typhoon, Chips! That's something I can understand." Then he gripped my arm. "What is it, Chips? You've been to college—*what is it?*"

There was nothing I could say. I left him and went up the outside companionways to the wheelhouse. All the deck officers were in there except the second mate who was bending over the pelorus on the flying bridge, still checking his observations. The captain came into the wheelhouse.

"I've authorized Sparks to send a distress call," he said.

Todd, the chief mate, said, "Captain, maybe if we went astern for a while we might shake it."

"Good idea, Mr. Todd." The captain called for full speed astern. The mechanical telegraph jangled and was answered from the engine-room. The engine whined to a stop, then picked up in reverse, making the ship throb like a giant heartbeat.

An hour later, when we had not moved, he ordered the engine to full ahead again. Then they tried reversing the engine quickly, several times. Nothing had any effect. We were as motionless as if we were imbedded in a cake of ice, but with the clear, warm water slipping past us, rising and falling in little swells that lapped gently against the hull. Also, whenever the engine was reversed, the magnetic compass-card whipped sharply around in a full half-circle in the opposite direction.

The radio operator, his face dripping with sweat and his clothes soaked, came in to report he could not get through.

"Too much interference," he said.

"What kind of interference?"

"I don't know, Captain. It's like static and it isn't. It covers all the bands. Once in a while I get a few weak signals, but that's all."

"Well, keep trying."

He ordered the engine stopped.

Without the accustomed noise and vibration the ship was like a dead ship, not quite real. I half believed it was all a dream. I left the wheel-house and started back down to the main deck and it was as if all my senses were muffled in thick layers of wool. I scarcely felt the deck my feet touched or the rails my hands gripped. Now and then shocks of reality came through to me and were quickly shut out.

The strain was beginning to tell on the men too. Four of the crew got into the ship's hospital, broke open a locker and stole a gallon bottle of grain alcohol. They started fighting among themselves. I saw the or-dinary who had been packing his gear. He had taken the suitcase and the duffel bag up to the boat-deck and stood near a lifeboat, staring at it. There were other men there too, in their lifejackets, obviously want-ing to lower the boats, but not quite daring to until the captain gave the order.

Just before sunset the vacuum dropped too low; the main turbine failed; then the generator kicked off the line. The little Diesel-powered emergency generator took over. The boiler fires were put out; the engine-room auxiliaries secured.

In the bleak, dimly-lighted port passageway two of the crew who dur-ing the trip had voiced their hatred of our second cook, Jantsen, because he was the only colored person on board, had thrown Jantsen down on the deck. One of them straddled Jantsen and was choking him and the other was on his knees beating at Jantsen's face with the bottom of both fists, hammerlike. There was room to reach over them and get a fire-extinguisher off the bulkhead. I swung it—I knocked out the one choking Jantsen and hauled the other off him.

"It's okay now, Jan."

He did not hear me; he ran down the passageway into the galley and came to the door with a meat-cleaver, threatening to kill anyone who came near him.

"You too!" he screamed at me.

A few minutes after this there was a high-pitched yelling and someone ran down the passageway on the other side toward the fore-deck. I started that way but before I got outside I heard a loud splash.

Two of the engine-room crew were standing at the gunwale staring down at the water.

"What happened?" I shouted.

They turned to me, their faces rigid with unbelief.

"He disappeared!" one of them said. His voice shook.

"Disappeared! You mean he sank out of sight?"

They stared at me and both of them shook their heads slowly. The other one said, "Disappeared! Like that! Soon as he hit!"

They did not seem to be drunk. Yet they were badly scared. Nor was there any sign of the man who had gone overboard. I left them and started up the companionways again and stopped on the starboard wing of the cabin-deck outside the wheelhouse.

Except for the coughing chatter of the emergency generator that supplied a few feeble lights, the ship was dead, a motionless hulk frozen fast in these wide miles of ocean. The last stain of red was rapidly being washed out of the western sky and the unearthly glow from the water was rising to supplant the darkness. I went into the wheelhouse.

The captain was sprawled face-down, half in the wheelhouse and half in the passageway behind it. The side of his face was turned to me and there was an ugly cut on his forehead. I wondered if he had stumbled and struck something or if someone had hit him. I started to bend over him and then I heard a scream that was unlike any of the others I had heard and a prolonged, racking cry that froze all other sounds, everything, even the beating of my heart:

"*It's coming on board!*"

For seconds a blank deathly silence hung in the wake of that cry. Then running feet pounded on the decks. There were stricken screams and other voices took up the shout. I ran out on the starboard wing.

I could not believe what I was seeing:

The water was rising. All around the ship it was rising in small spear-pointed waves, but only close up against the hull. Farther out, the sea was smooth, calm and undisturbed.

It was as if the ship were cradled in a nest of green-white flames that licked up the sides, clung, fell back, gathered themselves and rose higher —as if the steel plates of the hull were being consumed.

I stared at this seething caldron of flame-tipped water and all at once I knew—I knew with an instant, blinding impact that this water was alive. It was alive and possessed of an intelligence.

I could not have moved then if I had wanted to. Nor could I take this in its entirety. It was too vast and insupportable. At the same time, with part of my mind, I realized this could be the only explanation for a force—or an entity—powerful enough to stop the ship, to hold it motionless hour after hour, yet all the while remain, itself, fluid enough to allow the propeller to churn through it and schools of fish to swim in it.

I was aware of the panic, the blind terror of the crew as the first thick, rope-like, livid tentacle groped for the gunwale and spilled over on to the deck. As if in a dream or a flickering projection on a distant screen, I saw the men run. Some of them crashed unheeding into bulkheads, guy-wires, resistor-houses; stumbled over coamings, got up and ran in another direction. A few crawled out on their knees, praying loudly. Their sounds blended, became one, rose to me in waves like the panting, guttural grunts of some giant animal.

The radio operator plunged into the radio shack and slammed and locked the door. I heard the power hum of the transmitter and the liquid staccato ripple of the sending key. The second mate appeared on the boat-deck below and emptied his automatic pistol at the water, and then flung the gun away and ran inside. I saw Jantsen with the meat-cleaver, hacking at the hawser-thick arms of water. The blade bit through them into the metal ledge; still the water came on.

I went into the wheelhouse, found a spare lifejacket and put it on. When I got back out on the wing, the luminous water had lunged up in one sheer, steep wave completely surrounding the ship and was surging over in one solid mass. Both the fore- and after-decks were awash with it. It poured into the midship deckhouse through the open water-tight doors and was flowing up the outside companionways, vaulting them step by step in rippling heaves. Surrounding Number Three hatch where four of the men were praying, it rose over the coaming and converged on them.

Their screams cut through the other sounds as the water engulfed them. For an instant the heaped mounds of water were streaked with an iridescent play of color. Then the mounds subsided and flowed back off the hatch and there was no sign of the men, no sign they ever had been there at all.

The boat-deck below was covered. I became aware that the ship was settling and listing to starboard. I knew the engine-room had been filled and *it* was probably filling the holds. But the unimaginable force, or whatever it was, was also heeling the ship over. I braced myself against a stanchion as the water surged up the companionway and poured into the wheelhouse. A thick tentacle shot out and encircled my ankle.

I felt a sting not unlike an electric current, but not unpleasant. It was warm and vibrant. I caught my breath. The water gathered. Pulses of light and color shot back and forth in it. The thudding of my heart made a roaring in my ears. I heard a distant scream. I did not know if I had made it or not. I did not care. And in the instant that it rose and covered me and I lost consciousness, I knew an eternity, an infinity of things. . . .

When I awoke again, it was dawn. I was on the beach of what, I later learned, was the main island of Bikini. I still wore the lifejacket.

I soon realized that this spot where I had awakened was on the inshore, or the lagoon side, of the island, facing that enormous lagoon whose farthest limits I could not see. I walked along the beach to a point where the ocean was visible. There was no sign of the *Cambrian*, no evidence the ship had ever been near these waters. But I knew I could not have floated unconscious and face-up through the encircling reefs to the place where I had awakened.

In the long, solitary months I have had time to think; time to search, to find and piece together fragments of remembrance until I am now unshakably convinced that I was absorbed, fused into the body of what, for the lack of any other term I must call the monster, and then re-cast in my former shape and identity.

The monster *is*—it *becomes*—that which it absorbs. It is now neither good nor evil, but some of both. It has only one matrix or core: inexorable growth. It cannot be stopped, it cannot be destroyed, by our most powerful weapons. For it was born of our most powerful one. Born too, of our fear, our distrust, our suspicion and in a measure, of our cruelty. What it will become depends upon that balance, good or evil, existing on that ultimate, inevitable day when it has completed its final absorption.

I know this will be put down as a hoax or the fantasy of a mind deranged by hardship and solitude. I cannot blame anyone for that belief. For this goes beyond the realm of everyday common sense. But I have been in that other real realm and I have not much longer to live. I must go back to the monster, a part of which has followed this ship and is waiting for my return to the parent body. How else could I prove the reality of my conviction?

My only hope is that you who may read this do not have the seeds of that future absorption already planted within yourselves. For I fear that the radioactivity with which I am saturated, each atom linked to the body of the monster, will pass from me into the paper and ink I use. Can it pass through them, through other hands, perhaps through type and ink and paper again? I do not know. I hope not; I hope not.

JEZEBEL

by Murray Leinster

MURRAY LEINSTER (1896–   ) has perhaps more right to the title
of dean of science fiction than any other living author, unless it be
David H. Keller, whose output does not begin to match Leinster's.
He has contributed to virtually every magazine in the field, as well
as to *Collier's*, *The Saturday Evening Post*, and a host of others; he
has been widely anthologized; his books include *Space Platform*,
Sidewise in Time, *The Last Space Ship*, *Space Tug*, and *Great
Stories of Science Fiction*, an anthology edited by him. He divides
his time between a home on Long Island and his colonial home in
Virginia. He is married and the father of four children.

We could all feel a great deal safer if Mr. Thaddeus Binder were a little
more ambitious, or a little less successful, or if, perhaps, his dearest friend
Mr. Madden had caught him when he went after him with a stick of
driftwood. Unfortunately, in his retirement on pension from the electric-
light-and-power company, he does research. He reads Aristotle, Poincaré,
Ron Hubbard and Paracelsus. He gets ideas from them and tries them
out. And we'd be safer if he made atom bombs in his kitchen laboratory.
One of them might go off. That would simply be that. As it is——

He investigated the idea of compenetration, once. That is the philosophical notion that two things can occupy the same space at the same
time, and it sounds harmless. But when Mr. Binder got through with it,
not only himself but seventy-one other persons had been heaved violently into what can only be described as the middle of the week after
next. In the process they lost their small change, their zippers, the nails
out of their shoes and the fillings out of their teeth. They were also un-
pleasantly surprised.

That was mild, of course, but it's the suspense that hurts. Nobody
can guess what Mr. Binder will accomplish next. Even his best friend,
Mr. Madden, has grown suspicious. The other day Mr. Madden went
to call on him. Mr. Madden is also retired, from the career of skipper of

a charter-boat for fishing parties. His son runs the ancient fishing-boat now, and Mr. Madden disapproves. But the other day he went to Mr. Binder's house and rang the doorbell. Mr. Binder answered it.

"Why, George!" he said cordially, at sight of Mr. Madden's sunburned jowls. "George! Come in! I've got something to show you!"

"Hold it!" said Mr. Madden sternly. "I've troubles and I need consolation, but not one step do I come into your house if you've notions of showing me your scientific triumphs!"

"It's not a triumph," protested Mr. Binder. "It's a failure. It's only something I worked out from soap-bubbles."

Mr. Madden considered, then yielded.

"If it's only soap-bubbles," he conceded suspiciously, "it could be harmless. But I've got troubles. I've no mind to have them increased. Nothing controversial, now! I'm allergic to it!"

He stamped inside. Mr. Binder led the way happily to his kitchen. There were curtains at the windows, from the time before he was a widower. An ice-box whirred merrily by one wall. But beside another wall stood a work-bench and the chairs held burdens of coiled wires and tin cans full of rusty bolts, and there were mysterious substances in screw-top jars that once had held preserves. Mr. Binder cleared a chair by removing a breadboard, hand-drill and a cup and saucer with coffee in it.

"You'll be amused," said Mr. Binder ingratiatingly. "I got interested in soap-bubbles, and that led to surface tension, and that led to—well, George—I made something that you might as well call a vacuum. But it's a new kind of vacuum. It's solid."

Mr. Madden sat, four-square and with his knees apart.

"Well, now," he admitted, "that might not upset me. They use vacuums in electric bulbs and such. There's vacuum cleaners, though why anybody should worry about a dirty vacuum——"

Mr. Binder laughed delightedly. Mr. Madden thawed at this appreciation of impromptu wit. But he said mournfully:

"I've troubles on my mind, that boy of mine, running the old *Jezebel* that I took fishing parties out in for twenty years. I shouldn't ha' turned her over to him. He's got her up on a marine railway. A railway, understand! And he says she has to have a new engine. She's too slow, he says! Fishin' parties don't want speed. They want fish!"

Mr. Binder offered hospitality. He turned up the gas under a kettle on the gas stove. He put honey, cinnamon, nutmeg and a lavish slab of butter into a glass. He judgematically poured a huge hooker of brown liquid over it from a black bottle. He filled the glass with hot water, stirred it, and presented the result to Mr. Madden. Mr. Madden regarded it with lessened sternness. He took off his hat and coat, loosened his suspenders and relaxed the waistband of his trousers. He took the glass.

"The old demon rum himself," he said tolerantly. "You've bribed me to listen to you. All right, I'll listen. After, I'll tell you about my boy wantin' to put twelve hundred dollars in a new second-hand engine for the *Jezebel*. It's outrageous!"

Mr. Binder beamed. He went to his work-bench. He loosened the vise and removed a six-inch piece of wooden rod which had been held fast in it. One end of the rod glistened faintly. He showed it to Mr. Madden.

"You'd never guess it, George," he said happily, "but that's practically a vacuum on the end of this stick. Feel the wind!"

He held it close to Mr. Madden's weathered cheek. There was a distinct brisk wind blowing sidewise from the cut-off end. Mr. Madden raised his hand to take it, and Mr. Binder jerked it away.

"Not yet, George," he said apologetically. "You might get hurt if you don't understand it first."

"Then put it away," said Mr. Madden heavily. "I'll drink this drink and be gone. It's controversial!"

He sipped, shaking his head. Mr. Binder protested:

"Look, George! Like this!"

He picked up the breadboard. He presented the shiny end of the stick to it. There was a slight burping noise. There was a slight misty appearance. The wooden rod went through the breadboard. Mr. Binder withdrew it, and there was a neat hole there. Mr. Madden's jaw dropped. Mr. Binder picked up a section of sheet-iron. The noise was rather more like a hiccough than a burp. The wooden rod went through, leaving a hole. Mr. Binder picked up an empty bottle. The wooden rod cherruped. It made a hole in the glass bottle. There was again a misty appearance.

"Well, now!" said Mr. Madden, intrigued. "That's a fancy drill you've got there! What does the cutting?"

"What I call the vacuum," said Mr. Binder modestly. "It's really something that's got surface tension so high that it won't let anything touch it. Anything that comes in contact with it, it throws away. Sideways. Even air! That's why I call it a vacuum."

"Vacuum is as vacuum does," said Mr. Madden sententiously. "What're you going to do with it?"

"I can't do anything with it," said Mr. Binder regretfully.

"Hm, now!" said Mr. Madden. "It'd ought to be good for something!"

"It's just painted on the end of the stick," said Mr. Binder. "It's very easy to make. I did think I'd give it to the government for the boys in Korea. For bullet-proof clothes, you know. It can be painted on cloth."

Mr. Madden blinked.

"Bullet-proof clothes," he asked. "To put on a bayonet, now——"

Mr. Binder said regretfully, "Make believe this is a bullet." He picked up a spanner and swatted the end of the wooden stick. There was a noise. There was a darkish mist in the air. But the spanner didn't hit the stick. The stick went through the spanner. There was a hole. "If a bullet hits a piece of cloth with this solid vacuum on it, the bullet gets thrown away sidewise in powder. This solid vacuum don't like anything! A man with clothes on that were solid vacuum outside—you could turn a machine-gun on him, or shoot at him with a cannon, and nothing could get through to him."

"Ah!" said Mr. Madden with approval. "That's a fine, patriotic invention. What did the government say?"

"No use showing it," said Mr. Binder regretfully. "A man in a solid-vacuum suit couldn't sit down."

Mr. Madden looked his question. Mr. Binder pointed to the shiny end of the stick.

"This's the seat of his pants," he said. He touched the supposititious seat of somebody's pants to the seat of a kitchen chair. It went through. There was a hole.

"Hm," said Mr. Madden gravely. "They'd have to sit on the floor."

For answer, Mr. Binder touched the shiny stuff to the floor. It went through. He said, still bent over, "I haven't the nerve to let go of it. It ought to go on down to the center of the earth. I'd guess it would."

He sraightened up and put the stick back in the vise.

"I thought you'd be interested, George. Now, what's your trouble?"

Mr. Madden waved away the question. He was envisioning somebody wearing a suit like the shiny stuff on the end of the stick and who had sat down. Mr. Madden saw that he would go tumbling down through solid earth and rock, on downward indefinitely. There appeared to be drawbacks to solid vacuum as wearing apparel. But then he slapped his hand on his knee.

"Give him," he said authoritatively, "a ordinary seat to his pants. That's it! A man ain't often wounded just there, anyways."

But Mr. Madden shook his head and sighed.

"No. But he might stub his toe. If he fell flat on his face, it'd be just as bad as if he sat on his—in the usual way, George. And when fighting, a man might get careless and not watch where he walked."

"That's so," conceded Mr. Madden.

He sipped at his drink. Mr. Binder said, with a gesture toward the wooden rod in the vise, "You noticed I didn't dare put it down? There's a vacuum in front. It's always trying to get pulled into that vacuum. Only of course it couldn't be. If I pointed it up at the sky and let go, it'd go shooting off I don't know where. Straight up. Pulled by the vacuum. What's your trouble, George?"

Mr. Madden cleared his throat. He did have troubles. But Mr. Binder had proposed a problem, and Mr. Madden was not one to let an intellectual riddle go unsolved. He held up his hand.

"It's obvious," he said sternly. "Why didn't you realize it? You can paint that stuff on cloth. Take an umbrella and paint it with solid vacuum. Then you hold on to the handle and open the umbrella. You'll fly. Close the umbrella, and you'll come down. Just like that!"

But Mr. Binder shook his head yet again.

"Sometimes an airplane gets turned upside down," he said sagely. "It often happens. And if it hit the ground upside down—besides, George, where could you hang up an umbrella like that?"

Mr. Madden's glass was empty. Mr. Binder took it. Again he compounded honey, nutmeg, cinnamon and butter with hot water and a fluid from a black bottle. But as the butter melted he went back to the vise.

This time he took out the stick and dipped its shiny end into the two glasses. The effect was remarkable. For an instant it could be seen that the melted butter, attempting to touch the end of the stick, was thrown violently away sidewise in an infinitely thin sheet. It was actually only molecules thick. In consequence the butter-globules were broken into tiny droplets below microscopic size. The drink was stirred as no other drink was ever stirred before. It was literally homogenized. It was out of this world.

Mr. Binder returned the rod to the vise as Mr. Madden sampled it.

"Smooth!" said Mr. Madden in reverent astonishment. "Never was there such smoothness in human history! You're a rich man, Thaddeus! There's not a bar in the world won't buy batteries of these for mixers! Not a bar!"

"No," said Mr. Binder depressedly, as he sipped at his own glass. "If a bartender tried to clean one of these it would be too bad. If he dipped it too low it would powder the bottom of the glass and stir it in the drink, or go right through the bottom. No, George, it's just one of those inventions that's a good idea, but impractical!" And then he sighed and said encouragingly. "What's on your mind, George? You said you had some troubles."

Mr. Madden sighed in his turn.

"It's that boy of mine," he said pathetically. "He's got the old *Jezebel* up on a marine railway, and he says she's got to have a new engine. And there's been nothing the matter with that engine the past fifteen years. Twelve hundred dollars he wants to spend! Just to take people out to the fishing-grounds faster! And I've got to take the money out of the bank for him to waste on engines!"

Mr. Binder said "Tsk-tsk." He listened while Mr. Madden unburdened his soul. He mixed another hot buttered rum. He listened further to Mr. Madden's troubles. That is what a friend is for. Mr. Binder, being a friendly soul, gave Mr. Madden what comfort he could, but Mr. Madden was weeping for his twelve hundred bucks, and he could not be comforted.

At long last Mr. Binder said hesitantly, "George, there's something I could suggest. If this solid vacuum of mine could be made into uniforms for the boys in Korea, it'd be a military secret. But it can't. And it isn't practical for airplanes or drink-mixers. But it is a good vacuum. I could put some of it on the bow of the *Jezebel*. It'd try to pull the boat along. It might make her go faster, and I'm sure it'd save gasoline."

Mr. Madden blinked.

Mr. Binder went on meditatively, "And it ought to be safe. You don't run into things with boats, like cars. And this'd be just on the bow, and the boat'd be kept balanced by the rest of it, so it wouldn't start for the sky. And boats don't turn over—only sailboats—and moreover, I could put it on canvas, instead of the planks, so we could always take it off. Suppose I try it, George?"

Mr. Madden had been depressed on his arrival, but he was now uplifted. He had been suspicious, but he was now soothed. And he had been cagey, but this might save him some money.

They drove away from Mr. Binder's house in a taxi, with the materials for the application of solid vacuum to a charter-boat's bow in two paint-cans between their feet. And Mr. Madden was so moved with joy that he hummed melodiously as they rode. He had insisted on bringing the wooden rod as a sample of what was to be accomplished with the *Jezebel*. He beat time with it to his own melody as he rode.

"Now, George," said Mr. Binder, "you mustn't get your heart set on this! We can try, but there are lots of disappointments in this world. Maybe there's something we haven't thought of——"

"Nonsense!" said Mr. Madden exuberantly. "I'll own that it's a surprise to find that one of my own friends is a genius, but I shoulda known it! I wouldn't be surprised if the *Jezebel* hits ten knots with your stuff on her bow! Paint it right on, eh!"

"I'd better not," said Mr. Binder. "We might want to take it off again."

"Perish the thought!" said Mr. Madden. "The idea's revolting. With a good solid vacuum at her bow, the old *Jezebel* will be good as new and maybe more saving in gasoline besides!"

Their taxi darted past a station-wagon with a trick exhaust. The trick was to carry it up above the roof in a pipe, and let it loose in mid-air, where more people could smell it. Some of the fumes came in the taxi window. Mr. Madden began to cough. Mr. Binder thumped him encouragingly on the back. Mr. Madden dropped the wooden stick with the shiny end. He didn't notice. Mr. Binder didn't notice either.

But the rod tumbled to the floor, point-down. It burped slightly, and went through. It tumbled to the ground. Again it landed solid-vacuum-end down. It hiccoughed as it penetrated the asphalt. Gummy stuff like asphalt is more resistant to surface-tension—or vacuum—than more brittle materials. But the wooden rod vanished beneath the surface, leaving a neat small hole. It made a humming sound as it went through the macadam underlay of the asphalt. It sang happily as it went busily down through some four feet of packed clay to a steel pipe buried there. The pipe happened to be a high-pressure natural-gas-line. The solid vacuum cherruped and went into it. Natural gas from the heart of Texas awaited it. The pressure didn't push the wooden rod out again. Naturally. It couldn't. The end of the rod was vacuum. So the rod went into the gas-line, and then there was a geyser-like roar. Gas at fourteen hundred pounds to the square inch began to bellow up through the hole the pipe had left behind it. It erupted into the street, carrying sand, clay, macadam rocks and finally the asphalt. In seconds there was a hole a foot in diameter and growing bigger. But it actually developed under an ancient motor-truck carrying chickens in wooden crates. There was a racket as the stones pelted the bottom of the truck. The truck, insulted, backfired thunderously.

It rose off its hind wheels and darted ahead like an ancient female plucking up her skirts to flee a mouse. But it was not exactly a mouse from which it fled. The backfire had ignited the escaping gas. A lovely column of flame leaped skyward, howling. The driver of the truck cast a panic-stricken glance behind, burst into tears, and drove his truck into a fire-hydrant. It crashed. All the wooden cages broke and chickens spread their wings and flew frantically to and fro, while from the broken hydrant a charming fountain of water poured upward in the previously unembellished street.

But there was more. The little wooden rod went on. The surging gas tilted its back end, so that it went out of the gas-pipe on a slant. Two feet further on it struck a water-main and went blithely into it. Again is relative streamlining took effect. It swung about and went streaking along the pipe, in the water. As it went, it flung water laterally from its solid-vacuum front. Violently. It amounted to a traveling increase of pressure. The water-main cracked. The rod sped busily. The water-main opened along its length, poured water into the soil under the paving, searched for and found entry-ways into cellars, and the pavement swelled and rose while cellars received floods of pure cool water.

The rod went on again. There was a bend in the pipe, which it ignored. It buzzed its way out into yellow clay once more, found a conduit carrying telephone and fire-alarm signal lines, and made musical sounds as it cut through. It was followed by water fascinatedly trailing it to see what it would do. All the fire-alarms in the city rang furiously all at once. All the telephones went out of operation. The rod went buzzing on, found a concrete cellar-wall, buzzed through it, leaped into mid-air from sheer high spirits, and landed vacuum-point-down on the high-pressure boiler of an electric power-plant.

When it went out the bottom of the boiler, however, it emerged into the firebox. And here its career ended, because while what Mr. Binder called a solid vacuum could take care of any solid or mineral it might come upon, it couldn't do anything about heat. The eighteen hundred degrees of the firebox destroyed the solid vacuum at its point, and it was merely a little stick of wood when the water poured down out of the boiler to put out the furnace.

These events followed each other briskly. Still, it was a good thirty seconds between the time Mr. Madden strangled on exhaust-fumes and the roar of steam from the power-house. In that interval the taxi turned a corner and Mr. Binder and Mr. Madden went on oblivious to it all. In fact, when Mr. Madden stopped coughing and Mr. Binder stopped pounding his back, Mr. Madden said sentimentally: "Y'know, the more I think about it, the gladder I am that I've got a friend like Thaddeus Binder."

Little did he know.

Mr. Binder painted the first of the two coats on an old sail stretched about the *Jezebel*'s bow. When that had dried, he would swab it over with a particular reagent, and the sail would be coated with solid vacuum. The *Jezebel* was an ancient, stubby craft some forty feet long and something over twelve feet wide. She rested rakishly, stern to shoreward, on a cradle on a marine railway. About her there lay a thick aroma of oakum, paint, discarded bait, salt-water mud and general effluvium. She fitted her background. The canvas about her bow looked like an untidy diaper, and it was held in place by stout roofing nails. Mr. Binder carefully refrained from preparing his solid-vacuum surface all the way back to the nails, in case he needed to take the canvas off again. Mr. Madden sat on her deck underneath the awning-frame. Maybe he thought sentimental thoughts about how many lunches he had sold in advance to intending passengers at seventy-five cents a lunch, and then had maneuvered the *Jezebel* so they'd all be too seasick to eat anything.

Mr. Binder tested the first coat of his infinite-surface-tension solid-vacuum material. He swabbed it over with the reagent. He climbed a ladder leaning against the *Jezebel's* hull. Mr. Madden greeted him blithely.

"Well, can we try it now?"

Mr. Binder went forward and held his hand over the rail. He felt a distinct breeze blowing upward—air hurled sideways by the solid-vacuum coating just completed. If he'd put his hand astern from the side coating, he'd have found air blowing astern, or if he'd put his hand underneath the bottom of the solid vacuum he'd have felt wind there too. The stuff wasn't particular which way it heaved things. It just heaved them sideways to avoid their contaminating touch. This went even for air. It should go also for water. Mr. Binder went astern and nodded.

"I think it'll be all right to try now, George," he agreed.

Mr. Binder went ashore. To the office of the marine railway. He arranged for the cradle bearing the *Jezebel* to be lowered gently until the bow of the boat barely rested in the water. He climbed to the deck again. With a certain humor he went into the pilot-house, sticking up like a sore thumb astern, and waved instructions.

.The person in charge of the winch that hauled the cradle negligently reached down and lifted over the ratchet of the winch. The winch thereupon turned deliberately and whacked him in the solar plexus with a capstan-bar. He sat down, gasping. The *Jezebel* trundled down the inclined way toward the water.

"Hold it!" roared Mr. Madden. "Slow, now! Easy!"

The *Jezebel* went rolling faster. Mr. Madden bellowed instructions. They were wholly futile. *Jezebel* and all, the cradle splashed into the water. Wavelets reached up with a pretty eagerness to play tag with the charter-boat's bow.

When water tried to touch the canvas-covered bow, it was flung violently aside. It went in all directions in a thin, glistening, high-velocity sheet. When the *Jezebel* hit water, an appearance set up about her front parts which looked singularly like a liquid pinwheel twenty feet high. That was water getting away from before the boat, and leaving a vacuum there. Nature abhors a vacuum. So did the *Jezebel*. She tried to move into the vacuum and to fill it. The vacuum moved on before. The *Jezebel* hastened, flinging water higher and wider in her haste. The vacuum moved still faster, being fastened to her.

The *Jezebel* went out of the slip leading to the railway, exactly like a bat out of hell.

She had never made more than a groaning eight knots in all her existence, before, because her bow was bluff and clumsy and plenty of power was needed to overcome its resistance. It offered no resistance now. There was nothing ahead of it. She was making thirty-seven knots when she got out of the slip and headed for a sand-barge in tranquil passage to some unknown destination. When Mr. Madden in the pilot-house reacted from the straight paralysis of terror upon him, he swung the wheel, but fast. The *Jezebel* swung—heeling dangerously—and missed the sand-barge by six inches. She started down the harbor to pick up some speed.

At the very beginning, when she was going under fifty knots, she looked rather like a fireboat with all hoses working. But of course fireboats don't usually travel quite that fast. Somewhere between fifty and sixty knots, the *Jezebel* began to look more impressive. Spume and spray flung from her bows rose to a height of sixty feet or better—the height of a six-story building—and spread out on either hand. And there was plenty of water hitting her bows now, and every drop of it went somewhere. Some doubtless spurted down toward the bottom of the harbor. Some of it flowed astern. But an awful lot went into the air. There was something like six thousand tons of water thrown up to become airborne spray for every mile she traveled. And did she travel!

A quarter-mile from the sand-barge she was doing eighty knots. That was when she hit the Sunday-school picnic. The picnic was mounted on a large, ancient, paddle-wheel steamer, and everybody was going about looking benevolent, except the small boys who had sneaked out of sight and were fighting underneath the lifeboats and drawing pictures on white-painted surfaces.

From nowhere, but very swiftly, there loomed up a cylinder of flowing water, half a block wide and six stories high. It rushed upon and engulfed the Sunday-school picnic. Roaring waters swept the steamer. The roaring passed by, leaving the steamer rocking helplessly in a thick and blinding mist. Everybody who had been looking benevolent was soaked. Some of them even said naughty words. The steamer rocked so violently that little girls got seasick in all directions. The only persons on the steamer not thoroughly wetted and miserable and frightened were the little boys who had been fighting under the lifeboats.

This was an exterior picture of the *Jezebel*'s accomplishment during the first few seconds of activity. In the *Jezebel*'s pilot-house, nothing whatever was to be seen. She was surrounded by walls of rushing water. Rising water, thrown away sidewise by the solid vacuum at her bows. And the rising streams moved at such high velocity that they broke into tiny and ever tinier droplets and tiniest particles, until they were so small that they did not fall again. They were fog-particles. They floated in the air like the world-famous mists of Niagara.

But the *Jezebel* was blinded. She was invisible. A monstrous half-cylinder of vapor raced across the harbor, and it engulfed this ship and that, and no man knew what it could be, but all men feared it. Within the column—right behind that startling tumult like the snout of a terrified sea serpent—Mr. Madden uttered stricken cries and wrestled with the *Jezebel's* wheel.

There was a tug towing a long line of log-rafts down toward the sea. The lightning-like rush of white vapor roared upon the rafts. The *Jezebel* hit them. Her bows growled. The wooden rod had burped politely on hitting wood. The solid vacuum before the *Jezebel* made a deep-bass note as it flung aside the separate particles of log that tried to reach physical contact with it. The tug sped on, its foremost raft sliced through in the mist.

The straight line of the *Jezebel's* progress broke, as she was heading for a wharf. Mr. Madden clawed her around, and she heeled and made a ten-foot wave to go on and make trouble where it hit. She rushed toward an anchored tramp, and actually did pass under the overhang of its stern, and she pushed the tramp's bows under-water by the violence of her upward thrust. She swerved again as Mr. Madden turned her wheel at frantic random. She was throwing water upward at the rate of hundreds of tons per second, and she ran across the bow of a ferry-boat and drowned its fires and more than half-drowned its passengers.

"Turn it off!" howled Mr. Madden. "Turn it off! We got to turn it off!"

They were isolated from all of mankind in a universe of white mist. Mr. Binder said, "We can't."

Then the world went black about them. It was not that they were unconscious. It was that the *Jezebel* had gotten into the shallow water near shore alongside the more elegant and expensive shore-road section of the city. She was plowing through three feet of black mud. But it offered no hindrance to her passage. She threw it away with a continuous gesture. The *Jezebel* hit ninety knots traveling through mud some fifteen yards from shore. She heaved mud up; it floated magnificently over the road side at the water's edge; it coated trees, shrubs, houses, windows, and the elegantly attired strollers on the shore road. And Mr. Madden twisted madly at the wheel and veered out, cut through the stern of a low-lying garbage-scow on its way to sea, and flushed all the more malodorous refuse off into the harbor. Then the *Jezebel* streaked for the area thick with maritime traffic.

It should be understood that in all this Mr. Madden was going it blind. He was surrounded by an impenetrable white mist, stories high and half a block thick, which was the equivalent of the thickest fog that ever was on land or sea. He continued to wrench at the steering-wheel and howl for Mr. Binder to turn off the vacuum. Meanwhile the *Jezebel* cut circles and figures-of-eight and other charming arabesque figures in the water. She hit the anchor-chain of a ship loaded with live ammunition for foreign shores. The anchor-chain parted. She swamped a small boat carrying a shore-party ashore from a battle-ship, and swerved into a sandbar and sent a saffron cloud aloft, and ran under a bridge so close to one of its piers that Mr. Madden saw the mass of masonry at arms' length even through the mist.

The stream of vapor she left behind did not settle. It was too finely divided. It was like that artificial fog which is used in fighting oil-fires. And the *Jezebel* ran crazily here, and there, and everywhere, leaving monster masses of mist behind it, and all harbor traffic ceased to move. Ships cast anchor and unlimbered foghorns. Tugs blew whistles. Smaller craft rang bells, and bedlam arose upon the face of the waters.

Mr. Binder crawled aft and went into the pilot-house.

"Turn it off!" howled Mr. Madden as the bowsprit of a sailboat at anchor poked into view in the mist, caught in the pilot-house window, and neatly pulled one side of that small structure loose and carried it away astern. "Stop it! Cut it off! Do something!"

The *Jezebel* howled between the sterns of two ships that were drifting together, and steel plates met and crashed over her head. Mr. Madden wrenched at the wheel and wailed: "Sink her! We've got to stop! Sink her!"

Mr. Binder said mildly, "That's what I came to tell you about, George. She is sinking. I suppose there was a plug left open to drain her when she was up on the railway, and she's filling up." Then he added painfully, "It worries me, George. Because if we jump overboard, going as fast as this, we'll be knocked unconscious and drown. And when she starts to sink she's going to point bow downward, most likely, and head for the center of the earth. And we can't get out."

Mr. Madden opened his mouth. His eyes stared. Then he fainted peaceably.

When he recovered consciousness, there was a great quietude all about. The sun shone brightly. Waves lapped gently somewhere. Birds sang.

He heard a ripping sound. It sounded like somebody tearing more or less rotted canvas. It came again. Mr. Madden realized that the *Jezebel* was perfectly still. She did not rock, she did not have that faintly stirring alive feeling which all boats possess.

Slowly, groggily, incredulously, Mr. Madden staggered to his feet. He did not have to go out the pilot-house door. A wall was missing, providing a more convenient exit.

He stared blankly about him. The *Jezebel* was ashore on a slanting sandy beach. There was no sign of civilization anywhere about save a rusty tin can half-buried in the salty sand. Mr. Madden recognized his whereabouts. This was one of the Beach Islands, forty miles down-coast from the harbor in which the *Jezebel* had broken all records for speed and the creation of tumult.

The ripping of canvas came again. Mr. Madden tottered along the *Jezebel*'s deck. He looked over her bow. Mr. Binder stood on the beach, ripping off the canvas that had been coated with solid vacuum. He was handling it very carefully—only from the uncoated side. When he got a good-sized piece of it loose, he struck a match to it. It burned brightly. Mr. Madden smelled rank cloth and burning chemicals. He croaked: "Hey!"

Mr. Binder looked up and beamed at him. "Oh. Hello, George. We're all right, you see. When you fainted, George, I took the wheel. It looks like I very fortunately steered right out of the harbor and to sea. But when the *Jezebel* slowed down I made out where we were and steered accordingly."

"Slowed down?"

"Yes," said Mr. Binder mildly. "I didn't realize it, but it was very fortunate about the engine. When the *Jezebel* started to sink, the engine made her stern sink deeper than the bow. The bow started to come out of the water. The vacuum was lifted clear. So there wasn't as much of it in the water, and it didn't pull so hard. So we slowed."

Mr. Madden reached out his hand and steadied himself. He felt clammy, from cold sweat. Mr. Binder pulled off some more canvas and burned it. The bow of the *Jezebel* was almost clear of it.

"I headed along the coast," Mr. Binder explained, "until we were slowed away down. Then I headed for shore. We were almost sunk then, and the bow hardly touched water. I hit the beach not going too fast, and we just went up a little way. We'll have to get a tug to pull the *Jezebel* off, but I don't think she's damaged."

Mr. Madden closed his eyes. He was desperately grateful for the fact that he was still alive. But a tug to come forty miles and haul the *Jezebel* off, and go forty miles back again towing it . . . he shuddered.

"I thought I'd better get this canvas off," said Mr. Madden apologetically. "Somebody might come along and touch it, not knowing. But I made an interesting discovery, George! I think it'll please you. I don't think it's quite practical to use my solid vacuum as a way of pulling the *Jezebel* along, but I've got something just as good, for you."

Mr. Madden swept his eyes to heaven. Then he looked dazedly along the beach. He saw a rather heavy stick of driftwood at the edge of the waves.

"I'll tell you," said Mr. Binder interestedly. He held a strip of canvas—coated with solid vacuum—in his hands. He very carefully touched the back, the non-coated part only. He had it doubled so he could hold it. "See?"

Mr. Madden was speechless.

"The solid vacuum," said Mr. Binder, "won't let anything touch it. Friction can only happen when two things touch. And the solid vacuum throws away anything that touches it, but it won't throw away another solid vacuum! Because that can't touch! See? So if I have two solid-vacuum surfaces, George, and I rub them together, I have absolutely frictionless sliding!"

He beamed at Mr. Madden, mistaking Mr. Madden's stare for admiration.

"I'll tell you, George," he said happily. "All the stuff to make solid vacuum is on board. You'll go and get a tug to pull the *Jezebel* off, and pump it out, and plug the hole in it. And while you're gone I'll take the engine apart. And I'll coat the inside of the cylinder and the outside of the pistons with solid vacuum, and I'll coat the bearings and the things that run in them. And then the engine will be absolutely frictionless. You won't need a new one, you'll save money——"

He stopped. Mr. Madden descended with great deliberation from the deck of the stranded *Jezebel* to the sand. He walked away from Mr. Binder. He picked up a heavy stick of driftwood from the edge of the waves. He started back for Mr. Binder swinging it. . . .

He didn't catch Mr. Binder. Humanitarianism aside, it may be a pity. We could all feel much safer if he had, or if Mr. Binder were more ambitious or less successful, or something. Because Mr. Binder does research. If he only made atom bombs in his kitchen laboratory, say, it would be an improvement on the present state of things. One of them might go off. But he simply reads Aristotle and Poincaré and Ron Hubbard and Paracelsus and gets ideas from them and tries them out. Right now he is working on the idea that two and two has only been observed to total four, in a long sequence of what may be coincidences. He is investigating the theoretical possibility that two and two might some day produce an atavistic five. It sounds harmless, but nobody can guess what Mr. Binder will accomplish.

It's the suspense that hurts.

D. P. FROM TOMORROW

by Mack Reynolds

MACK REYNOLDS (1918–   ) is unusual in that, though a Californian, he does not live in that state. He has been widely published and widely anthologized, though he has written only *The Case of the Little Green Men* in book form, and edited *The Science-Fiction Carnival*, with Fredric Brown. At the present time he and his wife are living in Mexico.

The phone rang and Ed Kerry picked it up and said, *"Daily Star."*

He listened for a moment and said, "Yeah," and then, "Hold on a minute." He stuck a hand over the mouthpiece and said to the city room at large, "It's one of these drunks settling some bet. He wants to know when Lord Byron died."

Sam, over on the rewrite desk, said, "He died on April nineteenth, 1824."

Kerry said into the phone, "He died April nineteenth, 1824," and hung up.

Jake, the city editor, had been leaning back in his swivel chair, his feet up on the desk. He said to Sam, "How do you know?"

Sam shrugged and said, "Just happened to."

Jake said idly, "Offhand, I can't think of any information that makes less difference than when Byron died."

Ed Kerry said, "It's the queerest thing in this business. Some jerk phones in and wants to know what caliber gun it was that killed Lincoln, or maybe how many molecules there are in a drop of water. And what happens? Somebody in the city room always knows the answer. It's the same on every paper I ever worked for."

Jake growled, "You can't tell them to go get lost. These characters who phone into newspapers at the drop of a hat might stumble on the biggest story of the year ten minutes later. You don't want them phoning some other paper because they're sore at you for not telling them who got in the first punch in the Dempsey-Firpo fight."

Kerry said, "Yeah, but what gets me is that when these jerks ask their screwy questions, somehow or other they always get the right answer."

Somebody on rewrite said, "I remember once some drunk phoned in about four o'clock in the morning and wanted to know how tall Jumbo, Barnum's elephant, used to be. The guy who was working next to me says, 'eleven feet, six inches,' without even looking up from the story he was on."

Jake said, "It's because on a newspaper you got a whole room full of guys with a lot of general knowledge. Remember back in the 1940s or 1950s or whenever it was, they had this 'Information Please' program on the television?"

Sam said, "It was radio back then."

Jake growled, "What difference does it make? Anyway, these guys knew all the answers and there were only maybe three or four of them, mostly newspapermen. In a city room you've got a dozen or more men who've read so much that it starts . . ."

The phone rang again and, since nobody else stirred, Ed Kerry sighed and picked it up again. He said, "Yeah?" He repeated that a few more times and then, "Hold it, Ted. I'll ask Jake."

He looked over at Jake and said, "It's Ted Ruhling. He's over at Leo's. . . ."

"This is Ted's night off," Jake grunted.

". . . He says he's got a refugee over there with a story," Ed Kerry finished. The phone was still squeaking and he put the receiver back to his ear.

"A refugee, yet," Jake snorted. "What's Ted got in mind? He must be sober; when he's drunk he's got more story sense. We've had so many Martian refugee stories. . . ."

"This isn't a Martian," Kerry said. "It's a guy claims he's from another space-time continuum."

Somebody on rewrite said, "That does it. Now I've heard it all."

Jake began to say, "Tell Ted Ruhling to have himself a few more drinks and forget about . . . No, hold it. Tell him to bring the guy over here and we'll get the story. Maybe it'll be good for a humorous piece; besides, there's nothing going on anyway, we'll get some laughs."

Ed Kerry said into the phone, "It sounds like a real story, Ted. Jake says to rush the guy over here." He hung up.

Sam, over on rewrite, scratched himself reflectively. "I've seen a lot of stories in my thirty years in this racket, and I've seen a lot of stories about refugees. Refugees from Asia, refugees from Europe, refugees from South America and from Texas; even refugees from Luna and Mars. But I'll be a makron if I ever heard of a refugee from another space-time continuum."

Kitty Kildare bustled from her tiny office and hurried breathlessly toward Jake's desk.

Ed Kerry said softly, "Kitty looks like she's got another world beater. Tear down the front page, Jake."

Kitty gushed, "Jake, I really have something for tomorrow's column. Actually, I mean. Jake, this . . ."

Jake held up a weary hand to stem the tide. "Kitty," he said, "listen. That column is yours; you can put anything in it you want. It's none of my business. For some reason or other, people even read it. Don't ask me why."

Kitty Kildare simpered. "Now, Jake, you're always pulling my leg."

Jake shuddered.

Kitty went on, "But you'll see tomorrow. Actually, I mean." She bustled out of the city room and off to whatever story she had found to cover for her column.

Ed Kerry said wonderingly, "Kitty can get breathless over any story hotter than a basketball score."

Jake said, "What's another space-time continuum? Seems to me I read about it somewhere, or . . ."

Sam laughed. "Now we know Jake's secret vice. He hides in his room, locks the door, and reads science fiction."

The city editor scowled. "I don't get it."

Sam said, "Another space-time continuum is one of the favorite standbys of these science-fiction writers. You know. The general idea is that there are other, well, call them universes, existing side by side with ours. We aren't the only space-time continuum; we're only one of them."

"One theory is that there are an infinite number of continuums," Ed Kerry put in. "That means that somewhere everything is happening, has happened, and will happen."

Jake growled, "Shut up, Ed. Sam's explanation was getting bad enough, but . . ."

Sam said, "No. Ed's right. According to one theory, there are an infinite number of alternative universes, some of them almost identical to this one. For instance, in an infinite number of universes, Hitler won the second world war. In an infinite number of others, Hitler was never born. In still others, he spent his whole life as a paperhanger."

"Wait a minute, now," Jake said. "You mean to tell me that somewhere, in some other space-time whatever-y'call-it . . ."

"Continuum," Ed Kerry supplied.

"All right. Anyway, everything possible has happened, will happen, and is happening? *Everything*, no matter how unlikely?"

"That's the theory," Sam told him. "Consider, for instance, how improbable this space-time continuum in which we live really is."

Jake snorted, "Holy Wodo. Ted Ruhling has brought in some screwy stories in his time, but a refugee from . . ."

"Here he comes," somebody whispered.

"Okay, boys," Jake said softly. "The works. Somebody tell Jim to bring his camera."

Ted Ruhling wavered unsteadily toward the city desk, ushering along a little, wistful-looking character dressed in clothes that looked oddly out of style. The stranger's hair was going grey and his small face was much lined; he looked to be about forty.

Ruhling blinked at Jake and said, with considerable dignity, "This story is beyond the call of duty, y'realize, Jake. Oughta getta bonus. Wanta introduce Martin Cantine; refugee from another space-time continuum. Met him by accident in Leo's Bar." He slumped into a chair as though the effort of the introduction had exhausted him.

Jake got up and held out a hand to the little man. "Welcome to . . . uh, that is, welcome to our universe, Mr. Cantine."

Ed Kerry and Jim the photographer and several others crowded up with note-book and camera.

"Mr. Cantine," Kerry said excitedly, "what do you think of our space-time continuum's girls?"

"Shut up, Ed," Jake said from the side of his mouth.

But the little fellow answered seriously. "The same as I think of those in my own, of course."

Kerry said, as though disappointed, "You mean there's no difference?"

Martin Cantine found himself a chair, sat down, and said, earnestly, "I see that there must be some misunderstanding here. You gentlemen must realize that the continuum from which I fled was almost exactly like this one. Almost exactly. I note, for instance, that this city has identical buildings and in other ways is precisely like my own, except, of course, for the time element."

"Oh, oh," Sam said. "Here we go. The time element."

"What's different about the time element?" Jake asked cautiously.

The little fellow frowned worriedly. "I hope I can explain it to you. You see, the device which was constructed by my friends to enable us to flee our own period was designed to remove a living person from one space-time continuum and to place him in another. But it must be realized that in transporting ourselves to another *space* we at the same time, of necessity, transport ourselves also to another *time*. In all, we transport ourselves from another space, another time, and another space-time continuum. Actually, of course, the three are really one. Is that clear?"

"No," Ed Kerry said.

"Shut up, Ed," Jake growled. "Go on, Mr. Cantine."

Mr. Cantine was pleased that at least one person was following him. "Our device was set to remove me only slightly in *space,* and, consequently, only slightly in *time.* If I am correct, my time was about ten years after yours."

Jake closed his eyes for a long moment. Finally he opened them again and said, "Let's have that last again."

"In my space-time continuum," the little man said, "I lived about ten years in your future. In other words, in 2030."

"I get it," Sam said. "Ten years from now our space-time continuum will be like yours when you left—in most respects, that is. What you did was travel backward in time for ten years and to a slightly different continuum."

Ted Ruhling had managed to stay awake thus far. But now that he saw everything was under control he muttered, "Bonus," and slumped forward on the desk at which he was sitting.

Jake looked at him and grunted bitterly.

Ed Kerry said, "Well, let's get the rest of the story. Why did you leave home and come to our fair continuum?"

Martin Cantine frowned. "I thought you realized that I was a refugee. Didn't Mr. Ruhling explain on the phone?"

"Of course," Jake told him. "Now just what were you a refugee from, Mr. Cantine?"

The little man took a deep, dramatic breath. "From Gerald Twombly, the most vicious despot the world has ever seen!"

Ed Kerry choked on that. "Twombly!" he said, trying to hold his laughter. He swallowed hard, then said, very seriously, "How do you spell that?"

"Gerald Twombly. T-W-O-M-B-L-Y," Martin Cantine told him. "And now that you have been warned, you'll be able to defend yourself against this scourge."

"I missed something there," Jake said.

The little refugee explained, "As I pointed out, this continuum is almost exactly like mine. The principal difference is that you are ten years earlier in time; Gerald Twombly is not as yet in power. You have time to fight him, expose his nefarious schemes."

"Twombly," Ed Kerry said. "I *love* that name. Hitler, Mussolini, Caesar, Napoleon—none of them quite have the ring of Twombly."

Jake looked up at the clock on the wall. They were going to have to start work on the bulldog edition. Besides, he was getting tired of this nut. He nodded his head to Bunny Davis, down at the other end of the room, and she surreptitiously took up a phone and called the city hospital.

Ed Kerry was asking, "Just what form will this despotism take?"

Martin Cantine leaned forward earnestly. "The most vicious and bloody the world has ever known. People have forgotten, it has been so long since dictatorship has existed, how ruthless persons in power can become to maintain themselves. We've also forgotten that many of the devices that have been invented in the past one hundred years can be turned to horrible use by a police state. Truth serums, for instance, used ordinarily for psychiatry, but a terrible weapon in the hands of a secret police. Cybernetic-controlled wire and radio tapping devices that can listen to every conversation that takes place over instruments throughout the whole planet and immediately flash a report whenever anything the slightest degree removed from what is permissible is said. Radar . . ."

Jake yawned. "And just how did you manage to escape this guy . . . er, Twombly?"

Cantine frowned. "I am not the inventor of the S-T Invertor, but one of several who have been secretly removed to another continuum to escape Twombly's secret police. I am not exactly clear on the workings of the device."

"Shucks," Ed Kerry said. "I was afraid of that. Tell us what you do know about it." He was beginning to give up the pretense of taking notes.

Martin Cantine looked from one to the other, frowning. He was beginning to suspect the truth of the situation, and a red flush was creeping up his neck.

"I am afraid you gentlemen think I am exaggerating," he said tensely.

"I wouldn't exactly put it that way," Jake told him, stifling another yawn. "But part of it seems . . ."

The little man came to his feet, his expression tight. "I see," he said. He took a deep breath, then went on slowly, and very sincerely. "Even though you think me a charlatan, I beseech you, for your own sakes and for this continuum's—investigate this Gerald Twombly. You *must.* Or your space-time continuum will . . ."

Two white-coated interns came through the door and looked about questionably. Jake motioned to them and they advanced.

Jake said, a touch of unwonted kindliness in his gruff voice, "Here are two friends of yours, Mr. Cantine."

The little man looked about him unbelievingly. "But . . . but . . . you think I'm insane. You don't realize . . ." He shook off the hands of the interns, and spun about desperately to confront the city editor again.

He began to shout, "But you must . . . Gerald Twombly! . . . You must . . . !"

They led him out, struggling.

There was an embarrassed silence in the city room. The gag had not been as amusing as they had expected.

"Well, let's get to work," Jake said. "Kerry, you see if you can do up a stick or so on this Cantine. Gag it up a little, but don't go overboard. Jim, did you get a decent shot of the little guy? Those phony clothes he'd had made up for himself might make a . . ."

Sam, over on rewrite, said, "You know, the funny thing was that his story made a certain amount of sense."

Jake snorted. "Every nut's story makes a *certain* amount of sense. The only trouble is that, when you check it, it doesn't hold up."

"What'd ya mean, check it?" Sam said argumentatively. "What part of Cantine's story were you able to check?"

Jake growled, "For one thing, this guy Twombly. What a name for a dictator. Anyway, who ever heard of a Gerald Twombly? Did you Kerry . . . Jim . . . Bunny . . . Sam?"

They shook their heads. So did everyone else in the city room.

Jake shrugged. "Okay. There you are. This character says that in ten years Twombly's dictatorship is going to be so rugged that we'll all be wanting to take a powder out of here to another what'd'ya call it?"

"Space-time continuum," Sam said grudgingly.

"Yeah. Well, none of us have ever heard of him. Remember what I said earlier about all the general knowledge you find on a newspaper's staff? Okay, where's somebody that's even heard of this guy?"

"I guess you're right," Sam admitted. "But he seemed to be kind of a nice little duck."

"The nut factories are full of nice little ducks," Jake grunted. He tossed a story over to the rewrite man. "Here shut up and get to work or you'll be getting as screwy as he is."

Sam grinned and took up a pencil. "Okay, Jake."

Kitty Kildare hustled into the room, brandishing a sheaf of paper. "Jake," she said breathlessly, "wait until you see my column tomorrow. I'll have them dying, *dying*. Actually, I mean."

Jake shuddered. "Okay, what is it this time?"

She closed her eyes and breathed ecstatically. "A wonderful man; actually, I mean. I have the first interview he's *ever* given. He has a new political system he's advocating."

Ed Kerry said sarcastically, "I'll bet his name's Twombly."

Kitty turned and stared at him.

"How in the world did you know?" she said.

THE ALTRUISTS

by Idris Seabright

IDRIS SEABRIGHT (1911–   ) is a Kansan who also writes under other names. She has been widely published, both in the magazines and in anthologies. She and her husband live in California.

In an attempt to convey the maximum of information in the minimum of space, the *Guide to High Galactic Latitude Planetary Systems* is printed on preemtex as thin as gossamer, and its letter-press consists almost exclusively of conventional symbols. Even so, it occupies three huge volumes. The planet Skōs receives half a line in the second of these.

Malcolm Knight was reading the item about Skōs for the tenth time, frowning with the effort of translating the difficult symbology. "Skōs," he read, "sole satellite of long-period eclipsing binary, components red and blue-white. (For primaries' details see appropriate listing in Volume III.) Mass 9/10 earth normal, radius 11/10. Breathable air, drinkable water. Climate mild, uniform, equable. Three land masses. Inhabited by native nonhumanoid race, slurb, extremely friendly and hospitable. Restricted planet, landing only by permit. Coördinates . . ."

Malcom shut the book softly. He showed his long white teeth. The "restricted planet" entry meant only that the authorities felt that the "extremely friendly and hospitable" slurb might get the short end of the stick in casual contacts with human beings. Restrictions never applied to emergency landings, like his was going to be.

He had learned about Skōs by accident two years ago. A messmate of his, Charley Crane, had gone there with a landing party from the old *Euphrosyne,* and been much impressed with the place. He had praised not so much the physical beauty of the planet—though, to hear Charley tell it, it was an earthly paradise—as he had the character of the slurb.

"They're the kindest, most obliging, most hospitable creatures you ever saw in your life," he had said. "They seem to get a genuine kick out of doing anything at all they can for you. Why, if they'd had women we

wanted—they didn't, of course, and nobody knows how they reproduce—
we could have had them, and welcome."

"Um," Malcom had said.

"But outside of that. . . . They brought us fruits and nuts and meat.
The fruit was delicious. They waited on us hand and foot. They washed
and mended our clothes as well as they could. They cleaned our shoes.
They heated water for us to bathe in, and they'd have bathed us too, if
we'd let them. Anything we wanted, they did."

"How did you let them know what you wanted?" Malcom had asked.

"Oh, telepathy. You spoke in English, rather slowly, and they got the
idea. By the end of our visit, they were talking a little English themselves."

"It sounds pretty good," Malcom had said cautiously.

"It was, for the first week. Even now I like to remember the first
week. After that—I dunno. But you got sick of it."

"Why?" Malcom had wanted to know.

"It's hard to explain. But knowing that somebody would lie down and
die if he thought it would give you any pleasure makes you end up
hating him. It's not a natural thing. It makes you want to tear him up
into little bits.

"Can't you understand that, Mal? Maybe you can't. I always thought
you had more the Dictator and Slave complex than anybody I ever knew."

"Never mind about that," Malcom had said.

And now here he was, roughly about a thousand miles above the upper
atmosphere of Skōs, getting ready to land. Crane's words had roused a
hankering in him, or made him conscious of a hankering of which he
had been only dimly aware. It seemed to him that the slurb could give
him something he'd been looking for all his life.

Altruism. Because, when you came down to it, nobody was altruistic.
Parents, teachers, employers, officers, messmates—they all wanted something from you. If anybody did anything nice for you, he wanted to be
paid for it.

Even girls. Girls said they loved you, but they wanted something for
it. If it wasn't presents and good times—and it almost always was—they
still wanted fun for themselves. In a situation where a decent woman
should have been satisfied if you were happy, they wanted to be happy
too. Sometimes they complained. It was disgusting. No wonder he didn't
care much for girls.

But if Charley had been telling the truth, with the slurb it would be
different. For the two weeks or so before the rescue ship came for him,
he'd have a complete vacation. A vacation from human selfishness.

The little monocraft was spiraling down lightly. Malcom took a universal coördinate grid and began to jimmy it about over the emerging land masses of Skōs. He didn't think there'd be any trouble about his landing; he was almost sure there would not. He had the reputation aboard his ship, the *Tyche*, of being a steady and reliable element, a little rigid and overdisciplined. More than that, the monocraft wasn't expensive. Everyone knew its meteor shielding was far from thorough. For both those reasons his story of a quick, unexpected meteor which had pierced the imperviskin, endangering his air supply and making a planetary landing imperative, would be easily believed. The investigation about the wreck would be a formality.

Yes, he could get away with it. His task in the monocraft—plotting asteroid orbits around Skōs' double primary—made the story inherently probable. The asteroid project had been undertaken more for disciplinary reasons—to give the ratings something to do—than because it was of immediate vital interest. His messmates would congratulate him on not having been killed when the meteor broke the imperviskin. He'd enjoy a delightful little two weeks' vacation at the taxpayers' expense.

He glanced at the battery of gauges, and saw that the one that indicated air pressure within the cabin was falling rapidly. He'd better hurry. He didn't want to get into any real danger in carrying out his plan. He sent the monocraft into a faster whirl.

When Malcom reached the slurb village he was winded and irritable. He had sighted the village from the air, but had not dared set his craft down close to it. He was afraid that such convenient proximity might tend to belie his story of emergency and haste. So he had set up the automatic signaller—the rescue ship should come, he calculated, in not less than twelve or more than fourteen days—and then struck out across country toward the village. The country, though open and park-like, was dotted with thickets of some spiny-leaved sharp-thorned shrub. Malcom had his choice of clawing his way through the thickets, or of making unending detours. He had detoured; but to travel a distance of five miles, he had had to walk fifteen. The double red and white sun was high in the sky.

He stood looking at the village in silence. It was not impressive—a cluster of mud-plastered huts, in the shape of a segmented circle, around a slowly oozing spring. The spring ran out across a bed of clay that gave place to a swampy expanse of mud. There were humps that looked like submerged boulders in the mud. Around the village there was a fence, with an opening in one side, of the same spiny shrub he had already encountered.

Still Malcom was silent. It occurred to him, not for the first time, that an earth-type planet usually had a surprisingly close resemblance to earth. Except for the double sun in the sky, he might have been at home in the temperate zone on a pleasant day in early fall.

He put his hands to his lips and drew a deep breath. "Hey in there!" he bellowed. "Hurry up! Come on out!"

There was a stir within one of the huts. Then a slurb emerged.

Malcom's first reaction was of surprise that the *Guide* had called the slurb "nonhumanoid". His second was a nauseated recognition of what "nonhumanoid" meant.

The slurb had two arms, two legs, and a head; so has a lizard, and a lizard isn't human. It stood upright; so does a woodchuck, on occasion. It had two eyes in the front of its face, so its vision was probably binocular. But the slurb wasn't human, it wasn't even humanoid.

Perhaps it was the slurb's girth, which was enormous. The creature was literally as wide as it was tall. Perhaps it was the fact that it had a series of extra joints along the shoulder girdle and down the upper arm, so that its arms moved with the seemingly boneless flexibility of snakes. Perhaps it was the color of its sleek integument, which was a dirty off-white. Perhaps . . . Anyhow, the slurb was nonhumanoid.

Malcom inhaled shudderingly. He felt a disgust that had a moralistic tone. His anger fixed for a moment on Charley Crane—Charley, who had said that the slurb were funny but you soon got used to them—and then fastened firmly on the slurb. He drew his blaster from its holder. Was it for this he'd wrecked the monocraft, risked an investigation and possible prison? But wait—he might get into trouble if he blasted. Skōs was a restricted planet, after all. He'd give the slurb a chance.

"Get me something to eat," he said in loud, slow tones. "Be quick. And then heat water for a bath."

The slurb stood motionless. Malcom fingered his blaster. For a moment the slurb's fate—though not in the sense Malcom would have meant the phrase—hung in the balance. Then the slurb clasped its hands together behind its shoulder blades. It arched backward; the gesture seemed to be meant as a bow. It turned with surprising rapidity and went into the hut. It came back almost immediately with its hands full of purplish fruit.

Malcom enjoyed the next few days. Charley had been right, you soon got used to the funny looks of the slurb. They were no more disturbing than a lot of peculiar looking robots would have been. But the pleasure, the satisfaction, he got from their constant solicitous attention was unlike anything any conceivable robot could have afforded. It was—he could think of no other word for it—it was wonderful.

They made him a hut, bigger and better than any of theirs. They laid a bed for him of plushy sweet-scented forest boughs. They brought him delicious fruit and strange but savory meats. (Their cuisine was excellent.) They bathed him, they even shaved him with delicate care. But it wasn't their attentions, pleasant though these were in themselves; it was the spirit in which the slurb offered their services. They seemed to live only to please Malcom Knight.

Malcom felt like a man who, dying of thirst, has filled his belly with the precious stuff and now lies blissfully plunged in the cool sweet liquid.

So it went for four days. On the fifth something deeper in him awoke. Charley Crane had got sick of the slurb's attentions; what Malcom felt was not disgust but a sadistic curiosity.

How far would they go? Would they still like it, still sacrifice themselves to you, when what you asked them to do hurt? Something made him refrain from the worst outrages. Perhaps it was the fear of putting an end to a very good thing, perhaps it was the knowledge that if the slurb were obviously marked and damaged when the rescue ship arrived, he might have to answer for it. But on the sixth day he invented The Game.

It began innocently enough. He had the slurb line up—there were twenty-one of them, all, to his eyes, identical—while he threw gobs of mud at them. By the end of an hour he was throwing rocks at them with all his strength.

He made up a little score card. If he hit the slurb in the face, it counted ten. If he hit it in the chest, it counted three. If he hit the slurb on the knee—for some reason they were very sensitive about their knees—it counted fifteen. If he missed the slurb entirely, it had to go without its dinner. He was always trying to better his scores.

They did not dodge or protest. Sometimes when he got a whanger in on a knee they winced a little. He discovered that if you propel a rock toward a slurb by a blaster at minimum discharge, the wince is much more.

He began to have ideas. Weren't there people, people with money, who would get a great deal of pleasure out of the slurb? He thought there were. He was due for discharge from the patrol next year; if he could arrange to get a private ship. . . . And it wasn't as if the slurb would mind being sold to such people. They would enjoy it.

He slept late on the morning of the tenth day. The sky seemed gloomy and overcast, not much light was coming in through the door of his hut.

He yawned and stretched, turning luxuriously on his plushy couch. His plans in regard to the slurb had crystallized; in a year or two, at the most, he'd be back in a private ship and take a cargo of them off. There would be difficulties, of course. The whole thing would be ticklish. But the notion of having a cargo of slurb to sell had developed an unexpected business acumen in him. He was sure he could surmount the difficulties. It was just a question of knowing whom to bribe.

He rolled over on his side, wondering whether to try to sleep a little more. No, he was slept out. It was too bad that he'd have only a few more days with the slurb. But he could think of a lot of interesting variations of The Game in those days.

Meantime, he was getting hungry. He'd have breakfast. Without moving from his bed, he bellowed, "Breakfast! Bathwater! Hurry up!"

The seconds passed. There was no response.

Surprise made Malcom sit up. Once more he bellowed, "Breakfast! Damn it, hurry up!"

Still there was no response. Snorting with fury—he'd *fix* them, when they played The Game—he pulled on his pants, stuck his feet in his shoes, and went out.

The first thing that struck him was that the day was remarkably dark. Involuntarily he glanced toward the sky. The suns were well up, but only about half the disk of the white one was visible. The bigger dull red luminary was occluding it.

An eclipse, he supposed. Well, he'd think about it later. Meantime, where were those stinking god-damned slurb?

He looked in a hut and a hut and another hut. No slurb. He finally caught sight of them squatting in a symmetrical double square around the spring. They had plastered themselves with mud until they were nearly invisible. One slurb was sitting in the middle, almost on top of the spring.

Were they trying to hide from him? And in that limpbrain way? "Get up!" he shouted furiously. "Get to work!"

The slurb in the middle raised its head and looked at him. Its eyes were glassy and blank, and he could not tell whether it actually perceived him or not. Then its head dropped forward on its breast.

Malcom aimed a hard kick at the nearest slurb. He heard the whack as his foot connected with its ribs. It rolled with the impact and then crawled back an inch or two. It gave no other sign.

Malcom fingered his blaster. Would a jolt or two at medium discharge liven them up? But there was only a little juice left in the weapon by now, and it frightened him to think what he'd do if it didn't work.

In the end, he went back to his hut. He was hungry, angry, and a little afraid. The slurb's sudden inertia seemed contrary to the course of nature. And the day was getting darker and darker.

He sat on his bed for a while, swearing and cracking his knuckles. Then he went through the huts. He managed to get together a passable breakfast of somewhat overripe fruit. He had no idea where the slurb got the fruit from. How long would they be like this?

About noon he heard a noise outside. He went to the door opening and looked out hopefully. The whole twenty-one slurb were coming toward him, so mud-plastered as to be almost invisible. In both their hands they were carrying—Malcom squinted, to make sure in the heavy twilight— in both hands they were carrying big branches of the spiny shrub.

They stopped in front of his hut. There was a second's pause. Then the slurb in front said, in an oddly human voice, "Come on out."

For a moment Malcom was so surprised at the thing's having spoken English—they had never done anything except twitter and whoop at each other before—that he ignored the meaning of the words. Then he showed his teeth in a grin. Come out? When they were carrying those nasty branches? What kind of a fool did they take him for?

"Come out," the slurb repeated. To Malcom's ears the words were heavy with menace. Without any hesitation he twisted the dial on his blaster to full discharge and fired at the leading slurb. It was self-defense; they were obviously in a treacherous mood. Perhaps The Game yesterday had been a little too rough.

The slurb fell over. It kicked and writhed for an instant, and then lay still. It was probably dead.

That would show them. They had no way of knowing there was only the tiniest bit of juice left in his blaster. They'd think twice before they'd tell him to come out again.

He drew back within the hut. He was not as frightened as he might have been; the episode had a dreamlike, unreal quality. He even felt hopeful. Perhaps, now that he had shown the slurb who was boss, they'd go back to being their normal selves.

He was roused from his optimism by a crackling noise in his rear. He looked round in sudden instinctive fright. My God! Those devils! They'd set the hut on fire!

Whatever they were going to do to him, it couldn't be any worse than fire. In the thick dusk he saw that they had withdrawn from around the door opening. The hut was full of smoke and heat. The roof was beginning to burn. In sudden undignified haste Malcom plunged out of the hut.

The slurb closed in around him. In the glare of the burning shelter, their faces were impassive and glassy-eyed. They began to prod and lash at him with the spiny branches. Malcom was still wearing nothing but his trousers and his shoes. "Move," one of the slurb said. Malcom moved.

They prodded him toward the opening in the fence around the village. Was that all they had in mind, to get rid of him? Malcom, despite the painful lacerations his flanks and back were receiving, could have laughed in his relief. Then they got him to the gap and all jabbed at him simultaneously with their branches; he went through almost with alacrity.

They did not pursue him. When he was ten feet or so from the hole in the fence, he looked back. The slurb were plainly visible, silhouetted against the glare of the burning hut. They were busily filling in the gap in the spiny fence with thorny branches, and binding it together with vines.

He could, he supposed, do something. He toyed with the idea of setting their damned fence on fire. But then they would come after him again, and this time . . . No, he was lucky all they had done was push him out.

All the same, he was in an unpleasant fix. He couldn't stun anything larger than a weasel with the residual charge in his blaster, he had no shelter, and no immediate prospect of food. He wasn't even wearing a shirt. He felt a sudden passionate anger against Charley Crane, who had misled him so about the nature of the slurb. When the rescue ship came, he'd see what he could do about getting a punitive expedition organized against them. He would only have to tamper a little with the truth.

When the rescue ship . . . Oh. *Oh.* He suddenly perceived that he was in something considerably worse than an unpleasant fix. He had left a message in the automatic signaller, saying that he was taking shelter in the nearest slurb village. The rescuers would look for him there first. And when they found he wasn't there——

There was only one thing to do. He must get to the signaller. And wait there patiently until rescue came.

It was the only thing. He had to do it. But how in hell was he going to find the signaller in the dark?

For a moment Malcom felt despair. Then he brightened. Finding the signaller wasn't, after all, the only thing he could do. If he went a little farther into the parkland—he didn't want to stay too near the village, for fear the slurb would decide to attack him more decisively this time —if he went a little further, he could build a signal fire. There wasn't any immediate hurry about it, since the ship wasn't due for a couple of days. The slurb might change their minds before then. And if they didn't, his fire would be plainly visible from the air.

His self-confidence had come back. He even whistled softly as he walked away from the village. If only it weren't so damned dark. The light of the dim red sun did not illuminate; it made objects swim in a thick, depressing haze.

He'd make a camp. Sometimes it rained at night, and there was no sense in getting wet unnecessarily. He'd make a small fire, for comfort and warmth. And he ought to be able to find enough fruit, of one or another of the sorts the slurb had brought him, to get by.

He settled on a spot about a mile from the slurb village, an open space in front of a group of large-leaved trees. The country here was wooded, almost a forest in spots, and he had no difficulty in getting together a large pile of dry branches for his fire. He was less successful with his lean-to shelter, but it would, he supposed, keep off the worst of a heavy downpour. Oh, well. The rescue ship would be here at the latest in four days. *Damn* the slurb.

Now, food. He'd better make a small fire so he could find his way back to his camp. He stumbled about in the murk for an hour or so, his stomach growling, but in the bad light all the trees looked alike. He was just about to give up and return empty to his shelter when he found a lone tree covered with big mushy globes.

He picked all he could carry and took them back to his fire. In the ruddy light he saw that they were, as he had hoped, an orange fruit, rather like a persimmon, the slurb had given him once or twice. He wouldn't starve, anyway.

Now he could begin to wait. The red sun was almost on the horizon. In a little while it would be quite dark.

He piled branches on his fire. Slowly, to make it last, he peeled and ate two of the orange fruit. They were rather tasteless, but remarkably filling. He yawned. His belly was full, he'd had a hard day, and the warmth of the fire was making him sleepy. The *Guide* had not mentioned any dangerous animals on Skōs. He had time to kill. He slept.

He was wakened by a sudden intense stab of visceral pain. The sensation was so urgent and unexpected that it brought him bolt upright even before his eyes opened, in automatic defense.

He looked about him, sweating, his hand on his blaster. The slurb —an attack—he'd been wounded—those devils—they—— But his fire was burning calmly and brightly, his body was intact, and nothing moved in the forest. No, wait. Wasn't there a shimmer of . . . something . . . just at the edge of the circle of light made by his fire? Under the branches?

He leaned forward, peering urgently. No, it must have been his imagination. There was nothing visible except the light of his fire.

But in that case, what had happened? Had the orange fruit he had eaten griped him? But it hadn't been a pain like that, it had been like something from the outside and yet subjective. It had been as if his body had suffered without a visible wound or lesion, and yet from the outside.

In the end, he decided that he must have had a nightmare. He piled the fire high with branches, and sat down with his back against a tree trunk. But it was a long time before he went back to sleep.

Next day the white sun was still in eclipse. What ailed the thing, anyhow? He'd never heard of an eclipse lasting that long. Malcom spent the morning assembling an enormous pile of branches, the afternoon stripping the tree of all its ripe fruit. It was a long, dull day. There was no sign of the slurb.

When the final darkness came on, he felt restless and uneasy. He told himself that it was because he was hungry; the orange fruit made him feel stuffed, but left him unsatisfied. He built a big fire, much larger than the one last night, and sat as close to it as he could get, finding, in its searing warmth, a certain relief of his nervousness.

Four or five hours after sundown, at what would have been ten or eleven o'clock, he felt a second stab of pain.

Malcom's eyes darted uncertainly from side to side. His hand moved to his belly, to his head. Where had he been attacked? He was wide awake, his fire was blazing brightly, nothing had come near him. Had his brain received a message of pain, and given it to his body to feel?

He was drenched with sweat. Oh, he must have caught some fever, be coming down with a serious disease. It would have been a relief for him to think so. No, this was an infliction from without. And there was something oddly, inexplicably familiar in it. Not in the pain itself, whose intensity was altogether outside of his experience. But it was as if the impulses, the motives behind the pain had somehow had their origin with him.

A shimmer in the air between the firelight and the trees caught his eye. He stared at it with frightened apprehension. He was imagining—yes—no, he wasn't. Something impalpable was in motion in the air under the trees.

The moments passed. The shimmer was unmistakable now. The forest began to shiver and dance.

Its contours shifted and wavered while the branches softly dripped pale gold. They came back to solidity and then were gone once more in shimmering motion. Even the firelight began to quiver. As the dance continued, Malcom had the sudden wild idea that the forest was alive with mental force.

Mental force? Were the trees mental trees? He was seized by an abrupt stabbing paroxysm of pain in his chest. It hurt too much for him to be able to shriek. When he came out of it, the air was momentarily still. In his brief freedom he wondered: whose mental force?

The next attack was in the pit of his stomach, the one after that in his bladder and bowels. He vomited, he soiled himself. He lay in his own mess, filthy and miserable. This time, under the pain—and it made him sicker than the pain had—he sensed a thin edge of pleasure. It was not his pleasure, not even pleasure in his suffering. But it was there. Someone was enjoying himself very much.

The night wore on. The attacks, always more agonizing, came in long jets of pain and seemed to involve every part of his body indifferently. He thought it rained toward morning. He thought his fire went out.

The day came. It was brighter than yesterday, as the red sun withdrew slowly from the white primary. But it was not until late afternoon that Malcom could rouse himself to eat a little and try to clean himself. He was too weak to collect branches or try to kindle a fire. He looked forward to the coming night with sickening dread.

The torment began early, almost as soon as the sun had gone down. But except at first, it was not as bad as last night. That was not because the paroxysms of pain were less, but because they were so intense that Malcom was very soon delirious. Somebody was suffering, writhing and convulsed. Somebody shrieked, time after time. Somebody wondered how he could stand so much. It was not he.

A little before daybreak he fell into a coma. And then, instead of the nightmare glimpses of himself as he screamed and babbled and raved there was only a dark pit. Just before it closed over him he thought he saw an arc of light in the sky.

They came for him at last. It was a little before noon. He was conscious, but too exhausted to do anything more than open his eyes. Tenderly they lifted him in their boneless arms and carried him back to the village. They had built a new hut for him. They laid him on the plushy, fragrant bed and bathed his dirty body expertly.

On the second day Malcom had them carry him out of the hut. He was tormented by worry about the rescue ship. It ought to have been here by now. When the slurb were not quite as quick in obeying his command to carry him out as he thought they should be, he cursed at them—weakly, but in quite the old style.

When he was outside, he scanned the sky anxiously. No, there was nothing. He hadn't really expected to see anything—even if he had known where to look for the ship, he couldn't have picked it up without a scope.

He sighed. "Take me back," he said to his slurb. "No, wait. What's that, over on the other side of the spring? Take me there."

He had seen a flash of white. Eagerly and gently they obeyed him. When he got to the spot he saw that the white thing was a cross, made of two pieces of wood. On it somebody had painted his name, Malcom Knight, and his age, 29, in black paint.

For a moment he didn't understand. The rescue ship—had—that arc in the sky he remembered—had the ship——? Then he turned on the slurb, raging. "You filth! You stinking, stinking filth! Damn you, damn you. Why did you lie to them?"

There was a second's silence. Then one of the slurb stepped forward. "They didn't like you, Master. They wanted to hear you had died. We wanted them to be happy. We told them what would please."

Rage and despair fought against his weakness. He picked up a rock and threw it at them. He hit a knee. He threw again and again. In the end he fainted, and they had to carry him back to the hut.

It was nearly dark when he recovered consciousness. A slurb came in as soon as he called, with a bowl of delicious-smelling soup. Malcom pushed it aside. He had to know.

"Tell me," he said to the slurb, "why you brought me back from the forest. Why did you drive me out in the first place? Why didn't you take the men from the rescue ship to me? I want to know."

"Yes, Master," said the slurb obediently. It was silent, as if arranging its thoughts. "You see, Master, we lay eggs."

"Eggs?" Malcom felt anger rising in him again.

"Yes, Master. Whenever the red sun hides the white one, we lay eggs. That is what the lumps are, out in the mud."

"Well? What has your laying eggs got to do with your driving me out?"

"When we lay eggs, we want to be by ourselves. Oh, it was a good egg-laying, Master. There were never so many eggs before, so much wonderful pleasure in it. We drove you out to be by ourselves. We didn't tell the men where you were because we knew they didn't want to find you. And we brought you back because we knew we owed that lovely egg-laying to *you*.

"You are so strong, so ordering. When men order us about, it makes us lay more eggs. We would always lay them, of course, but not so many. That is why we like visitors. We soak up their pleasure when they order us or hurt us, as you did with the rocks. And we give their pleasure out again when we lay eggs."

Malcom sank back on his bed. He felt too sick for rage. Those paroxysms of pain in the forest—the horrid familiarity of what he had experienced—the feeling of pleasure underneath—oh, God. Charley Crane had said the slurb were telepathic. This was telepathy carried to its final limits. Their hospitality, their altruism—the slurb were psychic cannibals.

The slurb bent over him anxiously. "Are you well, Master? Give me an order, or throw a rock at me. Enjoy yourself. It will make the next egg-laying better."

Malcom shook his head feebly. *Next* egg-laying? He couldn't survive even the first night of another one. He'd be through.

Slurb began to enter the hut. They lined up around his bed. Anxiously and tenderly they regarded him, their boneless arms clasped behind their backs. "We only want you to be happy," chorused the slurb.

POTENTIAL

by Robert Sheckley

ROBERT SHECKLEY (1928–   ) was born in Brooklyn. He is one of the brighter stars among the younger writers of science fiction. He has been published in *Astounding Science Fiction*, *Galaxy Science Fiction*, *Today's Woman*, *Collier's*, and many other magazines.

He returned to consciousness slowly, aware of aches and bruises, and an agonizing knot in his stomach. Experimentally, he stretched his legs.

They didn't touch anything, and he realized that his body was unsupported. He was dead, he thought. Floating free in space——

Floating? He opened his eyes. Yes, he was floating. Above him was a ceiling—or was it a floor? He resisted a strong urge to scream; blinked, and his surroundings swam into focus.

He realized that he was in a spaceship. The cabin was a shambles. Boxes and equipment drifted around him, evidently ripped loose from their moorings by some sudden strain. Burnt-out wires ran across the floor. A row of lockers along one wall had been fused into slag.

He stared, but no recognition came. As far as he knew, he was seeing this for the first time. He raised a hand and pushed against the ceiling, drifted down, pushed again, and managed to grasp a wall rail. Holding this tightly, he tried to think.

"There is a logical explanation for all this," he said aloud, just to hear his own voice. "All I have to do is remember." Remember——

What was his name?

He didn't know.

"Hello!" he shouted. "Is there anyone here?" His words echoed between the ship's narrow walls. There was no answer.

He propelled himself across the cabin, ducking to miss the floating boxes. In half an hour he knew he was the only person aboard the ship.

He pushed himself back to the front of the ship. There was a padded chair there, with a long panel in front of it. He strapped himself into the chair and studied the panel.

It consisted of two blank screens, one much larger than the other. Under the large screen were two buttons, marked *vision-front,* and *vision-rear.* A dial beneath the buttons was calibrated for focus. The small screen was unmarked.

Not finding any other controls, he pushed the *vision-front* button. The screen cleared, showing black space with the brilliant points of the stars before him. He stared at it for a long time, open-mouthed, then turned away.

The first thing to do, he told himself, was to assemble all the knowledge at his disposal and see what he could deduce from it.

"I am a man," he said. "I am in a spaceship, in space. I know what stars are, and what planets are. Let me see——" He had a rudimentary knowledge of astronomy, less of physics and chemistry. He remembered some English literature, although he couldn't think of any writers except Traudzel, a popular novelist. He remembered the authors of several history books, but couldn't place their contents.

He knew the name for what he had: Amnesia.

Suddenly, he had a great desire to see himself, to look at his own face. Surely, recognition and memory would follow. He shoved himself across the room again, and started searching for a mirror.

There were lockers built into the walls, and he opened them hastily, spilling the contents into the weightless air. In the third locker he found a shaving kit and a small steel mirror. He studied the reflection anxiously.

A long irregular face, drained of color. Dark stubble growing on the chin. Bloodless lips.

The face of a stranger.

He fought down fresh panic and searched the cabin, looking for some clue to his identity. Quickly he pawed through the floating boxes, shoving them aside when they proved to contain nothing but food or water. He looked on.

Floating in one corner of the cabin was a sheet of scorched paper. He seized it.

"Dear Ran," it began. "The bio-chem boys have been doing some hurry-hurry last-minute checking on the pento. Seems there's a strong chance it might induce amnesia. Something about the strength of the drug, plus the near-traumatic experience you're undergoing, whether you're aware of it or not. *Now* they tell us! Anyhow, I'm dashing off this note at zero minus fourteen minutes, just as a refresher for you in case they're right.

"First, don't look for any controls. Everything's automatic, or it should be if this pile of cardboard and glue holds together. (Don't blame the technicians; they had practically no time to get it finished and away before flash-moment.)

"Your course is set for automatic planetary selection, so just sit tight. I don't suppose you could forget Marselli's theorem, but in case you have, don't worry about landing among some eighteen-headed intelligent centipedes. You'll reach humanoid life because it *has* to be humanoid life.

"You may be a bit battered after blastoff, but the pento will pull you through. If the cabin is messy, it's because we just didn't have time to check everything for stress-strain tolerances.

"Now for the mission. Go at once to Projector One in Locker Fifteen. The projector is set for self-destruction after one viewing, so make sure you understand it. The mission is of ultimate importance, Doc, and every man and woman on Earth is with you. Don't let us down."

Someone named Fred Anderson had signed it.

Ran—automatically using the name given in the letter—started looking for Locker Fifteen. He found at once where it had been. Lockers Eleven through Twenty-five were fused and melted. Their contents destroyed.

That was that. Only the scorched paper linked him now with his past, his friends, all Earth. Even though his memory was gone, it was a relief to know that the amnesia had an explanation.

But what did it mean? Why had they thrown the ship together in such a rush? Why had they placed him in it—alone—and sent him out? And this all-important mission—if it was so vital, why hadn't they safeguarded it better?

The note raised more questions than it answered. Frowning, Ran pushed himself back to the panel. He looked out the screen again, at the spectacle of the stars, trying to reason it out.

Perhaps there was a disease. He was the only person not infected. They had built the ship and shot him out to space. The mission? To contact another planet, find an antidote, and bring it back——

Ridiculous.

He looked over the panel again, and pushed the button for *vision-rear*.

And almost fainted.

A glaring, blinding light filled the entire screen, scorching his eyes.

Hastily he cut down the field of focus, until he was able to make out what it was.

A nova. And the letter had mentioned the flash-moment.

Ran knew that Sol was the nova. And that Earth was consumed.

There was no clock on the ship, so Dr. Ran had no idea how long he had been traveling. For a long time he just drifted around dazed, coming back to the screen constantly.

The nova dwindled as the ship speeded on.

Ran ate and slept. He wandered around the ship, examining, searching. The floating boxes were in the way, so he started to pull them down and secure them.

Days might have passed, or weeks.

After a while, Ran started to put the facts he knew into a coherent structure. There were gaps and questions in it, probably untruths as well, but it was a beginning.

He had been chosen to go in the spaceship. Not as a pilot, since the ship was automatic, but for some other reason. The letter had called him "Doc." It might have something to do with his being a doctor.

Doctor of what? He didn't know.

The makers of the ship had known Sol was going nova. They couldn't, evidently, rescue any sizable portion of Earth's population. Instead, they had sacrificed themselves and everyone else to make sure of rescuing him.

Why him?

He was expected to do a job of the greatest importance. So important that everyone had been subordinated to it. So important that the destruction of Earth itself seemed secondary, as long as the mission was accomplished.

What could that mission be?

Dr. Ran couldn't conceive of anything so important. But he had no other theory that came even close to fitting the facts as he knew them.

He tried to attack the problem from another viewpoint. What would he do, he asked himself, if he knew that Sol was going nova in a short time, and he could rescue only a limited number of people with a certainty of success?

He would have sent out couples, at least one couple, in an attempt to perpetuate human stock.

But evidently the leaders of Earth hadn't seen it that way.

After a time, the small screen flashed into life. It read: *Planet. Contact 100 hours.*

He sat in front of the panel and watched. After a long time the digits changed. *Contact 99 hours.*

He had plenty of time. He ate, and went back to work getting the ship into what order he could.

While he was storing boxes in the remaining lockers, he found a carefully packaged and fastened machine. He recognized it as a projector at once. On its side was engraved a large "2."

A spare, he thought, his heart pounding violently. Why hadn't he thought of that? He looked into the viewer and pushed the button.

The film took over an hour. It started with a poetic survey of Earth; flashes of her cities, fields, forests, rivers, oceans. Her people, her animals, all in brief vignettes. There was no sound track.

The camera moved to an observatory, explaining its purpose visually. It showed the discovery of the Sun's instability, the faces of the astrophysicists who discovered it.

Then the race against time began, and the rapid growth of the ship. He saw himself, running up to it, grinning at the camera, shaking someone's hand, and disappearing inside. The film stopped there. They must have stored the camera, given him the injection, and sent him off.

Another reel started.

"Hello, Ran," a voice said. The picture showed a large, calm man in a business suit. He looked directly at Ran out of the screen.

"I couldn't resist this opportunity to speak to you again, Dr. Ellis. You're deep in space now, and you've undoubtedly seen the nova that has consumed Earth. You're lonely, I daresay.

"Don't be, Ran. As representative of Earth's peoples, I'm taking this final chance to wish you luck in your great mission. I don't have to tell you that we're all with you. Don't feel alone.

"You have, of course, seen the film in Projector One, and have a thorough understanding of your mission. This portion of film—with my face and voice on it—will be automatically destroyed, in the same way. Naturally, we can't let extraterrestrials in on our little secret yet.

"They'll find out soon enough. You can feel free to explain anything on the remainder of this film to them. It should win you plenty of sympathy. Make no reference, of course, to the great discovery or the techniques that stemmed from it. If they want the faster-than-light drive, tell them the truth—that you don't know how it's propagated, since it was developed only a year or so before Sol went nova. Tell them that any tampering with the ship will cause the engines to dissolve.

"Good luck, Doctor. And good hunting." The face faded and the machine hummed louder, destroying the last reel.

He put the projector carefully back in its case, tied it into the locker, and went back to the control panel.

The screen read: *Contact 97 hours.*

He sat down and tried to place the new facts into his structure. As background, he remembered vaguely the great, peaceful civilization of Earth. They had been almost ready to go for the stars when the Sun's instability was found. The faster-than-light drive had been developed too late.

Against that background he had been selected to man the escape ship. Only him, for some unfathomable reason. The job given him was thought more important, evidently, than any attempts at race-survival.

He was to make contact with intelligent life, and tell them about Earth. But he was to withhold any mention of the greatest discovery and its resulting techniques.

Whatever they were.

And then he was to perform his mission——

He felt as though he could burst. He couldn't remember. *Why* hadn't the fools engraved his instructions on bronze?

What could it be?

The screen read, *Contact 96 hours.*

Dr. Ran Ellis strapped himself into the pilot chair and cried from sheer frustration.

The great ship looked, probed and reported. The small screen flashed into life. *Atmosphere–chlorine. Life–nonexistent.* The data was fed to the ship's selectors. Circuits closed, other circuits opened. A new course was set up, and the ship speeded on.

Dr. Ellis ate and slept and thought.

Another planet was reported, examined and rejected.

Dr. Ellis continued thinking, and made one unimportant discovery.

He had a photographic memory. He discovered this by thinking back over the film. He could remember every detail of the hour-long spectacle, every face, every movement.

He tested himself as the ship went on, and found that the ability was a constant. It worried him for a while, until he realized that it was probably a factor in his selection. A photographic memory would be quite an asset in learning a new language.

Quite an irony, he thought. Perfect retention—but no memory.

A third planet was rejected.

Ellis outlined the possibilities he could think of, in an effort to discover the nature of his mission.

To erect a shrine to Earth? Possibly. But why the urgency, then, the stressed importance?

Perhaps he was sent out as a teacher. Earth's last gesture, to instruct some inhabited planet in the ways of peace and co-operation.

Why send a doctor on a job like that? Besides, it was illogical. People learn over millennia, not in a few years. And it just didn't fit the *mood* of the two messages. Both the man in the film and the note-writer had seemed practical men. It was impossible to think of either of them as altruists.

A fourth planet came into range, was checked and left behind.

And what, he wondered, was the "great discovery"? If not the faster-than-light drive, what could it be? More than likely a philosophical discovery. The way man could live in peace, or something like that.

Then why wasn't he supposed to mention it?

A screen flashed, showing the oxygen content of the fifth planet. Ellis ignored it, then looked up as generators deep in the body of the ship hummed into life.

Prepare for landing, the screen told him.

His heart leaped convulsively, and Ellis had a momentary difficulty breathing.

This was it. A terror filled him as gravitation tugged at the ship. He fought it, but the terror increased. He screamed and tore at his straps as the ship started to go perceptibly *down.*

On the big screen was the blue and green of an oxygen planet.

Then Ellis remembered something. "The emergence from deep space into a planetary system is analogous to the emergent birth-trauma." A common reaction, he told himself, but an easily controllable one for a psychiatrist——

A psychiatrist!

Dr. Randolph Ellis, psychiatrist. He knew what kind of doctor he was. He searched his mind for more information, fruitlessly. That was as far as it went.

Why had Earth sent a psychiatrist into space?

He blacked out as the ship screamed into the atmosphere.

Ellis recovered almost at once as the ship landed itself. Unstrapping, he switched on the vision-ports. There were vehicles coming toward the ship, filled with people.

Human-appearing people.

He had to make a decision now, one that would affect the rest of his time on this planet. What was he going to do? What would his course of action be?

Ellis thought for a moment, then decided he would have to play by ear. He would extemporize. No communication would be possible until he had learned the language. After that, he would say that he was sent from Earth to . . . to——

What?

He would decide when the time came. Glancing at the screens, he saw that the atmosphere was breathable.

The side of the ship swung open, and Ellis walked out.

He had landed on a subcontinent called Kreld, and the inhabitants were Kreldans. Politically, the planet had reached the world-government stage, but so recently that the inhabitants still were identified with the older political divisions.

With his photographic memory Ellis found no difficulty learning the Kreldan language, once a common basis had been established for key words. The people, of the common root Man, seemed no more foreign than some members of his own race. Ellis knew that this eventuality had been predicted. The ship would have rejected any other. The more he thought of it, the more he was certain that the mission depended on this similarity.

Ellis learned and observed, and thought. He was due, as soon as he had mastered the tongue sufficiently, to meet the ruling council. This was a meeting he dreaded, and put off as long as he could.

Nevertheless, the time came.

He was ushered through the halls of the Council Building, to the door of the Main Council Room. He walked in with the projector under his arm.

"You are most welcome, sir," the leader of the council said. Ellis returned the salutation and presented his films. There was no discussion until everyone had seen them.

"Then you are the last representative of your race?" the council leader asked. Ellis nodded, looking at the kindly, seamed old face.

"Why did your people send only you?" another council member asked. "Why weren't a man and woman sent?" The same question, Ellis thought, that I've been asking myself.

"It would be impossible," he told them, "for me to explain the psychology of my race in a few words. Our decision was contained in our very sense of being." A meaningless lie, he thought to himself. But what else could be say?

"You will have to explain the psychology of your race sometime," the man said.

Ellis nodded, looking over the faces of the council. He was able to estimate the effect of the beautifully prepared film on them; they were going to be pleasant to this last representative of a great race.

"We are very interested in your faster-than-light drive," another council member said. "Could you help us attain that?"

"I'm afraid not," Ellis said. From what he had learned, he knew that their technology was pre-atomic, several centuries behind Earth's.

"I am not a scientist. I have no knowledge of the drive. It was a late development."

"We could examine it ourselves," a man said.

"I don't think that would be wise," Ellis told him. "My people consider it inadvisable to give a planet technological products beyond their present level of attainment." So much for theory. "The engines will overload if tampered with."

"You say you are not a scientist," the old leader asked pleasantly, changing the subject. "If I may ask, what are you?"

"A psychiatrist," Ellis said.

They talked for hours. Ellis dodged and faked and invented, trying to fill in gaps in his knowledge. The council wanted to know about all phases of life on Earth, all the details of technological and social advances. They wondered about Earth's method of pre-nova detection. And why had he decided to come here? And finally, in view of coming alone, was his race suicidally inclined?

"We will wish to ask you more in the future," the old council leader said, ending the session.

"I shall be happy to answer anything in my power," Ellis said.

"That doesn't seem to be much," a member said.

"Now Elgg—remember the shock this man has been through," the council leader said. "His entire race has been destroyed. I do not believe we are being hospitable." He turned to Ellis.

"Sir, you have helped us immeasurably as it is. For example, now that we know the possibility of controlled atomic power, we can direct research toward that goal. Of course, you will be reimbursed by the state. What would you like to do?"

Ellis hesitated, wondering what he should say.

"Would you like to head a museum project for Earth? A monument to your great people?"

Was that his mission, Ellis wondered? He shook his head.

"I am a doctor, sir. A psychiatrist. Perhaps I could help in that respect."

"But you don't know our people," the old leader said concernedly. "It would take you a lifetime to learn the nature of our tensions and problems. To learn them in sufficient intimacy to enable you to practice."

"True," Ellis said. "But our races *are* alike. Our civilizations have taken like courses. Since I represent a more advanced psychological tradition, my methods might be of help to your doctors——"

"Of course, Dr. Ellis. I must not make the mistake of underestimating a species that has crossed the stars." The old leader smiled ruefully. "I myself will introduce you to the head of one of our hospitals." The leader stood up.

"If you will come with me."

Ellis followed, with his heart pounding. His mission must have something to do with psychiatry. Why else send a psychiatrist?

But he still didn't know what he was supposed to do.

And, to make it worse, he could remember practically none of his psychiatric background.

"I think that takes care of all the testing apparatus," the doctor said, looking at Ellis from behind steel-rimmed glasses. He was young, moon-faced, and eager to learn from the older civilization of Earth.

"Can you suggest any improvements?" he asked.

"I'll have to look over the setup more closely," Ellis said, following the doctor down a long, pale-blue corridor. The testing apparatus had struck a complete blank.

"I don't have to tell you how eager I am for this opportunity," the doctor said. "I have no doubt that you Terrans were able to discover many of the secrets of the mind."

"Oh, yes," Ellis said.

"Down this way we have the wards," the doctor said. "Would you care to see them?"

"Fine." Ellis followed the doctor, biting his lip angrily. His memory was still gone. He had no more psychiatric knowledge than a poorly informed layman. Unless something happened soon, he would be forced to admit his amnesia.

"In this room," the doctor said, "we have several quiet cases." Ellis followed him in, and looked at the dull, lifeless faces of three patients.

"Catatonic," the doctor said, pointing to the first man. "I don't suppose you have a cure for that?" He smiled good-naturedly.

Ellis didn't answer. Another memory had popped into his mind. It was just a few lines of conversation.

"But is it ethical?" he had asked. In a room like this, on Earth.

"Of course," someone had answered. "We won't tamper with the normals. But the idiots, the criminally insane—the psychotics who could never use their minds anyhow—it isn't as though we were robbing them of anything. It's a mercy, really——"

Just that much. He didn't know to whom he had been talking. Another doctor, probably. They had been discussing some new method of dealing with defectives. A new cure? It seemed possible. A drastic one, from the content.

"Have you found a cure for it?" the moon-faced doctor asked again.

"Yes. Yes, we have," Ellis said, taking his nerve in both hands. The doctor stepped back and stared.

"But you couldn't! You can't repair a brain where there's organic damage—deterioration, or lack of development——" He checked himself.

"But listen to *me*, telling *you*. Go ahead, Doctor."

Ellis looked at the man in the first bed. "Get me some assistants, Doctor." The doctor hesitated, then hurried out of the room.

Ellis bent over the catatonic and looked at his face. He wasn't sure of what he was doing, but he reached out and touched the man's forehead with his finger.

Something in Ellis' mind clicked.

The catatonic collapsed.

Ellis waited, but nothing seemed to be happening. He walked over to the second patient and repeated the operation.

That one collapsed also, and the one after him.

The doctor came back, with two wide-eyed helpers. "What's happening here?" he asked. "What have you done?"

"I don't know if our methods will work on your people," Ellis bluffed. "Please leave me alone—completely alone for a little while. The concentration necessary——" He turned back to the patients.

The doctor started to say something, changed his mind and left quietly, taking the assistants with him.

Sweating, Ellis examined the pulse of the first man. It was still beating. He straightened and started to pace the room.

He had a power of some sort. He could knock a psychotic flat on his back. Fine. Nerves—connections. He wished he could remember how many nerve connections there were in the human brain. Some fantastic number; ten to the twenty-fifth to the tenth? No, that didn't seem right. But a fantastic number.

What did it matter? It mattered, he was certain.

The first man groaned and sat up. Ellis walked over to him. The man felt his head, and groaned again.

His own personal shock-therapy, Ellis thought. Perhaps Earth had discovered the answer to insanity. As a last gift to the universe, they had sent him out, to heal——

"How do you feel?" he asked the patient.

"Not bad," the man answered—in English!

"What did you say?" Ellis gasped. He wondered if there had been a thought-transfer of some sort. Had he given the man his own grasp of English? Let's see, if you reshunted the load from the damaged nerves to unused ones——

"I feel fine, Doc. Good work. We weren't sure if that haywire and cardboard ship would hold together, but as I told you, it was the best we could do under the——"

"Who are you?"

The man climbed out of bed and looked around.

"Are the natives gone?"

"Yes."

"I'm Haines, Representative of Earth. What's the matter with you, Ellis?"

The other men were reviving now.

"And they——"

"Dr. Clitell."

"Fred Anderson."

The man who called himself Haines looked over his body carefully. "You might have found a better host for me, Ellis. For old time's sake. But no matter. What's the matter, man?"

Ellis explained about his amnesia.

"Didn't you get the note?"

Ellis told them everything.

"We'll get your memory back, don't worry," Haines said. "It feels good to have a body again. Hold it."

The door opened and the young doctor peered in. He saw the patients and let out a shout.

"You did it! You are able——"

"Please, Doctor," Ellis snapped. "No sudden noises. I must ask not to be disturbed for at least another hour."

"Of course," the doctor said respectfully, withdrew his face and closed the door.

"How was it possible?" Ellis asked, looking at the three men. "I don't understand——"

"The great discovery," Haines said. "Surely you remember that? You worked on it. No? Explain, Anderson."

The third man walked over slowly. Ellis noticed that the vacuous faces were beginning to tighten already, shaped by the minds in back of them.

"Don't you remember, Ellis, the research on personality factors?"

Ellis shook his head.

"You were looking for the lowest common denominator of human-life-and-personality. The source, if you wish. The research actually started almost a hundred years ago, after Orgell found that personality was independent of body, although influenced and modified by it. Remember now?"

"No. Go on."

"To keep it simple, you—and about thirty others—found that the lowest indivisible unit of personality was an independent nonmaterial substance. You named it the M molecule. It is a complex mental pattern."

"Mental?"

"Nonmaterial, then," Anderson said. "It can be transferred from host to host."

"Sounds like possession," Ellis said.

Anderson, noticing a mirror in a corner of the room, walked over to examine his new face. He shuddered when he saw it, and wiped saliva from its lips.

"The old myths of spirit-possession aren't so far off," Dr. Clitell said. He was the only one wearing his body with any sort of ease. "Some people have always been able to separate their minds from their bodies. Astral projection, and that sort of thing. It wasn't until recently that the personality was localized and an invariant separation-resynthesis procedure adopted."

"Does that mean you're immortal?" Ellis asked.

"Oh, no!" Anderson said, walking over. He grimaced, trying to check his host's unconscious drool. "The personality has a definite life span. It's somewhat longer than the body's, of course, but still definitely within limits." He succeeded in stopping the flow. "However, it can be stored dormant almost indefinitely."

"And what better place," Haines put in, "for storing a nonmaterial molecule than your own mind? Your nerve connections have been harboring us all along, Ellis. There's plenty of room there. The number of connections in a human brain have been calculated at ten to the——"

"I remember that part," Ellis said. "I'm beginning to understand." He knew why he had been chosen. A psychiatrist would be needed for this job, to gain admittance to the hosts. He had been especially trained. Of course the Kreldans couldn't be told yet about the mission or the M molecule. They wouldn't take kindly to their people—even the defectives—being possessed by Earthmen.

"Look at this," Haines said. Fascinated, he was bending his fingers backwards. He had discovered that his host was double-jointed. The other two men were trying out their bodies in the manner of a man testing a horse. They flexed their arms, bunched their muscles, practiced walking.

"But," Ellis asked, "how will the race . . . I mean, how about women?"

"Get more hosts," Haines told him, still trying out his fingers. "Male and female. You're going to be the greatest doctor on this planet. Every defective will be brought to you for cure. Of course, we're all in on the secret. No one's going to spill before the right time." He paused and grinned. "Ellis—do you realize what this means? Earth isn't dead! She'll live again."

Ellis nodded. He was having difficulty identifying the large, bland Haines in the film with the shrill-voiced scarecrow in front of him. It would take time for all of them, he knew, and a good deal of readjustment.

"We'd better get to work," Anderson said. "After you have the defectives on this planet serviced, we'll refuel your ship and send you on."

"Where?" Ellis asked. "To another planet?"

"Of course. There are probably only a few million hosts on this one, since we're not touching normals."

"Only! But how many people have I stored?"

There was the sound of voices in the hall.

"You really are a case," Haines said, amused. "Back into bed, men—I think I hear that doctor. How many? The population of Earth was about four billion. You have all of them."

EYE FOR INIQUITY

by T. L. Sherred

T. L. SHERRED writes from Michigan. He is a comparatively recent addition to the lists of writers in the genre, but his work is among the most novel and memorable.

We were both surprised the first time I made a ten-dollar bill. My wife sat there and her eyes were as wide as mine. We sat a while, just looking at it. Finally she reached over to my side of the table and poked at it a little gingerly before she picked it up.

"It looks just like a real one," she said thoughtfully; "looks good, feels good."

I told her I didn't know. "Let me see it once," and she handed it over to me.

I rubbed it gently between my fingers and held it up to the light. The little whorls, so delicately traced on a geometric lathe, were clear and clean; the features of Alexander Hamilton were sharp, the eyes grimly facing to the west. The paper was reasonably crisp, the numbers solidly stamped.

I couldn't see a single thing wrong with it.

My wife is more practical than I. She said, "Maybe you can't see anything wrong with it yourself. But I want to know if they'll take it at the supermarket. We need butter."

They took the ten-dollar bill at the supermarket; we got two pounds of butter, some coffee and some meat, and I bought some magazines with the change. We went home to think it over and chased the kids outside so we could talk without interruption.

Jean looked at me. "Now what?"

I shrugged. "So we make some more ten-dollar bills. You trying to tell me we don't need any more?"

She knew better than that. "Talk sense, Mike McNally. That ten-dollar bill means that we'll have meat tomorrow instead of macaroni. But that doesn't answer my question; now what?"

I told her I wanted to think it over.

"No, you don't. Any thinking is going to be done on a corporate basis." She meant it. "If you're going ahead with this—well, I'm in it, too."

"Fair enough," I told her. "Let's wait until the kids get to bed and we'll get it straightened out. In the meantime get that other bill out again. I need a new battery, and the right front tire isn't going to last much longer."

She agreed that was fair, and took the other bill—and, I'll say right here, that it was the *only* bill we had left, with payday three days away—out of her purse. She laid it on the coffee table in front of me, smoothing out the creases.

"All right," she said. "Go ahead."

I shifted the ten-dollar bill a little closer to me, leaned my elbows on the table, and concentrated.

Almost immediately the duplicate began to take shape; first in outline, then in color, then in fine lines of script and curlycued detail. It took about five seconds in all, I suppose. We hadn't as yet attempted to time it.

While Jean carefully examined the duplicate, I made two more, three in all besides the original. I gave Jean back the original and one of the duplicates to boot and went down to price new batteries. It was a warm day, so I piled the kids into the car and took them along with me for the ride.

After the kids get to bed and after the dishes are washed and left to dry on the sink, the house is quiet. Too quiet, sometimes, when I think how fast little children grow up and leave home. But that's a long time away, especially for the little guy. Jean brought in the beer, and we turned on the Canadian station that doesn't have commercials. They were playing Victor Herbert.

"Well?" Jean, I could tell, was a little nervous. She'd had all day to think things over with the children not underfoot. "I see they took them, all right."

"They" and "them" were the bills and the people that had sold me the tire and the battery. "Sure," I said. "Nothing to it."

Jean put down her beer and looked me straight in the eye. "Mike, what you're doing is against the law. Do you want to go to jail, and do you want the kids to know their father——"

I stopped her right there. "You show me," I challenged her, "where what I'm doing is against the law."

"Well——"

I didn't let her get started. "In the first place, those bills are not counterfeits. They're just as real as though they were made right in

Washington. They're not copies, because 'copy' implies that in some way they attempt to emulate the original. And these don't emulate anything—they're real! Just as real as could be—I showed you that on the microscope and you agreed to that."

I was right, and she knew it. I was perfectly confident that even the atoms in the original bill and the duplicates were identical.

I had her there. She just sat and looked at me, with her cigarette burning away in the ashtray. I turned up the radio a little louder. Neither of us said anything for a while.

Then she asked, "Mike, was anyone else in your family ever able to do this, anyone that you know for sure?"

I didn't think so. "My grandmother was always having some presentiments about things that came true about half the time, and my mother was always able to find things that were lost. My Aunt Mary is still having the wild and woolly dreams she's had all her life, but that's as far as it goes, if you except the fact that my own mother was born with a caul and when I was real small, before she died, she always used to insist that I would learn to make money just when I needed it the most."

Jean said, "What about that relative of yours that was burned alive in Belfast?"

I was insulted. "That was County Monaghan, which is a long way from Ulster. And it was my great-grand-aunt Brigid-Nora. And she was burned because her father was Spanish, and because she always had plenty of gold and food during the Great Famine; not because she was a witch."

"Your grandmother always used to say she was a witch."

"Logical way to reason," I said. "Brigid-Nora was from the Connaught side of the family. You know, like the Walloons and the Flemings, or the Prussians and the Bavarians."

"Never mind your Irish history. You said your mother——"

"Yes, she said I'd have plenty of money just when I needed it most. But you're a mother yourself; you know how mothers feel about their offspring."

Jean sighed, and split the last bottle evenly between our glasses. "Your mother certainly knew her little boy. 'Just when you need it most!' Mike, if this doesn't work out I'm going to go back to work. I can't stand this—this no-meat, no-clothes, no-nothing diet any more. I can't take this sort of life much longer!"

I knew that. I couldn't take it much longer myself. Borrowing five here, then there, driving a car that hadn't been in corporate existence for twelve years, getting gas and oil on a pay-you-Friday basis, wearing suits that—well, you know what I mean. I didn't like it. And the two kids would wait a long time before they got to live in a house their father could buy on a foreman's pay.

Regardless of what they say in comic strips, I really proposed in the rumble seat of a Whippet roadster; otherwise, I hadn't been on my knees in front of anyone since I was a boy. But that night I just got down on the floor in front of Jean and we really had it out; all the things that people usually don't say, but think. I told her what I wanted and she told me what she wanted and we both made sloppy spectacles of ourselves. Finally we got up and went to bed.

The next morning I was up before the kids, which, for me, is exceptional. The first thing I did after breakfast was to call up my boss and tell him what he could do with his job. An hour after that *his* boss called me up and hinted that all would be forgiven if I reported for work on the afternoon shift as usual. I hinted right back for a raise and waited until he agreed. Then I told him what he could do with his job. We sat out in the kitchen for almost an hour that morning making duplicate ten-dollar bills, with Jean keeping track until we got up to two thousand dollars in cold, hard, green cash—more money than we had ever had at one time in our whole married or single life. Then we dressed the kids and took a cab downtown. Shopping. Shopping for cash, with no looks at the price tags. Oh, Jean tried to sneak a look every once in a while, when she thought I didn't see, but I always ripped the tag off and stuck it in my pocket.

The bicycle and the scooter and the bigger things we had delivered; the rest we carried. The landlord's wife was immensely surprised when we came back home in another cab with the trunk full of packages; she wanted to express her sympathy over the sudden event that had caused us to go away in one taxi and return in another. Nothing serious, she hoped. We said no, it wasn't serious, and shut the door.

Well, that was the beginning. Two or three days of steady buying will buy an awful lot of clothes. In three weeks we had all we could wear and were thinking seriously of buying some things for the house. The stove we have was on its last legs before we bought it, and the furniture is all scratched and marred from when the kids were still crawling and spilling things.

But we didn't want to buy any furniture until we could find a place to live out in the country, and all the places we looked at in our Sunday drives were either too much or too far or too something. So I called Art's Bar, where I hang out sometimes on paynights.

"Art," I asked, "do you remember that real-estate man that wanted to sell me that cottage before he found out I didn't have the money?"

Sure, he remembered. "As a matter of fact, he's here right now trying to sell me some insurance. Why?"

I told him I might want to see him about a new house.

"Then come on down and get him out of my hair. I need more insurance like I need more rocks in my head. You coming down here or do you want me to send——?"

No, I'd come down there. I don't want anyone except relatives to see the crummy place where I live. Even relatives like to rub it in.

The real-estate man—even if his name was important, I couldn't remember it now—had gone over to DeBaeker's grocery for bread. He'd be right back, Art said.

All right. I could wait. I asked Art for a short beer, and he slid it deftly down to my favorite corner. It tasted a little too cold, and I warmed it a bit with my hands. This mechanical refrigeration is all right when business is rushing, but when business is slow the beer in the coils gets too cold for my taste.

"Art," I said, "the paper isn't here yet. What have you to read besides the *Neighborhood Shopper?*"

Art looked up from the cash-register tape. "I don't know, Mike. There's a whole bunch of mail I opened that I haven't had a chance to look at yet. There might be the last *Bar News* in there. Take a look for yourself while I see how much dough the night man was off last night."

He shoved over the morning mail. I used to help out Art every once in a while to make myself a few extra dollars, and he knew there wasn't anything in the mail beside the usual advertising circulars, which he had no objection to my reading.

There was no *Bar News* there, and I idly turned over the pile, glancing at advertising puffs for spigots and coil cleaners and sham glasses. Then I saw it, and looked closer. I might add that I read everything, from streetcar transfers to medicine labels to the *Men Wanted* posters in the post office.

This particular circular was a copy of others that every small businessman gets from his post office or Federal Reserve District. This one was just like all the rest, with warning of flaws or errors or careless workmanship in the usual number of counterfeit bills always in circulation. This warning caught me where it hurt.

It said:

WATCH FOR THIS
TEN DOLLAR BILL

*Federal Reserve Note, Series G, serial number G 69437088 D.
Series 1934 D, with 7 printed four lower corners on obverse of
bill. Portrait of Alexander Hamilton.*

THIS IS AN EXCELLENT
COUNTERFEIT!

*and can be distinguished at first glance only by above serial
number on face of bill. Special warning to groceries and cloth-
ing stores; all detected so far have been from these businesses. It
is thought that since so few bills have been detected these bills
are only samples being tested for public reception. If you see
one of these bills, detain the passer on some reasonable pretext
and call . . .*

and it gave the Federal Building telephone number.

That was enough for me. I crumpled up the circular and dropped it
to the floor with my ears waiting for it to explode. Art rolled up the tape
and dropped it in the cash drawer. I sat there, thankful I was sitting. My
knees wouldn't have held me.

Art drew himself a short beer. "Find anything good?"

I managed to take a shaky breath. Anything good? Hell, Art was never
going to know just how good, or how bad, I felt.

"Art," I said, "I want another beer. Better give me something stronger
with it." So I paid Art, got a shot and a beer, which I'm not used to, and
sat back trying to get my breath back under control. I didn't realize how
stupid I'd been until Art came back from the cash register with the
duplicate ten in his hand.

"Here, Mike. You'd better take this ten back—pay me later, unless you
want a lot of silver. Too early in the day for me, and the last two guys
that came in had twenties. Okay?"

You bet it was okay. "Sure, Art. I know how it is." I took the ten from
his outstretched fingers with a hand that quivered. "As a matter of fact,
I shouldn't have given you that ten at all." You bet I shouldn't. "I've got
the right change right here——" and I dumped a handful on the bar.
"You better have one with me, yourself."

Art had another short beer; I finished my drink, and I went out to the
car and sat in it and quietly had the male equivalent of hysterics. I made
it home all right, and made it to bed without saying much to my wife.
And then I lay there half the night, thinking.

Now, I don't consider myself to be a crook, nor did I want to be one.
I hadn't thought about it too much because those ten-dollar bills looked
too good to me and Jean. But I had a decision to make: was I going to

go ahead with this, or was I going to go back to the dog-eat-dog life I'd given myself and my family?

Money? Well the Government prints it, sends it to the bank, and from there to the man who actually spends it. After passing through scores or hundreds of hands, each time acting as a buying or selling catalyst for the national economy, it wears out—the paper becomes worn or torn. Then it is totaled, shipped back to Washington, and destroyed. But not all of it.

Inevitably some would be lost, burned by fire or drowned by water, or maybe even buried in unknown pits by anonymous misers to rot in useless solitude. A billion dollars in crisp green currency would issue from the Mint, to return worn and foreshortened by thousands of missing dollars. Would it be wrong to replace some of those lost units? The Government would still have to replace no more than they had originally printed; the people that spent the money would suffer no inflationary loss of their savings; industry would get full value and possibly even increased sales.

That's the way I had figured—no one would lose, and one family would benefit—mine. But now I had been proved wrong by some bank teller, by some sharp-eyed comparison of similar numbers. The innocents had lost when they had taken my duplicates, lost because all counterfeit money is automatically confiscated. Uncle Sam brooks no false images. Perhaps even some of my friends, some of my acquaintances, had lost because of me, and all because I had been stupid enough to use the same bill for all my duplicates.

The disgusted ceiling stared down at me and I made a mental note never to tell my wife. I'd solve this my own way, without getting her into it, and I went to sleep long after I had given up trying to find a way out.

When I got up the next morning, I duplicated a five-dollar bill.

It worked all right. There really wasn't any reason why I shouldn't be able to duplicate any one I wanted; it was just that the ten had been the first one I tried, and that only because it was the only one in the house. And it felt better to me to have a pocket full of tens than a pocket full of fives. I guess it would to most people.

When I made the first five, I looked through my billfold and took out all the fives I had, and made one more of each one. Then I went through Jean's purse and did the same. When I was finished, I had about a dozen copies, and about a dozen originals, and I felt rather proud of myself. I leaned back in my chair and began to figure the probability of some bank teller's noticing that the numbers of two five-dollar bills were identical, if the bills came into the bank two days or two weeks apart.

Then the handful of bills and I went out to do my shopping.

I think the best thing to do would be to tell what I did for the next few months. The first bunch of fives I got rid of in different stores, one or two in each one. Every once in a while I would be able to convert four five-dollar bills into a twenty, or into a pair of tens. Then I would duplicate the bigger bill, and spend the original and the copy in two widely separated stores.

In two or three months I was in more business places, more bars, and more odd shops than I'd been in the past ten years. But I did have one bit of trouble; it got so that the clerks would good-naturedly wail when I went into a store, and complain that I must be a millionaire, because I never seemed to have less than a five or a ten or a twenty. I didn't like the idea of having attention called to me in such a way, even though nothing but pleasant conversation came out of it. So the only thing I could do was to spend a lot of time and traveling so that I hit the same stores as seldom as possible. I had a little black book with all the addresses I'd visited, with a note in my own private code telling what I'd bought.

Every week or so I'd drop down to the bank and deposit what seemed to be a reasonable figure. And what a pleasant feeling it was to be able to walk into a bank with a bankbook and a fistful of money to put in! It was really the first time in my life that I had ever used a bank for anything else but a place to get money orders, or to cash in a savings bond that my boss had insisted I pay for with the pay-roll deduction plan.

It even got so the clerks in the bank would give me a big smile and say, "Business must be doing all right, Mr. McNally." I'd give them a pontifical frown and complain that the country was going to the dogs with high taxes. I knew that was what I was expected to say. Anyone who deposits every week, just as regular as clockwork, better than a hundred dollars is bound to complain about taxes. The more deposited, the louder the bellow.

And we bought a new car. Well, not exactly new, but it was only a year old. These big cars depreciate a lot the first year. The salesman who sold it to me must have thought he was pulling a fast one when he got rid of that gas-eater, but that didn't worry me any. The more gas it used, the more chances I got to get into a gas station where I could get rid of another bill. I always had wanted a big car anyway. My old car I sold to the junkman, with a twinge of regret when he hauled it away with the fenders throbbing gently in the wind.

My wife, who all this time never did find out about the mess I had almost gotten into with the original setup, had for the first time in her life all the clothes, all the household appliances, all the little luxuries she wanted. But she wanted to buy a house.

"Mike," she said, "there's a lot of houses around Twelve Mile Road. Let's get some place where the kids can play."

I told her no dice, and managed to make it stick. After all, I had just a little bit better than a down payment in the bank, and I didn't want to take any chances until I had the ability to take care of all the expenses that would be bound to arise with the purchase of a new home.

So we just stayed where we were, with the landlady's eyes popping every time we came home with something new. She tried to pump, but we don't pump very well with people we don't like.

There was one place where I had trouble, and it was the one place I didn't want it. Naturally, I couldn't stop going to Art's Bar. I had been going in there for years, and the last thing I wanted was to have someone think I was going high hat. On top of that, I enjoy playing cards, and I like to drink beer. So I dropped in there just as often as I always did, and tried to think of answers for all the questions that were shot at me. When someone who's always been on the verge of bankruptcy—and most of Art's customers are that way; it was a family bar—suddenly shows up with good clothes and a new car and the ability to buy a friend a beer once in a while, then questions are bound to arise. I told them I was doing this and doing that, and still didn't satisfy their curiosity.

Finally I called the man who'd been trying to sell me some more insurance for years. He came out to the house and gave me one of his high-pressure sales talks. I pretended to be taking notes of his figures, but I wasn't. I was checking his sales pitch. I bought some more insurance and memorized a lot of the words and phrases he used. The next time at Art's when someone asked me what I was doing for a living I told them I was selling insurance, and went into the sales talk I'd memorized. They let me alone after that, apparently convinced.

Late in 1951 we bought our house. (We still live there, if you're curious. Drop in and see us some time, if you're ever around the Utica Road, near Rochester. It's the big one on the far corner, near the golf course.) We paid spot cash for the whole thing, on a seventy-by-two-hundred-foot lot. The kids fell in love with it at first sight, naturally, and I think it was the slide and the swings in the backyard that did it. It didn't take long before they were just as brown as Polynesians, and it didn't take long before Jean was the same. She spent—and spends—more time digging in the yard planting flowers than I do sleeping.

It was really a wonderful life. We'd get up when we felt like it—in the summer, when the kids weren't in school—and sit around until we felt like doing something. When we found something to do we did it without counting out in advance what we could afford to spend. If we wanted to stay overnight in town we did it, and we stayed at whatever hotel we wanted to. And when we registered at the hotel we didn't have to ask first how much the room was, and Jean could go right into the lobby with me without feeling self-conscious about the clothes she happened to be wearing. It amused me a little when I figured that out; before we'd had enough money we used to feel self-conscious no matter what we were wearing, no matter how well we were dressed. Now we didn't care how we looked.

Once we registered at the Statler when we came back from a little ride to Tilbury, Ontario, and Jean and I and the kids were wearing shorts. We just went to our room, had a good night's sleep, had breakfast, and were home before we even thought of how many stares we'd collected in the glittering lobby. We thought that over, analyzed it, and began to laugh.

When the kids got out of school in the summer of 1953, we went for a long trip, this time to Wisconsin Dells, and then to the Black Hills. When we got back, in the middle of August, the mailbox was full of the usual advertising, and after a cursory glance at the collection, I threw it all into the incinerator, which was a mistake. That was in August. In September we had a caller.

It was one of these Indian-summer days, with the breeze and the warm sun, and the overtones of the children playing in the yard.

"My name," he said, "is Morton. Frank Morton. I'm with the Bureau of Internal Revenue."

Jean almost collapsed.

"Nice place you have here, Mr. McNally," he said. "I've always admired it."

I thanked him for that. "We like it, Mr. Morton. The kids like it here away from the traffic." I couldn't think of anything else to say.

He agreed. "As a matter of fact, my boy comes over to play here quite often."

I was surprised at that.

"You must have seen him," Morton went on. "Fat little fellow!"

I knew who he meant. "Little Frankie? Why, sure! He likes my wife's cookies. Doesn't he, Jean?"

Jean said that reminded her of what she had in the oven, and excused herself to let me face the music alone. I didn't mind; I'd always told her that all this was my idea, and I'd take care of whatever happened. I knew she'd be right out in the kitchen with her ear right up against the door.

"That isn't what I was after, Mr. McNally. This is just what you might call a friendly call, in a way."

I liked that. "Always glad to have you, Mr. Morton. You must live in that house across from the grocery store."

Yes, he did. "I say a 'friendly call,' but it's partly business. As I told you, I'm with Internal Revenue."

Into my throat again with my heart. "Internal Revenue. Oh, yes."

"You see, Mr. McNally, little Frankie has had so much fun playing with your children I thought I'd save you a little trouble. Since I live right down the street, I think the least I could do is to be a good neighbor."

I couldn't make out what he was driving at. All I could do was be polite, and ask him to keep talking. And he did.

"You see, since I work in the Bureau, a lot of forms and things pass over my desk. The other day the name and address on one looked familiar. I took a second look and knew it must be you. You're the only McNally on the street that I know of, so I thought I'd stop by on the way home from work and tip you off."

Tip me off to what?

"Well," he said, "this was one of the regular forms the Bureau sends out. Apparently someone who has charge of your file sent you a letter asking you to come down and talk about a discrepancy in your tax return. And you apparently ignored the letter."

I opened my mouth to say something and thought better of it. Morton hurriedly went on.

"Now, Mr. McNally, I know you were gone most of the summer, and, since this is in my department, and since we're neighbors, I know that things get lost in the mail, and I thought I should drop by and tell you you must have never gotten any notice to appear. It might be a good idea for you to call in person, and explain what must have happened. It'd save you a lot of trouble, in the long run. Just tell them I stopped by on a friendly call."

He had more to say about that, but I think the situation really was that he didn't like the man who was in charge of my file, and wanted to warn me to get out from under before this someone really dropped the boom.

We talked for a little while longer about his boy and mine and the things people talk about when they've met for the first time, and he left with an apologetic smile. He already felt he'd gone out of his way to mind someone else's business, and he felt guilty. I did my best to ease things, and Jean came out of the kitchen just before he left with a plate of cookies for Morton's wife.

We watched him go down the curving flagstone walk that had cost me two hundred duplicate dollars; we watched him walk briskly to his own house half a block away. I asked Jean if she wanted a cigarette. She shook her head.

"No. Not right now." She sat limply in the nearest chair. "Now what's going to happen to us?"

I told her I didn't know. But I'd take care of it.

She gave that short sarcastic laugh she saves for special occasions. "Yes, you'll take care of it. Like you take care of a lot of things. I knew you'd get in trouble sooner or later." She began to sniffle.

I didn't know whether to get mad or to act sympathetic. When a woman cries, I don't think either one works. After I tossed a few words around I realized nothing was going to do much good, so I picked up my hat and went for a ride. I got into a card game at Art's, twenty miles away, where I hadn't been for some time. Art was so glad to see me he bought the house and me a beer, which, for Art, is exceptional. When I got home Jean was in bed pretending to be asleep. I let her keep up the pretense, and went to sleep myself.

The next morning, bright and early, with my heart in my mouth and lead in my shoes, I was standing in line at the counter in the Federal Building. I told them what I was there for, and they passed me through three different hands and two different desks until I got to the man with my file.

The man had big ears and a bad disposition. His name was Johnson, and he made it quite clear that to me it was *Mr.* Johnson. He got right down to cases.

"You're lucky, McNally, that Frank Morton went out of his way to be neighborly, as he calls it. But that's neither here nor there. You haven't filed any income-tax return for 1951, 1952, *and* for 1950. Why?"

I wasn't going to let him get me mad, but I knew I could make him blow his top. I detest public servants with an inferiority complex.

"Well, Johnson," I said, "for a good reason. For 1952, 1951, *and* 1950, I had no income."

That was just the answer he was looking for, and wasn't expecting. He shuffled papers like mad, unable to believe his luck.

"Well, now, McNally," he said triumphantly, "that's a rather peculiar statement. You have a house that is assessed at eight thousand dollars, and worth three times that. Right?"

Of course he was right. Taxes are low where I live, with the jet-engine plant paying most of the bills.

"And you have no income for three years, McNally, none at all?"

"Johnson," I told him sorrowfully, "I am a very law-abiding individual. I am quite familiar with the income-tax rules"—which I wasn't—"and I am also a very thrifty person. My wife makes all my suits and raises all our food. I don't need income, but to overcome boredom I am thinking of applying for a government job, in the customer-relations department. Anything else, Mr. Johnson?"

No, there was nothing else. But "you'll quite possibly hear from us a little later, McNally." When I left he was frantically scribbling away with a red pencil. I certainly wish I didn't have such a lousy temper, but in for a lamb, in for a sheep. All I could do was to wait for the wheels to roll over me, with Johnson pressing the starting button.

The wheels rolled, and apparently missed me. We didn't hear from the Bureau of Internal Revenue all the rest of the year, and when next May came around Jean and I had almost forgotten. We decided it would be nice if we took a little trip, and found out that to go to Europe it would be necessary to get a passport. We applied for one. That must have been the trigger that made someone think we were trying to get out of Federal jurisdiction. We got no passports, but I got a summons.

It really wasn't a trial. There was no judge there, and I had no lawyer. We just sat down in uncomfortable chairs and faced each other. There isn't much use mentioning any names, so I won't. It was just a meeting to see if things could be settled without a trial; most likely because trials take up time and money. They were fairly decent, but it boiled down to this:

"Mr. McNally, you have a house, a car, and a bank account."

The bank account wasn't big, and I mentioned that.

"Big enough for someone with no income. And we can prove—actually *prove*—Mr. McNally, that in the past three years you have spent for tangibles almost twenty thousand dollars. Your scale of living is and has been running at a hundred dollars every week—or better."

I could do nothing but admit it, and compliment their thoroughness. They were not impressed.

"So, Mr. McNally, that is why you are here now. We see no use in subjecting you to the inconvenience of a trial, with all the attendant publicity."

They waited for me to agree with them, so I did.

"What we are primarily interested in, Mr. McNally, is not the exact amount of your income—although that is an extremely serious question, which must be adjusted to our satisfaction before this is all over."

That made me sit straight in the chair.

"Not so much in the amount, Mr. McNally, but the source. Just who are you working for, and how do you do it?"

"Do what?"

They were very patient, elaborately so. "How do you take the bets, Mr. McNally? How do they get bets to you, and how do you pay off when you win or lose?"

"What bets?" I asked blankly. "What are you talking about?"

If you've never seen a collective lip being curled, you don't know what you've missed.

"Come now, Mr. McNally. Come now! We're all men of the world, if you want to put it that way. We know that you have a source of income. What we want to know—and we are *very* curious—is how you manage to run your business without using any means of communication we have been able to find."

They paused to let me consider; then: "We'll be frank with you, sir— we're puzzled. Puzzled so much that perhaps we can come to some sort of arrangement allowing you to pay your past-due taxes without penalty."

I began to laugh. First I laughed, and then I roared.

"I suppose," I said, "that you're the source of all the clicks and static we've been hearing on the telephone lately. And I imagine you're the source of all these cars and trucks that have been breaking down within a block of my house." They admitted it with their faces. "And you can't find out how I take bets, and how I pay off. And I'll bet that you're our new milkman, and our new baker!"

They let me laugh myself out, and they didn't like it. One of the government men stood up and towered over me.

"Mr. McNally, this is no laughing matter for you. You came here under your own power, and you may leave the same way if you so choose. But there is one thing I can definitely assure you: that you will be back here under less comfortable, more formal circumstances just as soon as we have presented the evidence we have against you to a Federal jury."

That didn't sound so good to me, and they all saw it.

"Did you, sir, ever stop to think what would happen to your wife and children if a true bill were presented against you? Are you prepared to face the penalty for deliberately neglecting to file an income-tax return for three consecutive years? You cannot, regardless of how you are communicating with your runners, conduct a gambling business from a jail cell. Had you thought of that, Mr. McNally?"

The income tax? Well, there was one slim chance—I hated to do it, but a chance was a chance. I knew I didn't want Jean to get mixed up in anything I had started, and I knew that with the thing out in the open there would be bound to be some kickback that would affect the kids. And children shouldn't be exposed to trouble. They get enough of that when they're adults.

The government men kept hammering at me and I kept thinking. A slim chance was better than no chance at all. Then they gave me my cue. Someone was saying:

". . . And you can't sit there and tell us you got all that income out of thin air!"

I broke in. "What did you say?"

"We were talking about the impossibility of your proving——"

"No. Go back a little. What you said about money out of thin air?"

The collective smirked. "Let's not be too literal, Mr. McNally. We know you got the money; we want to know where and how you got it."

I told them. "Out of thin air, like you said." I slid out my billfold. "You might compare the numbers on these bills," and I passed out a handful. "The best place in the world to get money is right out of the air —no germs on it that way."

So they checked the serial numbers, and they compared the bills, and they began to scream like a herd of frustrated stallions. They were still screaming when I left, under my own power.

Probably the only reason they let me go was because I was so completely frank about everything.

"Never mind where I got the money," I said. "You admit you couldn't tell one from the other. If you'll come out to my house tomorrow I'll show you where they came from; keep me here and you'll be no further ahead than you are now."

One of them suggested they could follow other leads and nail me in the end—even if it took a couple of years.

"But wouldn't you rather clean this up all in one shot? You know I wouldn't get far if I tried to skip, and I have no intention of doing that. Give me a chance to get things lined up—no, I have no one working with or for me, if that's what you're thinking—and tomorrow you get everything out in the open."

I didn't try to lose the car that followed me all the way home. Then I talked Jean into taking the kids over to her mother's the next morning, and drank three cans of beer before I could go to sleep.

The next morning I was shaved, dressed, and breakfasted when Jean and the kids pulled out of the driveway, bound for Grandma's. I knew that they would have a tail of some kind, but that was all to the good. When she was barely out on the main highway, away from the house, according to agreement, the Marines would land. They did—two quiet, insignificant-looking little men I had never seen before. But I've seen too many movies not to be able to spot a shoulder holster when I see one.

They were extremely polite, came in as though they were walking on expensive eggs. I gave them a pleasant smile and a can of beer apiece.

They introduced themselves as Internal Revenue and Secret Service, and I blinked at that. What was the Secret Service doing here?

He told me.

"Secret Service is charged with the responsibility," he said, "of detecting and handling counterfeit money."

Well, I knew it had been a slim chance. All I could do was ride the horse, now that I'd ordered the saddle. I cleared my throat.

"Well, gentlemen, I asked you here deliberately. I think the best thing to do is to get this straightened out once and for all." Secret Service grunted. "And the best way to do it is make a clean breast of things. Right?"

"Right!"

I reached in my pocket. "Take a look at these. Are they counterfeit? Or are they good?" And I passed them a sheaf of bills.

Secret Service took them over to where the morning sun was glaring through the blinds and took a lens from his pocket. He stood there for quite some time before he came back to sit down.

I asked him, "Are they good, or are they bad?"

Secret Service grunted. "Perfectly good. Good as gold. Only they all have the same numbers."

"Fine," I said. "You probably don't get paid very much. Take them with you when you go." The temperature dropped forty degrees. I didn't have to be a mind reader to know why.

"No, I'm not trying to bribe you. I thought it would be a good illustration of what I said yesterday—that's right, you weren't there. Someone said that money doesn't come out of thin air. Well, this money did."

Internal Revenue believed that just as much as Secret Service, and said so.

I shrugged. "So you want a better sample?"

They nodded.

They had nothing to lose.

"How much money have you got on you? I don't mean silver, although I might be able to fix you up there, too, but bills. Dollar bills, fives, tens, twenties. . . ." I tried to be funny. "Since you're not elected, I don't think you have any big bills." The joke fell flat, but between them they dug up about sixty dollars in bills of different denominations, and I spread them out as neatly as I could on the coffee table.

"All right, now; this is what I meant——" and I made sure that they were comfortably settled around the glass-topped surface. The first bill up in the right corner was a dollar, and I told them to watch the surface of the table right next to it. I looked at the bill and concentrated.

The surface of the glass clouded, and the duplicate began to appear, nice and green and shiny. When it was complete, I leaned back and told the pair to pick up the dollar and its mate and feel free to examine them. While they had the new one over under the light, looking at it from all angles, I did a quick job on the rest of the money and went out to the kitchen for more beer.

They were so intent on the first one they never saw me leave. When they turned back to me I was sitting there with a cigarette, three full cans, and an expectant smile. Then they looked at the coffee table and saw the rest of the duplicates.

Secret Service looked at the bills, at the ones he had in his hand, and at Internal Revenue. "Good God Almighty," he said, and collapsed into his chair.

It took some time for them to get their breath; longer still for them to be able to ask sensible questions.

"You probably won't believe me," I warned. "I still don't believe it myself."

Secret Service looked at Internal Revenue. "After that," he said, "I'll believe anything. Come on, McNally, you've got yourself into a mess. Let's hear you get yourself out of it."

That I wouldn't go for. "I'm in no mess; you are. I'll make a million of those bills if you want, or if you don't, all I can do is spend a few years in prison. Now, if I'm in trouble, I'll stay in it. On the other hand, if you'll give me a clean bill of health I'll come across. Okay?"

Secret Service snorted. "My job is to nail the source of counterfeit money. Bud, you're all through!"

I kept after him. "Suppose you can say you've dried up the source. Suppose you can prove that to yourself, and your boss. Do I get a clean sheet? And do I get an okay for back taxes if I pay up?"

Internal Revenue hesitated. "Back taxes can always be paid up, with a penalty, if we think there was no criminal intent."

"And how about you?" I said to Secret Service. "Okay with you?"

But he was just as bullheaded as me. "No, McNally. You stuck out your neck, and chopped it off yourself. You'll make no more progress with U. S. Currency."

I kept right after him. "All you can get me for is possession of what you call counterfeit money. It looks good to me. Maybe the numbering machine stuck, or something."

"Yeah? No numbering machine in here. You made that stuff right here in front of my eyes!"

"Did I?" I asked. "Maybe it was just a magic trick. The hand is quicker than the eye, you know."

He was definite about that. "Not quicker than my eye. You made that money right here in front of me. I don't know how you did it, but I'll find out."

That was what I wanted him to say. "You saw me make money right in front of you? Without a printing press or anything? What would a jury say to that? What would they think about your sanity—and yours?" I turned to Internal Revenue. "And you still don't know how I did it, and you never will, unless I tell you. Right? What do you say?"

Internal Revenue wagged his head and moaned. "Right, I'm afraid."

Secret Service swore. "You too? You want to let this—this counterfeiter get away with that? Why——"

I mentioned the old one about sticks and stones may break my bones and he snorted hard enough to blow the rest of the bills off the coffee table. No one picked them up.

"Well, how about it?" I prodded. "While you're thinking about it, I'll get another beer."

"Oh no, you don't" he yelped, and tried to follow me into the kitchen. Internal Revenue pulled him back into his chair and leaned over. I could hear them whispering frantically while I pretended to have trouble finding the beer opener. I let them whisper for two or three minutes until I went back into the living-room and found the opener where it had been all the time. I opened the cans and sat back. Secret Service had a face like Thor.

"Make up your mind yet?" I inquired. "I'd like to coöperate, but not at the point of a gun."

His frown grew darker. "Got a telephone? I'll have to get my boss in on this."

Internal Revenue winced. "Yes, there's a phone. I've spent three months listening in on it." While Secret Service went to the phone to mutter briefly into it, I grinned. I know just how long Jean can talk to her mother saying absolutely nothing.

Secret Service came back and sat down. "He's pretty close to here. Five minutes."

We sat drinking cold beer until the boss showed up. Five minutes was a poor estimate. Three would have been better. I looked out the window and watched a telephone company truck drop off an undistinguished repairman, and sit there with the motor running. Sharp babies, these Federals.

So we went through the whole routine again with the coffee table and the bills and I had the place littered with money before they all gave up. I began to wonder if there was enough beer.

The boss said, "What guarantee have I that this will stop?"

I said, "When you find out how I do it you'll be your own guarantee. Okay——"

The boss said, "No. There are a lot of things to be straightened out first. For one thing——"

I snapped at him, "Let's get this straight. I'll tell you how I make the money. I'll give you the gadget to take with you so you'll know I can't make any more. All you have to do is promise never to prosecute me for what's gone by in the past. Now, there's no strings to my offer—there'll be no more money made, and you let me alone for the rest of my life. If either of us ever breaks the agreement, everything is off and the other can do what he likes."

He jumped on one word. "Gadget! You make this stuff, really make it? It isn't just an optical illusion?"

I nodded. "I really make it, right in front of you, and if we do business you take the gadget with you right out the front door. Never again will I make a dime, and that's a promise!"

The boss looked at Secret Service and Secret Service looked at Internal Revenue. They all looked at me and I excused myself. When I came out of the bathroom they weren't too happy; the boss did the talking.

"McNally, God help you if you're lying. We'll coöperate, only because we have to. But, all right; we won't prosecute for anything you've done in the past. But, if you ever pull anything like this again, you're going to rue the day you were born. Just to show you I mean business, this could mean all our jobs. Counterfeiting is a felony, and we're letting you get away with it. Understand that?"

He barked out the words, and I knew he meant just what he said. But I meant what I'd said, too. I told him that was fair enough, as far as I was concerned.

"It better be. Now, start talking. How do you do it?"

I laughed. "I discovered it by accident. You can do it yourself. Here; this coffee table . . ."

They looked down at it. "What about it?"

"You're the boss," I told him. "You do it first. Just put one of those bills on the glass and think about it. Think about how nice it would be if you had another one just like it. Think about where your next pay is going to go."

I'll give the boss credit. He hated to make a fool of himself, but he tried. He really tried. He took a bill out of his billfold and dropped it skeptically on the glass top. He shifted uncomfortably under the stares of the other two, and gave me one glare before he started concentrating on the money. Nothing happened.

He looked up at me and opened his mouth. I shook my head.

"This is no joke," I said softly. "You're the first one that knows this— even my wife doesn't," which was quite true.

He was game, and tried to concentrate. I motioned to Secret Service and Internal Revenue to move away with me, on the basis that the boss might find it a little easier without three men panting over him. We moved a few feet away and I took a sip of my beer.

I almost choked when I heard a gasp from the boss. I eagerly bent over the table again. The same thing was happening; the mist, the green color, the final completed bill. The boss sat up and wiped his forehead. "Uh," he said.

"Let me try that," said Secret Service and Internal Revenue, almost in unison, and they in turn bent over the table. The same thing happened.

They all sat back and waited for me to talk. I sat back and waited for them to ask questions. The boss asked the first one.

"How do you do it?"

I told him the absolute truth. "I don't know. I was just sitting here with my wife one night, glooming about what we owed, when she took out the last ten dollars we had. She flipped it on the table to show me how short we were going to be, and I just sat there moping about life in general. The next thing you know we had two ten-dollar bills. And that was it."

They all moved back and looked at the coffee table.

The boss said, "Where did you get this—this portable mint?"

"From my relatives," I said. I went on to tell him about the banshees and the leprechauns and he didn't believe a word of it. But Secret Service did. Later I found out his name was Kelly.

"So what do we do now?" said the boss in an irritated voice.

"I told you that you could have the gadget," and I meant it. "I've got a home, a car, and enough money in the bank. I always thought I could write stories if I had the chance, and I've been waiting for a good one. I think this is it. Take the table, and good health with it."

He looked at the table again. "And anyone can work it—anyone at all?"

"I suppose so. You just did it yourself."

Without an instant's hesitation he smashed the muzzle of the gun down at the coffee table. There was an agonized tinkling crash that sounded feminine; and then there was nothing but brittle shards on the rug.

"Take this—thing outside," he commanded, and Secret Service carried the wooden frame of the table out on the front porch. The boss jumped on the skeleton until it shattered, and Secret Service himself brought a can of gasoline from the pseudo-telephone truck.

We all watched the wood burn until there were ashes that the wind carried away when I stirred them gently with my foot. Then they left together, without saying another word. I never saw any of them again; Kelly I recognized from his newspaper picture when he was promoted some years later.

So that's the story. I never made any duplicate bills again; my promise made, the table destroyed, the ashes lost in the breeze. I write a little on the side occasionally, and with my limited talent I don't sell too many stories. It's a good thing I had money in the bank when the table was burned; money isn't as easy to get as it once was.

Sometimes I regret losing the coffee table—it was an old family heirloom. And money was so easy to make when I had it, that life was a dream. But it's just as well that the boss smashed and burned it. If he had kept it for a while, he would have found out it was just a table, that *I* had made the bills while they were so intent on the money. It was my ancestry, and not theirs. But what they don't know will never hurt them. I kept my promise, and I'll go on keeping it. But I made no promises not to duplicate anything else.

Right now there's a lot of people engaged in the business of finding and restoring old automobiles. Next year I'm going to France to take a look at a Type 51 Bugatti. They cost forty thousand dollars to make twenty years ago, and there're only fourteen in existence. A fellow named Purdy who lives in New York would pay a good price for a fifteenth, I understand. And while I'm in Europe I'll just stop in and look at some rare books and stamps and coins. They tell me that's a good business, too—perfectly legal, and far more profitable than writing stories like this.

KINDERGARTEN

by Clifford D. Simak

CLIFFORD SIMAK (1904–   ) is an editor of the Minneapolis *Star*. His is one of the best-known names in science fiction. He has contributed to most of the magazines in the field, and has been widely anthologized, beginning with *The Best in Science Fiction* and *Strange Ports of Call*. He is the author of a classic novel in the genre, *City*, as well as of other books.

He went walking in the morning before the Sun was up, down past the old, dilapidated barn that was falling in upon itself, across the stream and up the slope of pasture ankle-deep with grass and summer flowers, when the world was wet with dew and the chill edge of night still lingered in the air.

He went walking in the morning because he knew he might not have too many mornings left; any day, the pain might close down for good and he was ready for it—he'd been ready for it for a long time now.

He was in no hurry. He took each walk as if it were his last and he did not want to miss a single thing on any of the walks—the turned-up faces of the pasture roses with the tears of dew running down their cheeks or the matins of the birds in the thickets that ran along the ditches.

He found the machine alongside the path that ran through a thicket at the head of a ravine. At first glance, he was irritated by it, for it was not only unfamiliar, but an incongruous thing as well, and he had no room in heart or mind for anything but the commonplace. It had been the commonplace, the expected, the basic reality of Earth and the life one lived on it which he had sought in coming to this abandoned farm, seeking out a place where he might stand on ground of his own choosing to meet the final day.

He stopped in the path and stood there, looking at this strange machine, feeling the roses and the dew and the early morning bird song slip away from him, leaving him alone with this thing beside the path which looked for all the world like some fugitive from a home appliance shop.

But as he looked at it, he began to see the little differences and he knew that here was nothing he'd ever seen before or heard of—that it most certainly was not a wandering automatic washer or a delinquent dehumidifier.

For one thing, it shone—not with surface metallic luster or the gleam of sprayed-on porcelain, but with a shine that was all the way through whatever it was made of. If you looked at it just right, you got the impression that you were seeing into it, though not clearly enough to be able to make out the shape of any of its innards. It was rectangular, at a rough guess three feet by four by two, and it was without knobs for one to turn or switches to snap on or dials to set—which suggested that it was not something one was meant to operate.

He walked over to it and bent down and ran his hand along its top, without thinking why he should reach out and touch it, knowing when it was too late that probably he should have left it alone. But it seemed to be all right to touch it, for nothing happened—not right away, at least. The metal, or whatever it was made of, was smooth to the hand and beneath the sleekness of its surface he seemed to sense a terrible hardness and a frightening strength.

He took his hand away and straightened up, stepped back.

The machine clicked, just once, and he had the distinct impression that it clicked not because it had to click to operate, not because it was turning itself on, but to attract attention, to let him know that it was an operating machine and that it had a function and was ready to perform it. And he got the impression that for whatever purpose it might operate, it would do so with high efficiency and a minimum of noise.

Then it laid an egg.

Why he thought of it in just that way, he never was able to explain, even later when he had thought about it.

But, anyhow, it laid an egg, and the egg was a piece of jade, green with milky whiteness running through it, and exquisitely carved with what appeared to be outré symbolism.

He stood there in the path, looking at the jade, for a moment forgetting in his excitement how it had materialized, caught up by the beauty of the jade itself and the superb workmanship that had wrought it into shape. It was, he told himself, the finest piece that he had ever seen and he knew exactly how its texture would feel beneath his fingers and just how expertly, upon close examination, he would find the carving had been done.

He bent and picked it up and held it lovingly between his hands, comparing it with the pieces he had known and handled for years in the museum. But now, even with the jade between his hands, the museum

was a misty place, far back along the corridors of time, although it had
been less than three months since he had walked away from it.

"Thank you," he said to the machine and an instant later thought
what a silly thing to do, talking to a machine as if it were a person.

The machine just sat there. It did not click again and it did not move.

So finally he left, walking back to the old farmhouse on the slope above
the barn.

In the kitchen, he placed the jade in the center of the table, where he
could see it while he worked. He kindled a fire in the stove and fed in
split sticks of wood, not too large, to make quick heat. He put the kettle
on to warm and got dishes from the pantry and set his place. He fried
bacon and drained it on paper toweling and cracked the last of the eggs
into the skillet.

He ate, staring at the jade that stood in front of him, admiring once
again its texture, trying to puzzle out the symbolism of its carving and
finally wondering what it might be worth. Plenty, he thought—although,
of all considerations, that was the least important.

The carving puzzled him. It was in no tradition that he had ever seen
or of which he had ever read. What it was meant to represent, he could
not imagine. And yet it had a beauty and a force, a certain character,
that tagged it as no haphazard doodling, but as the product of a highly
developed culture.

He did not hear the young woman come up the steps and walk across
the porch, but first knew that she was there when she rapped upon the
door frame. He looked up from the jade and saw her standing in the
open kitchen doorway and at first sight of her he found himself, ridicu-
lously, thinking of her in the same terms he had been thinking of the
jade.

The jade was cool and green and she was crisp and white, but her
eyes, he thought, had the soft look of this wondrous piece of jade about
them, except that they were blue.

"Hello, Mr. Chaye," she said.

"Good morning," he replied.

She was Mary Mallet, Johnny's sister.

"Johnny wanted to go fishing," Mary told him. "He and the little
Smith boy. So I brought the milk and eggs."

"I am pleased you did," said Peter, "although you should not have
bothered. I could have walked over later. It would have done me good."

He immediately regretted that last sentence, for it was something he
was thinking too much lately—that such and such an act or the refrain-
ing from an act would do him good when, as a matter of plain fact, there

was nothing that would help him at all. The doctors had made at least that much clear to him.

He took the eggs and milk and asked her in and went to place the milk in the cooler, for he had no electricity for a refrigerator.

"Have you had breakfast?" he asked.

Mary said she had.

"It's just as well," he said wryly. "My cooking's pretty bad. I'm just camping out, you know."

And regretted that one, too.

Chaye, he told himself, quit being so damn maudlin.

"What a pretty thing!" exclaimed Mary. "Wherever did you get it?"

"The jade? Now, that's a funny thing. I found it."

She reached a hand out for it.

"May I?"

"Certainly," said Peter.

He watched her face as she picked it up and held it in both hands, carefully, as he had held it.

"You *found* this?"

"Well, I didn't exactly find it, Mary. It was given to me."

"A friend?"

"I don't know."

"That's a funny thing to say."

"Not so funny. I'd like to show you the—well, the character who gave it to me. Have you got a minute?"

"Of course I have," said Mary, "although I'll have to hurry. Mother's canning peaches."

They went down the slope together, past the barn, and crossed the creek to come into the pasture. As they walked up the pasture, he wondered if they would find it there, if it still was there—or ever had been there.

It was.

"What an outlandish thing!" said Mary.

"That's the word exactly," Peter agreed.

"What is it, Mr. Chaye?"

"I don't know."

"You said you were given the jade. You don't mean . . ."

"But I do," said Peter.

They moved closer to the machine and stood watching it. Peter noticed once again the shine of it and the queer sensation of being able to see into it—not very far, just part way, and not very well at that. But still the metal or whatever it was could be seen into, and that was somehow uncomfortable.

Mary bent over and ran her fingers along its top.

"It feels all right," she said. "Just like porcelain or——"

The machine clicked and a flagon lay upon the grass.

"For you," said Peter.

"For me?"

Peter picked up the tiny bottle and handed it to her. It was a triumph of glassblower's skill and it shone with sparkling prismatic color in the summer sunlight.

"Perfume would be my guess," he said.

She worked the stopper loose.

"Lovely," she breathed and held it out to him to smell.

It was all of lovely.

She corked it up again.

"But, Mr. Chaye . . ."

"I don't know," said Peter. "I simply do not know."

"Not even a guess?"

He shook his head.

"You just found it here."

"I was out for a walk——"

"And it was waiting for you."

"Well, now . . ." Peter began to object, but now that he thought about it, that seemed exactly right—he had not found the machine; it had been waiting for him.

"It was, wasn't it?"

"Now that you mention it," said Peter, "yes, I guess it was waiting for me."

Not for him specifically, perhaps, but for anyone who might come along the path. It had been waiting to be found, waiting for a chance to go into its act, to do whatever it was supposed to do.

For now it appeared, as plain as day, that someone had left it there.

He stood in the pasture with Mary Mallet, farmer's daughter, standing by his side—with the familiar grasses and the undergrowth and trees, with the shrill of locust screeching across the rising heat of day, with the far-off tinkle of a cowbell—and felt the chill of the thought within his brain, the cold and terrible thought backgrounded by the black of space and the dim endlessness of time. And he felt, as well, a *reaching* out of something, of a chilly alien thing, toward the warmth of humanity and Earth.

"Let's go back," he said.

They returned across the pasture to the house and stood for a moment at the gate.

"Isn't there something we should do?" asked Mary. "Someone we should tell about it?"

He shook his head. "I want to think about it first."

"And do something about it?"

"There may be nothing that anyone can or should do."

He watched her go walking down the road, then turned away and went back to the house.

He got out the lawn mower and cut the grass. After the lawn was mowed, he puttered in the flowerbed. The zinnias were coming along fine, but something had gotten into the asters and they weren't doing well. And the grass kept creeping in, he thought. No matter what he did, the grass kept creeping into the bed to strangle out the plants.

After lunch, he thought, maybe I'll go fishing. Maybe going fishing will do me——

He caught the thought before he finished it.

He squatted by the flowerbed, dabbing at the ground with the point of his gardening trowel, and thought about the machine out in the pasture.

I want to think about it, he'd told Mary, but what was there to think about? Something that someone had left in his pasture—a machine that clicked and laid a gift like an egg when you patted it.

What did that mean?

Why was it here?

Why did it click and hand out a gift when you patted it?

Response? The way a dog would wag its tail?

Gratitude? For being noticed by a human?

Negotiation?

Friendly gesture?

Booby trap?

And how had it known he would have sold his soul for a piece of jade one-half as fine as the piece it had given him?

How had it known a girl would like perfume?

He heard the running footsteps behind him and swung around and there was Mary, running across the lawn.

She reached him and went down on her knees beside him and her hands clutched his arm.

"Johnny found it, too," she panted. "I ran all the way. Johnny and that Smith boy found it. They cut across the pasture coming home from fishing . . ."

"Maybe we should have reported it," said Peter.

"It gave them something, too. A rod and reel to Johnny and a baseball bat and mitt to little Augie Smith."

"Oh, good Lord!"

"And now they're telling everyone."

"It doesn't matter," Peter said. "At least, I don't suppose it matters."

"What is that thing out there? You said you didn't know. But you have some idea. Peter, you must have some idea."

"I think it's alien," Peter reluctantly and embarrassedly told her. "It has a funny look about it, like nothing I've ever seen or read about, and Earth machines don't give away things when you lay a hand on them. You have to feed them coins first. This isn't—isn't from Earth."

"From Mars, you mean?"

"Not from Mars," said Peter. "Not from this solar system. We have no reason to think another race of high intelligence exists in this solar system and whoever dreamed up that machine had plenty of intelligence."

"But . . . not from this solar system . . ."

"From some other star."

"The stars are so far away!" she protested.

So far away, thought Peter. So far out of the reach of the human race. Within the reach of dreams, but not the reach of hands. So far away and so callous and uncaring. And the machine——

"Like a slot machine," he said, "except it always pays in jackpots and you don't even need a coin. That is crazy, Mary. That's one reason it isn't of this Earth. No Earth machine, no Earth inventor, would do that."

"The neighbors will be coming," Mary said.

"I know they will. They'll be coming for their handouts."

"But it isn't very big. It could not carry enough inside it for the entire neighborhood. It does not have much more than room enough for the gifts it's already handed out."

"Mary, did Johnny want a rod and reel?"

"He'd talked of practically nothing else."

"And you like perfume?"

"I'd never had any good perfume. Just cheap stuff." She laughed nervously. "And you? Do you like jade?"

"I'm what you might call a minor expert on it. It's a passion with me."

"Then that machine . . ."

"Gives each one the thing he wants," Peter finished for her.

"It's frightening," said Mary.

And it seemed strange that anything at all could be frightening on such a day as this—a burnished summer day, with white clouds rimming the western horizon and the sky the color of pale blue silk, a day that had no moods, but was as commonplace as the cornfield earth.

After Mary had left, Peter went in the house and made his lunch. He sat by the window, eating it, and watched the neighbors come. They came by twos and threes, tramping across the pasture from all directions, comirg to his pasture from their own farms, leaving the haying rigs and the cultivators, abandoning their work in the middle of the day to see the strange machine. They stood around and talked, tramping down the thicket where he had found the machine, and at times their high, shrill voices drifted across to him, but he could not make out what they said, for the words were flattened and distorted by the distance.

From the stars, he'd said. From some place among the stars.

And if that be fantasy, he said, I have a right to it.

First contact, he thought. And clever!

Let an alien being arrive on Earth and the women would run screaming for their homes and the men would grab their rifles and there'd be hell to pay.

But a machine—that was a different matter. What if it was a little different? What if it acted a little strangely? After all, it was only a machine. It was something that could be understood.

And if it handed out free gifts, that was all the better.

After lunch, he went out and sat on the steps and some of the neighbors came and showed him what the machine had given them. They sat around and talked, all of them excited and mystified, but not a single one of them was scared.

Among the gifts were wrist-watches and floor lamps, typewriters and fruit juicers, sets of dishes, chests of silver, bolts of drapery materials, shoes, shotguns, carving sets, book ends, neckties, and many other items. One youngster had a dozen skunk traps and another had a bicycle.

A modern Pandora's box, thought Peter, made by an alien intelligence and set down upon the Earth.

Apparently the word was spreading, for now the people came in cars. Some of them parked by the road and walked down to the pasture and others came into the barnyard and parked there, not bothering to ask for permission.

After a time, they would come back loaded with their loot and drive away. Out in the pasture was a milling throng of people. Peter, watching it, was reminded of a county fair or a village carnival.

By chore-time, the last of them had gone, even the neighbors who had come to say a few words with him and to show him what they'd gotten, so he left the house and walked up the pasture slope.

The machine still was there and it was starting to build something. It had laid out around it a sort of platform of a stone that looked like marble, as if it were laying a foundation for a building. The foundation was about ten feet by twelve and was set level against the pasture's slope, with footings of the same sort of stone going down into the ground.

He sat down on a stump a little distance away and looked out over the peace of the countryside. It seemed more beautiful, more quiet and peaceful than it had ever seemed before, and he sat there contentedly, letting the evening soak into his soul.

The Sun had set not more than half an hour ago. The western sky was a delicate lemon fading into green, with here and there the pink of wandering clouds, while beneath the horizon the land lay in the haze of a blue twilight, deepening at the edges. The liquid evensong of birds ran along the hedges and the thickets and the whisper of swallows' wings came down from overhead.

This is Earth, he thought, the peaceful, human Earth, a landscape shaped by an agricultural people. This is the Earth of plum blossom and of proud red barns and of corn rows as straight as rifle barrels.

For millions of years, the Earth had lain thus, without interference; a land of soil and life, a local corner of the Galaxy engaged in its own small strivings.

And now?

Now, finally, there was interference.

Now, finally, someone or something had come into this local corner of the Galaxy and Earth was alone no longer.

To himself, he knew, it did not matter. Physically, there was no longer anything that possibly could matter to him. All that was left was the morning brightness and the evening peace and from each of these, from every hour of each day that was left to him, it was his purpose to extract the last bit of joy in being alive.

But to the others it would matter—to Mary Mallet and her brother Johnny, to the little Smith boy who had gotten the baseball bat and mitt, to all the people who had visited this pasture, and to all the millions who had not visited or even heard of it.

Here, in this lonely place in the midst of the great cornlands, had come, undramatically, a greater drama than the Earth had yet known. Here was the pivot point.

He said to the machine: "What do you intend with us?"

There was no answer.

He had not expected one.

He sat and watched the shadows deepen and the lights spring up in the farm houses that were sprinkled on the land. Dogs barked from far away and others answered them and the cowbells rang across the hills like tiny vesper notes.

At last, when he could see no longer, he walked slowly back to the house.

In the kitchen, he found a lamp and lit it. He saw by the kitchen clock that it was almost nine o'clock—time for the evening news.

He went into the living-room and turned on the radio. Sitting in the dark, he listened to it.

There was good news.

There had been no polio deaths in the state that day and only one new case had been reported.

"It is too soon to hope, of course," the newscaster said, "but it definitely is the first break in the epidemic. Up to the time of broadcast, there have been no new cases for more than twenty hours. The state health director said . . ."

He went on to read what the health director said, which wasn't much of anything, just one of those public statements which pretty generally add up to nothing tangible.

It was the first day in almost three weeks, the newscaster had said, during which no polio deaths had been reported. But despite the development, he said, there still was need of nurses. If you are a nurse, he added, won't you please call this number? You are badly needed.

He went on to warm over a grand jury report, without adding anything really new. He gave the weather broadcast. He said the Emmett murder trial had been postponed another month.

Then he said: "Someone has just handed me a bulletin. Now let me see . . ."

You could hear the paper rustling as he held it to read it through, could hear him gasp a little.

"It says here," he said, "that Sheriff Joe Burns has just now been notified that a Flying Saucer has landed on the Peter Chaye farm out near Mallet Corners. No one seems to know too much about it. One report is that it was found this morning, but no one thought to notify the sheriff. Let me repeat—this is just a report. We don't know any more than what we've told you. We don't know if it is true or not. The sheriff is on his way there now. We'll let you know as soon as we learn anything. Keep tuned to this . . ."

Peter got up and turned off the radio. Then he went into the kitchen to bring in the lamp. He set the lamp on a table and sat down again to wait for Sheriff Burns.

He didn't have long to wait.

"Folks tell me," said the sheriff, "this here Flying Saucer landed on your farm."

"I don't know if it's a Flying Saucer, Sheriff."

"Well, what it is, then?"

"I wouldn't know," said Peter.

"Folks tell me it was giving away things."

"It was doing that, all right."

"If this is some cockeyed advertising stunt," the sheriff said, "I'll have someone's neck for it."

"I'm sure it's not an advertising stunt."

"Why didn't you notify me right off? What you mean by holding out on a thing like this?"

"I didn't think of notifying you," Peter told him. "I wasn't trying to hold out on anything."

"You new around here, ain't you?" asked the sheriff. "I don't recollect seeing you before. Thought I knew everyone."

"I've been here three months."

"Folks tell me you ain't farming the place. Tell me you ain't got no family. Live here all by yourself, just doing nothing."

"That's correct," said Peter.

The sheriff waited for the explanation, but Peter offered none. The sheriff looked at him suspiciously in the smoky lamplight.

"Can you show us this here Flying Saucer?"

By now Peter was a little weary of the sheriff, so he said, "I can tell you how to find it. You go down past the barn and cross the brook . . ."

"Why don't you come with us, Chaye?"

"Look, Sheriff, I was telling you how to find it. Do you want me to continue?"

"Why, sure," the sheriff said. "Of course I do. But why can't you . . ."

"I've seen it twice," said Peter. "I've been overrun by people all the afternoon."

"All right, all right," the sheriff said. "Tell me how to find it."

He told him and the sheriff left, followed by his two deputies.

The telephone rang.

Peter answered it. It was the radio station he'd been listening to.

"Say," asked the radio reporter, "you got a Saucer out there?"

"I don't think so," Peter said. "I do have something out here, though. The sheriff is going out to take a look at it."

"We want to send out our mobile TV unit, but we wanted to be sure there was something there. It be all right with you if we send it out?"

"No objections. Send it along."

"You sure you got something there?"

"I told you that I had."

"Well, then, suppose you tell me . . ."

Fifteen minutes later, he hung up.

The phone rang again.

It was the Associated Press. The man at the other end of the wire was wary and skeptical.

"What's this I hear about a Saucer out there?"

Ten minutes later, Peter hung up.

The phone rang almost immediately.

"McClelland of the *Tribune*," said a bored voice. "I heard a screwball story . . ."

Five minutes.

The phone rang again.

It was the United Press.

"Hear you got a Saucer. Any little men in it?"

Fifteen minutes.

The phone rang.

It was an irate citizen.

"I just heard on the radio you got a Flying Saucer. What kind of gag you trying to pull? You know there ain't any Flying Saucers . . ."

"Just a moment, sir," said Peter.

He let the receiver hang by its cord and went out to the kitchen. He found a pair of clips and came back. He could hear the irate citizen still chewing him out, the voice coming ghostlike out of the dangling receiver.

He went outside and found the wire and clipped it. When he came back in again, the receiver was silent. He hung it carefully on the hook.

Then he locked the doors and went to bed.

To bed, but not immediately to sleep. He lay beneath the covers, staring up into the darkness and trying to quiet the turmoil of speculation that surged within his brain.

He had gone walking in the morning and found a machine. He had put his hand upon it and it had given him a gift. Later on, it had given other gifts.

"A machine came, bearing gifts," he said into the darkness.

A clever, calculated, well-worked-out first contact.

Contact them with something they will know and recognize and need not be afraid of, something to which they can feel superior.

Make it friendly—and what is more friendly than handing out a gift?

What is it?

Missionary?

Trader?

Diplomat?

Or just a mere machine and nothing more?

Spy? Adventurer? Investigator? Surveyor?

Doctor? Lawyer? Indian chief?

And why, of all places, had it landed here, in this forsaken farmland, in this pasture on his farm?

And its purpose?

What had been the purpose, the almost inevitable motive, of those fictional alien beings who, in tales of fantasy, had landed on Earth?

To take over, of course. If not by force, then by infiltration or by friendly persuasion and compulsion; to take over not only Earth, but the human race as well.

The man from the radio station had been excited, the Associated Press man had been indignant that anyone should so insult his intelligence, the *Tribune* man had been bored and the United Press man flippant. But the citizen had been angry. He was being taken in by another Flying Saucer story and it was just too much.

The citizen was angry because he didn't want his little world disturbed. He wanted no interference. He had trouble enough of his own without things being messed up by a Saucer's landing. He had problems of his own—earning a living, getting along with his neighbors, planning his work, worrying about the polio epidemic.

Although the newscaster had said the polio situation seemed a little brighter—no new cases and no deaths. And that was a fine thing, for polio was pain and death and a terror on the land.

Pain, he thought.

I've had no pain today.

For the first time in many days, there has been no pain.

He lay stiff and still beneath the covers, examining himself for pain. He knew just where it lurked, the exact spot in his anatomy where it lurked hidden out of sight. He lay and waited for it, fearful, now that he had thought of it, that he would find it there.

But it was not there.

He lay and waited for it, afraid that the very thought of it would conjure it up from its hiding place. It did not come. He dared it to come, he invited it to show itself, he hurled mental jibes at it to lure it out. It refused to be lured.

He relaxed and knew that for the moment he was safe. But safe only temporarily, for the pain still was there. It bided its time, waited for its moment, would come when the time was right.

With careless abandon, trying to wipe out the future and its threat, he luxuriated in life without the pain. He listened to the house—the slightly settling joists that made the floor boards creak, the thrum of the light summer wind against the weathered siding, the scraping of the elm branch against the kitchen roof.

Another sound. A knocking at the door. "Chaye! Chaye, where are you?"

"Coming," he called.

He found slippers and went to the door. It was the sheriff and his men.

"Light the lamp," the sheriff said.

"You got a match?" Peter asked.

"Yeah, here are some."

Groping in the dark, Peter found the sheriff's hand and the book of matches.

He located the table, slid his hand across the top and felt the lamp. He lit it and looked at the sheriff from across the table.

"Chaye," the sheriff said, "that thing is building something."

"I know it is."

"What's the gag?"

"There's no gag."

"It gave me this," the sheriff said.

He threw the object on the table.

"A gun," said Peter.

"You ever see one like it?"

It was a gun, all right, about the size of a .45. But it had no trigger and the muzzle flared and the whole thing was made of some white, translucent substance.

Peter picked it up and found it weighed no more than half a pound or so.

"No," said Peter. "No, I've never seen one like it." He put it back on the table, gingerly. "Does it work?"

"It does," the sheriff said. "I tried it on your barn."

"There ain't no barn no more," said one of the deputies.

"No report, no flash, no nothing," the sheriff added.

"Just no barn," repeated the deputy, obsessed with the idea.

A car drove into the yard.

"Go out and see who's there," said the sheriff.

One of the deputies went out.

"I don't get it," complained the sheriff. "They said Flying Saucer, but I don't think it's any Saucer. A box is all it is."

"It's a machine," said Peter.

Feet stamped across the porch and men came through the door.

"Newspapermen," said the deputy who had gone out to see.

"I ain't got no statement, boys," the sheriff said.

One of them said to Peter: "You Chaye?"

Peter nodded.

"I'm Hoskins from the *Tribune*. This is Johnson from the AP. That guy over there with the sappy look is a photographer, name of Langly. Disregard him."

He pounded Peter on the back. "How does it feel to be sitting in the middle of the century's biggest news break? Great stuff, hey, boy?"

Langly said: "Hold it."

A flash bulb popped.

"I got to use the phone," said Johnson. "Where is it?"

"Over there," said Peter. "It's not working."

"How come at a time like this?"

"I cut the wire."

"Cut the wire! You crazy, Chaye?"

"There were too many people calling."

"Now," said Hoskins, "wasn't that a hell of a thing to do?"

"I'll fix her up," Langly offered. "Anyone got a pair of pliers?"

The sheriff said, "You boys hold on a minute."

"Hurry up and get into a pair of pants," Hoskins said to Peter. "We'll want your picture on the scene. Standing with your foot on it, like the guy that's just killed an elephant."

"You listen here," the sheriff said.

"What is it, Sheriff?"

"This here's important. Get it straight. You guys can't go messing around with it."

"Sure it's important," said Hoskins. "That is why we're here. Millions of people standing around with their tongues hanging out for news."

"Here are some pliers," someone remarked.

"Leave me at that phone," said Langly.

"What are we horsing around for?" asked Hoskins. "Let's go out and see it."

"I gotta make a call," said Johnson.

"Look here, boys," the sheriff insisted in confusion. "Wait——"

"What's it like, Sheriff? Figure it's a Saucer? How big is it? Does it make a clicking noise or something? Hey, Langly, take the sheriff's picture."

"Just a minute," Langly shouted from outside. "I'm fixing up this wire."

More feet came across the porch. A head was thrust into the door.

"TV truck," the head said. "This the place? How do we get out to the thing?"

The phone rang.

Johnson answered it.

"It's for you, Sheriff."

The sheriff lumbered across the room. They waited, listening.

"Sure, this is Sheriff Burns. . . . Yeah, it's out there, all right. . . . Sure, I know. I've seen it. . . . No, of course, I don't know what it is. . . . Yes, I understand. . . . Yes, sir. . . . Yes, sir. I'll see to it, sir."

He hung up the receiver and turned around to face them.

"That was military intelligence," he said. "No one is going out there.

No one's moving from this house. This place is restricted as of this minute."

He looked from one to another of them ferociously.

"Them's orders," he told them.

"Oh, hell," said Hoskins.

"I came all the way out here," bawled the TV man. "I'm not going to come out here and not . . ."

"It isn't me that's doing the ordering," said the sheriff. "It's Uncle Sam. You boys take things easy."

Peter went out into the kitchen and poked up the fire and set on the kettle.

"The coffee's there," he said to Langly. "I'll put on some clothes."

Slowly, the night wore on. Hoskins and Johnson phoned in the information they had jotted down on folded copy paper, their pencils stabbing cryptic signs as they talked to Peter and the sheriff. After some argument with the sheriff about letting him go, Langly left with his pictures. The sheriff paced up and down the room.

The radio blared. The phone banged constantly.

They drank coffee and smoked cigarettes, littering the floor with ground-out stubs. More newsmen pulled in, were duly warned by the sheriff, and settled down to wait.

Someone brought out a bottle and passed it around. Someone else tried to start a poker game, but nobody was interested.

Peter went out to get an armload of wood. The night was quiet, with stars.

He glanced toward the pasture, but there was nothing there to see. He tried to make out the empty place where the barn had disappeared. It was too dark to tell whether the barn was there or not.

Death watch or the last dark hour before the dawn—the brightest, most wonderful dawn that Man had ever seen in all his years of striving?

The machine was building something out there, building something in the night.

And what was it building?

Shrine?

Trading post?

Mission house?

Embassy?

Fort?

There was no way of knowing, no way that one could tell.

Whatever it was building, it was the first known outpost ever built by an alien race on the planet Earth.

He went back into the house with the load of wood.

"They're sending troops," the sheriff told him.

"Tramp, tramp, tramp," said Hoskins, dead-pan, cigarette hanging negligently to his underlip.

"The radio just said so," the sheriff said. "They called out the guard."

Hoskins and Johnson did some more tramp-tramping.

"You guys better not horse around with them soldier boys," the sheriff warned. "They'll shove a bayonet . . ."

Hoskins made a noise like a bugle blowing the charge. Johnson grabbed two spoons and beat out galloping hoofs.

"The cavalry!" shouted Hoskins. "By God, boys, we're saved!"

Someone said wearily: "Can't you guys be your age?"

They sat around, as the night wore on, drinking coffee and smoking. They didn't do much talking.

The radio station finally signed off. Someone fooled around, trying to get another station, but the batteries were too weak to pull in anything. He shut the radio off. It had been some time now since the phone had rung.

Dawn was still an hour away when the guardsmen arrived, not marching, nor riding horses, but in five canvas-covered trucks.

The captain came in for just a moment to find out where this goddam obscenity Saucer was. He was the fidgety type. He wouldn't even stay for a cup of coffee. He went out yelling orders at the drivers.

Inside the house, the others waited and heard the five trucks growl away.

Dawn came and a building stood in the pasture, and it was a bit confusing, for you could see that it was being built in a way that was highly unorthodox. Whoever or whatever was building it had started on the inside and was building outward, so that you saw the core of the building, as if it were a building that was being torn down and some one already had ripped off the entire exterior.

It covered half an acre and was five stories high. It gleamed pink in the first light of the morning, a beautiful misty pink that made you choke up a little, remembering the color of the dress the little girl next door had worn for her seventh birthday party.

The guardsmen were ringed around it, the morning light spattering off their bayonets as they stood the guard.

Peter made breakfast—huge stacks of flapjacks, all the bacon he had left, every egg he could find, a gallon or two of oatmeal, more coffee.

"We'll send out and get some grub," said Hoskins. "We'll make this right with you."

After breakfast, the sheriff and the deputies drove back to the county seat. Hoskins took up a collection and went to town to buy groceries.

The other newsmen stayed on. The TV truck got squared off for some wide-angle distance shots.

The telephone started jangling again. The newsmen took turns answering it.

Peter walked down the road to the Mallet farm to get eggs and milk. Mary ran out to the gate to meet him. "The neighbors are getting scared," she said.

"They weren't scared yesterday," said Peter. "They walked right up and got their gifts."

"But this is different, Peter. This is getting out of hand. The building . . ."

And that was it, of course. The building.

No one had been frightened of an innocent-appearing machine because it was small and friendly. It shone so prettily and it clicked so nicely and it handed out gifts. It was something that could be superficially recognized and it had a purpose that was understandable if one didn't look too far.

But the building was big and might get bigger still and it was being erected inside out. And who in all the world had ever seen a structure built as fast as that one—five stories in one single night?

"How do they do it, Peter?" Mary asked in a hushed little voice.

"I don't know," he said. "Some principle that is entirely alien to us, some process that men have never even thought of, a way of doing things, perhaps, that starts on an entirely different premise than the human way."

"But it's just the kind of building that men themselves would build," she objected. "Not that kind of stone, perhaps—maybe there isn't any stone like that in the entire world—but in every other way there's nothing strange about it. It looks like a big high school or a department store."

"My jade was jade," said Peter, "and your perfume was perfume and the rod and reel that Johnny got was a regular rod and reel."

"That means they know about us. They know all there is to know. Peter, they've been watching us!"

"I have no doubt of it."

He saw the terror in her eyes and reached out a hand to draw her close and she came into his arms and he held her tightly and thought, even as he did so, how strange that he should be the one to extend comfort and assurance.

"I'm foolish, Peter."

"You're wonderful," he assured her.

"I'm not really scared."

"Of course you're not." He wanted to say, "I love you," but he knew

that those were words he could never say. Although the pain, he thought
—the pain had not come this morning.

"I'll get the milk and eggs," said Mary.

"Give me all you can spare. I have quite a crowd to feed."

Walking back, he thought about the neighbors being frightened now
and wondered how long it would be before the world got frightened,
too—how long before artillery would be wheeling into line, how long
before an atom bomb would fall.

He stopped on the rise of the hill above the house and for the first time
noticed that the barn was gone. It had been sheared off as cleanly as if
cut with a knife, with the stump of the foundation sliced away at an
angle.

He wondered if the sheriff still had the gun and supposed he had. And
he wondered what the sheriff would do with it and why it had been
given him. For, of all the gifts that he had seen, it was the only one that
was not familiar to Earth.

In the pasture that had been empty yesterday, that had been only
trees and grass and old, grassed-over ditches, bordered by the wild plum
thickets and the hazel brush and blackberry vine, rose the building. It
seemed to him that it was bigger than when he had seen it less than an
hour before.

Back at the house, the newspapermen were sitting in the yard, looking
at the building.

One of them said to him, "The brass arrived. They're waiting in there
for you."

"Intelligence?" asked Peter.

The newsman nodded. "A chicken colonel and a major."

They were waiting in the living-room. The colonel was a young man
with gray hair. The major wore a mustache, very military.

The colonel introduced himself. "I'm Colonel Whitman. This is
Major Rockwell."

Peter put down his eggs and milk and nodded acknowledgment.

"You found this machine," said the colonel.

"That is right."

"Tell us about it," said the colonel, so Peter told them about it.

"This jade," the colonel said. "Could we have a look at it?"

Peter went to the kitchen and got the jade. They passed it from one to
the other, examining it closely, turning it over and over in their hands,
a bit suspicious of it, but admiring it, although Peter could see they
knew nothing about jade.

Almost as if he might have known what was in Peter's mind, the
colonel lifted his eyes from the jade and looked at him.

"You know jade," the colonel said.

"Very well," said Peter.

"You've worked with it before?"

"In a museum."

"Tell me about yourself."

Peter hesitated—then told about himself.

"But why are you here?" the colonel asked.

"Have you ever been in a hospital, Colonel? Have you ever thought what it would be like to die there?"

The colonel nodded. "I can see your point. But here you'll have no——"

"I won't wait that long."

"Yes, yes," the colonel said. "I see."

"Colonel," said the major. "Look at this, sir, if you will. This symbolism is the same . . ."

The colonel snatched it from his hands and looked.

"The same as on the letterhead!" he shouted.

The colonel lifted his head and stared at Peter, as if it had been the first time he had seen him, as if he were surprised at seeing him.

There was, suddenly, a gun in the major's hand, pointing at Peter, its muzzle a cold and steady eye.

Peter tried to throw himself aside.

He was too late.

The major shot him down.

Peter fell for a million years through a wool-gray nothingness that screamed and he knew it must be a dream, an endless atavistic dream of falling, brought down through all the years from incredibly remote forebears who had dwelt in trees and had lived in fear of falling. He tried to pinch himself to awaken from the dream, but he couldn't do it, since he had no hands to pinch with, and, after a time, it became apparent that he had no body to pinch. He was a disembodied consciousness hurtling through a gulf which seemed to have no boundaries.

He fell for a million years through the void that seemed to scream at him. At first the screaming soaked into him and filled his soul, since he had no body, with a terrible agony that went on and on, never quite reaching the breaking point that would send him into the release of insanity. But he got used to it after a time and as soon as he did, the screaming stopped and he plunged down through space in a silence that was more dreadful than the screaming.

He fell forever and forever and then it seemed that forever ended, for he was at rest and no longer falling.

He saw a face. It was a face from incredibly long ago, a face that he once had seen and had long forgotten, and he searched back along his memory to try to identify it.

He couldn't see it too clearly, for it seemed to keep bobbing around so he couldn't pin it down. He tried and tried and couldn't and he closed his eyes to shut the face away.

"Chaye," a voice said. "Peter Chaye."

"Go away," said Peter.

The voice went away.

He opened his eyes again and the face was there, clearer now and no longer bobbing.

It was the colonel's face.

He shut his eyes again, remembering the steady eye of the gun the major had held. He'd jumped aside, or tried to, and he had been too slow. Something had happened and he'd fallen for a million years and here he was, with the colonel looking at him.

He'd been shot. That was the answer, of course. The major had shot him and he was in a hospital. But where had he been hit? Arm? Both arms seemed to be all right. Leg? Both legs were all right, too. No pain. No bandages. No casts.

The colonel said: "He came to for just a minute, Doc, and now he's off again."

"He'll be all right," said Doc. "Just give him time. You gave him too big a charge, that's all. It'll take a little time."

"We must talk to him."

"You'll have to wait."

There was silence for a moment.

Then: "You're absolutely sure he's human?"

"We've gone over every inch of him," said Doc. "If he isn't human, he's too good an imitation for us ever to find out."

"He told me he had cancer," the colonel said. "Claimed he was dying of cancer. Don't you see, if he wasn't human, if there was something wrong, he could always try to make it look . . ."

"He hasn't any cancer. Not a sign of it. No sign he ever had it. No sign he ever will."

Even with his eyes shut, Peter felt that he was agape with disbelief and amazement. He forced his eyes to stay closed, afraid that this was a trick.

"That other doctor," the colonel said, "told Peter Chaye four months ago he had six more months to live. He told him . . ."

Doc said, "Colonel, I won't even try to explain it. All I can tell you is that the man lying on that bed hasn't got cancer. He's as healthy a man as you would wish to find."

"It isn't Peter Chaye, then," the colonel stated in a dogged voice. "It's something that took over Peter Chaye or duplicated Peter Chaye or . . ."

Doc said, "Now, now, Colonel. Let's stick to what we know."

"You're sure he's a man, Doc?"

"I'm sure he's a human being, if that is what you mean."

"No little differences? Just one seemingly unimportant deviation from the human norm?"

"None," Doc said, "and even if there were, it wouldn't prove what you are after. There could be minor mutational difference in anyone. The human body doesn't always run according to a blue-print."

"There were differences in all that stuff the machine gave away. Little differences that came to light only on close examination—but differences that spelled out a margin between human and alien manufacture."

"All right, then, so there were differences. So those things were made by aliens. I still tell you this man is a human being."

"It all ties in so neatly," the colonel declared. "Chaye goes out and buys this place—this old, abandoned farm. He's eccentric as hell by the standards of that neighborhood. By the very fact of his eccentricity, he invites attention, which might be undesirable, but at the same time his eccentricity might be used to cover up and smooth over anything he did out of the ordinary. It would be just somebody like him who'd supposedly find a strange machine. It would be . . ."

"You're building up a case," said Doc, "without anything to go on. You asked for one little difference in him to base your cockeyed theory on—no offense, but that's how I, as a doctor, see it. Well, now let's have one little fact—fact, mind you, not guess—to support this idea of yours."

"What was in that barn?" demanded the colonel. "That's what I want to know. Did Chaye build that machine in there? Was that why it was destroyed?"

"The sheriff destroyed the barn," the doctor said. "Chaye had nothing to do with it."

"But who gave the gun to the sheriff? Chaye's machine, that's who. And it would be an easy matter of suggestion, mind control, hypnotism, whatever you want to call it . . ."

"Let's get back to facts. You used an anesthetic gun on this man. You've held him prisoner. By your orders, he has been subjected to intensive examination, a clear invasion of his privacy. I hope to God he never brings you into court. He could throw the book at you."

"I know," the colonel admitted reluctantly. "But we have to bust this thing. We must find out what it is. We have got to get that bomb back!"

"The bomb's what worries you."

"Hanging up there," the colonel said, sounding as if he'd shuddered. "Just hanging up there!"

"I have to get along," replied the doctor. "Take it easy, Colonel."

The doctor's footsteps went out the door and down the corridor, fading away. The colonel paced up and down a while then sat down heavily in a chair.

Peter lay in bed, and one thought crashed through his brain, one thought again and again:

I'm going to live!

But he hadn't been.

He had been ready for the day when the pain finally became too great to bear.

He had picked his ground to spend his final days, to make his final stand.

And now he had been reprieved. Now, somehow, he had been given back his life.

He lay in the bed, fighting against excitement, against a growing tenseness, trying to maintain the pretense that he still was under the influence of whatever he'd been shot with.

An anesthetic gun, the doctor had said. Something new, something he had never heard of. And yet somewhere there was a hint of it. Something, he remembered, about dentistry—a new technique that dentists used to desensitize the gums, a fine stream of anesthetic sprayed against the gums. Something like that, only hundreds or thousands of times stronger?

Shot and brought here and examined because of some wild fantasy lurking in the mind of a G-2 colonel.

Fantasy? He wondered. Unwitting, unsuspecting, could he have played a part? It was ridiculous, of course. For he remembered nothing he had done or said or even thought which gave him a clue to any part he might have played in the machine's coming to the Earth.

Could cancer be something other than disease? Some uninvited guest, perhaps, that came and lived within a human body? A clever alien guest who came from far away, across the unguessed light-years?

And that, he knew, was fantasy to match the colonel's fantasy, a malignant nightmare of distrust that dwelt within the human mind, an instinctive defense mechanism that conditioned the race to expect the worst and to arm against it.

There was nothing feared so much as the unknown factor, nothing which one must guard against so much as the unexplained.

We have to bust this thing, the colonel had said. We must find out what it is.

And, that, of course, was the terror of it—that they had no way of knowing what it was.

He stirred at last, very deliberately, and the colonel spoke.

"Peter Chaye," he said.

"Yes, what is it, Colonel?"

"I have to talk to you."

"All right, talk to me."

He sat up in the bed and saw that he was in a hospital room. It had the stark, antiseptic quality, the tile floor, the colorless walls, the utilitarian look—and the bed on which he lay was a hospital bed.

"How do you feel?" the colonel asked.

"Not so hot," confessed Peter.

"We were a little rough on you, but we couldn't take a chance. There was the letter, you see, and the slot machines and the stamp machines and all the other things and . . ."

"You said something about a letterhead."

"What do you know about that, Chaye?"

"I don't know a thing."

"It came to the President," said the colonel. "A month or so ago. And a similar one went to every other administrative head on the entire Earth."

"Saying?"

"That's the hell of it. It was written in no language known anywhere on Earth. But there was one line—one line on all the letters—that you could read. It said: 'By the time you have deciphered, you'll be ready to act logically.' And that was all anybody could read—one line in the native language of every country that got a copy of the letter. The rest was in gibberish, for all we could make of it."

"You haven't deciphered it?"

He could see the colonel sweating. "Not even a single character, much less a word."

Peter reached out a hand to the bedside table and lifted the carafe, tipped it above the glass. There was nothing in it.

The colonel heaved himself out of his chair. "I'll get you a drink of water."

He picked up the glass and opened the bathroom door.

"I'll let it run a while and get it cold," he said.

But Peter scarcely heard him, for he was staring at the door. There was a bolt on it and if——

The water started running and the colonel raised his voice to be heard above it.

"That's about the time we started finding the machines," he said. "Can you imagine it? A cigarette-vending machine and you could buy cigarettes from it, but it was more than that. It was something watching you. Something that studied the people and the way they lived. And the stamp machines and the slot machines and all the other mechanical contrivances that we have set up. Not machines, but watchers. Watching all the time. Watching and learning . . ."

Peter swung his legs out of bed and touched the floor. He approached swiftly and silently on bare feet and slammed the door, then reached up and slid the bolt. It snicked neatly into place.

"Hey!" the colonel shouted.

Clothes?

They might be in the closet.

Peter leaped at it and wrenched the door open and there they were, hung upon the hangers.

He ripped off the hospital gown, snatched at his trousers and pulled them on.

Shirt, now! In a drawer.

And shoes? There on the closet floor. Don't take time to tie them.

The colonel was pushing and hammering at the door, not yelling yet. Later he would, but right now he was intent on saving all the face he could. He wouldn't want to advertise immediately the fact that he'd been tricked.

Peter felt through his pockets. His wallet was gone. So was everything else—his knife, his watch, his keys. More than likely they'd taken all of it and put it in the office safe when he'd been brought in.

No time to worry about any of them. The thing now was to get away.

He went out the door and down the corridor, carefully not going too fast. He passed a nurse, but she scarcely glanced at him.

He found a stairway door and opened it. Now he could hurry just a little more. He went down the stairs three at a time, shoelaces clattering.

The stairs, he told himself, were fairly safe. Almost no one would use them when there were the elevators. He stopped and bent over for a moment and tied the laces.

The floor numbers were painted above each of the doors, so he knew where he was. At the ground floor, he entered the corridor again. So far, there seemed to be no alarms, although any minute now the colonel would start to raise a ruckus.

Would they try to stop him at the door? Would there be someone to question him? Would——

A basket of flowers stood beside a door. He glanced up and down the corridor. There were several people, but they weren't looking at him. He scooped up the flowers.

At the door, he said to the attendant who sat behind the desk: "Mistake. Wrong flowers."

She smiled sourly, but made no move to stop him.

Outside, he put the flowers down on the steps and walked rapidly away.

An hour later, he knew that he was safe. He knew also that he was in a city thirty miles away from where he wanted to go and that he had no money and that he was hungry and his feet were sore from walking on the hard and unyielding concrete of the sidewalks.

He found a park and sat down on a bench. A little distance away, a group of old men were playing checkers at a table. A mother wheeled her baby. A young man sat on a nearby bench, listening to a tiny radio.

The radio said: ". . . apparently the building is completed. There has been no sign of it growing for the last eighteen hours. At the moment, it measures a thousand stories high and covers more than a hundred acres. The bomb, which was dropped two days ago, still floats there above it, held in suspension by some strange force. Artillery is standing by, waiting for the word to fire, but the word has not come through. Many think that since the bomb could not get through, shells will have no better chance, if any at all.

"A military spokesman, in fact, has said that the big guns are mere precautionary measures, which may be all right, but it certainly doesn't explain why the bomb was dropped. There is a rising clamor, not only in Congress, but throughout the world, to determine why an attempt was made at bombing. There has as yet been no hostile move directed from the building. The only damage so far reported has been the engulfment by the building of the farm home of Peter Chaye, the man who found the machine.

"All trace has been lost of Chaye since three days ago, when he suffered an attack of some sort and was taken from his home. It is believed that he may be in military custody. There is wide speculation on what Chaye may or may not know. It is entirely likely that he is the only man on Earth who can shed any light on what has happened on his farm.

"Meanwhile, the military guard has been tightened around the scene and a corridor of some eighteen miles in depth around it has been evacuated. It is known that two delegations of scientists have been escorted through the lines. While no official announcement has been made, there is good reason to believe they learned little from their visits. What the building is, who or what has engineered its construction, if you can call the inside-out process by which it grew construction, or what may be expected next are all fields of groundless speculation. There is plenty of that, naturally, but on one has yet come up with what might be called an explanation.

"The world's press wires are continuing to pile up reams of copy, but even so there is little actual, concrete knowledge—few facts that can be listed one, two, three right down the line.

"There is little other news of any sort and perhaps it's just as well, since there is no room at the moment in the public interest for anything else but this mysterious building. As so often happens when big news breaks, all other events seem to wait for some other time to happen. The polio epidemic is rapidly subsiding; there is no major crime news. In the world's capitals, of course, all legislative action is at a complete standstill, with the governments watching closely the developments at the building.

"There is a rising feeling at many of these capitals that the building is not of mere national concern, that decisions regarding it must be made at an international level. The attempted bombing has resulted in some argument that we, as the nation most concerned, cannot be trusted to act in a calm, dispassionate way, and that an objective world viewpoint is necessary for an intelligent handling of the situation."

Peter got up from his bench and walked away. He'd been taken from his home three days ago, the radio had said. No wonder he was starved.

Three days—and in that time the building had grown a thousand stories high and now covered a hundred acres.

He went along, not hurrying too much now, his feet a heavy ache, his belly pinched with hunger.

He had to get back to the building—somehow he had to get back there. It was a sudden need, realized and admitted now, but the reason for it, the source of it, was not yet apparent. It was as if there had been something he had left behind and he had to go and find it. Some thing I left behind, he thought. What could he have left behind? Nothing but the pain and the knowledge that he walked with a dark companion and the little capsule that he carried in his pocket for the time when the pain grew too great.

He felt in his pocket and the capsule was no longer there. It had disappeared along with his wallet and his pocket knife and watch. No matter now, he thought. I no longer need the capsule.

He heard the hurrying footsteps behind him and there was an urgency about them that made him swing around.

"Peter!" Mary cried out. "Peter, I thought I recognized you. I was hurrying to catch you."

He stood and looked at her as if he did not quite believe it was she whom he saw.

"Where have you been?" she asked.

"Hospital," Peter said. "I ran away from them. But you . . ."

"We were evacuated, Peter. They came and told us that we had to leave. Some of us are at a camp down at the other end of the park. Pa is carrying on something awful and I can't blame him—having to leave right in the middle of haying and with the small grain almost ready to be cut."

She tilted back her head and looked into his face.

"You look all worn out," she said. "Is it worse again?"

"It?" he asked, then realized that the neighbors must have known—that the reason for his coming to the farm must have been general knowledge, for there were no such things as secrets in a farming neighborhood.

"I'm sorry, Peter," Mary said. "Terribly sorry. I shouldn't have . . ."

"It's all right," said Peter. "Because it's gone now, Mary. I haven't got it any more. I don't know how or why, but I've gotten rid of it in some way."

"The hospital?" she suggested.

"The hospital had nothing to do with it. It had cleared up before I went there. They just found out at the hospital, that is all."

"Maybe the diagnosis was wrong."

He shook his head. "It wasn't wrong, Mary."

Still, how could he be sure? How could he, or the medical world, say positively that it had been malignant cells and not something else—some strange parasite to which he had played the unsuspecting host?

"You said you ran away," she reminded him.

"They'll be looking for me, Mary. The colonel and the major. They think I had something to do with the machine I found. They think I might have made it. They took me to the hospital to find out if I was human."

"Of all the silly things!"

"I've got to get back to the farm," he said. "I simply have to get back there."

"You can't," she told him. "There are soldiers everywhere."

"I'll crawl on my belly in the ditches, if I have to. Travel at night. Sneak through the lines. Fight if I'm discovered and they try to prevent me. There is no alternative. I have to make a try."

"You're ill," she said, anxiously staring at his face.

He grinned at her. "Not ill. Just hungry."

"Come on then." She took his arm.

He held back. "Not to the camp. I can't have someone seeing me. In just a little while I'll be a hunted man—if I'm not one already."

"A restaurant, of course."

"They took my wallet, Mary. I haven't any money."

"I have shopping money."

"No," he said. "I'll get along. There's nothing that can beat me now."

"You really mean that, don't you?"

"It just occurred to me," Peter admitted, confused and yet somehow sure that what he had said was not reckless bravado, but a blunt fact.

"You're going back?"

"I have to, Mary."

"And you think you have a chance?"

He nodded.

"Peter," she began hesitantly.

"Yes?"

"How much bother would I be?"

"You? How do you mean? A bother in what way?"

"If I went along."

"But you can't. There's no reason for you to."

She lifted her chin just a little. "There is a reason, Peter. Almost as if I were being called there. Like a bell ringing in my head—a school bell calling in the children . . ."

"Mary," he said, "that perfume bottle—there was a certain symbol on it, wasn't there?"

"Carved in the glass," she told him. "The same symbol, Peter, that was carved into the jade."

And the same symbol, he thought, that had been on the letterheads.

"Come on," he decided suddenly. "You won't be any bother."

"We'll eat first," she said. "We can use the shopping money."

They walked down the path, hand in hand, like two teen-age sweethearts.

"We have lots of time," said Peter. "We can't start for home till dark."

They ate at a small restaurant on an obscure street and after that went grocery shopping. They bought a loaf of bread and two rings of bologna and a slab of cheese, which took all of Mary's money, and for the change the grocer sold them an empty bottle in which to carry water. It would serve as a canteen.

They walked to the edge of the city and out through the suburbs and into the open country, not traveling fast, for there was no point in trying to go too far before night set in.

They found a stream and sat beside it, for all the world like a couple on a picnic. Mary took off her shoes and dabbled her feet in the water and the two of them felt disproportionately happy.

Night came and they started out. There was no Moon, but the sky was ablaze with stars. Although they took some tumbles and at other times wondered where they were, they kept moving on, staying off the roads, walking through the fields and pastures, skirting the farmhouses to avoid barking dogs.

It was shortly after midnight that they saw the first of the campfires and swung wide around them. From the top of a ridge, they looked down upon the camp and saw the outlines of tents and the dull shapes of the canvas-covered trucks. And, later on, they almost stumbled into an artillery outfit, but got safely away without encountering the sentries who were certain to be stationed around the perimeter of the bivouac.

Now they knew that they were inside the evacuated area, that they were moving through the outer ring of soldiers and guns which hemmed in the building.

They moved more cautiously and made slower time. When the first false light of dawn came into the east, they holed up in a dense plum thicket in the corner of a pasture.

"I'm tired," sighed Mary. "I wasn't tired all night or, if I was, I didn't know it—but now that we've stopped, I feel exhausted."

"We'll eat and sleep," Peter said.

"Sleep comes first. I'm too tired to eat."

Peter left her and crawled through the thicket to its edge.

In the growing light of morning stood the building, a great blue-misted mass that reared above the horizon like a blunted finger pointing at the sky.

"Mary!" Peter whispered. "Mary, there it is!"

He heard her crawling through the thicket to his side.

"Peter, it's a long way off."

"Yes, I know it is. But we are going there."

They crouched there watching it.

"I can't see the bomb," said Mary. "The bomb that's hanging over it."

"It's too far off to see."

"Why is it us? Why are we the ones who are going back? Why are we the only ones who are not afraid?"

"I don't know," said Peter, frowning puzzledly. "No actual reason, that is. I'm going back because I want to—no, because I have to. You see, it was the place I chose. The dying place. Like the elephants crawling off to die where all other elephants die."

"But you're all right now, Peter."

"That makes no difference—or it doesn't seem to. It was where I found peace and an understanding."

"And there were the symbols, Peter. The symbols on the bottle and the jade."

"Let's go back," he said. "Someone will spot us here."

"Our gifts were the only ones that had the symbols," Mary persisted. "None of the others had any of them. I asked around. There were no symbols at all on the other gifts."

"There's no time to wonder about that. Come on."

They crawled back to the center of the thicket.

The Sun had risen above the horizon now and sent level shafts of light into the thicket and the early morning silence hung over them like a benediction.

"Peter," said Mary, "I just can't stay awake any longer. Kiss me before I go to sleep."

He kissed her and they clung together, shut from the world by the jagged, twisted, low-growing branches of the plum trees.

"I hear the bells," she breathed. "Do you hear them, too?"

Peter shook his head.

"Like school bells," she said. "Like bells on the first day of school—the first day you ever went."

"You're tired," he told her.

"I've heard them before. This is not the first time."

He kissed her again. "Go to sleep," he said and she did, almost as soon as she lay down and closed her eyes.

He sat quietly beside her and his mind retreated to his own hidden depths, searching for the pain within him. But there was no pain. It was gone forever.

The pain was gone and the incidence of polio was down and it was a crazy thing to think, but he thought it, anyhow:

Missionary!

When human missionaries went out to heathen lands, what were the first things that they did?

They preached, of course, but there were other things as well. They fought disease and they worked for sanitation and labored to improve the welfare of the people and tried to educate them to a better way of life. And in this way they not only carried out their religious precepts, but gained the confidence of the heathen folk as well.

And if an alien missionary came to Earth, what would be among the first things that he was sure to do? Would it not be reasonable that he, too, would fight disease and try to improve the welfare of his chosen charges? Thus he would gain their confidence. Although he could not expect to gain too much at first. He could expect hostility and suspicion. Only a pitiful handful would not resent him or be afraid of him.

And if the missionary——

And if THIS missionary——

Peter fell asleep.

The roar awakened him and he sat upright, sleep entirely wiped from his mind.

The roar still was there, somewhere outside the thicket, but it was receding.

"Peter! Peter!"

"Quiet, Mary! There is something out there!"

The roar turned around and came back again, growing until it was the sound of clanking thunder and the Earth shook with the sound. It receded again.

The midday sunlight came down through the branches and made of their hiding place a freckled spot of Sun and shade. Peter could smell the musky odor of warm soil and wilted leaf.

They crept cautiously through the thicket and when they gained its edge, where the leaves thinned out, they saw the racing tank far down the field. Its roar came to them as it tore along, bouncing and swaying to the ground's unevenness, the great snout of its cannon pugnaciously thrust out before it, like a stiff-arming football player.

A road ran clear down the field—a road that Peter was sure had not been there the night before. It was a straight road, absolutely straight, running toward the building, and it was of some metallic stuff that shimmered in the Sun.

And far off to the left was another road and to the right another, and in the distance the three roads seemed to draw together, as the rails seem to converge when one looks down a railroad track.

Other roads running at right angles cut across the three roads, intersecting them so that one gained the impression of three far-reaching ladders set tightly side by side.

The tank raced toward one of the intersecting roads, a tank made midget by the distance, and its roar came back to them no louder than the humming of an angry bee.

It reached the road and skidded off, whipping around sidewise and slewing along, as if it had hit something smooth and solid that it could not get though, as if it might have struck a soaped metallic wall. There was a moment when it tipped and almost went over, but it stayed upright and finally backed away, then swung around to come lumbering down the field, returning toward the thicket.

Halfway down the field, it pivoted around and halted, so that the gun pointed back toward the intersecting road.

The gun's muzzle moved downward and flashed and, at the intersecting road, the shell exploded with a burst of light and a puff of smoke. The concussion of the shot slapped hard against the ear.

Again and again the gun belched out its shells point-blank. A haze of smoke hung above the tank and road—and the shells still exploded at the road—this side of the road and not beyond it.

The tank clanked forward once more until it reached the road. It approached carefully this time and nudged itself along, as if it might be looking for a way to cross.

From somewhere a long distance off came the crunching sound of artillery. An entire battery of guns seemed to be firing. They fired for a while, then grudgingly quit.

The tank still nosed along the road like a dog sniffing beneath a fallen tree for a hidden rabbit.

"There's something there that's stopping them," said Peter.

"A wall," Mary guessed. "An invisible wall of some sort, but one they can't get through."

"Or shoot through, either. They tried to break through with gunfire and they didn't even dent it."

He crouched there, watching as the tank nosed along the road. It reached the point where the road to the left came down to intersect the crossroad. The tank sheered off to follow the left-hand one, bumping along with its forward armor shoved against the unseen wall.

Boxed in, thought Peter—those roads have broken up and boxed in all the military units. A tank in one pen and a dozen tanks in another, a battery of artillery in another, the motor pool in yet another. Boxed in and trapped; penned up and useless.

And we, he wondered—are we boxed in as well?

A group of soldiers came tramping down the righthand road. Peter spotted them from far off, black dots moving down the road, heading east, away from the building. When they came closer, he saw that they carried no guns and slogged along without the slightest semblance of formation and he could see from the way they walked that they were dog-tired.

He had not been aware that Mary had left his side until she came creeping back again, ducking her head to keep her hair from being caught in the low-hanging branches.

She sat down beside him and handed him a thick slice of bread and a chunk of bologna. She set the bottle of water down between them.

"It was the building," she said, "that built the roads."

Peter nodded, his mouth full of bread and meat.

"They want to make it easy to get to the building," Mary said. "The building wants to make it easy for people to come and visit it."

"The bells again?" he asked.

She smiled and said, "The bells."

The soldiers now had come close enough to see the tank. They stopped and stood in the road, looking at it.

Then four of them turned off the road and walked out into the field, heading for the tank. The others sat down and waited.

"The wall only works one way," said Mary.

"More likely," Peter told her, "it works for tanks, but doesn't work for people."

"The building doesn't want to keep the people out."

The soldiers crossed the field and the tank came out to meet them. It stopped and the crew crawled out of it and climbed down. The soldiers and the crew stood talking and one of the soldiers kept swinging his arms in gestures, pointing here and there.

From far away came the sound of heavy guns again.

"Some of them," said Peter, "still are trying to blast down the walls."

Finally the soldiers and the tank crew walked back to the road, leaving the tank deserted in the field.

And that must be the way it was with the entire military force which had hemmed in the building, Peter told himself. The roads and walls had cut it into bits, had screened it off—and now the tanks and the big guns and the planes were just so many ineffective toys of an infant race, lying scattered in a thousand playpens.

Out on the road, the foot soldiers and the tank crew slogged eastward, retreating from the siege which had failed so ingloriously.

In their thicket, Mary and Peter sat and watched the building.

"You said they came from the stars," said Mary. "But why did they come here? Why did they bother with us? Why did they come at all?"

"To save us," Peter offered slowly. "To save us from ourselves. Or to exploit and enslave us. Or to use our planet as a military base. For any one of a hundred reasons. Maybe for a reason we couldn't understand even if they told us."

"You don't believe those other reasons, the ones about enslaving us or using Earth as a military base. If you believed that, we wouldn't be going to the building."

"No, I don't believe them. I don't because I had cancer and I haven't any longer. I don't because the polio began clearing up on the same day that they arrived. They're doing good for us, exactly the same as the missionaries did good among the primitive, disease-ridden people to whom they were assigned. I hope——"

He sat and stared across the field, at the trapped and deserted tank, at the shining ladder of the roads.

"I hope," he said, "they don't do what some of the missionaries did. I hope they don't destroy our self-respect with alien Mother Hubbards. I hope they don't save us from ringworm and condemn us to a feeling of racial inferiority. I hope they don't chop down the coconuts and hand us——"

But they know about us, he told himself. They know all there is to know. They've studied us for—how long? Squatting in a drugstore corner, masquerading as a cigarette machine. Watching us from the counter in the guise of a stamp machine.

And they wrote letters—letters to every head of state in all the world. Letters that might, when finally deciphered, explain what they were about. Or that might make certain demands. Or that might, just possibly, be no more than applications for permits to build a mission or a church or a hospital or a school.

They know us, he thought. They know, for example, that we're suckers for anything that's free, so they handed out free gifts—just like the quiz shows and contests run by radio and television and Chambers of Commerce, except that there was no competition and everybody won.

Throughout the afternoon, Peter and Mary watched the road and during that time small groups of soldiers had come limping down it. But now, for an hour or more, there had been no one on the road.

They started out just before dark, walking across the field, passing through the wall-that-wasn't-there to reach the road. And they headed west along the road, going toward the purple cloud of the building that reared against the redness of the sunset.

They traveled through the night and they did not have to dodge and hide, as they had that first night, for there was no one on the road except the one lone soldier they met.

By the time they saw him, they had come far enough so that the great shaft of the building loomed halfway up the sky, a smudge of misty brightness in the bright starlight.

The soldier was sitting in the middle of the road and he'd taken off his shoes and set them neatly beside him.

"My feet are killing me," he said by way of greeting.

So they sat down with him to keep him company and Peter took out the water bottle and the loaf of bread and the cheese and bologna and spread them on the pavement with wrapping paper as a picnic cloth.

They ate in silence for a while and finally the soldier said, "Well, this is the end of it."

They did not ask the question, but waited patiently, eating bread and cheese.

"This is the end of soldiering," the soldier told them. "This is the end of war."

He gestured out toward the pens fashioned by the roads and in one nearby pen were three self-propelled artillery pieces and in another was an ammunition dump and another pen held military vehicles.

"How are you going to fight a war," the soldier asked, "if the things back there can chop up your armies into checkerboards? A tank ain't worth a damn guarding ten acres, not when it isn't able to get out of those ten acres. A big gun ain't any good to you if you can't fire but half a mile."

"You think they would?" asked Mary. "Anywhere, I mean?"

"They done it here. Why not somewhere else? Why not any place that they wanted to? They stopped us. They stopped us cold and they never shed a single drop of blood. Not a casualty among us."

He swallowed the bit of bread and cheese that was in his mouth and reached for the water bottle. He drank, his Adam's apple bobbing up and down.

"I'm coming back," he said. "I'm going out and get my girl and we both are coming back. The things in that building maybe need some help and I'm going to help them if there's a way of doing it. And if they don't need no help, why, then I'm going to figure out some way to let them know I'm thankful that they came."

"Things? You saw some things?"

The soldier stared at Peter. "No, I never saw anything at all."

"But this business of going out to get your girl and both of you coming back? How did you get that idea? Why not go back right now with us?"

"It wouldn't be right," the soldier protested. "Or it doesn't seem just right. I got to see her first and tell her how I feel. Besides, I got a present for her."

"She'll be glad to see you," Mary told him softly. "She'll like the present."

"She sure will." The soldier grinned proudly. "It was something that she wanted."

He reached in his pocket and took out a leather box. Fumbling with the catch, he snapped it open. The starlight blazed softly on the necklace that lay inside the box.

Mary reached out her hand. "May I?" she asked.

"Sure," the soldier said. "I want you to take a look at it. You'd know if a girl would like it."

Mary lifted it from the box and held it in her hand, a stream of starlit fire.

"Diamonds?" asked Peter.

"I don't know," the soldier said. "Might be. It looks real expensive. There's a pendant, sort of, at the bottom of it, of green stone that doesn't sparkle much, but——"

"Peter," Mary interrupted, "have you got a match?"

The soldier dipped his hand into a pocket. "I got a lighter, Miss. That thing gave me a lighter. A beaut!"

He snapped it open and the blaze flamed out. Mary held the pendant close.

"It's the symbol," she said. "Just like on my bottle of perfume."

"That carving?" asked the soldier, pointing. "It's on the lighter, too."

"Something gave you this?" Peter urgently wanted to know.

"A box. Except that it really was more than a box. I reached down to put my hand on it and it coughed up a lighter and when it did, I thought of Louise and the lighter she had given me. I'd lost it and I felt bad about it, and here was one just like it except for the carving on the side. And when I thought of Louise, the box made a funny noise and out popped the box with the necklace in it."

The soldier leaned forward, his young face solemn in the glow from the lighter's flame.

"You know what I think?" he said. "I think that box was one of them. There are stories, but you can't believe everything you hear . . ."

He looked from one to the other of them. "You don't laugh at me," he remarked wonderingly.

Peter shook his head. "That's about the last thing we'd do, Soldier."

Mary handed back the necklace and the lighter. The soldier put them in his pocket and began putting on his shoes.

"I got to get on," he said. "Thanks for the chow."

"We'll be seeing you," said Peter.

"I hope so."

"I know we will," Mary stated positively.

They watched him trudge away, then walked on in the other direction.

Mary said to Peter, "The symbol is the mark of them. The ones who get the symbol are the ones who will go back. It's a passport, a seal of approval."

"Or," Peter amended, "the brand of ownership."

"They'd be looking for certain kinds of people. They wouldn't want anybody who was afraid of them. They'd want people who had some faith in them."

"What do they want us for?" Peter fretted. "That's what bothers me. What use can we be to them? The soldier wants to help them, but they don't need help from us. They don't need help from anyone."

"We've never seen one of them," said Mary. "Unless the box was one of them."

And the cigarette machines, thought Peter. The cigarette machines and God knows what else.

"And yet," said Mary, "they know about us. They've watched us and studied us. They know us inside out. They can reach deep within us and know what each of us might want and then give it to us. A rod and reel for Johnny and a piece of jade for you. And the rod and reel were a *human* rod and reel and the jade was Earth jade. They even know about the soldier's girl. They knew she would like a shiny necklace and they knew she was the kind of person that they wanted to come back again and . . ."

"The Saucers," Peter said. "I wonder if it was the Saucers, after all, watching us for years, learning all about us."

How many years would it take, he wondered, from a standing start, to learn all there was to know about the human race? For it would be from a standing start; to them, all of humanity would have been a complex alien race and they would have had to feel their way along, learning one fact here and another there. And they would make mistakes; at times their deductions would be wrong, and that would set them back.

"I don't know," said Peter. "I can't figure it out at all."

They walked down the shiny metal road that glimmered in the starlight, with the building growing from a misty phantom to a gigantic wall that rose against the sky to blot out the stars. A thousand stories high and covering more than a hundred acres, it was a structure that craned your head and set your neck to aching and made your brain spin with its glory and its majesty.

And even when you drew near it, you could not see the dropped and cradled bomb, resting in the emptiness above it, for the bomb was too far away for seeing.

But you could see the little cubicles sliced off by the roads and, within the cubicles, the destructive toys of a violent race, deserted now, just idle hunks of fashioned metal.

They came at last, just before dawn, to the great stairs that ran up to the central door. As they moved across the flat stone approach to the stairs, they felt the hush and the deepness of the peace that lay in the building's shadow.

Hand in hand, they went up the stairs and came to the great bronze door and there they stopped. Turning around, they looked back in silence.

The roads spun out like wheel spokes from the building's hub as far as they could see, and the crossing roads ran in concentric circles so that it seemed they stood in the center of a spider's web.

Deserted farmhouses, with their groups of buildings—barns, granaries, garages, silos, hog pens, machine sheds—stood in the sectors marked off by the roads, and in other sectors lay the machines of war, fit now for little more than birds' nests or a hiding place for rabbits. Bird songs came trilling up from the pastures and the fields and you could smell the freshness and the coolness of the countryside.

"It's good," said Mary. "It's our country, Peter."

"It was our country," Peter corrected her. "Nothing will ever be quite the same again."

"You aren't afraid, Peter?"

"Not a bit. Just baffled."

"But you seemed so sure before."

"I still am sure," he said. "Emotionally, I am as sure as ever that everything's all right."

"Of course everything's all right. There was a polio epidemic and now it has died out. An army has been routed without a single death. An atomic bomb was caught and halted before it could go off. Can't you see, Peter, they're already making this a better world. Cancer and polio gone—two things that Man had fought for years and was far from conquering. War stopped, disease stopped, atomic bombs stopped—things we couldn't solve for ourselves that were solved for us."

"I know all that," said Peter. "They'll undoubtedly also put an end to crime and graft and violence and everything else that has been tormenting and degrading mankind since it climbed down out of the trees."

"What more do you want?"

"Nothing more, I guess—it's just that it's circumstantial. It's not real evidence. All that we know, or think we know, we've learned from inference. We have no proof—no actual, solid proof."

"We have faith. We must have faith. If you can't believe in someone or something that wipes out disease and war, what can you believe in?"

"That's what bothers me."

"The world is built on faith," said Mary. "Faith in God and in ourselves and in the decency of mankind."

"You're wonderful," exclaimed Peter.

He caught her tight and kissed her and she clung against him and when finally they let each other go, the great bronze door was opening.

Silently, they walked across the threshold with arms around each other, into a foyer that arched high overhead. There were murals on the high arched ceiling, and others paneled in the walls, and four great flights of stairs led upward.

But the stairways were roped off by heavy velvet cords. Another cord, hooked into gleaming standards, and signs with pointing arrows showed them which way to go.

Obediently, walking in the hush that came close to reverence, they went across the foyer to the single open door.

They stepped into a large room, with great, tall, slender windows that let in the morning sunlight, and it fell across the satiny newness of the blackboards, the big-armed class chairs, the heavy reading tables, case after case of books, and the lectern on the lecture platform.

They stood and looked at it and Mary said to Peter: "I was right. They were school bells, after all. We've come to school, Peter. The first day we ever went to school."

"Kindergarten," Peter said, and his voice choked as he pronounced the word.

It was just right, he thought, so humanly right: The sunlight and the shadow, the rich bindings of the books, the dark patina of the wood, the heavy silence over everything. It was an Earthly classroom in the most scholarly tradition. It was Cambridge and Oxford and the Sorbonne and an Eastern ivy college all rolled into one.

The aliens hadn't missed a bet—not a single bet.

"I have to go," said Mary. "You wait right here for me."

"I'll wait right here," he promised.

He watched her cross the room and open a door. Through it, he saw a corridor that went on for what seemed miles and miles. Then she shut the door and he was alone.

He stood there for a moment, then swung swiftly around. Almost running across the foyer, he reached the great bronze door. But there was no door, or none that he could see. There was not even a crack where a door should be. He went over the wall inch by inch and he found no door.

He turned away from the wall and stood in the foyer, naked of soul, and felt the vast emptiness of the building thunder in his brain.

Up there, he thought, up there for a thousand stories, the building stretched into the sky. And down here was kindergarten and up on the second floor, no doubt, first grade, and you'd go up and up and what would be the end—and the purpose of that end?

When did you graduate?

Or did you ever graduate?

And when you graduated, what would you be?

What would you be? he asked.

Would you be human still?

They would be coming to school for days, the ones who had been picked, the ones who had passed the strange entrance examination that was necessary to attend this school. They'd come down the metal roads and climb the steps and the great bronze door would open and they would enter. And others would come, too, out of curiosity, but if they did not have the symbol, the doors would not open for them.

And those who did come in, when and if they felt the urge to flee, would find there were no doors.

He went back into the classroom and stood where he had stood before.

Those books, he wondered. What was in them? In just a little while, he'd have the courage to pick one out and see. And the lectern? What would stand behind the lectern?

What, not *who.*

The door opened and Mary came across the room to him.

"There are apartments out there," she said. "The cutest apartments you have ever seen. And one of them has our names on it and there are others that have other names and some that have no names at all. There are other people coming, Peter. We were just a little early. We were the ones who started first. We got here before the school bell rang."

Peter nodded. "Let's sit down and wait," he said.

Side by side, they sat down, waiting for the Teacher.